W9-BPL-401

DISCARD

Also by Justina Ireland

Vengeance Bound

PROMISE of SHADOWS

JUSTINA IRELAND

SIMON & SCHUSTER BFYR

NEW YORK   LONDON   TORONTO   SYDNEY   NEW DELHI

An imprint of Simon & Schuster Children's Publishing Division
1230 Avenue of the Americas, New York, New York 10020

For information about special discounts for bulk purchases, please contact Simon & Schuster Special Sales at 1-866-506-1949 or business@simonandschuster.com.
The Simon & Schuster Speakers Bureau can bring authors to your live event. For more information or to book an event, contact the Simon & Schuster Speakers Bureau at 1-866-248-3049 or visit our website at www.simonspeakers.com.
Book design by Lucy Ruth Cummins
The text for this book is set in Adobe Caslon Pro
Manufactured in the United States of America
2 4 6 8 10 9 7 5 3 1
Library of Congress Cataloging-in-Publication Data
Ireland, Justina.
Promise of shadows / Justina Ireland.—First edition.
pages cm
Summary: As a human/god offspring, Zephyr Mourning is destined for a life of servitude but when she uses a forbidden dark power to kill the minor god who murdered her sister she is sent to Tartarus, where she discovers that she may be the Nyx, a dark goddess prophesied to change the balance of power.
ISBN 978-1-4424-4464-5 (hardcover)
ISBN 978-1-4424-5357-9 (eBook)
[1. Gods—Fiction. 2. Goddesses—Fiction. 3. Murder—Fiction. 4. Prison—Fiction.
5. Prophecies—Fiction. 6. Mythology, Greek—Fiction.] I. Title.
PZ7.I6274Pro 2014
[Fic]—dc23
2013002959

For Madeline. Don't let anyone take your wings.

PROMISE *of* SHADOWS

CHAPTE

ON

I MOVE MY SHOVEL, PUSHING THE MUD BACK AND FORTH AT A GLACIAL pace. Next to me, my friend Cass moves just as slowly. They have a saying down here in Tartarus: *There's no need to hurry when you've got forever to get the job done.* The saying is just one of many. It's easy to be clever when you're staring eternity in the face.

I've just dumped a load of dirt on top of my steadily growing pile when Cass speaks.

"I think you got a visitor," she says, looking past me toward the guard shack at the far edge of the plain. We work on the line with a few hundred others, digging a ditch the same way we have every day since I got to the Pits. The lowest point in the Underworld, the Pits of Tartarus is a bleak place. A muddy plain edged by a forest of black trees, the sky a constant twilight, it's a place reserved for criminals and lowlifes. All we do here is dig, moving the mud into long rows. I'm not sure why we dig all the time, since no one ever tells us anything except when to work, when to rest, and when to eat. I'm not even sure the work serves a purpose beyond keeping us from killing each other, and we still manage to do that just fine.

Cass elbows me hard in the side, and I wince. My ribs are still bruised from our most recent attack. A couple of Fae who thought kicking me to death would get them out of Tartarus or at least get them some respect. Thanks to Cass, all it got them was dead.

She nudges me again, and this time I groan. "That hurts."

"It's the Messenger this time," she says, jutting her chin toward the figure at the far end of the line. "They're getting serious." I don't look up. The last thing I need is the guard taking his whip to my back.

Panic rises, tightening my chest. I take a deep breath and force it down. I cannot freak out. "You don't know that he's here for me," I tell Cass. The words are more for me than for her. One of the guards, who are all minotaurs, starts to move in our direction, and I lower my voice. "If he's here for me, they'll let me know." I hold my breath until the half-bull, half-man creature heads back the other way. I don't want to get in trouble for talking. Cass doesn't really mind the punishments the bulls hand out. I do.

I'm not as strong as she is.

"Mourning!"

The bull's voice echoes across the plain, carrying down along the line of prisoners toiling in the dirt. I keep my head down and my shovel moving, not bothering to acknowledge the shout and buying some time to compose myself. It starts to rain, and I sigh. It's the least of my problems, but the downpour gives me something to focus on besides my visitor.

Rain in Tartarus means a lot of different things. Today it's a fine mist of excrement falling from the sky. It's like having an outhouse upended over your head. Cass keeps telling me that at some point I'll get used to it, but she's been here longer than anyone else. There's no time in the Underworld, but from what I can tell of her penchant for togas, she's been here a while. Like, centuries. I don't think I'll be kicking around here that long. Too many people want me dead.

And the weather sucks.

The best way to keep the muck out of my eyes and mouth is to keep my head down and wait until it passes. I'm a smart girl, so that's what I do. Deep down, I'm hoping that the guard won't call me again.

"Mourning. Zephyr Mourning. Get your lazy carcass down here, Godslayer."

I wince at the tone in the guard's voice. I've waited too long to answer, and now I'm in for it. The bulls down here are no better than the prisoners, just as violent and rude. What do you expect from a minotaur? I'm not very good at taking a punch, and I have no desire to provoke the guard any further, so I plant my shovel in the mud and jog in the direction of the shout.

I slow down to a walk when I see a familiar figure walking beside the bull, a whip-thin man with a shock of white-blond hair. The "Messenger" Cass called him. But she's old school, and most vættir these days refer to him by his given name, Hermes. The Messenger of the Gods. He carries an oversize golf umbrella and picks his way around the larger muck puddles. The wings on his ankles flutter in agitation. His blue eyes glow in the constant dusk of Tartarus, their metallic blued-steel sheen denoting his Æthereal blood and causing the other prisoners to subtly shift away from him. There's too much shine to them for him to be anything but Exalted, and even the dumbest vættir knows better than to cross paths with one of the favored sons and daughters of the universe. Their powers are so vast that they are gods among gods.

Still, all the æther in the universe can't keep the rain from splattering Hermes. His impeccably tailored dove-gray suit has several dark spots. It serves him right. Only Hermes would wear couture to hell.

A few feet still separate me and Hermes when a fight breaks out on the line. A couple of Fae grapple, their wrestling match carrying them right into our path. The scent of their rage pushes away the stink of the rain, and for once I'm grateful for my ability to smell emotions. Their anger is the acrid aroma of burning flesh, which is better than the bathroom scent of the rain. Whatever they're fighting about, it's clear that the Fae hate each other. This is more than a normal Tartarus scuffle.

The Fae are more intent on their fight than on the Æthereal walking toward them. They go down a couple of feet away from Hermes, landing in a deep puddle. The contents splash up and across the legs of Hermes's pants, soaking them with crap and mud. I swallow the hysterical laugh that threatens to bubble up.

This can't end well.

Everyone freezes for a moment, even the fighters on the ground. They're all waiting for Hermes's wrath, for the outpouring of æther that follows any Æthereal temper tantrum. But this is Tartarus, and there's no æther here. Hermes is as powerless as the rest of us.

That doesn't stop him from closing the umbrella and swinging it at the nearest Fae. The fiberglass snaps as it catches the slim man across the face, snapping his head back with an audible crunch. The other Fae tries to scramble away, but Hermes is much faster. With one hand he hauls the Fae up by the scruff before slamming him face-first into the soft mud. Then, with the detached expression of a man buying groceries, Hermes holds the flailing Fae down until he no longer moves.

Bile burns the back of my throat, and it's hard to breathe. I push down the fear that makes me want to run away, to keep running until I can forget the coldness in Hermes's eyes as he killed a man.

Cass appears next to me with a sigh. Even though I can smell the mixed fear and relief from the rest of the vættir, I get nothing from her. Cass's emotions are always a mystery. "Great, now I'll never get that food ration he owes me." She's serious. Cass never jokes about anything.

Life is cheap in Tartarus.

A couple of bulls run over to haul away the two Fae. Their bodies will be thrown beyond the tree line so that the unseen things that live in the woods can feast on them instead of on us. I relax so my expression doesn't reflect the horror I feel. Hermes straightens, tossing away his ruined umbrella. "Hey, Zephyr," he says as he adjusts his suit.

Cass slides back into the work crew as I cross my arms. It feels like a lifetime since I last saw Hermes. Time passes differently in Tartarus, so I have no idea how long it's actually been. A month? A year? Some days it feels like it was just yesterday that I landed here. Others, it feels like I've been here my entire life.

No matter how long it's been, I can't forget that he's the one who put me in Tartarus. I thought he was more than just my sister's boyfriend. I thought of him as family, the big brother I never had. And he turned me in to the Æthereal High Council. That's what I get for trusting an Æthereal.

Never trust the gods.

Reminding myself of his betrayal centers me. "Hey, Hermes. If it isn't my favorite psycho . . . pomp." My voice is even. I've learned a few things down here, especially from Cass. I won't let him know how his presence fills me with a burning rage that blurs my vision and makes me want to scream.

He gives me a wide smile, his chiseled cheekbones looking even sharper. "Funny. Did you think of it yourself?"

I sigh, feigning boredom. "What do you want? Can't you see I have a very important ditch to dig?"

Hermes's lips twitch. At least he still appreciates sarcasm. He clears his throat. "I'm here to speak with you on behalf of the Æthereal High Council."

I shrug. "Okay." I'm not sure what else I'm supposed to say. I was never important enough to garner the High Council's notice before they sent me to Tartarus. Not many of the vættir are. We're second-class citizens, lucky to avoid the gods' notice.

"This is a private interview," Hermes says. He eyes the nearest bull. The minotaur straightens, steam puffing out of his bovine nostrils as he snaps to attention.

"You may use the nearby gatehouse, Exalted, if it suits your needs." The minotaur executes a clumsy bow, muck flying off one of his massive horns and landing on Hermes's pants.

Hermes sighs and pinches the bridge of his nose before he remembers that his hands are covered in crap. Rage tightens his mouth as he gives the half-man, half-bull creature a limp-wristed wave to lead the way. We follow the guard to a nearby outbuilding in silence. Only the set of Hermes's shoulders belies his utter disgust.

This would be hilarious if I wasn't sick with dread.

We make our way through the steady rain to the gatehouse, where the bull remains outside while we go in. The room is small. It's little more than a shack, really. Rough-hewn boards keep out the storm, and the floor is made of hard-packed earth. Dark fire flickers in the hearth, casting no light but warming the room nonetheless. A rickety table and chair lean against the wall opposite the fireplace, and a handful of pixies sealed in glass globes cast the only light in the room. The pixies emit a sickly yellow glow when they see us, one of them tapping on his prison insistently.

"Hey. Hey! Let me out before the bull comes back. I'll pay you." I ignore the bug. Anyone foolish enough to try to bribe me must be new to hell. He must not know who I am, or that I don't care about his money, because there's no way I'm ever leaving Tartarus.

Godslayers don't get parole.

I try to scrape as much of the sludge off my face as I can, before I see the well in the far corner of the room. The water has the same sulfurous rotten-egg smell as all the water here in the Pits, but at least it doesn't smell like an outhouse in August. There's a grate near the well, and I upend the bucket over my head while standing on it. I repeat this two more times before I'm satisfied I've gotten the worst of the mess off. No sense in trying to get completely clean. This is Tartarus, after all.

I hold a full bucket out to Hermes. He shakes his head in distaste before thinking twice and dipping a lemon-yellow pocket square into the water. He gingerly wipes the dark streaks off his pale skin. I dump the rest of the water over my head before tossing the bucket back in the corner.

"The Underworld seems to agree with you," he remarks as he starts to put away the handkerchief, thinks twice, and throws it on the sad-looking table.

I squeeze the excess water out of my blue, ropy locks and snort. What does he see? The front I keep up so the weaker inmates won't mess with me? Just because I've learned how to hide my fear doesn't mean I'm not scared. "It's hell, H. I don't think it agrees with anyone."

He purses his lips. "No æther, which means no real magic, it's perpetually dark, the sky rains excrement, and there are monsters waiting for a chance to devour the unwitting. I honestly don't see what your problem is."

His sense of humor is still as dry as the Sahara. It's too bad I don't find him funny anymore. I extend my talons and growl. "Give me one reason why I shouldn't turn your face into confetti, Betrayer."

Hermes's blued-steel gaze flashes. "Because it's the last thing Whisper would've wanted you to do."

Agony arcs through my chest, and I look away so he won't see the pain of my loss in my gaze. Whisper. I can't think of my sister without remembering the last time I saw her, her chest a gaping wound, her blood soaking into the concrete of the patio. She was my best friend and now she's gone. My talons slide back under my fingernails. I wasn't really going to attack him, anyway. "She loved you, you know. Even though she knew you'd eventually leave her."

He clears his throat and looks away. I'm glad that I've managed to make him uncomfortable. Some of the water from my hair has managed to find its way into my mouth, and I spit onto the floor. "You didn't come here to discuss my sister. What do you want?"

He sighs. "Still just as ladylike as ever. The High Council has sent me down here to inquire how it was that you managed to kill an Æthereal."

I smirk. This is the third inquisitor the Council has sent down since I got here. The first two left with nothing, and Hermes will too. Just because he used to screw my sister doesn't mean I owe him anything. "Just lucky, I guess."

His lips thin in irritation before he sighs. "I bear this message for you." He takes a shining white rock from his pocket, and I take a step back in surprise. He holds an æther stone, a magically charged rock that would fetch a good price in the Pits. Before I can ask what he plans to do with it, he drops it on the ground between us. Light surges upward and snaps into sharp focus. I can't help the hitch of breath in my chest.

Standing before me is a too-real image of my mother. The last time I saw the form before me, she was leaving for a battle, her claymore propped on her shoulder. Ruby-red hair knotted into locks that reached her waist, skin the color of midnight, and wings of deepest red and black. "Blood on coal," Whisper used to call them when we'd watch her fly off to battle. I know that it isn't really her. She's dead, her shade somewhere in the Elysian Fields, enjoying eternal happiness. The projection is the Æthereal equivalent of Princess Leia's plea to Obi-Wan. Still, I can't stop myself from reaching out to her like I've always wanted.

My mother's voice cuts through my mind after all these years, an unwanted phantom. *You're the daughter of an Æthereal, Zephyr. Try to stop being such an incredible disappointment.* I can even see the way her dark face would scrunch up at me, as though I was the one problem in her life that she couldn't solve.

The memory is the opposite end of the emotional spectrum from the woman gazing at me lovingly from the projection. "Zephyr, I know you probably aren't happy to see me, but I need you to answer Hermes's questions. It is of the utmost importance that the High Council be able to understand how you killed Ramun Mar."

I swallow dryly. Who is this woman? There's love shining in

her eyes, and she seems gentle and affectionate. This stranger is nothing like my mother. That Mourning Dove once flew me up to ten thousand feet and then dropped me, all to teach me how to fly.

"There's no room for mistakes in battle," she called as I fell, screaming until my sister, Whisper, flew up to catch me. It's amazing I ever learned to fly after that terrifying introduction to the sky.

The message plays, but I'm finished listening to the lying image before me. I fight back angry tears before I kick the æther stone toward the corner. It falls into the well with a wet plunk. I fight to keep my words steady. "If you think that's going to get me to talk, then you don't know me at all."

"Do you think that's what your mother would want?"

I turn around once my eyes have stopped burning, the threat of tears avoided. "That woman doesn't exist. Never did. I don't know how you did it, but it's a pretty sad attempt to get me to talk. Why don't you just tell me what you want from me?" The words come out as a plea. I bite my lip, my eyes sliding away from his all-too-knowing blue ones.

"Aw, Peep," he whispers, and the pet name cuts through me, the pain sharper and fresher than the ache of his betrayal. He reaches for me but at the last moment draws back, and I know he's thinking about our last meeting.

He's remembering that I might not have been caught by the Æthereals if he hadn't tricked me.

I hate him even as I love him with all my heart. He made my sister so happy, and that made me happy. Deep down I'd always hoped he would stay with Whisper, marry her like people do on television. I had this idea of a huge wedding, one that everyone in the Aerie would attend. There'd be cake, and I'd be Whisper's maid of honor. It would be just like a movie.

I made the mistake of telling her that one time, and she just laughed, the sound high and brittle like glass breaking. "Zeph, you know that Æthereals don't marry vættir. Especially not Exalteds like Hermes. I'm just grateful for the time that we have together. One day you'll understand that."

Hermes sighs and leans back against the wall of the gatehouse, drawing me out of the memory and putting a physical distance between us that's a match for the emotional one. "The High Council needs you to cooperate because a war is brewing over you, kiddo. The kind of war that the vættir might not survive."

"Why me? What did I do?"

A bark of laughter escapes from him. "What, besides kill an Æthereal? No big deal there, Godslayer." He shakes his head, a small smile playing around his lips before he turns serious again. "You killed one of the unkillable. People want to know how. They want to know if it can happen again. And if they're next."

I smile tightly. "Sounds like Hera's been working overtime." At my trial she'd advocated for my death more than any of the other gods.

Hermes nods slowly. "That's putting it mildly. She's been on the warpath since you were sent here last year, and things are only getting worse."

The air whooshes out of my lungs. I feel like I've been punched.

"A year? I've been here a year?" I imagine all the things I've missed in a year. If I'd been in the Mortal Realm, I would've finally gone to high school, a real school with norms. Homecoming, prom, football games, all the things regular people get to do. That's what I would've spent the last year doing. Not digging ditches and fighting to stay alive.

After I failed my Trials, I thought a normal life was finally in my reach. Harpies who cannot pass the Trials are either given menial positions or expelled from the Aerie, forced to spend the rest of their lives trying to blend in among the norms, full-blooded humans. Most Harpies dread the modern world and opt to work in the Aerie's laundry or kitchens, but I dreamed of the day when I'd no longer have to live in the Aerie. Freedom seemed like a blessing, not a curse.

But then I accidentally killed an Æthereal and ended up in Tartarus, ruining all my plans. And now I find out that I've lost a year in what felt like a few months.

Hermes's eyes dart away from mine, and he shrugs in response. "Time passes differently down here."

"You think?" I begin to pace as his words sink in. I'm finally realizing that my imprisonment is permanent. I'm not going to go to high school, or college, or anywhere else in the Mortal Realm. I'm going to be forever stuck here in Tartarus, covered in sludge and pretending to be brave. A year has passed, and I feel just like I did the last time I saw Hermes. Desperate, confused, and incredibly lost.

I stop pacing and cross my arms, trying to school my face to blankness. *Arrows are useless without a bow.* It's an old Harpy saying. No sense wallowing in might-have-beens. "Are we finished?" I snap.

Hermes startles, my sharp tone unfamiliar. "What?" he asks in surprise. I've never raised my voice at him. I've always given him the deference that the Exalteds demand, even as he snuck into the house late at night to meet with my sister. But now I'm not thinking about class structures and the proper forms of address, or even the way my sister lit up when she saw him. I'm just thinking about the year of my life that I lost.

"Are you done with me or what? I have to get back before someone steals my shovel."

His expression goes from shocked to sad, and I have to turn away from the pity on his face. "What happened to you, Peep? You're different. I almost didn't recognize you when I arrived. You're rougher now."

I sigh and sit in the room's only chair, leaning my head back against the wall's rough wood. "Tartarus happened to me, H. That's all. Just Tartarus."

CHAPTER TWO

HERMES CONTINUES TO QUESTION ME, BUT IT'S HALFHEARTED AND I'M uncooperative. Down here where the æther is nonexistent he's powerless, and there's no reason for me to give up the answers he needs. I may be depressed, but I'm not suicidal.

If he finds out the truth, my life sentence in Tartarus will be exchanged for a death sentence.

After a while the Exalted stands with a sigh. "Stay here. I'll be back in a moment." Then he flashes out of existence.

I should wonder where he's going, what he's doing. But I don't. Instead I'm just grateful for the chance to get a few minutes of shut-eye. As soon as he's gone, I close my eyes and doze off a little. But I'm not really asleep. Instead I'm remembering.

I'd been on the run for a couple of weeks, running from safe house to safe house as I tried to avoid Hera's Acolytes, a band of minor Æthereals and vættir vigilantes who work on behalf of the gods. The vættir in the Acolytes weren't any different from the rest of us vættir. We all had the misfortune of having a little human blood mixed in with our Æthereal lineage, keeping us out of the Æthereal Realm and firmly stuck in the Mortal Realm. Being a vættir is a bum deal.

Kicked out of paradise all because one of our ancestors got frisky with a mortal. But after a while you get used to being treated like crap, especially since the trade-off is a magical ability of some sort.

The Acolytes were hunting me down because I'd killed one of their own, a low-level god named Ramun Mar. I'd only killed Mar because he'd killed my sister, Whisper. Death is the punishment for vættir who mess around with Æthereals, but the Acolytes are the only ones who enforce such archaic beliefs. After I killed Ramun Mar, the Acolytes wanted me dead too. I had other ideas.

I was standing in the middle of a farmer's field in upstate New York with a shredded wing from my latest attempt to outrun the Acolytes. Dark pressed in all around me, the night ominous as I waited to be attacked again. The Acolytes had been chasing me for two weeks, a game of cat and mouse that had left me tired and injured. I didn't think they'd stop now, but my busted wing needed time to heal. Time I was sure I didn't have.

A sudden rustle of the grass was the first sign that I wasn't alone. I spun around, a knife waiting to be thrown balanced on my fingertips. I wasn't going to die easily.

Hermes raised his hands in surrender. "It's me, Peep. It's me. Relax, okay?"

I put the knife away at the sound of the nickname and sagged a little in relief. Fresh tears pricked my eyes. "Hermes?"

He nodded, and I launched myself into his arms. He was stiff and unyielding, but I didn't care. I sobbed into his shoulder. "Whisper is dead. The Acolytes killed her."

"I know."

"Why, Hermes? Why would they kill her? She was a good Harpy. She did whatever they told her to do. Why would the Acolytes kill her?"

He hesitated, and at first I thought he wouldn't tell me. But then he sighed and looked away. "Because of me. Someone found out that she was seeing me," he said, his voice low. He gently pushed me away from him and straightened his suit jacket, fussing over invisible lint on his shoulders. He'd always dressed up, and even that night he wore a stylish lime-colored suit that made me feel even dingier than I was.

"Oh gods, what do I do now, Hermes? Every time I run, they find me. And now my wing is ruined, and I have no way to go on." I began to shake as it sank in. I was a sitting duck, one with a broken wing and no chance of survival.

"Don't worry, Peep. I promised Whisper a long time ago that I'd keep you safe, and I will." He tilted his head at me and pursed his lips. "You haven't made it easy, you know."

I wiped away my tears and snorted in disbelief. "Hera's Acolytes have shown up everywhere I've gone. I was supposed to wait patiently for you while they tore out my heart?"

Hermes didn't respond, he just sighed and adjusted his cuffs. "Well, let's go. I don't have all millennium."

"Where are we going?"

"Somewhere safe."

My mother and Whisper were both dead, so the only place

that would be safe for me was the Elysian Fields. I'd heard of people fleeing to the Underworld to escape being punished by the Acolytes before, but that usually involved suicide. However, Hermes could take me there without the inconvenience of my death.

I reached for his hand, and a split second before I took it I wondered why he was so fidgety. But then we were soaring through the realms in a beam of light. The stress of the past couple of weeks melted away in an instant. Hermes would keep me safe. He loved my sister. He'd keep a promise to her.

We settled, my eyes still dazzled by the light of our passage. I blinked to clear my vision. The Elysian Fields were even more perfect than I'd imagined. White marble columns rose into a too-blue sky, like everything had been built in the clouds. Birds soared and butterflies flitted, and my heart felt light. It was impossible to be afraid in such a beautiful place, and for the first time in weeks my fear ebbed away. All I had to do was find my sister, and everything would be fine.

Before I could thank Hermes, he clamped a damper on my wrist.

I stared at the silver bracelet, the contrast between the bright metal and my brown skin taking a long moment to sink in. The enchanted bracelet on my wrist was a relic from a time when Æthereals owned the vættir as slaves. There was no way I could protect myself with it on.

"Hermes," I said, my voice a pained whisper. "What have you

done?" I yanked my hand back and reached for power, any power, but it was too late.

"This is the best place for you right now," Hermes said. I reached out to strike him, but my hand was caught by a large minotaur. His bull's head looked strange atop his human body. I realized with a start that he wasn't wearing a glamour to hide his strange nature, but he was wearing a silver collar of servitude. I knew where I was.

Out of the frying pan and into the fire. I was in the Æthereal Realm, the land of the gods.

"I thought maybe you'd smell the lie on me before I got you here," Hermes said. His expression was agonized, but it didn't help the anger eating away at my middle.

"I can only smell the emotions of humans. And you aren't human." I hurled the words at him like an insult as the minotaur dragged me away. The gods tell us the vættir are the ones who are flawed, our human blood compromising us. But it's the gods who betray the ones they love without remorse.

"Aren't you afraid the bulls will find you napping in their guard shack?"

I open my eyes, pulling myself out of the memory. Cass slinks through the door, almost quieter than a mouse. I still heard her though. "I'll wake up long before they enter, the way they clomp around everywhere. Besides, the psychopomp told me to wait here."

"An Exalted here to visit you. That can't be good." She goes to the well in the corner and uses the bucket to wash off like I did earlier. Her shoulder-length blond hair clings to her neck, and for a moment I wish I had hair as straight as hers. But Harpies have hair that easily tangles, and mine is a shocking royal blue that hangs down my back in snarled locks. I should cut it short like Cass's, at least to my shoulders. But a Harpy's locks are second only to her wings in importance. Since I no longer have my wings, I'm reluctant to give up my hair.

I run my fingers over the twisted hair nervously, wondering what it looks like. It feels longer, and I wonder if it's changed somehow. I wish I could see it. There are no mirrors in Tartarus.

"You didn't answer my question."

"What question?" I lean forward and meet her flat gaze. Cass has the best poker face, ever. Her emotions never show in her eyes, not like so many others here. I think it's why she's so deadly. No one ever sees it coming.

"Hermes, Messenger of the Gods. What's he doing flitting around Tartarus?"

I shrug. "You know why I'm here. Why do you think he's here?"

It's a rhetorical question, but Cass answers anyway. "To question you. To figure out how you snuffed out an Æthereal." She plays with the ragged end of her hair for a moment before releasing it. "You must really scare them if they're willing to send Hermes down to the Underworld to question you directly."

"Maybe." I sit back, thinking hard. "There's something else going on, something I don't understand. Hermes was talking about a war, and he seemed really concerned about it. But I always thought Æthereals enjoyed their wars."

Cass shrugs. "Of course the Æthereals love wars. How else are they supposed to break up the centuries? Sex and killing are their primary amusements." There's no trace of bitterness in Cass's voice, but maybe that's because she's just speaking the truth. Wars are as common to the gods as manipulating the lives of others to suit their whims. The history lessons we had in the Aerie were filled with nothing but the Exalteds vowing to kill one another, usually after an Æthereal slept with someone they weren't supposed to. I think they actually like fighting. It must be pretty lame to be immortal after the first few thousand years. A nice war would be a change of pace.

But that doesn't explain Hermes's shiftiness. I know he's hiding something, but what? I wish I could smell Æthereal emotions; it would be a big help. Assuming they actually have them. "I can't understand why the Æthereal Council would pull out all of the stops to figure out how I killed one of Hera's low-level thugs."

"I know. It would make more sense for them to just kill you and get it over with."

I snort. "Gee, thanks."

"Well, you're a Harpy. What would you do if faced with an enemy?" Cass sits on the edge of the table, hands held out toward the dark fire. Sitting is a luxury in Tartarus. There's no idle time here. Days are marked by work punctuated by meals and rest. Hanging out in the shack without worrying about getting killed is a pretty nice change of pace.

I shake my head. "I'd run. That's what I would do. But then again, I'm not technically a Harpy."

"Is this about your wings again?"

I shake my head and bite back a laugh. On the way to Tartarus my wings were ripped from me, the price for my passage to the Underworld. Everyone down here has lost something, even Cass. Although I'm not sure what she lost. I've never been brave enough to ask.

"No, Cass, this isn't about my wings, thanks for asking. I'm a coward, Cass. Harpies are brave, and I'm not."

"Says who?"

I shift in my seat. "The Matriarch. I failed my Trials." I'd tried to explain to Cass what a big deal it was to fail such an important test before, but she wouldn't listen to me.

Cass tilts her head and studies me. "So just because some woman who isn't even here says you aren't a Harpy, you're not a Harpy? Even though you have the hair and the talons and used to have the wings? That doesn't make sense. A dog is still a dog, even if it doesn't bark."

"It's complicated. Let's not have this argument again," I say. Because when she puts it that way, it does sound silly.

I rub my hands over my face, trying to push aside the sting of my past failures and figure out what I'm missing. There has to be some other reason that Hermes came to question me, and not just the fact that I killed Ramun Mar. I can't believe that's all there is to it. Otherwise the Exalteds would've just killed me. Why keep me alive? Just to continue questioning me?

What is it I'm missing? What could make a lowly vættir interesting enough that the Æthereal High Council gets involved?

Before I can figure it out, the room explodes with light. I blink, and the spots clear to reveal Hermes standing a few feet away. Cass is already gone, the swinging door the only evidence of her hasty flight.

Hermes doesn't notice, just grabs my arm and hauls me out of the chair. "Hey! What are you doing?" I ask.

"Taking you to see Hades."

I yank my arm free and take a step back. "Why?"

Hermes sighs and grasps my arm, this time more gently. "Because there are questions that need answers, and if you won't answer them for me, maybe you'll answer them for the King of the Dead."

Before I can respond, the world falls away in a burst of light, and when my vision clears, I'm standing outside a massive building. It's not a castle. More like a temple, or at least the bastard love child of a temple and a castle. Hundreds of steps lead up to darkness framed by black marble columns rising into towers. The structure is carved into the mountainside, like the land is vomiting forth Hades's domain. Massive bowls of dark fire flicker in between the columns, their midnight flames casting no light but making the structure more ominous. The twilight sky beyond makes the place look like something from a horror movie.

I take a step backward and damn near fall off the cliff behind me.

Hermes steadies me and sighs. "You should've answered my questions, kiddo. Now they're bringing in the big guns." He shoves me toward the entryway, away from the sheer cliff face behind us. "Trust Hades. He's honest, not like the rest of the Æthereals."

"You mean like you?"

He doesn't answer my question, just straightens his suit, which is once again brightly cream colored. He must've gone home and changed in between popping back and forth around the realms.

"Hades has no love for the High Council. Right now he's going to be your best ally." Hermes takes a step back, and I frown.

"You're not coming with me?" I want to take the words back as soon as they're out of my mouth. They're the words of a child, not an inmate of Tartarus.

Hermes's expression softens, and he pushes his hand through his hair. He spends a lot of time in the Mortal Realm, and it shows. From the old stories he's always been the most human of all the Æthereals. "I'm afraid not. Just answer his questions, and you'll be fine, Peep. Go ahead, he's expecting you." He swallows and gives me a slight smile. "By the way, I also keep my promises. Even if it doesn't seem that way."

I look at the black marble columns carved out of the mountain in front of me and heave a sigh. "That's not exactly comforting."

But when I turn around, I am completely alone.

CHAPTER THREE

I ENTER THE TEMPLE/CASTLE THING SLOWLY, EXPECTING TO BE ATTACKED at any moment. My boots echo loudly on the marble floor of Hades's mansion. Everything here is dark, darker, darkest. A long hallway stretches before me, and the sight reminds me of a haunted house my mother took us to when I was a kid. Mom thought it was important for Whisper and me to mix with the human kids who lived in the town near the Aerie. She thought it was good for vættir to remember that we were both human and Æthereal, and not some flawed version of one or the other. Not everyone in the Aerie agreed with her, and most of our trips to town we made by ourselves.

It was something Whisper carried on after Mom was gone, but I don't remember any of the trips with her being as stressful as the ones with my mom.

It was Halloween, the only day of the year when we were allowed to go into town without a glamour, a kind of magic spell, to hide our massive wings. The town had set up a haunted house, and while Whisper was eager to go inside, I was terrified. Mom wasn't hearing any of it though. "Go with your sister, or you can walk back to the Aerie by yourself. I won't have a coward in my line." I cried and begged her not to make me go, while Whisper watched with a blank expression. Six years older than me, she had mastered the Harpy way of hiding emotions by the age of twelve. At six, I hadn't.

And I never would.

I had nightmares about that haunted house for years. And every night when I would wake from sleep, my throat clogged with a scream, I would see my mother and the disappointment in her eyes.

Now, in this place so like that haunted house of memory, I swear to myself that I will not show my fear. I hold tight to the thought and study my surroundings. Randomly placed fire bowls warm the space with their dark fire, and decorative columns that glow silver light the way. I hold my hand up to one and recognize a familiar tingle. Æther. Somehow Hades has brought æther down to the Underworld and sealed it away. I wonder why the King of the Dead would need æther. All of the lords of the Underworld use erebos, which is plentiful here. A dark power made of shadows, erebos is the opposite of æther, which derives its power from light. It seems like a wasted effort to bring that much æther across the Rift, the nothingness that divides the worlds, just to light up a room.

Unless, of course, Hades keeps it to remind his visitors how powerful he is. All that trapped æther has certainly put me on my guard.

I square my shoulders and march down the hallway. I won't let Hades intimidate me. I've spent the past year in the Pits of Tartarus. There's very little I haven't seen or done to survive. I'm not telling the High Council how I killed Ramun Mar. Not even the King of the Dead. Especially not him.

Because if I say I struck down an Æthereal with dark lightning, I'll be dead before I finish the story.

At the end of the hallway is a door that glows with a welcoming light. I figure that's supposed to be my goal, so I head toward it. Halfway to my destination there's a strange noise. Breathing, a heavy chuffing sound that makes me pause and turn around.

I immediately wish I hadn't.

The breathing comes from a giant, three-headed hound. A cerberus, one of the watchdogs of the hells. This one's a Rottweiler the size of an elephant, with glowing red eyes and slavering jaws. Right now he's sniffing the ground with one of his heads, while the other two scent the air. I have no doubt it's my scent that's intrigued him.

Aw, hells.

I take a slow step backward toward the glowing door. Maybe it's my breathing; maybe it's my pounding heart. Whatever it is, all three of the heads snap in my direction, and growls issue from each of the beast's throats.

Fear freezes me for a split second before I turn around and run like my life depends on it.

Behind me the demon dog takes off as well. The scrabbling of its nails echoes throughout the hall, and I look over my shoulder to see how close I am to becoming puppy chow. The thing crouches, preparing to leap. My feet tangle around each other and I go down just as the thing springs at me. I land on my belly with an *oof*, skidding forward a little on my face while the cerberus leaps over me. The marble is cool against my cheek, but there's no time to enjoy the sensation. I push up and climb to my feet. A little ways away, the cerberus turns around within the small space between the columns that line the hall. I frown, because it looks like the thing's gotten bigger.

That can't be good.

The beast takes a slow step forward, growling in stereo. I want to say something inane like "Nice puppy," but my throat is frozen in fear. I take a deep breath and try to push away the terror that makes me clumsy. I roll my head around, shake out my arms, and stomp my feet, hoping to get the adrenaline flowing. There's no way I can just jump over the damn thing to get to the illuminated door, which is so close that the demon dog's tail whaps the doorframe. But maybe I can go under it. There are a few inches between the beast's belly and the ground, and marble is slippery.

I take a deep breath. "It's just like sliding into home," I mutter to myself. This is probably not the time to think about how I always got picked last for sports.

Before I let myself consider the many ways this could go wrong, I take a couple of steps backward then run forward as fast as I can. The ginormous dog lets loose a surprised bark and runs toward me. When I'm close enough to smell the thing's sulfurous breath, I throw my arms up and kick my feet out like I'm about to score the winning run in the World Series.

The demon dog gives a yelp, and I think maybe I'm going to make it, until the thing's leftmost head snaps at me. I throw my arm across my eyes rather than have the thing chew my face off. Long teeth sink into my right arm, and I can't swallow my cry of pain.

Looks like the home team just won.

The cerberus yanks me backward and up into the air, my feet dangling above the ground. The massive head shakes me back and forth, tossing me around like a chew toy. I swing my legs away from the other heads, which snap at me. The agony in my arm is crippling, and it's hard to think about anything else but the teeth grinding against my bones. Tears burn a hot path down my cheeks, and my cries of pain are almost as loud as the demon dog's growls. Blackness threatens to overtake me. I shake my head, chasing it away. I didn't spend the past year fighting off the dregs of vættir society just to let some overgrown mutt eat me for lunch.

I will not die today.

In desperation I extend my talons and try to claw out the beast's eyes, but they're too far away for me to reach. My razor-sharp nails skitter off the side of the massive head. The creature's hide is too thick for my talons to penetrate, and all I succeed in doing is pissing off the beast a little more.

Bummer.

I swing left and then right, trying to work up enough momentum to wrap my legs around the thickly corded neck. I try this several times without success, all while the other two heads are snapping and snarling. Every time I try to lift my legs up, the head holding me gives another shake, and I don't do anything but moan and kick the beast weakly in the side.

My abs ache with the effort, and I realize it's time for plan B. Or is it C? I think hard, trying to force my brain into gear. It's not easy with the way my arm hurts, but I remember watching a dog-training show with Whisper, and the trainer mentioned the sensitivity of a dog's nose. I'm not sure why I remember that, but I do.

Figuring it's worth a shot, I pull my fist back and punch the cerberus in the nose. It's weak and awkward. Even months of toiling in the Pits hasn't improved my left hook. The punch is somewhere between sad and pathetic.

The cerberus gives me a playful shake in response.

I cry out as a muscle tears in my upper back. There's a popping sensation and my arm throbs. The fresh pain in my shoulder makes me think it's dislocated. Thankfully, the adrenaline surging through my veins will keep the worst of the pain at bay for a little while longer. But I'm not sure I even have that much time left.

I'm getting a little desperate. My talons are no use against the creature, and I have no other weapons. I can't keep swinging my legs out of the way of the other heads. I'm too tired. And if one of the other maws locks onto my legs, I'll be torn apart.

I close my eyes and begin to summon my forbidden power. It's dangerous, and using it in Hades's hall is a stupid move. But I'm out of options.

I'm just not ready to die.

"Daisy, drop her right now."

The mouth locked on my arm releases, and I fall to the ground, rolling around in misery. When I try to move my arm, agony runs up the limb. Yep, definitely dislocated. The first time I dislocated the thing was back in the Aerie during one of our hand-to-hand combat lessons. My partner was a much better fighter than I was, and she wanted to make sure everyone knew it. I ended up with a dislocated shoulder and a few cracked ribs. She got ranked first for our class.

"Are you well?" Persephone's voice rolls over me, and I prop myself up with my good arm. Pain makes my vision swim. In the Mortal Realm I would've started healing by now, but the lack of æther in the Underworld means that I'm on my own. There's no way I can fix this right now. Cass is going to have to pop it back into place when I get back to the Pits.

The old training from back in the Aerie kicks in. I hurriedly dash away my tears and stand, ignoring the screaming from my shoulder. My breath catches as I climb to my feet, and I force myself to exhale normally. Never let the enemy see you in pain. "Yeah, just peachy. Shouldn't you have that thing on a leash?" My voice is just the right amount of sarcastic and bitchy. I'm pretty proud of myself, since nausea clutches at my stomach, and I just want to sit down and bawl.

The cerberus sits next to Persephone, and she strokes him idly as she studies me. "I wanted to see if Tartarus taught you how to survive."

A bitter laugh bursts from my mouth before I can stop it. I have to fight back a moan. Even laughing makes my arm hurt. I hold my right arm close to my body with my left, trying to immobilize it. It's better than nothing. "Well, it looks like I haven't learned anything down here. Your puppy almost ate me alive."

A slight smile curves her lips. In the dim light of the hall I can't see the color of her eyes, just the Æthereal shine of them. "You learned how to not give up, to keep trying even in the face of overwhelming odds. That is something many never learn, vættir and Æthereal alike."

Standing here in Hades's hall, it's easy to remember the last time I saw her. Persephone was one of the Exalteds on the High Council during my trial. It was her vote, the tiebreaker, that sent me to Tartarus rather than to my death and oblivion. Then I was grateful to her. Now? Not so much.

"Exalted, thank you for your help. But the King of the Dead is expecting me." I take an experimental step toward the door. The motion makes my stomach heave. How am I supposed to present myself to Hades when I can barely stand? I lean against one of the nearby pillars of æther. By touching the pillar of untapped power I should be able to draw enough out to chase away the pain a little. But I feel no different. My shoulder throbs and doesn't heal any. I want to cry.

Persephone sighs and walks over. She digs her fingers into

my injured shoulder, and I can't bite back my scream. I fall to my knees. "Harpies do not show fear. But you do. So if you are not a Harpy, then what are you, Zephyr Mourning?" I can't ask her what she's talking about. All I can do is make little whimpering sounds as her fingers knead my injured shoulder.

Without warning she grabs my arm and lifts it up, popping the shoulder back into place. My scream echoes down the hallway, and the cerberus lies down with a whine. Then she plunges one of her hands into the pillar, the other still on my shoulder. The pain is replaced by a gentle warmth. The warmth changes, going from soothing to a deep burn. I gasp and Persephone's eyes go wide. She pulls her hand away and takes a hurried step back. I moan, my stomach churning and my head pounding. For a little bit I think I'm going to puke all over Hades's hall. But then the sensation passes, and I'm able to climb to my feet.

Persephone watches me, the amusement gone. I suddenly feel like an ant under a magnifying glass. "What are you?" she asks me again, her copper eyes intense.

"Nothing. I'm just a vættir." I stand as straight as I can, my hand still resting against the pillar.

"Yes, of course." She considers me a moment longer and then steps aside. "You are a strange bird, Zephyr Mourning."

I don't say anything, just nod in acknowledgment. As I walk past her, the black leaves in her blond hair stretch toward me with a rustle. The movement creeps me out, and I walk a little faster.

I hate Æthereals.

"Zephyr Mourning?"

I stop and turn around at Persephone's call. "Yes?"

"What was that power you were reaching for before I arrived?"

Fear stabs my heart with a sharp sliver of panic. I swallow and can't help but remember the first time I used my forbidden power.

I was ten and practicing for my casting final. I couldn't seem to get the mage light to dance the way it was supposed to. It was a simple spell, a calling of æther into an orb, one of the most basic magic spells ever. It was easy for everyone else in my class, but not for me. I could barely summon the æther. Every time I managed to manipulate it into a ball, it would promptly explode. Not only that but summoning the power hurt, like inadvertently biting my tongue while eating. Not a huge pain, but enough that I didn't really like my magic sessions.

The teacher clucked and told me to practice at home. "You're doing everything correctly. As far as I can tell you're just not putting forth enough effort," she said with her gray eyebrows drawn together. After class she called me over to her desk and handed me a sheet of homework. "Here are some exercises to practice at home. A proper Harpy can summon at least enough æther to light her way during dark nights. If you can't manage that, I'm going to have to fail you."

Her words left me cold. A failing mark in a basic magic class was suicide. My mother was a Harpy of the Enigma line, the most skilled fighters our Aerie had. Fail a class? I might as well tell my mother I was a pacifist.

At home I followed the exercises to the letter, but I felt like I was doing something wrong. Pulling the power to me felt unnatural, like writing with my foot. So I closed my eyes and tried it again, this time feeling the power rather than pulling it as I had been. It felt much more natural, and when I opened my eyes, the orb before me glowed silver and black, but mostly black. I stared at it with wonder until Whisper came into the room and batted the thing away with a birdlike screech.

"You can't ever do that again. Do you understand me?" she said, shaking me to emphasize each word. The fear in her face scared me more than the panic lacing her voice, and I nodded.

"They'll kill you for using erebos," she whispered, as though she was afraid someone might overhear us.

"But I can't summon the orb any other way. I'm going to fail basic magic," I wailed, on the verge of tears. I could already imagine my mother's rage.

Whisper watched me for a long moment before going to her chest and digging around in the bottom. She was much older than me, only a year away from the Trials we all take in our seventeenth year. I felt like she knew things that I didn't, mysterious things that made her seem so much more adult than me.

She pressed a small, bright stone into my hand. "Here. This will give you a boost."

"What is it?"

"Æther stone. Just pull the magic from there instead of yourself. Wear it in your boot the day of your test and you should be fine."

I passed my magic exam, and that was only because the æther stone helped me through the thing. I made sure to never enroll in another spell-casting course. All of my instructors thought that I was just terrible at using magic, the same way I was bad at everything else. But magic was less important than my lack of skill with a sword, or my hesitation when it came to killing. As far as the Aerie was concerned, I was a huge disappointment, and my lack of magical ability was just one more reason I sucked.

I never used that dark power again until the night I killed Ramun Mar. It was only after he was dead, his body a smoking ruin, that I realized why Whisper was so afraid that day she found me. Erebos was unnatural.

If I was the kind of creature that could use it, what did that make me?

That's the reason the vættir can't wield erebos. How can we be trusted with a power so destructive it can destroy gods?

So instead of telling Persephone the truth, I tilt my head and blink. "Power? What power? There's no magic in the underworld, Exalted." It's a terrible lie, but mostly because I'm such a bad liar. Harpies don't lie. We can smell the truth in each other's emotions. So what's the point?

"There is magic in the underworld. There is erebos." Persephone's eyes seem to burn a hole right through me, and it takes everything I have not to squirm like a kid caught stealing the last cookie from the cookie jar.

I force a laugh, the sound hollow and flat. "Only the Lords of the Underworld can use erebos."

"Yes. And the shadow vættir."

I shrug. "The shadow vættir are extinct."

"That is true." Her tone is curt, and I know I struck a nerve. It gives me an odd sense of pleasure, pissing her off. Persephone spends most of her time down here, but she is still a bright, like most Æthereals. She's just as powerless as Hermes down here. That probably got old after the first couple millennium.

I consider the columns of æther around us. Hades must've brought all this raw power down here for his wife, so she wouldn't feel so helpless. It makes the King of the Dead a touch less scary.

Persephone sighs and hugs herself. "That is all, Zephyr Mourning. Thank you." She hesitates, and then shrugs. "It really was for the best."

"What was?"

She opens her arms to take in the space around us. "Sending you here to the Underworld. Tartarus was the safest place for you after you killed one of Hera's generals. You would not have been able to run from Ramun Mar's brother forever, you know."

"I'm not afraid of Ramun Sol, and I'm not afraid of Hera," I say before walking toward the lit doorway at the end of the hall. But it's a lie.

I am utterly terrified of them.

CHAPTER FOUR

I WALK THROUGH THE DOOR, NERVOUSNESS ONCE AGAIN PUTTING ME on edge. The first thing I register is the dark god standing at the far end of the room, his back to me. It would be impossible to miss Hades. Erebos swirls around him, shrouding him in a mantle of hypnotically shifting shadows.

I tear my eyes away from Hades and take in the room. I imagined the chamber of the King of the Dead would be dark and brooding, like something taken out of a Tim Burton movie. Shrunken heads and deep shadows, with the skeletons of past foes hanging from the rafters. *Edward Scissorhands* meets *The Nightmare Before Christmas*, with a dash of *Beetlejuice* thrown in for kicks. But the chamber is round and bright, with columns and walls made of white marble. Light pours in from giant squares of æther nestled in between decorative columns. The darkest thing in the room is Hades himself. His back is still to me when he speaks.

"Do you know why you are here, Zephyr Mourning?"

Hades's voice is rich and deep, like an evening-news anchor. I blink. It takes a moment for his words to penetrate. There's something about the shifting darkness around him that mesmerizes, and I'm having trouble focusing.

"Yes," I finally answer.

"So, then, what do you have to tell me?" He turns toward me, and I get a glimpse of an ancient warrior's uniform under the darkness, a pale shift overlaid by a silver breastplate, his arms adorned with leather gauntlets. There's some sort of design on his arms, but the shadows hide its meaning. The Underworld magic clings to him like a cape, flowing down from the top of his head so that it's impossible to see where his hair ends and the erebos begins. I'm sure it's an effect that's meant to impress, and it does.

I don't bother to wonder why he's dressed for war.

He steps away from the window, which looks out onto some far-off desert landscape where people shoot at each other. It doesn't look like any part of the Underworld that I know. At first I think the windows are actually TVs, but then the scene changes to people sitting on a lawn enjoying a picnic, while little kids run around gathering up colored eggs. I remember the time Whisper and I went to town for the annual Easter egg hunt, and yearning clenches my stomach.

"Is that the Mortal Realm?" I say before I think about who it is I'm asking.

Hades nods. "Not part of my domain, but I enjoy watching anyway."

I turn to look at the other windows, and slowly I realize that they look out over different parts of the realms. There are toga-wearing gods walking through the sky plazas of the Æthereal Realm and the river valley of the Du'at, part of the Underworld. The Pits of Tartarus show hundreds of vættir toiling in the mud, and the Folkvangr is in the middle of a snowstorm. I keep turning, looking for the window that will show me the Elysian Fields, hoping that maybe I'll get a glimpse of my sister.

"The Fields are right there to your left. Today is the bacchanalia."

Hades's words barely register. I've already found it, a scene of drunken debauchery. Satyrs chase wood nymphs through a clearing, while ram-horned berserkers raise mugs of some foamy drink. Vættir of all kind feast and dance and make merry. I can't imagine my mom hanging out in the middle of a drunken revelry, but I look for Whisper among the participants. My sister never found a party she didn't like.

Disappointment is beginning to hollow out my middle when the screen goes dark, and Cass's face replaces the image of the Elysian Fields.

I look over my shoulder at Hades, whose arms are now crossed, his expression hard. "Why have you refused to answer the questions of the Æthereal High Council?"

I wrap my arms around my middle. I want to see my sister so very badly that it's hard to think about anything else. For a long moment I consider telling him the truth. Hades could strike me down for being unnatural, and I'd be dead. I could join the revelry in the Elysian Fields.

But then Cass's warning returns to me. She told me one night that not all shades make it to the afterlife, that sometimes the trip across the Underworld is too dangerous. "There are things that will devour a shade for just a taste of life," she said. "That's why we try so hard to survive the Pits. Because not making it to the afterlife would be so much worse."

I swallow the confession that lingers on the tip of my tongue and say instead, "I don't think it's in my best interest."

He frowns as he considers my words. "Who told you this? Cassiphone Pellacis?"

My brow furrows. Is he reading my mind? Or just guessing? "What does Cass have to do with this?"

"Do you know who your newfound companion is?"

I shake my head, trying to make sense of this sudden turn in conversation. "Cass is my friend."

"Cassiphone Pellacis is a liar and a fraud, just like her father. He betrayed his people, and she is not much better. The crimes she has committed are even more legendary than yours, my little Godslayer."

His tone rubs me the wrong way, and a familiar anger returns. But like always I don't acknowledge the emotion, just push it down deep, where it simmers. If I keep my mouth shut, he'll just send me back to the Pits. After all, he's not the first inquisitor the Æthereal High Council has sent.

He's just a little scarier than the rest.

Hades walks toward me, the darkness around him shrouding his steps so that he appears to glide. I take a step back, but he doesn't seem to notice. "She is heartless and not to be trusted."

I think of all the times Cass has saved my life. I swallow hard. "People can change." My voice comes out as a squeak.

Hades's gaze burns through me. His eyes are the same bright silver as my own, and it's a little like looking into a mirror. I wonder if my father was some distant offspring of Hades, or maybe even Zeus. Mom just told me he was an Æthereal, although Whisper used to hint that he was an Exalted. I never believed that, but seeing eyes the same color as mine looking at me has me wondering and thinking about family ties.

In that moment I remember that Hades is Hermes's uncle, for whatever that's worth. Maybe Hermes put in a good word for me, and the King of the Dead will take pity on me and just send me back to the Pits.

"Have *you* changed, Zephyr Mourning?" he asks, his voice dangerously low.

Goose bumps rise up on my arms, but I ignore them. My heart is in my throat, pounding out my fear in an irregular rhythm. I ignore it all and try to remember that I have survived a year in Tartarus.

I lift my chin. "Yes."

Hades studies my face, and I wonder if he has the power to see the stains on my soul, like Anubis. Or maybe he really is reading my mind. "For the better? Have you changed for the better?"

I start to answer, but then I remember the Fae that Hermes so casually killed this morning. Before, I would've been horrified and upset. Now, not so much. It was another terrible moment in a string of nightmares, so uneventful that I barely registered the loss of life.

The Matriarch at the Aerie would say that I'm getting battle hardened, like forging iron into steel. Stronger, more adaptable. But I don't feel like a better person. I feel like I'm losing something important about myself.

I don't tell Hades this. Instead I just shrug.

Hades says nothing, his expression blank. I wish I could tell what he wants from me. After all, what will the Æthereal High Council do if I don't answer their questions? Cass's musings come back to me. Are they just planning to kill me anyway?

I try not to think about it.

The dark god gestures to the window behind me. "Let me show you the crimes of Cassiphone Pellacis, and you can decide whether you want to call her a friend or not."

I'm not sure why he's so hung up on me being friends with Cass. Is it because he thinks she's the reason I'm not talking? I say nothing, just turn around. All of the windows fall away, and reality turns in on itself until Hades and I stand in the middle of a meadow. The tang of the ocean drifts in the air, and far off in the distance is the bluest water I have ever seen. It makes me ache for home, for the Aerie and the way it overlooked the sea.

"Where are we?"

"An ancient place. Watch, and see the kind of girl you call 'friend.'"

I open my mouth to argue, but I'm distracted by a commotion in the village that lies down in the valley below us. Half the town explodes in a fireball. People run screaming from the buildings, pouring out in every direction, their words of fear unintelligible. They aren't speaking any language that I know, although the words do sound like a pale imitation of Æthereal.

I don't need to understand the language to know that the villagers are scared.

The first explosion is quickly followed by another, and then another. People run in every direction, some toward far-off boats, others up the hill past where Hades and I stand in the meadow. I try to figure out what's causing the damage. It's not like they had explosives when Cass walked the Mortal Realm. Her time on earth was a few thousand years before dynamite.

My question is answered when Cass walks toward us. She wears a rust-colored toga, and her golden hair whips around her head in an angry cloud. Her face is twisted in rage, and as the villagers flee in her wake, she screams one word, over and over again. She throws bolts of æther at the buildings she passes, destroying homes and people with the same mindless cruelty as a child kicking over blocks. I don't even know if she notices the men and women she incinerates. Her focus is on the hill where Hades and I stand. She draws even with us. Shock reverberates through me as I realize her toga was once white. The rust coloring is dried blood.

Cassiphone screams again. "HERA!"

The scene before us shimmers, and the bitch-goddess herself

appears on the far edge of the field. Hera looks just like she did at my trial, dark hair braided on top of her head, an ivory toga draped around her curvaceous figure. Cass turns in response to Hera's arrival, and I half lurch toward both of them before Hades places a calming hand on my arm.

"This is just an echo of memory. Hera is not really here."

I nod, but my jaw is still clenched, and I have to force myself to relax. I may not know what is going on here, but one thing is certain: If Hera is involved, it can't be anything good. She argued the loudest at my trial for a death sentence, and it was her Acolytes that killed my sister. If there's trouble, you can pretty much guarantee Hera is somehow responsible.

"Cassiphone Pellacis, you have destroyed my temple and my village. Your bloodshed has not gone unnoticed. I am here now, at your behest. State your reason for summoning me." Hera's tone is haughty, but at least she speaks Æthereal, so I can understand what she's saying.

Cassiphone growls low in her throat. Her hands are clenched into fists. "Murderer."

Hera's too-red lips curve into a smile, slow and cruel like the wicked stepmother in a fairy's tale. "You will have to be more specific."

Cass responds by throwing a gout of flame at Hera. The Æthereal blocks the attack easily. The battle is on, æther and flame flying in all directions. It's strange to see a battle without movement, the energy flashing between them the only indication of violence. Harpies fight like street brawlers, magic a necessary evil, but not our preferred method. We like to draw blood.

At least, we're supposed to.

The back-and-forth between Hera and Cassiphone is strangely subdued, and it isn't until Cass goes to her knees that I realize she's been losing this entire time. I take a half step forward before I remember that I can't help her. This is a battle she lost long ago. My heart hurts for her as she wobbles and finally collapses with a moan.

Hera advances, clucking her tongue as she approaches Cass, who lies flat on her back. "He never would have been yours, anyway. It was just a matter of time before he found a more suitable match."

Cass coughs and mutters something, blood foaming on her lips. Hera frowns. "What did you say, girl?"

"She said it never mattered because she loved him."

Hera and I both turn to the opposite edge of the meadow, where a tiny woman stands with her hands on her hips. Her scarlet hair reaches her waist, and her dress is made of tiny pearls. Her golden eyes shine with rage, and she taps her foot impatiently. I'm not sure who she is, but Red is not happy.

"This is no business of yours, Aphrodite," Hera snaps. I blink in surprise, because the goddess on the edge of the meadow looks nothing like I imagined her to be. The goddess of love, this woman is fierce, like she would be at home hunting bears.

"You destroyed young love, Hera. This is my business," Aphrodite snaps. While the two goddesses argue, Cass struggles into a sitting position. Neither Aphrodite nor Hera are paying attention to her, and she uses their distraction to her advantage. Cass lashes out at Hera, scoring a direct hit in the middle of the goddess's back. The Exalted spins around with a shriek, her face twisted with rage.

"This isn't over," Cass snarls at the goddess as she slowly climbs to her feet. Her expression is fierce, her spine straight despite the fatigue that makes her hand shake as she points at Hera. "I will destroy you, Hera. No matter how long it takes."

Before Hera can retaliate, Hermes flashes into the meadow. He moves faster than I've ever seen him move before. One moment he's beside Cass, the next there's a flash of light and the two of them are gone.

The scene dissolves, and Hades's chamber slowly comes back into focus, along with all of the windows. The window on the Elysian Fields is dark, but I glance at it longingly, anyway.

"So now you know the kind of person you have chosen as your companion."

I close my eyes for a long moment and take a deep breath. It pains me, realizing how little I know about Cass. Attacking an enemy while their back is turned is dishonorable, but who cares? Does it really matter when someone's saved your ass more times than you can count? And sure she killed a lot of innocent people trying to find Hera, but Cass has also spent gods know how long in the Pits of Tartarus. I kind of feel like she's served her time.

"Nothing you've shown me has changed my mind. She's still my friend." I hate that Cass had to go through something so painful, but at the same time I like knowing someone else has a score to settle with Hera. It makes me feel less alone.

"She is a Pellacis. She will lie to you, and she will eventually betray you in order to get what she wants. It is the nature of her kind. Pellacis are inherently dishonest."

I've never heard of a Pellacis, but Hades is talking as if they're some kind of vættir, like a Fae or a Mer. Beyond that, his meaning is clear. Cass will sell me out if given half a chance. It's the Æthereal version of good cop/bad cop. Come clean with us now, kid, and we'll go easy on you.

But it's a wasted effort. Cass doesn't know my secret, and I still trust her more than I trust any god.

So I say nothing, just cross my arms and meet his bright gaze.

Hades looks at me a long moment before nodding. "As you wish." He stares off into the distance, his metallic eyes thoughtful. Why would he take such a roundabout way to get me to spill my guts? It's weird, but I don't really get Æthereals anyway. They all seem a little off, and I wonder if it's because all that power fries their brains.

Plus, it's probably a tactic that works more often than not. Lucky for me I've seen enough cop shows to know the hard sell when I see it. I'm better off keeping my mouth shut.

Hades's gaze once again lights on me. "So you refuse to answer the Æthereal High Council's questions."

"I don't have anything to tell them." It's the truth. But I still hold my breath, waiting for his response. What's the worst he can do to me? Feed me to one of his demon dogs? That would suck, but there's not much I can do except keep quiet and hope everyone forgets about me.

Hades makes a sound that is curiously close to a sigh. "Next time they will not ask so nicely."

I let out my breath in relief before I pause. "What do you mean?"

"The courtesies you have been shown thus far have been in deference to your mother. She was a respected general, and there are few who did not owe her some small favor. But you have quickly evaporated even that small bit of goodwill. Hera and the others of her ilk will now advocate for your outright death." He turns away, but not before I see a flash of emotion pass over his stoic face. Sadness? Anger? Is the emotion directed at me?

More important, why does he care?

My curiosity is cut short by his next words. "Hera is pushing to have you summoned to the Æthereal Realm again. She is still unhappy with how the last trial went, and the longer you survive down in the Pits the more supporters she gains."

I'm not a genius, but I can figure out what he's not saying: I'm dead, it's just a matter of when and how. It's one thing to know I have to fight to survive, another to know my end is near no matter what.

But what can I do about it?

Fear leaves me cold, and I whisper, "Yeah, okay." I tug nervously at one of my locks and try to find the bright side. But it's really hard to do anything but imagine the hundreds of ways I could die. That does nothing to help the churning of my stomach.

I half expected Hades to lie, to make empty promises about how well I would be treated if I just tell the High Council what they want to know. But he didn't. He just laid the truth out for me without any fanfare. And as much as it hurts, I actually appreciate it.

Maybe Hermes was trying to help me. But I can't really see him getting me out of this one.

Hades's expression, at least what I can see of it between the tendrils of darkness, is pensive. It strikes me that he's a somber god, without the flamboyance of Hermes or the selfish dramatics of most of the bright Exalteds. It's fitting for an Æthereal who spends so much time around the dead.

Hades suddenly opens his arms, and before I can retreat out of his reach, I am wrapped up in a hug. It's a strange sensation, and his darkness wraps around me in a comforting embrace. I want to stiffen, to resist even this small measure of affection. But the darkness is calming. Reassuring. I need a little of that right now. I close my eyes and hug him back, surprised by how right the act seems.

"You will always be safe here in the Underworld," Hades says, tightening the embrace before letting me go. "I knew your mother well, and I still visit her from time to time. It would sadden her to see her daughter treated so shabbily. Please believe that I will never let any harm come to you while you are in my domain."

His words don't do anything to stop the sick feeling in my middle. Instead I just wonder how he knew my mother. I know that she did several missions here in the Underworld. Did she meet Hades then? Were they maybe something more?

Hades takes a step back, and I push the questions from my mind. I can't really imagine my mother with anyone, let alone Hades. She wasn't one to let sentiment override her judgment. Whoever my father was, I know I was the result of a breeding contract, not some torrid affair. Love just isn't in the cards for Harpies.

In the back of my mind a little voice whispers, *What about your sister?* But Whisper proves my point. She let herself fall in love and ended up dead.

Hades retreats across the room, but the darkness doesn't follow him. For a moment it clings to my skin, soothing my pain. The ever-present ache in my chest, a constant companion since the day Whisper was killed, eases. I want to make Hades's dark cloak my own, to let it erase the burden of loss and failure that weighs on me.

But the darkness isn't mine, and to try to claim it would be a death sentence. So instead of cradling the erebos close, I shove it away while taking a step back.

Hades watches me, his gaze too knowing. "The darkness seems placated by you."

I turn away so he won't see my expression, which I'm sure is full of longing. "I'm a Godslayer. The darkness knows its own." I bite my tongue and hope that Hades doesn't notice the slip. Way to almost confess, Mourning.

Hades says nothing, and after a long moment, when I feel more centered, I turn around. "Is that it, then? Am I free to return to the Pits?"

"If that is your wish." He seems reluctant to let me go, and I wonder what this is really about. I should be beneath the notice of the King of the Dead. After all, I'm just another inmate of the Pits.

I look back toward the window that earlier showed the Elysian Fields. Hades notices, and asks, "Would you like to see your mother?"

"What's the catch?"

His eyebrows raise. "There is no catch. The offer was without conditions."

I hesitate. "Yes. Yes, I'd like to see her."

The window lights up, and there is my mother. Her blue-black skin glows like it never did in life. Her long red snarls are piled on top of her head, and she wears a dress. Her black-and-red wings seem to glow, less terrifying in death, almost cheerful. She sits with a group of other Harpies, laughing over something. I blink and look at the image again.

"Umm, are you sure that's my mother?"

"Yes. The shades are different from how they were in life. The Elysian Fields are a place of forgetting."

I nod, because I get what he's trying to say. It's hard to be angry when you can't remember what it was that you were pissed about.

I step back from the window. "Thank you," I say. I pause, considering my next words. "My sister, Whisper. Do you think I could see her, too? Just for a quick moment," I hurriedly add as his expression darkens. I hate the weakness in my voice, the slight tremor at the end. But the empty ache in the middle of my chest is back. I think that maybe if I can see her one last time, if I can see that she's happy in the afterlife, that some of the hurting will go away. Maybe I won't be so scared about everything. Maybe I can face my impending death with dignity.

"I am sorry. I cannot."

The yearning in my middle disappears, burned away by a familiar rage. This time I don't try to silence it. "Can't or won't?"

"Cannot."

"Why not? Just a second. I swear, I'll never ask you for anything again."

The whorls of darkness snap, and Hades tenses. "I cannot show you your sister because she is not here. Her shade never arrived in my domain."

His answer steals my breath away, and my chest tightens. "She never arrived?"

"Your sister is not in the afterlife."

His words unhinge something in me. The thought that Whisper isn't in the Elysian Fields breaks something in my heart. I want to lie on the ground and never get up.

I see her again, lying on the patio, her chest a gaping red mess. I know she was dead. She has to be in the Fields. If she isn't in the afterlife, where is she?

And does Hermes know her shade is adrift somewhere in the realms?

The only thing that's gotten me through my time in Tartarus was the belief that I would one day see my family again in the

Elysian Fields, that I could still earn a place in the afterlife. And now . . .

Now I have nothing.

Suddenly there's no point in going on. Why care where my shade ends up? Either way I'll just be alone. I don't know the woman who Hades just showed me in the Elysian Fields. My mother and I were never all that close, anyway. Mom was a drill sergeant, a taskmaster trying to make me something I was not. It was Whisper who cared for me, who taught me to fly and worked hard to make sure I could pass my lessons. My mother was just a specter who appeared in between wars. I can't spend eternity without Whisper.

I almost blurt out what Hades wants to know. Tell him about my abilities so he can end me here and now. I could tell him everything about the night Ramun Mar was killed, how I was so angry and scared and when I reached for the power, the darkness came, eager and willing and oh so destructive. I want to tell him everything. I want to just be done with it all.

But as I open my mouth to spill my one remaining secret, I stop. Because maybe that's just want he wants me to do. Maybe that's why he was kind to me. Hermes's smiling blue-steel eyes come back to me. What if this has all been an act? What if he's only pretending to be nice to get me to confess everything?

What if Hermes is part of this? Maybe the little pep talk was so I'd trust Hades and confess to using the dark power. Then he could deliver the coup de grâce and end me once and for all.

My anger returns, my grief forgotten. Æthereals are all the same.

"You're lying," I say, my voice soft. Something dark and anxious jumps low in my belly. As soon as the words are out of my mouth, I realize it's probably not the smartest thing in the world to insult an Exalted like Hades. The Exalteds are stronger than other Æthereals, and Hades is near the top of the food chain.

And me? I'm pretty close to the bottom.

But I can't seem to stop myself. My rage churns and fills me with the shadows that I recognize from the night I confronted Ramun Mar. The tiny voice in the back of my mind urges me to calm down, to be cautious. But I can't.

I won't.

Hades stills, his dark aura snapping with temper. Strangely, it seems to echo my own emotional state. "Why would I lie? What is the benefit in denying you access to your sister?"

I don't answer his question. Because if he's not lying, then my sister is gone. Not in the afterlife, just *gone*. She was once there, and now she's *nowhere*. My brain can't process that fact. My heart won't let me think that someone I loved so much could just cease to exist.

"I said you're lying. You're a liar. You're all liars." Hot tears pour down my cheeks. I know they make me look weak, but I don't care. I'm beyond caring. I am nothing but grief and rage. "You're all alike, lying when it suits you, cruel for the fun of it. Sleeping with whoever you want even though it could mean their death." I dash away my tears, breathing deep to keep myself from having a full-fledged breakdown.

But something of my words has penetrated Hades's somber demeanor, and behind the churning darkness his eyes narrow. "Who? Who am I like, Zephyr Mourning?"

Awareness prickles along my arms, and too late I realize I've pushed him too far. One does not offend a god and live to tell about it. But my anger and pain and sorrow are too wide for me to see reason, and I open my mouth when I would be better off keeping it shut.

"The High Council. All you Æthereals are the same. I don't know why I ever thought I could trust you. You probably never even met my mother. It's all just a lie to get me to confess how I killed Ramun Mar."

Hades pauses, and for a second I think maybe he won't punish me for my behavior. But then the whole of his darkness draws back from him, so that for one shining moment his form is revealed. The inky aura looms over him like a snake about to strike.

"Insolent puppy," he says. Time seems to slow into that single moment, and my anger withdraws enough for me to realize that I have seriously screwed up.

The dark wave rushes around Hades and over me, sweeping me up. It's no longer the welcoming friend it was earlier. Now the darkness has intent. I can feel it as it whispers over my skin. The erebos sighs in a hundred different voices. It steals my air and burns my nerve endings. I'm on fire while drowning and being

CHAPTER FIVE

I WAKE SLOWLY. MY BODY TAKES ITS TIME COMING BACK ONLINE, fingertips tingling and toes wiggling. I've just registered the grass tickling my nose and the headache forming behind my eyelids when the full effect of Hades's punishment slams into me.

I roll over with a groan. I feel like I've been beaten with a sack of doorknobs. Everything throbs, even my teeth. My nerve endings are seared. When I try to move, fresh pain shoots through me. I close my eyes and take deep breaths. Maybe I can just lie here forever. I'd make a pretty good rock.

Nausea ripples through my middle. I want to sit up. Maybe puke a little. But that would involve movement. I can't do anything more strenuous than breathe.

The pain begins to ebb, but I don't move. I open my eyes and blink in surprise. I stare up into the same twilight sky that I've looked at for the past year.

"Rise and shine, princess," Cass says, kicking my foot. "You missed chow."

I roll over before climbing to my knees. My head pounds and I hurt all over, but it's better than being dead.

torn to pieces. It flows through the center of me, tearing away something vital. I try to scream out my pain, but the darkness steals even that bit of release.

I am tossed and turned in a sea of pain and rage and disappointment. I reach out, attempting to wield some of my own forbidden power. For a single shining moment the darkness abates, reluctant to hurt me. But it's pointless. The erebos quickly begins devouring me again, Hades's intent pushing it forward. My abilities are nothing compared to his, a raindrop trying to attack the ocean.

I surrender to my punishment, going limp as the dark energy tears me apart atom by atom. My last thought before I lose consciousness is relief.

At least I finally know how I die.

"Where are we?" I glance around, taking in the scenery. There's actually grass here, and the wood line is closer. A lot closer.

"The bulls got a sudden order to move us after the rain stopped. We're going into the woods." Cass holds out her hand and helps me lever myself to my feet.

"The woods? But I thought going in there was certain death."

Cass gives me a look. "It is. I think someone is trying to make a point."

A couple of Fae walk past me, giving me serious stink eye. One whispers something to the other, and I shrink into myself as the willowy blondes study me. "Oh gods."

Cass sighs. "Yeah. It's going to be really hard to keep you alive."

I swallow and nod. "I understand. Well, thanks for all you've done. I mean, you're probably one of the best friends I've ever had." I don't add that she's one of the only friends I've ever had. Life in the Aerie doesn't really lend itself to closeness.

Thinking about Cass abandoning me dredges up old memories of a boy with dark eyes and an easy smile. He was the one who gave me the nickname Peep, after those marshmallow chicks that come out in the spring. But he wasn't a Harpy, and in the end he left me just like everyone else.

She gives me a strange look. "You're a good friend too, Zeph. But that wasn't a declaration of your death. It was merely a statement of fact." She pauses and looks around. "Come on, let's fall in line before the bulls notice."

We slip into the line of vættir, trailing behind a satyr with a shovel propped on his shoulder. It reminds me that my shovel is gone. It's going to be really hard to dig without one. Assuming I live long enough to make it to the work site.

My body still aches a little, but as we start walking, my discomfort fades into the background. There's an anxious sensation deep in my stomach that I don't recognize. It makes me want to run into the shadows behind the trees or pick a fight with the satyr in front of me. It's a strange urge to have. I'm not really one to break the rules.

But I've also never been so close to dying before.

The trees press in on us, turning the twilight to night. There are deep shadows in between the twisted black trunks of the trees, and I press closer to Cass on instinct. "Don't touch the trunks. The trees are carnivorous," she says just as the satyr in front of us trips over an exposed root and falls. He lands against the trunk of one of the trees and screams as the bark envelops him. The spoiled-lemon stink of his fear is overwhelming, and I have to hold my breath. Cass carefully steps around the tree, avoiding the satyr's flailing arms as he is completely encased in smooth, shining bark.

The line keeps moving. No one even turns around to see what happened. That's the thing about Tartarus. Everyone can hear you scream. They just don't care. I reach down to pick up his shovel and keep walking.

I should feel something, be sad about his death or at least horrified. But I didn't know him, and I needed a shovel. I'm too busy trying to figure out how I'm going to survive to feel much beyond my own desperation.

We keep walking, picking our way around the deadly trees. I watch the ground to make sure I don't trip and try to forget that very soon I'll be dead. Whether at the hands of my fellow inmates or the Æthereals or this forest is really the only question. My sadness makes my shoulders droop, and I consider throwing myself against a tree just to get it over with. Maybe my restless shade will be able to find Whisper, wherever she ended up.

Cass nudges me with her elbow, and I look up. "What's wrong?" she asks, perceptive as always. I hastily detail everything that happened, from the strange meeting with Persephone to the revelation that Whisper isn't in the Elysian Fields and my punishment for talking back to a god. She winces when I describe how the darkness overwhelmed me.

"You're lucky to even be here."

I nod. "I know."

"Not many vættir can even survive contact with a wave of erebos." Cass grabs me by the arm and pulls me out of the way of a grasping vine. I swat at the vine with my shovel, making contact. The thing lets loose a high-pitched scream as it darts away.

Cass continues to look at me like she's waiting for me to confess my darkest secret. Maybe I should finally tell her. It's not like I have a lot of time left. I owe her so much. The least I could give her would be this small truth.

I open my mouth, ready to tell her everything, when there's a chorus of screams from the front of the line of vættir winding its way through the forest. "What's going on?"

Cass snaps to attention just as vættir begin to run toward us. Their screams meld with the rancid-citrus stink of their fear, and my head pounds. Her hand is a vise on my arm. "Look."

A creature moves through the forest, its hulking mass knocking over trees as it lets loose a hoarse roar. The head of the thing resembles a giant lion, but a scorpion's tail lashes out at the fleeing vættir, while an eagle's wings beat the air in agitation. I take a step back, and my mouth goes dry. "Is that a manticore?"

"No, chimera. But this is our chance." Cass pulls me sideways, away from the approaching beast but also in the opposite direction of the fleeing inmates.

"Wait, our chance for what?" I ask as I run to keep up with Cass. I really don't have much choice. She's pulling me by the arm, and she's incredibly strong. It's either run or let my arm get yanked out of the socket, and once was enough.

"To escape," she says, and it's enough to make me dig in my heels.

"Whoa, wait. Wait just a minute here. We can't escape. Where are we supposed to go?"

Behind us the screams are getting louder, the roar of the beast echoing through the trees. Cass sighs. "We go to the Mortal Realm. I can get us to Charon, at the river crossing. We'll convince him to get us across. You can hide in the Mortal Realm, at least for a little while. The Æthereals aren't as strong there."

I shake my head, despair weighing heavily in my middle. "They'll still find me."

"Maybe. Either way we can at least find out what happened to your sister." Cass grabs my arm and pulls me along, and I don't resist.

"What do you mean we can find my sister?" I run to keep up with her, and she lets go of me to swing her shovel at a clinging vine that drops down at us.

"If her shade never made it to the Underworld, then it has to be in the Mortal Realm somewhere. We can help her move on."

"But what if it isn't? What if she isn't there?"

Cass stops and looks me dead in the eye. "Then the Nyx can find her."

My bark of laughter bounces off the trees. "Really, Cass? The Nyx isn't real. It's just a story adults tell children to help them sleep at night."

Cass sighs and starts jogging again. "If your sister didn't cross over, then the Nyx is real. That's why we need to find out if her shade is still in the Mortal Realm or not."

I pick up the pace to keep up. "I don't understand."

"Disappearing shades is one of the signs of the Nyx's return. So if your sister's shade is missing, then it might mean the Nyx has finally returned."

"Returned? What are you saying? You mean the Nyx was a real thing once?"

Cass nods. "A long time ago. I'm surprised you don't know

that." Her words are heavy with importance, and her tone is kind of insulting. Why would I think that a made-up hero is real? What does she think I am, a little kid?

I shake my head, pushing aside my irritation. "But, if she was real, what happened to her?"

"Not her, him," Cass says, as she starts moving faster. "He was a real person." She looks over her shoulder at me but doesn't stop running. "My father killed him."

CHAPTER SIX

AFTER CASS'S CONFESSION THERE'S NOTHING TO DO BUT RUN. SHE picks up the pace enough that I don't have breath to ask anything else, and I half wonder whether she planned it that way. I've never seen much emotion from Cass, but there is definitely an energy about her right now that seems kind of excited.

But what's she excited about?

We zigzag through the trees as quickly as we can, while my brain turns over our conversation. The Nyx. It's a childhood story my sister used to tell me, the shadowy vættir equivalent of Santa Claus. Mom wasn't one for fanciful stories, or bedtime stories at all. Her idea of entertainment was letting me color battle maps of past victories.

But Whisper? She liked to dream.

Thinking about my sister takes me back to our small house in the Aerie where Whisper and I shared a room. Like most houses in the Aerie ours was small, consisting of only two bedrooms, a practice studio where Mom drilled us on hand-to-hand combat, and a bathroom. There was no kitchen because all meals were delivered by the Aerie, rations allotted according to status. Since Mom was a general, we ate pretty well. We were even lucky enough to own a television, an uncommon luxury in the austerity of the Aerie.

At night when I was too restless to sleep, Whisper would tell me stories about the creation of the realms or the latest gossip about this Æthereal or that one. I don't know how old I was when she first told me the story of the Nyx. Young enough to still be afraid of the dark, but old enough that I shouldn't have been. I'd watched the shadows from the tree outside our window move against the wall, imagining it to be some kind of ravening monster when Whisper had called out in the dark.

"Peep, are you okay? You smell like a lemon meringue pie that's gone bad."

"I'm scared. Can I come sleep with you?"

Whisper sighed. She was a teenager and too old to want to share her bed with an annoying little sister. "Yes. Come on."

I'd vaulted out of my bed and into hers, burrowing under the covers. She pushed my wings out of the way until we were lying side by side. "You know, you don't have anything to be afraid of."

"I know. Fear makes me stupid, and as long as I know what's making me afraid I should be able to dismantle the emotion with fact." It was what Mom told me all the time.

Whisper laughed, her voice low. "No, you don't have anything to be afraid of because the Nyx will protect you."

"My teacher says the Nyx isn't real. She says it's just something that weak people use to feel better about their circumstances."

"The teachers here don't know everything, Peep." And then

Whisper's voice had taken on the dreamy tone that meant she was telling a story. "Long ago, before the realms were split, gods and men lived in harmony. Their children, the vættir, united the best in each of them. The vættir had the abilities of the gods tempered with the emotions of mortals. But Cronus was a jealous god and despised humans. So he commissioned the drakans to split the worlds, and that is what they did.

"The dark Æthereals retreated to the Underworld, where the erebos was strongest. The bright Æthereals rose up to the Æthereal Realm, where they looked down on those who couldn't manipulate æther like they could. And the vættir were bound to the Mortal Realm with their human relatives, their mortal blood preventing them from freely crossing the Rift separating the realms."

Whisper shifted in the bed, her head resting against mine. "For a time things were good, but the bright Exalteds weren't happy just ruling over their weaker cousins. They wanted more. They wanted to rule over the Mortal Realm as well."

"What does this have to do with the Nyx?"

"I'm getting to that, Peep. Just give me a second." She took a deep breath and exhaled. "Where was I?"

"The Æthereals were about to start the Æthereal Wars."

In the dark I couldn't see her nod, but I could feel it. "That's right. So the Æthereals went to war, which you know because it's all we learn about in school. But eventually the vættir won the war because of the Nyx, a warrior who was able to use the erebos, the deepest shadows, like a weapon. He swore that as long as he drew breath, vættir would never be oppressed by the Æthereals. He was the champion of all vættir, and if someone was in trouble, he would save them."

"Oh yeah? So where is he now?"

"He's dead. He was betrayed long ago by his beloved, and killed by a sword made of bright. But as he lay dying, he swore he would return, that not only would he avenge his murder, but that he would slay the bright Exalteds who killed him."

"But if he's dead, how is he going to save me from the shadows?"

Whisper tickled my side, and I had to fight to suppress my giggle. If Mom heard us playing around, there was no telling what she'd do. "That's the point of the story, Peep. You don't need the Nyx to save you. The Nyx used the dark to protect the vættir. So why should the vættir fear the shadows?"

Cass halts suddenly and I run into her back, the memory evaporating like smoke. There's an ache in my chest, and I miss my sister all over again. Does it ever get any easier?

"We need to rest a little," Cass says. I just nod, too out of breath to do anything else. I lean over, my hands on my knees while my body tries to recover. I haven't run like that since the night Whisper died. I didn't really miss it.

After my heart rate returns to something close to normal, I straighten. I still clutch my shovel, and when I loosen my grip on it, my knuckles ache. "Ugh. How far did we go?"

Cass shakes her head. "Not far, but we need to find something to eat, or we'll collapse."

I nod, because she's right. Thirst and hunger aren't felt in the Underworld like they are in the Mortal Realm, but they still affect us. I've seen people drop dead while working on the line because they were too scared to take a break to eat or drink.

I look around, taking in the creeper vines and the black trees. We're in a different part of the forest than we were when the chimera attacked. The trees are farther apart, and a few are heavy with a strange, prickly fruit. They look like an eggplant with spikes, weighty and tear shaped. "Can we eat those?"

Cass looks up and shrugs. "We won't know unless we try."

I reach for one of the fruits, and Cass grabs my wrist. "Use your shovel to knock it down, just in case." I think of Venus flytraps, and how they emit a sweet scent to attract bugs. Cass is right. The trees are carnivorous. Maybe the fruit is just a lure to attract prey.

Cass raises her shovel and swats at some low-hanging fruit while I do the same. The heavy fruit falls off the trees easily enough, landing in the leaf litter covering the ground. Cass uses her shovel to split hers open, and I do the same. As soon as we do, the creeper vines dive down, devouring the fruit.

"If you actually want to eat them, you're going to have to make sure you're free of the tree line first. The nudges love them."

I spin around, shovel raised, while next to me Cass takes up a similarly aggressive stance. A blond-haired guy with too-blue eyes raises his hands, his surprise hitting me in waves of black licorice.

"Whoa, whoa, ladies. I come in peace. I'm just looking for something to eat too." There's no scent of a lie to his words, and

I lower my shovel while Cass keeps hers raised.

"Where'd you come from?" I ask. Not Tartarus. He's entirely too clean to have worked the Pits. His jeans and T-shirt look new and modern. Plus, I definitely would've remembered his eyes, a metallic blue that glows with an inner light. If he isn't a full-blooded Æthereal, he's got to be close. Maybe that's why Cass is giving him some serious stink eye.

He grins sheepishly and rubs the back of his neck. "Actually, I come from a small town called Ulysses's Glen. It's in Virginia." Now that he mentions it, I can hear the slightest hint of an accent in his voice. I look at Cass for guidance. She says nothing, so I continue the interrogation.

"How'd you get down here?" And why would anyone willingly come to Tartarus? Maybe I've been in the Underworld too long, but suspicion curdles my stomach, and I'm about one bad answer away from clobbering pretty boy with my shovel. Or letting Cass hit him with her shovel. Whatever.

"Um," he looks around and then lets out a sigh. "My brother. He can trip the Rift." Cass gives me a confused look, and the blond guy hurriedly explains, "You know, travel across the Rift. Anyway, we came down here looking for someone, but then there was a chimera stampede, and we got separated. I'm Blue, by the way."

There's no hint of a lie. He smells as honest and open as his smile, and any lingering doubts evaporate. "Nice to meet you, Blue. I'm Zephyr, and this is Cass. So the fruit? They're okay to eat?"

"Yeah, but we should probably take them beyond the tree line."
He points to where the trees open up to a blood-red sky.

That sky stops me. "What's going on?" I've never seen the sky in
Tartarus look so . . . violent. Sure the rain sucks, but on clear days
the sky is usually gray like a permanent twilight, that moment in
the Mortal Realm just after the sun sets and before the world is
plunged into darkness. But this red sky? It's terrifying.

"My brother said it's a sign that war is brewing," Blue says,
jumping up to pull one of the heavy, spiky fruits down. Since he's
much taller than us he doesn't have to rely on the reach of the
shovel to pick the fruit. He tosses it to me, and then does the same
for Cass before getting one for himself.

"How would he know?" Cass asks as we walk to the tree line
and that bleeding sky.

"Well, he kind of grew up down here. He knows the Underworld
better than anyone I've ever met."

I've never heard of a vættir growing up in the Underworld, but
I spent my entire life in the Aerie until I was arrested and sent to
Tartarus. There's a lot I don't know.

Outside the trees the land looks different from the Pits. The
ground is hard, not the soft mud I'm used to. Blue grass grows in
waist-high clumps, and black boulders dot the landscape. It's a lot
warmer here than the Pits, and even without a sun it feels nice.
This part of the Underworld might look like something out of a
nightmare with its red sky, but it doesn't smell bad. There's none

of the scent of offal that clings to the Pits, and without a bunch of other vættir I'm not overwhelmed by the scent of emotions. It's actually kind of okay, if you can call hell nice.

Cass points to a far-off yellow river that winds through the landscape. "That's the Acheron. We'll follow it until we get to the Styx." Her voice is low, her words only for me. I remember that the Styx is where Charon, the Ferryman, plies his trade. If we want to get across to the Mortal Realm, he's going to be our best bet.

We sit on a couple of the boulders and eat our fruit. Cass waits until Blue tears into his before taking a bite. I follow her lead. And promptly gag. The inside of the fruit is meaty, like eating a too-rare steak. It's also salty, and the flavor is somewhere between a hamburger and a rotten pineapple. It's all I can do to choke it down.

"No telling how long until we eat again," Cass says, her meaning clear. We have a long way to the Ferryman. And at the pace Cass sets, I'm going to need every bit of sustenance I can get.

Blue grins as I try to force myself to eat the foul fruit. "It's a bit of an acquired taste."

"No joke," I say. I chew a mouthful and swallow it. "How long have you been down here?"

"Oh, since school ended. I'm not sure how long that's been. You know time's all weird here."

I nod, thinking of my lost year. It's hard not to be bitter about losing so much of my life. But I guess it could be worse. I could be dead.

His words suddenly sink in, and I turn to him. "Wait, did you say school? What kind of school do you go to?" I'm not asking because I really care, more because I'm wondering what kind of vættir he is, and it would be rude to ask him directly.

He shrugs. "Just a regular norm school. The town where I live, Ulysses's Glen, is made up of all vættir. Well, vættir and their families. There are a few norms in town, but most of them are married to vættir. Anyway, we go to school like human kids and everything, but it's an all-vættir public school. I'm a junior. Well, I'll be a senior when I get back. Assuming I ever find my brother."

I stare at my fruit as I consider his words. A town full of vættir living normal lives. No killing. No wars. That sounds heavenly.

In a place like that I could be more than just a failure.

Cass shifts on her rock, her green eyes boring into Blue. The metallic shine is brighter. "What are you doing down here, again?"

Blue grins at her, ignoring the narrowed glare she shoots at him. "I told you—I'm looking for a friend."

Cass watches him. "I thought you were looking for your brother?"

"I'm actually trying to find both. My brother and a friend of ours."

Cass pushes off her rock, flipping the peel of her fruit away from her. "What does he look like? Maybe we've seen him."

There's a mischievous glimmer in Blue's eyes. "My brother or my friend?"

"Let's start with your friend."

Blue leans back. He radiates the cut-grass scent of curiosity.

"Maybe you have. But I'm looking for a her, not a him."

Cass crosses her arms, her gaze steely. "Vættir?"

"Of course. But she's not going to be in the Pits."

I take a small bite of the fruit and swallow it with some effort. This time the meaty taste of it makes my belly roil with nausea. "Why, is she dead?"

He shakes his head. "No, she's a Harpy. You really think one of the killing kind is going to muck around in the Pits?" He asks it in a teasing tone, but his words turn my blood cold. Is he talking about me?

Blue keeps talking in between eating bites of his fruit. "I figure she's probably still in the Underworld, though. Maybe hanging out in the Killing Fields or even one of the lesser hells where the dark Æthereals stay, like the Du'at or the Folkvangr or something."

Cass gives me a meaningful look. Blue is too intent on finishing the rest of his fruit to catch it. But I know what she's trying to tell me. I'm most likely the only Harpy in Tartarus. My kind are big rule followers, and we don't end up in Tartarus as much as the other races of vættir. This golden boy with the too-blue eyes is probably looking for me.

But why?

As I watch Blue toss away his fruit peel, I think maybe he's playing with us, that Cass and I walked into a trap. But then I realize that I don't have wings anymore, and he hasn't seen my talons since my hands are covered in muck and fruit. There's no way he knows that I'm the only Harpy in the Pits.

Blue finishes his fruit and jumps to his feet. "You guys want some more?" I shake my head, but Cass nods. He grins. "I'll be right back." As soon as he darts into the tree line, Cass is on her feet.

"Come on, we need to ditch the pretty boy while we can."

CHAPTER SEVEN

I DON'T MOVE, AND CASS GRABS MY ARM, TRYING TO PULL ME ALONG. "Zeph, we need to get a move on before he gets back."

I throw the remainder of my fruit on the ground and wipe my mouth with the back of my hand. "Why?"

She blinks owlishly at me. "Are you joking?"

I shake my head. "No. I'm not. Tell me why we should ditch him."

She stares off into the woods. "I don't trust him. Did you see his eyes? Brighter than new coins. How do we know he isn't Æthereal?"

"He's not. Trust me. His emotions stink way too bad for him to be a god. I wouldn't be able to smell anything if he was Æthereal."

"So you trust him?"

"Well, no. But I don't distrust him. It's more I'm just waiting to see what happens."

Cass turns to me and stills. She's strangely intense, more so than usual. For the first time since I've met her fear uncurls slowly in my belly. "What?"

"What do you smell from me?"

"What?" It's not the question I'm expecting, and the sudden change in direction catches me off guard.

"You've been by my side for a long time, and I'm just now learning that you can smell emotions."

Crap. I swallow a sigh. "That's because it's not really something Harpies brag about."

Cass is still looking at me like I'm a bug under a magnifying glass. "How's it work?"

I shrug. "I don't know. It's a Harpy thing. Like our talons. Emotions have similar scents. Like fear? It's usually some kind of spoiled citrus. And happiness? Always smells good, like cookies or cake." I don't add that I'm sort of uncomfortable about the gift. All Harpies can scent out emotions, but some are better than others. I may have failed at every last thing related to battle, but I rocked the sniffing out emotions part. The problem is most people don't really like you to know what they're feeling. It's a bit like reading minds: It's best if people just don't know you can do it.

Just when I think Cass is going to let it go, she says again, "So what do you smell from me?"

I stand and wipe my dirty hands on my even dirtier pants. "Why, Cass? We're friends. What does it matter?"

"I want to know. You've never asked me why you couldn't smell my emotions."

"I never said I couldn't smell your emotions," I say.

"Can you?"

I shift from foot to foot. "No. But really, it's none of my business,

Cass. I don't care." I don't want to know why I can't smell anything from Cass. Honestly, it's nice to be around someone without
knowing their every feeling.

"I'm not a god, you know." She tugs at a loose string on her toga
before dropping her arms down by her sides. "I'm a vættir."

"Good. So drop it then. Blue's going to be back at any moment,
and I don't want to have this conversation with an audience." I
might kind of like Blue, but that doesn't mean I want him to know
I can sniff out how he's feeling.

Cass watches me, and then finally nods. "You aren't going to ask
me why you can't smell my emotions?"

I want to ask her. I really do. Especially since she's making such
a big deal about it. But one of the things I love about Cass is
that she reminds me so much of my sister. And after I discovered
Whisper's secrets, our relationship was never the same. Whisper
taught me long ago that prying is a big mistake. So as much as I
want to ask Cass why I never smell any emotion from her, I don't.
I'd rather have her friendship than her secrets, and I have a sinking
suspicion that I can't have both.

"Cass," I say with a sigh. "I trust you. It isn't important. Besides,
just a few hours ago Hades pretty much told me that I'm dead
meat. As much as I want to play twenty questions with you, we
have bigger things to worry about right now."

The words are no sooner out of my mouth than a scream rips
through the air, like the sound of tires skidding across pavement. I
know without a doubt it came from the direction Blue headed into

the woods. But it didn't sound like him. The noise was guttural and foreign, like it came from an animal. I begin to shake and Cass grabs my arm. She doesn't look afraid, more concerned.

"You were saying," she drawls.

"Ha-ha." Another scream tears through my middle, leaving my heart pounding. The skin on my arms has pimpled, and I swallow thickly. "Tell me you know what that is."

She shakes her head while tugging me away from the woods. "I think it would a good idea to start running."

Another scream splits the day, and Blue comes running toward us through the tall grass. "Go! Go!" he yells, waving us ahead of him. I get a glimpse of blond hair and height before he sprints past us, not looking back to see if we follow.

We take off running, Cass quickly outpacing me. Blue weaves into a field of waist-high blue grass, and we follow. I feel clumsy as I run, like my feet are asleep. I trip and fall, and everything falls away as the voice in my brain yells, *Get up, get up, GETUP!* On the ground I can't see anything but the blue grass, the red sky beyond an ominous warning. I try to climb to my feet, but it's difficult. The ground shakes beneath my hands, causing small stones to jump.

Something very, very big is approaching.

I stumble to my feet and start running, glancing back over my shoulder as I do. Whatever is chasing us seems like it would be too big to hide in the tall grass, but I don't see anything. That just makes me run faster. I'm not the world's best fighter, but I'm an excellent runner.

Still, Blue and Cass have easily outdistanced me, their forms far ahead in the tall blue grass. We can't see what's chasing us, but we aren't waiting to find out, either.

I finally catch up to Cass and Blue. He skids to a sudden stop, and I crash into him. His arm wraps around my waist to steady me, the sickly stink of his fear overwhelming.

"What is it? Why are you so afraid?" I gasp.

"Drakan," he says.

I shake my head, not believing him. "No. Drakans aren't real." They can't be real, otherwise I might just lose my damn mind. Drakans are the biggest, scariest thing in the Underworld. They supposedly created the Rift, but no one's ever seen one before. Now I'm thinking maybe that's because they don't survive the meeting.

A drakan would be bad, worse than a manticore. I'm not sure I'm fast enough to outrun a drakan, if that's what is really chasing us.

But the rotten-orange scent of Blue's fear convinces me that he's telling the truth, or at least thinks he is. "If you don't believe me, feel free to stay here and get eaten by an imaginary monster." He looks around, releasing me as he does. "Come on, this way."

We start running again, the kind of flat-out sprint that spins a web of agony along my side. I push my hand into the hollow beneath my rib cage, hoping I can somehow will the stitch away. The pain grounds me, so that I don't have a chance to let my fear paralyze me. That's a good thing, I guess.

The tall grass thins out and the terrain changes to shining black rock. My bones rattle as my feet slam into the hard surface. I'm starting to fall back, Cass and Blue leaving me far behind. If I can't kick it into high gear, I'm going to be monster chow.

I really, really miss my wings right now.

Far ahead of me Cass and Blue stop suddenly, and it doesn't take long for me to catch up to them. When I draw up alongside them, I can see why they halted.

The black rock gives way to air. Far below us, yellow water crashes over jagged and deadly rocks. On the other side of the chasm are piles of bones that look sort of like buildings. I bend over, gasping for breath. "What now?" I ask.

Blue glances over at me. His eyes glow, they're so bright. His Æthereal blood must be incredibly strong. He sighs, like he can't believe he's been burdened with such terrible luck. "I don't know."

"We don't have all millennium, so we should probably decide on something sooner rather than later," Cass says, her gaze locked on the way we came. She doesn't even look winded, while I'm pretty sure I'm going to pass out if I don't catch my breath.

Blue pushes his hand through his hair. He looks back at the cliff again and throws his hands up into the air. "We're going to have to jump."

Cass makes a choked noise. "We will never make that," she says.

The blond boy grins, and my heart gives an unexpected leap. He's gorgeous. "Well, it's either jump or be eaten by the drakan. Me, I'm willing to give it a try." He apparently has a death wish. Why are all the pretty boys insane?

Without any more discussion Blue backs up a few feet and sprints forward, jumping at the last possible second. For a long moment I have the aching fear that he'll fall. I imagine his body twisted and broken on the rocks below. But then he's on the other side, his feet skidding across the black rock as he slides to a stop. He stands on the far side of the chasm, and his laughter drifts back to us.

"As easy as pie!" he yells across the gap.

Cass looks at me and shrugs. "Good luck," she says. Then she's backing up while she hikes up the skirts of her toga, tucking them up between her legs so they don't trip her when she runs. She sprints past me, her arms windmilling as she flies through the air. She moves so fast that she's on the other side before I even have a chance to worry.

"Oh gods," I say. I consider the jump, my stomach turning over. If I still had my wings, I would've already been across the chasm. But my wings are long gone and in their place is a newfound fear of going splat.

On the other side of the gap Cass's waving arms urge me to hurry, and when the ground begins to tremble I know why.

I turn and look over my shoulder, but I still can't see anything. After a second I finally figure out why. The monster bearing down on us matches the sky, its enormous body a shimmering mass that reflects its surroundings. The only sense I have of its size is the way the grass moves from its passage. From what I can tell the creature is huge, like an angry, invisible house moving through the grass.

Fear freezes me, and I fight to push the emotion away. I'm small and insignificant. Everything comes crashing down on me at once. Whisper and the way she looked when I found her, my trial, Hermes's abandonment, the vague promise of doom by Hades. So much has happened to me in the past year, and I'm suddenly just so exhausted.

I'm tired of being afraid.

The entire mass of the creature regards me, waiting for me to do something. But I'm so sore and tired, and a wave of defeat washes over me. I just can't see the point in fighting anymore.

I just have to face the fact that I'm not a survivor. Why should I even bother?

So instead of running, instead of fighting, instead of freaking out like I should, I just sit there and wait to be eaten.

No wonder I failed my Trials.

A strange sense of calm comes over me, and I study the creature as it studies me. It has no form that I can discern, but I can sense its massiveness. It looms over me, pressing down and invading the space. But it's less a physical presence and more an awareness. The creature feels dark, even though it's completely invisible. It is fear and anxiety given physical form, and I understand why Blue ran. He said it was a drakan, and if he's right, then this is one of the fearsome creatures who separated the realms in the first place, using their might to divide up the universe. I guess I should be terrified just thinking about that.

But the reality is I just don't care anymore. It's hopeless. At least now I know how I die.

"Are you seriously going to sit there and wait for it to eat you, or are you going to cross the chasm?"

The voice comes out of nowhere, jolting me out of my pity party. I turn, and a boy with long dark hair and pale skin strides through the grass toward me. He stands straight, completely unfazed by the giant monster nearby. Like Blue, his clothes are modern and on the fashionable range of things. But it's not the familiar smirk that makes my heart pound. It's the way he's looking at me.

I would recognize those fathomless dark eyes anywhere.

"Tally?"

He nods and drops down into a crouch beside me. "Why are you sitting on the ground, Peep?"

"I . . . I was waiting for it to eat me." I'm not entirely sure that I'm not already dead. How else do I explain my childhood friend suddenly appearing in the Underworld?

"That's pretty dumb. Especially since it's actually giving you a chance to cross." He studies me, his jaw tight. His brows are pulled together in a scowl. There's a hardness to him that was never there before, but that's not saying much since it's been almost ten years since I saw him last.

I look back at the drakan, and Tally sighs. "Well, come on. I'll help you cross if you're afraid."

"It's not going to eat me?"

He smiles. "Drakans don't exactly eat people. But they don't really enjoy them trespassing, either. They're very territorial."

"Oh." I'm still having trouble wrapping my mind around the

fact that I am not about to be devoured. "How do you know all that?"

He shrugs. "I've learned some things in the past few years."

I look from Tally to the nearly invisible monster behind him. "So you're sure it's not going to eat me?"

Tally sighs. "Yes. Now let's go, Peep, before it changes its mind," he says impatiently, standing and holding out his hand.

I open my mouth to argue with him just like I would've in the good old days, but then the thing looming over us lets out a chuffing sound that may or may not be laughter. I clamp my mouth shut. It's strange that Tally appears and all of a sudden the monster stops chasing me. But now isn't the time to think about it. "Thank you," I grit out.

I take his outstretched hand. The contact sends a tingle down my arm, and I snatch my hand back. He watches me, his frown disappearing and one eyebrow raising in question. "Problem?"

"No, uh, sorry." I take his hand and he easily lifts me to my feet. The tingle where our hands connect spreads up my arm to my entire body. There's a flash of cold, and then I'm standing next to Cass.

I snatch back my hand. "What in the hells was that?"

"Teleportation. It's kind of Tallon's specialty," the blond boy with the too-blue eyes answers with a grin.

"Tallon?"

He shrugs. "I don't really go by Tally anymore."

I turn back to Tally—Tallon now—and shake my head. "You never did that when we were kids."

He shrugs. "I grew into my talents." There's a hint of something in his voice, and I'm pretty sure that he's not just talking about teleportation. My face heats but I barely notice it. I'm still trying to wrap my brain around a vættir who can teleport. That's not exactly a normal talent.

And Tallon isn't just any vættir. He's the boy I used to chase through the woods of the Aerie. I clear my throat. My insides are in turmoil, but I'm determined not to let him see a single shred of it. "So, what brings you to the Underworld?"

Blue grins and throws his arm across Tallon's shoulders. "The scenery, of course."

Tallon rolls his eyes. "We're here to rescue you."

der aches as I remember my last run in with one of the demon dogs. I swallow hard.

"Okay, not fun. So what's the plan?"

Cass raises an eyebrow. "Why do we need a plan? Aren't you getting rescued?"

Tallon and Blue still argue a little ways off, and I shake my head. "I'm not waiting on them. What's your plan?"

Cass points toward the yellow river in the distance. "That's the Acheron. If we follow it south to the Styx, we could get the Ferryman to take us across to the Mortal Realm."

"The Ferryman's gone," Tallon says as he and Blue return. Blue's expression is somewhere between sheepish and irritated. Tallon just frowns. His scowl could melt rock.

Cass's brows draw together. "Gone? Gone where?"

Tallon shrugs. "Wherever it is he goes when travel's been restricted. Hades closed down escorted travel between the realms. War's brewing."

"With who?" I ask, but no one answers me. I take that to mean they don't know.

I sigh and turn to Cass. "Well, we can't just stay here and wait for the cerberus to come and get us."

Cass nods. "We need to get going." She gives Tallon a low bow. "Thank you for saving my friend. But we must take our leave." It's clear that Cass doesn't trust the guys, even though I know Tallon from way back when. I wonder what kind of life she's had that even friends could be enemies.

I think of her standing on that hill long ago, challenging an Exalted to a contest that she had no chance of winning. What else don't I know about Cass?

Tallon doesn't acknowledge Cass's dismissive thanks. "You won't get far without the Ferryman."

I cross my arms. "So, what's the plan?"

"I'll take you both across the Rift. Like I said, I came here to save you."

"Who sent you?"

Tallon gives me a small, wistful smile. "Nanda."

My heart aches as I think of the woman who was more of a mom to me than my real mother. Her visits were the highlight of my childhood. She'd blow into town like a whirlwind, a smiling, laughing Harpy who defied the conventions of the Aerie. Sometimes she'd have Tallon in tow, sometimes her bossy daughter Alora. But no matter how long she stayed or when she came to visit, Nanda brought happy times with her.

She'd been in the same year group as my mother, but unlike my mother she'd given up her spot in the Aerie after only a short while. I never knew why; I just knew that the life Nanda lived was a promise of something more, something beyond the restrictive life of the Aerie.

It was a life I had wanted at one point, especially after I failed my Trials. But then Ramun Mar killed Whisper, and my entire existence was thrown into a tailspin.

"Why now?" I ask, my brain grasping to make sense of this sudden turn of events.

"Alora had a vision," Blue says, looking bored. I wonder if he feels the same way I do about the so-called visions of Alora. I was always sure she was just being a jerk when she would claim to have "seen" things when we were kids. Mostly because her "visions" always ended up with her getting to go first, or getting the better piece of dessert.

"We're going to take you to the Mortal Realm. Nanda will be able to explain everything," Tallon says, his voice softening slightly. He still looks sort of gloomy, but now it's more like he heard a sad song, not like he wants to pummel someone.

Cass shakes her head. "How are you going to get us across?"

Blue throws his arm across Tallon's shoulders. "My boy here has the peculiar ability to trip the Rift. He can get us across the realms."

Tallon doesn't say anything, and I study him, trying to see past the attractive exterior. There's apparently a lot I don't know about him.

Cass sighs. "How do we know we can trust you?" she asks, getting right to the heart of the matter.

Blue grins, completely unfazed. "Ah, that's the tricky thing about trust, isn't it?" The answer seems to mollify Cass some, and even though she doesn't lose her defensive posture, she does seem to relax a little.

"So are you guys coming or not?" Tallon asks, shrugging off Blue. Now that's the impatient little boy I remember. I grin and tug on his hair.

"Lead on! Tallyho!" I say, just like we used to when we were kids.

He doesn't say anything, just rolls his eyes and sets off toward the river in the direction that Cass wanted to go. Blue follows him, giving me an apologetic smile. Cass stands next to me, and we watch the guys walk away.

"I would guess that the kid you knew has changed some."

I nod. Now, like Cass, I wonder if I can trust the brooding man my childhood friend has changed into.

We walk for what feels like forever. There's no time in the Underworld, but it still feels like hours. We alternate our walking with running, covering a large distance before Tallon finally calls a halt. We stand on a slight rise, and the view is impressive. To our left is the Acheron, as yellow and wide as it was when we left the cliff. To the south is the Styx, a black ribbon of water that still seems impossibly far away. And to our right is more of that black forest that makes me very, very nervous.

As soon as we stop, Cass heads over to find out what Tallon's plans are, and Blue comes over to sit next to me on a large rock.

"So, you're the infamous Zephyr Mourning."

I nod. "Yep." I like Blue and his playful attitude. It's a welcome relief from Tallon's sulkiness. The entire walk he's done nothing but bark out orders, yelling at me when he thought I wasn't running fast enough. Give me a pair of wings, and I'd show him.

But even though I'm fond of Blue, I don't trust him. To be fair, there aren't many people I trust these days.

"You said you and Tallon were brothers," I say suddenly.

He raises an eyebrow at me. "We are. Half brothers. We share a mother."

"I never saw you at Nanda's house." We never went to Nanda's house; she always came to visit us at the Aerie. But I'm willing to bet Blue doesn't know that.

Blue's normally friendly expression shutters, and he sighs. "I didn't grow up with Nanda like Tallon did. I just visited her during the summers, until it was time to start high school." There's a whisper of sadness in his voice, and the scent of rain on asphalt stings my nose. I want to pry, but it's obviously a topic surrounded with pain, so I change the subject.

"How come you never came with Nanda to the Aerie?"

Blue grins. "Dragons aren't allowed. Too dangerous."

I laugh. "You're a dragon?"

"Hey, don't sound so impressed. You're the Godslayer. That's way more awesome."

"What did you just call me?" He actually said Godslayer like it was a good thing, instead of the insult it's meant to be. Godslayers are worse than murderers. We defy the natural order of things. A Godslayer kills Æthereals, who are supposed to be eternal.

"Zephyr Mourning, Godslayer and Hero to the Vættir," Blue says, announcing it like I'm the main act in a circus. I just blink at him. My confusion apparently shows on my face. "You haven't heard the stories?" he asks.

"What stories?"

Blue clears his throat and begins to tell the story like he's the voice-over for a movie trailer. "Zephyr Mourning, brave Harpy and loving sister, found her dear sister slain by the hand of the General of the Acolytes, the dread Ramun Mar." He pauses to boo and hiss, and then launches back into the story. "But Zephyr could not let such an insult pass, and she called down the blackest of lightning to avenge her sister and punish the dastardly Ramun Mar. And for her brave defense of family, she was exiled to the Pits of Tartarus."

"Where'd you hear that?" I ask. I can't breathe, and my heart beats triple time.

He shrugs, sobering suddenly. "It's what everyone's saying. Just a rumor, that's all."

But it isn't a rumor. It's the truth. And if Blue heard that I used black lightning to kill Ramun Mar, that means the Æthereal High Council has too. Somehow my secret has gotten out.

The Æthereal High Council has been playing with me all this time. They know that I can use the erebos.

I'm already dead. I just didn't know it.

Terror clutches at my brain, silencing whatever Blue is saying. Tallon calls him over, and he walks off while I try not to burst into panicked tears. I have to get out of the Underworld. We don't have time to rest.

Hades sees everything that happens in his realm. What if the chimera attack was just a distraction to get me alone so that some Æthereal assassin could take me out? What if Blue and Tallon are really here to kill me?

I take a deep breath and fight back the hysteria. I have to try to think about this rationally. If the High Council wanted me dead, they wouldn't have to send anyone. They could've paid off one of the inmates back in the Pits. More than likely all of the attempts on my life over the past year have been as a result of one bribe or another. I probably have Cass to thank for their collective failure.

So where does that leave me now? It's just a matter of time before Hera and the rest of the Æthereal High Council get tired of playing with me and demand my death. It's better if I'm in the Mortal Realm when that happens. The Æthereals have less influence there, and if I'm lucky, I can lay low for the next twenty years until everyone forgets about me.

Suddenly, getting to the Mortal Realm isn't just about saving my sister's shade, but about saving my life as well.

Tallon strolls over while Cass and Blue disappear into a nearby cluster of trees. Tallon stops when he sees my expression. "Are you okay?"

I nod but don't say anything. I don't want to tell him what I suspect, that the Æthereal High Council is hunting me. Tallon was always a cautious kid. I don't want him to change his mind about getting me and Cass out of hell.

It seems to be enough for him. He drops down into a crouch and pulls at the grass. "Cass and Blue went to go find something to eat. We need to make it to the Styx before we can cross, and from what I can tell of the terrain that's still a ways away."

"Okay."

He seems to take the hint that I'm not in the mood to talk. Tallon stands and walks off, staring into the distance back the way we came. Heartbeats pass before his soft curse cuts through my haze of fear.

"What is it?" I ask.

"Come see for yourself."

I jump off the rock and stand next to Tallon, close enough that I'm aware of the heat he gives off but far enough away that we aren't touching.

From our vantage point we can see two cerberus chasing down a pack of far-off vættir. We're obviously not the only ones who had the bright idea to use the chimera attack as a chance to escape. If we'd been walking at a more relaxed pace, they would've caught up to us instead of them.

I have a feeling Cass and I are next on the menu.

"We need to get going," I say, my heart in my throat.

Tallon nods. "It's going to be a hard sprint to the Styx." There's warning in his voice, like he thinks I'm the weakest one here.

Unfortunately he's right.

Cass and Blue come running out of the forest with their arms full of the prickly, purple things. I have to swallow a groan.

Tallon hears me. "They're kind of an acquired taste," he says, a glimmer in the dark depths of his eyes.

"Yeah, that's what Blue said," I grumble.

"Here," Cass says, shoving one of the fruits at me. "Eat quickly. We need to get moving."

"You heard the cerberus?"

"Kind of hard to miss," Blue says around a mouthful of fruit.

Tallon rips open his fruit and takes a bite while heading down the hill. "Let's eat while we walk. We don't have time to sit around like a bunch of blue hairs at lunch."

I shoot him a dirty look, even though I know he really means old women, not me and my blue Harpy hair. Still. It's kind of a jerky thing to say.

We start walking. The others eat their fruit without a word, but once again I can barely choke mine down. It isn't very appetizing, and my belly rebels at every bite. It takes everything I have not to gag.

As we walk, the screams and shouts of the vættir behind us start to fade. We still pick up the pace once everyone has finished eating. I get a stitch in my side after only a few steps, but I don't say anything.

I'll survive a little pain in my side. I may not survive staying in the Underworld.

CHAPTER NINE

WITH THE FEAR OF THE CERBERUS MOTIVATING US, WE MAKE GOOD time. It's probably because my growing dread that we'll be caught hurries my steps. The screams of the vættir have faded but haunt my memory. I can't let that happen to me.

I spend a long time trying to think about nothing, just focusing on keeping my feet moving. Our pace continues to be brutally fast, but no one complains. Even Tallon manages to stop scowling, although I prefer the frown to the worry that now creases his brow. We need to hurry. If I'm caught, I'm dead. It's as simple as that.

The cerberus will either tear me to pieces or take me back to the Pits. I won't spend long in the Pits before I'm taken before the Æthereal High Council and executed. I'm not sure what will happen to Cass, but I doubt her fate will be much better. There's an urgency to her movements that makes me think she doesn't want to return to Tartarus either.

Deep down I almost want the cerberus to attack. Something inside me wants to take on the demon dogs, to teach them a lesson they'll never forget. The craving for violence is a strange discovery, like finding out I suddenly have an extra toe. I recognize it as part of me and yet completely separate, a foreign impulse that I know comes from some facet of my personality I've yet to discover. It's a very Harpy response to jump blindly into a fight. It's also a drive I've never had before, and the unfamiliar feeling isn't welcome. It makes me anxious, and that's something I don't need right now. I push the emotion aside and try to ignore it. I already know that I stand absolutely no chance against a cerberus. No need to tempt the Fates.

We keep walking. The sky doesn't get any brighter or darker, and there's no way to tell how long we've been traveling. Hours or days. Lethargy has begun to seep deep into my bones. All I want is to lie down for a little while and take a nap, cerberus be damned.

I smell the river long before I see it, the stench of rotting flesh and dead fish wafting across the plain toward us. It smells like hatred and lies, and I wonder if that's why some vættir refer to the Styx as the River of Deceit. Harpies aren't the only vættir who can smell emotions, and it makes as much sense as any other explanation.

The terrain shifts from the tall blue grass to charred brown grass. It reminds me of the Mortal Realm, and for a moment I think we must be very close to home.

"Did we cross over?" I ask, my tone hopeful. Cass walks beside me, while the boys lead the way in front of us.

She shakes her head. "No, a lot of the Underworld looks like the Mortal Realm since it was all one world before the drakans created the Rift. It's only Tartarus that's bad. The rest of the Underworld is almost normal."

Just when I'm pretty sure that I cannot take another step, we climb a rise and the Styx is right there, a black ribbon of water cutting through the landscape.

I want to cheer, but it seems wrong somehow. Now the stink of the water is strong enough to make me gag, and I cover my nose and mouth. Blue has the same reaction as me. Cass and Tallon are completely unaffected.

The Styx is like nothing I've ever seen before. Rivers in the mortal realm are brown and rowdy, their currents full of debris. Even the Acheron was full of motion, the yellow water tumbling over stones in its dash to meet up with the Styx. The Styx is flawless. The black water is smooth and undisturbed, a dark mirror that reflects the blood-red sky overhead. There's no sign that the water is even moving. The river is a midnight swath that stretches off in both directions as far as the eye can see. It's still and quiet, and it terrifies me.

Blue marches up next to Cass and peers into the water. "So if I jump in there will I be invincible?"

"Try it," Tallon says. There's a teasing tone in his voice. He even smiles a little.

Maybe I'm not the only one excited to get out of here.

"More than likely you'd end up getting eaten by one of the creatures that live in the river's depths," Cass says, her eyes scanning the surface of the water.

Blue takes a step back. I know how he feels. If the fear of river monsters wasn't enough, now that the possibility of returning to the Mortal Realm is so close, I'm filled with an anxious excitement. I never really thought we'd make it out, and now that it's about to happen, I can't stop myself from bouncing. The thought of going home after all this time makes me light-headed. Getting to the Mortal Realm will solve all of my problems.

Right now I have to believe that.

Tallon sighs and points to a whirlpool a few feet from the river's edge. "There's the portal. I can only take two people at a time, so we'll have to take turns. I'll jump in and take Blue and Peep across first, and then return for you."

Cass shakes her head. "No. What's to make you come back for me?"

Blue nods. "She's right. Take the girls first. The cerberus aren't going to be coming for me. I'll be okay."

I take a step backward, away from the dark water eddying nearby. My nervous excitement drains away. I'm not sure I want to jump into a whirlpool. It doesn't really seem safe. "Maybe you guys should go first."

Tallon gives me a sharp look. "It's perfectly safe."

Cass shakes her head. "Blue's right. He'll be fine waiting here by himself."

I hear what she's not saying, and my face heats in embarrassment. She knows that I'm scared, and that I'm a train wreck when it comes to defending myself. She wants us to go first because I have no chance of surviving a run-in with a cerberus on my own.

I sigh. "Fine." I want to cop an attitude, to call her out for doubting me. But she's right. Cass knows me too well. I can't defend myself against a cerberus. I was lucky to even survive last time. It was only Persephone's timely intervention that saved me from becoming a dog treat.

I don't know whether to hug Cass for her generosity or scream in frustration at my complete and utter lameness.

Tallon holds out his hand to me, and once again the electric tingle shoots down my arm. Cass already holds his other hand. We step into the water, which is oddly warm. I gag at the stench. This close I can taste the dead fish in the air. I clamp my mouth closed and try to take as few breaths as possible.

Tallon adjusts his grip on my hand before looking over to Cass. The water barely covers Tallon's hips, but it's a little more than waist high on me and hits her in the center of her chest. I never realized how small she was.

Tallon looks down at me. "Are you ready?" I give a quick nod.

He steps forward, and we go under. I hold my breath and squeeze my eyes closed. There's a moment of warmth, and then blistering cold.

And then I am nowhere.

I wake suddenly. It's strange, because I don't remember falling asleep. It takes me a moment before I remember the portal, and Tallon.

And the Mortal Realm.

I sit up. Little explosions of pain protest the movement, and I know I pushed myself too hard trying to get to the Styx. I ignore the aches. It's hard to think about a little hurt when the sun is shining on your face.

The sun. Actual sunshine. It's bright and warm and utterly amazing. I giggle, euphoria sweeping over me. I made it. It's almost impossible to believe.

But this is definitely the Mortal Realm. I sit in the middle of a cow pasture, and a little ways off a few black-and-white cows moo their disapproval at me. I look around, noting the trees, a nearby pond, and the sweet, sweet scent of somewhere that isn't the Underworld. Everything is so blessedly normal.

If this is a dream, I don't want to wake up.

I creakily climb to my feet, feeling much older than I am. I'm lucky to be alive. The old stories are full of cautionary tales about what happens to heroes who try to travel the Underworld. I've managed to escape Tartarus, outrun a chimera and a pack of cerberus, and make the jump across the Rift dividing the realms. That's pretty impressive, even for one of the old heroes.

But for a failure like me? It's a gods-damned miracle.

Now I just have to find my sister's shade. I don't have any idea where to start, and the realization dampens my joy a little, but not much. Because I've already done the impossible by escaping the Underworld. For the first time since I discovered that her shade wasn't in the Elysian Fields I feel like I have a real chance of helping her. And that's kind of awesome, as long as I don't remember that the gods want me dead.

There's a rustling sound, and Cass stumbles into view. For the first time since I met her in Tartarus, she actually seems lost and maybe a little uncertain. She spots me and walks over. Cass glances around. "Where are we?"

"I think it's a cow pasture."

She sniffs. "The Mortal Realm hasn't changed much."

I fight back a smile. "When exactly were you sent to the Underworld?"

"Right after the Spartan War. A very long time ago."

I think of the rustic clothing of the villagers in the memory Hades showed me, and I nod. That had to be about two, maybe three thousand years ago. Cass's head is going to explode. Gods, she's missed so much. How in the hells am I supposed to explain something like the Internet to someone who doesn't even understand indoor plumbing?

I nod and push aside my worry. One thing at a time. I need to make sure we have a place to hide so the gods can't find us. Then I need to figure out how to find Whisper's missing shade. She has to be my first priority once I'm safe. She always took care of me, and now I need to return the favor. Everything else can wait.

"Zephyr! Cass! Hey, where are you guys?" Blue yells, his shout causing the cows to meander away from us.

"Over here!" I answer. I hold out a hand to Cass, and she helps me climb to my feet.

Now that I'm standing, I can see Blue splashing in the pond a little ways away. Tallon is nowhere to be seen. But then he surfaces, pushing his long dark hair out of his face. I blink, because I can't really believe what I'm seeing.

Is Tallon really smiling?

His entire face transforms. He was handsome before, even scowling. But now, with his full lips twisted into a smile and the barest hint of dimples . . .

He's absolutely gorgeous.

Even as a kid Tallon wasn't a big smiler. He always seemed to have very grown-up things on his mind, something Whisper and I always teased him about. But no matter how serious things were, I could always get him to laugh. I considered it one of my special talents. Getting to see him like this again, happy and carefree and completely unguarded, it unlocks something in me. I want to see more of this Tallon.

I stop and just watch him. He jumps on Blue and ducks him under the water. Tallon's shirt is off, and I get a glimpse of a black shoulder tattoo and biceps before he goes back under the water. I've never seen muscles like that on a guy in real life. Just on TV. To be honest, I haven't been around many guys, period. There weren't any men in the Aerie, only the occasional visitors, and they were always escorted by one of the high-ranking officers. I've definitely never seen anyone as unbelievably beautiful as Tallon.

I push my hand against my stomach. There's a fluttering hunger there that I'm sure has nothing to do with food. My mouth is dry, and I can't seem to tear my eyes away from Tallon. Last time I saw him, he was just a boy, but he's not anymore. He's different, and so am I. I wonder what it would be like to kiss him. Would it be like the TV shows, where girls seem to be struck stupid by kissing the guy they like? Would it make me feel alive, like soaring over the treetops?

Would it make me feel brave?

Cass lays a hand on my shoulder. "Zephyr, are you okay?"

I jump, and force a smile. "Um, yeah. Just daydreaming."

She follows the direction of my stare and sighs. "Be careful what you dream about. Some things are more dangerous than they seem."

I look over at Tallon and frown. "What do you mean?"

"How much do you know about him?"

"Who, Tallon?"

Cass's gaze meets mine. "Yes."

I force a laugh. A tendril of guilt creeps through me, because not too long ago I was wondering if Tallon and Blue could be assassins. Obviously I was wrong to suspect them, so hearing Cass echo my earlier thoughts is not comforting. "Cass, I've known Tallon since I was a kid. Gods, we aren't going to go through this again, are we?"

"What kind of vættir is Tallon, then? I've never heard of a vættir that can cross the realms."

Neither have I, but I'm not about to let Cass's suspicions cloud my mind or dampen my good mood. "I don't know, and I don't care. Can you please just drop it?"

Cass doesn't answer me at first, just turns and watches the boys.

"I think maybe you should be a little more cautious. People can change, Zeph."

I sigh. "I feel like I've gotten this lecture before," I mutter.

Cass turns back to me. "What?"

"Nothing."

Blue waves at us before Tallon pushes him under. He surfaces, laughing and sputtering. "What are you waiting for? You know you smell as bad as we do."

Blue's right. Our clothes carry the stink of the Styx, not to mention the accumulated sweat of our headlong flight through Tartarus. Cass's toga is dirt streaked and grimy, and I'm sure my purple basilisk-leather clothes from the Pits don't look much better.

I nudge Cass. "Let's go swimming. We can argue about this later."

She looks at the pond, then at me. "Do you think it's deep?" she asks.

"Only one way to find out." I plop down on the grass and unstrap my boots. They're the only remnant I have left of my life before I landed in Tartarus.

The thought makes me sad, but I push it aside by remembering that Nanda sent Tallon to the Underworld to find me. Whisper is gone, but there's still someone who cares about me. Even though it's been years since I saw her, Nanda didn't forget about me.

The boys have swum out to the middle of the pond, and Blue waves at us. Tallon just watches us with dark, serious eyes, his smile once again hidden. "Come on in; the water's fine!" Blue calls.

I stand and stretch, then run past Cass and into the water. It's warm out, either late spring or early summer. The sun beats down on me as I splash through the shallows, breathing in the clean, fresh air of the pasture. Even the smell of the far-off cows isn't enough to dim my good mood. I probably smell worse than they do.

The water where I stand is chest deep, but Cass has only waded in as far as her knees. "Come on, Cass!" I say, splashing water at her.

She frowns. "I can't swim."

"You should still be able to touch right here."

Without answering she walks farther into the water.

The water is cool, but not cold. The bottom is slimy, and I'm anxious to get out far enough that I can swim rather than squish through mud. The pond is on the large side, but the bottom quickly slopes downward. About twenty feet from the shore I'm treading water, and I turn around and wave at Cass.

"I can't touch here, just so you know."

She nods, and I leave her to her own devices.

I swim out quickly to the middle, where the boys paddle in a circle. I duck under, diving until I can touch the bottom before flipping over and heading back toward the surface. The pond isn't the cleanest in the world, but it's better than anything in the Underworld. The water washes away the last traces of hell, and when I surface, it feels like I'm finally getting a second chance.

"What are you doing in my pond?"

I clear the water out of my eyes. A couple of feet away from me a water sprite stands on the surface of the pond, her transparent arms crossed and her foot tapping. She's made entirely of water, and her hair moves down her body like a waterfall. I tread water and do a few kicks backward, trying to get closer to the shore.

One the other side of her the boys stop swimming and tread water. "Whoa," Blue says. The sprite doesn't seem concerned with the boys, just me.

I offer a friendly smile. "I'm sorry. I was just trying to get clean."

The sprite stamps her foot, which causes water to splash in all directions. "It's bad enough those stupid cows wade in when it gets too hot, but at least they don't know any better. Don't you know better than to go jumping into other vættir's ponds?"

"Yes. Look, I'm really sorry. I'll just swim back to shore—"

"Oh you will, will you? What makes you think I'll just let you leave?" Her words are filled with menace, and it strikes me that maybe she's just spoiling for a bit of a fight. She can't get much company out here in the middle of a cow pasture, and sometimes a decent brawl is just as satisfying as a nice long chat with friends.

But I'm not about to fight a water sprite, especially in her domain.

Blue swims over to me. "Hey, Lyss, we're really sorry. We just got back from the Underworld, and we didn't think to introduce you to Zephyr."

The sprite says nothing, just gestures in our direction. Blue is lifted up by a wave and deposited back next to Tallon.

"My quarrel isn't with you, Blue. The girly knows the rules. She has trespassed, and now I demand a tribute."

I paddle backward a little more, hoping that I can maybe get to shore. "A tribute? Look, I don't have anything to give you. I said I was sorry." I turn around and begin paddling for shore, once again running away from battle.

Before I can get very far, I'm pulled under, water going up my nose and in my mouth. I close my eyes and kick at the hand wrapped around my ankle. I make contact before the sprite can phase back to water, and she lets me go. I break the surface, coughing and choking.

"That's enough, Lyss. Leave her alone," Tallon yells.

Cass still stands exactly where she was before I went under. I have to warn her. She doesn't know how to swim, and for all her badassery she wouldn't stand a chance against a water sprite. I yell to get her attention. "Cass, you have to get out! There's a—" My words are cut off by Lyss dragging me back under. She lets go before I have a chance to kick at her again, and I'm just about to break the surface when I'm dragged back under. Water is in my nose and mouth, and my lungs scream for air. I can't make contact with the sprite. She phases from her water form to her physical form and back too quickly. If this keeps up, she's going to drown me, and my first day back in the Mortal Realm will be a spectacular failure.

Fear and rage settle deep into my middle. They cut through

me, and I sense my darkness rising up, answering the call of my panic. It's just like the night I killed Ramun Mar, but this time the darkness is different. It feels like a living thing, an old friend who has just been waiting for the chance to help. Without even calling it, my darkness rises. It shrouds me in reassurance. I welcome the confidence it brings. It feels like I can do anything with the darkness at my side.

The attack ceases. I break the surface, coughing and heaving. The erebos surrounds me like a mantle, buoying me up until I stand on the surface of the water. It's stronger than the last time I called it, over a year ago. But it feels so right, even more so than the night it killed Ramun Mar for me.

The darkness knows what I want, and it's happy to obey.

The sprite is a few feet away, standing on the water as well. She phases from water to flesh, and her eyes are wide.

"I'm sorry," she says. "I—I was just playing. It's not a big deal. Really. I'm sorry."

I barely register her apology. Instead I'm drinking in her fear. The sour scent makes me feel strong, and it would be so easy to give her a taste of pain, to let her know what it's truly like to be afraid.

The darkness agrees with me. It asks me to release it, as loud as a roar and as quiet as a whisper. I remember what my sister said long ago: *You must control the darkness. You can't ever give in to it.* But the shadows want to make me happy, and I deserve a little happiness.

A few creeping tendrils of darkness race across the water and wrap around Lyss's arms, the greater mass of shadows still swirling around my feet. The sprite's stammering speech is abruptly halted. The sharp, soured musk of the sprite's fear comes to me across the water, followed quickly by the stagnant-water scent of her resignation. She knows as well as I do that I would have no problem ending her life.

That knowledge scares me, but the emotion is so far away, so detached, that I don't even bother examining it.

"Let her go, Zephyr."

I slowly turn toward the voice. Tallon treads water near my feet, his dark eyes watching me intently.

"Why should I?"

"Because she's done nothing wrong. There's no need to punish her."

"She started it." I turn back to the sprite, who is now crying, sobs shaking her shoulders. Her fear has coalesced into desperation, a rotten-fruit scent that belongs in a garbage dump, not a pond in the middle of nowhere.

"You're better than this, Peep." Tallon's voice is low. He reaches through the darkness and grabs my ankle in a gentle grip. The physical contact combined with the childhood nickname is enough to break through the haze of rage. I look down at him, and I suddenly feel very guilty.

I'm acting like a spoiled brat.

I ask the darkness to release the sprite. It responds immediately, the inkiness that radiates out from my feet retracting and wrapping back around me. I breathe deeply and wait for the cold rage to fade, and as it does, I'm lowered back into the water.

The sprite falls into the water as well, and I turn toward her. "I'm sorry," I say. She watches me with tear-bright metallic-green eyes.

"You're real. I always thought you were just a myth, something to make us feel better." She sniffles and swipes at her tears. "I can't believe you're real."

I have no idea what the sprite's talking about. Exhaustion weighs on my shoulders, and I take a deep breath, trying to clear away the last of the darkness that clings to me. I can feel it in my belly, restless for release. It's stronger than ever, and I wonder if Hades's punishment in the Underworld has broken me somehow. Did the wave of erebos he sent at me break the dam I spent so many years trying to build? How do I get my shadows under control again? Right now it feels like a living thing, a caged tiger pacing inside of me. How do I keep myself from using it, when it's so easy?

I swim back to the shore, past a silent Tallon. I climb out of the water past Cass, who follows me with a bland expression. Fear hurries my steps. My secret is out, and now I am a walking target. But worse than the fear is the shame that heats my cheeks. It makes me feel dirty and ashamed, using the erebos. It just isn't natural.

I am a monster.

Cass walks alongside me, her step light. "You wanted to kill her." There's no judgment in her voice.

I nod. I swallow hard to try to force down the sudden lump in my throat. "I don't understand it. I worked so hard to control the shadows, to keep them buried. What's happening to me?"

"Nothing. It's who you are, Zeph."

"And who am I?" I ask, my voice rising.

Cass looks over her shoulder to where the boys are. They tread water and talk to the sprite. They aren't even paying attention to us. "Let's find a spot where we won't be overheard."

We walk to where my boots lie in the grass, and I pull them on my still-wet feet. Then we make our way to where the cows have gathered under a leafy oak. I tread carefully so that I won't step on the surprises nestled in the grass. I look over my shoulder at Cass. I'm shocked to see that she's actually floating a few inches above the ground.

"How are you doing that?" I ask, pointing at her feet. She looks down and shrugs.

"It's easy, just using a little æther to levitate. You could probably do it as well."

I shake my head. "I'm not so hot with æther."

Cass nods and sighs. "That's to be expected, I suppose. The Nyx is supposed to be of the dark. You could probably use the erebos to levitate though. You kind of just did."

My heartbeat echoes in my ears. "Wait, back up. What did you just say? The Nyx? You're joking, right?"

Cass shakes her head. "Back in the old days there were two classes of vættir, the bright and the shadow. The dark gods are just as guilty of taking human lovers as the bright, and the offspring were shadow vættir. They were the same as the bright vættir, only their powers were tied to erebos instead of æther. The Nyx was just supposed to be a particularly strong shadow vættir, a god or goddess constrained to flesh."

I wave my hand in irritation. "I've heard of shadow vættir. I thought they were all gone. You know, extinct."

Cass shakes her head. "As far as I know there are still shadow vættir in the Mortal Realm."

"But why would you think I was the Nyx if there are all kinds of these shadow vættir running around?"

Cass sighs. "There aren't as many shadow vættir around as in the old days. And when you killed Ramun Mar you fulfilled the first part of the prophecy promising the Nyx's return. How many vættir can destroy an Æthereal?"

I shift nervously from foot to foot. Prophecies are no small thing to the vættir, but this can't be true. Cass must be delusional from crossing back into the Mortal Realm, because this noise about me being the Nyx is crazy talk.

I try to change the subject. "So what happened to all of these shadow vættir who can use the erebos?"

"The Acolytes have been quietly killing us off for the past thousand years." Both Cass and I startle as Tallon walks up, Blue trailing behind. Tallon's words remind me of the day Whisper found out I could use the erebos. "They'll kill you if they knew," she said. I'd thought she was exaggerating. Maybe she wasn't.

Tallon doesn't look at me, and the small slight cuts me deeper than it should. Instead he's focused on Cass. "Do you really think she's the Nyx?"

Cass moves between us. Flames flare up in her hands, and she crouches into a defensive stance. "I do. What's your concern with her?"

An answering fire flares up around Tallon, and a couple of oddly curved short swords appear in his hands. His scowl is back, his expression stern. I barely recognize him. Maybe Cass was right. What if after all this time I don't know him anymore?

"The vættir have been waiting for her return for centuries. I know who you are, Pellacis. There's no way I'm going to let you betray the dark champion again."

"What makes you think I betrayed him the first time?" Cass says, the flames climbing up her arms and flaring brightly. I take a step back to avoid the heat. "I've spent the past few thousand years waiting for the Nyx to return. I never betrayed Elias. I loved him."

"'She shall return to you in the darkest of the dark, her presence an ever-present spark,'" Blue says, reciting something. His words cut through both Tallon's and Cass's aggression, and their fires gutter out. Tallon still has his swords, though.

Blue points to me. "Your eyes seemed to glow when we were walking through Tartarus, you know. The silver really stands out."

"Yes," Cass says. She looks back at me over her shoulder. "It was the first thing I noticed about her when she arrived in the Pits." She turns back to Tallon. "That's one of the reasons I believe she's the true Nyx."

Tallon nods. "It makes sense."

They're talking about me like I'm not even here, and I stomp my foot in irritation. "Will someone please tell me what you're all talking about?" It comes out sounding hysterical, and I clamp my mouth shut.

Blue gives me a pitying look, but his next words are directed at Cass and Tallon. "She's right. If she grew up in an Aerie, she's probably never even heard of the Prophecy of the Promise. Remember the stories Nanda used to tell?"

Tallon grimaces. "Gods, yes. The cult of Athena."

Blue nods slowly. "We should let Nanda explain all this."

Tallon sighs and turns to me. "Blue's right. Nanda knows more about this than we do. She'll be able to explain it to you better than anyone."

Cass nods. "Then let us make haste to Nanda's."

My heart leaps at the thought of seeing my nest mother again, but I squash the feeling. I shake my head and cross my arms. "No. I'm not going anywhere until you guys tell me just what's going on." I need some answers.

My expression must show my resolve. Tallon sighs. His swords disappear, and he makes a dismissive motion with his hands. "We think you might be the Nyx, Peep. We told you Alora had a vision after word got out about you being a Godslayer, but I didn't tell you what she saw. In the vision Alora saw you leading an army of vættir in battle. Killing an Æthereal was the first sign of the Prophecy of the Promise, but Alora's vision proved that you were the Nyx. That's why we went to the Underworld to save you."

My mouth falls open. The idea of me, a failure and a terrible coward, leading anyone anywhere is so laughable it makes my brain short-circuit. I force a laugh, but it comes out sounding hysterical. "Ha-ha, good joke, guys."

Cass pats my arm. "It's okay. It'll take a little bit to get used to the idea."

I ignore her placating tone and swallow hard. My heart is beating so loud that it echoes in my ears. "Who is this imaginary vættir army going to fight?"

Cass gives me a side-eyed look. "The Æthereals, Zeph. You're supposed to help the vættir win their independence from the Æthereals once and for all."

I shake my head. "Not me. I'm not the Nyx." But from the way they're all looking at me, I'm starting to feel like maybe I'm wrong.

CHAPTER TEN

IT TURNS OUT THAT WE AREN'T THAT FAR FROM WHERE NANDA LIVES. IN
fact Tallon brought us across the Rift to their hometown in the
Mortal Realm, Ulysses's Glen. I guess he figured that we were
going to Nanda's whether we wanted to or not.

The guys know the water sprite that I almost killed. Lyss. That
makes me feel even worse about losing control. No wonder Tallon
can't even look at me. She's probably his girlfriend or something.
Especially since Blue asks him, "Hey, are you still going to ask
Lyss to borrow her car?" with an eye waggle that hints at them
being more than just friends. Tallon could just flash us to his aunt's
house, but I get the sense that bringing everyone across the Rift
wore him out. While we stand under the tree, Tallon trudges back
to the pond to ask for the sprite's car keys.

Blue sighs and stretches. "Let's hope she says yes. If not, it's
going to be a long walk."

"How far are we from Nanda's house?" I ask, trying not to
watch Tallon talking to the water sprite. I don't know why I even
care that he's smiling at her.

"I don't know, like ten miles, maybe?" Blue says, jolting me back to the conversation. I tear my eyes away from the pond.

"Why'd he drop us so far away?" I ask.

"Ulysses's Glen is full of vættir, but not all of them are okay with some of Tallon's lesser-known talents," he confides. Blue says it a little nervously, so I don't ask him what he's talking about. I get the feeling that Tallon's ability to trip the Rift is as hush-hush as my shadows used to be. That makes me feel even more exposed now that my secret is out.

Before we leave, I walk over to the edge of the pond to the sprite. She watches me warily, and I clear my throat. "I'm sorry," I say. I don't add that I was about to tear her apart piece by piece. I get the feeling she knows why I'm apologizing.

I'm surprised when she grins at me and inclines her head. "It's an honor to have almost been killed by the Nyx. A Promise made," she says.

"A Promise kept," I answer, without even thinking. It was something my mom always said, even though no one else in the Aerie ever did. It's the right response. My answer makes the sprite smile even wider. I walk away feeling a little less like a monster.

No one says much on the drive to Nanda's house. Blue drives, while Tallon rides in the passenger seat. Cass and I sit in the back. She's never ridden in a car before, and it shows. It took some convincing to even get her into the car, and now she's as nervous as a cat in a dog park. Every little movement of the car has her clutching at her seat belt, her eyes darting side to side. I try to distract her by making jokes, but I doubt she even hears me. It's kind of nice

to see her a little ruffled. At least now I know she really is vættir.

I eventually just let her be, my thoughts tangling inevitably around this whole Nyx business. I can't stop thinking about this prophecy thing, and the growing noise of the darkness inside me. I've never been that angry about anything before. And the way the darkness came to me ... I should be concerned. I fought the power for so long, but I barely even had to reach for it just now. What would've happened if Tallon hadn't stopped me? Would I really have killed the sprite? I can't go around killing people who irritate me. That's just not okay.

In the back of my mind a little voice wonders, *But what if it is? What if that's what makes you the Nyx?*

Even if killing is what the Nyx is supposed to do, how can I fulfill some prophecy and find my sister? From the old stories I get the feeling that fulfilling prophecies is kind of a full-time gig. It doesn't seem like it would leave a lot of time for anything else, and I have to find out what happened to Whisper.

That's assuming one of the Exalteds doesn't show up to kill me. If this whole Nyx thing is true, I can't imagine the Æthereal High Council sitting back and letting me turn into a general who will lead a vættir army against them. That's just not their style.

All of this is overwhelming, and I almost miss the simplicity of life in the Pits. I wish I knew what to do next. I wish my stomach didn't feel like a blender set on high. Most important, I wish I wasn't so certain that I'm going to fail.

Blue stops the car in front of a smallish house on a treelined

street. There's nothing all that remarkable about it. The house is white, and a wooden swing rocks slowly in the breeze on the front porch. The only things that set the house apart from its neighbors are the flowers that grow in abundance, covering just about every surface available. Fat Gerber daisies occupy pots, while morning glories climb a trellis, and rosebushes crowd the beds. Even the lawn is unusually lush and green compared to its neighbors. It's very pretty, especially after so much time in Tartarus.

Cass leans between the seats to talk to Blue. "Your aunt's a nymph?"

He shakes his head. "Harpy. Close enough." I think it's his idea of a joke, since nymphs are a peaceful bunch, but it's lost on Cass.

There's an odd stillness about the house that makes me uneasy. "Is she expecting us?" Nanda isn't the kind to sit in her house and wait for guests. She'd be more likely to sit on the porch and run toward the car when we arrive, cracking our ribs with one of her hugs as soon as she got the chance.

"No," Tallon says. His scowl is back. "We weren't supposed to get back until the end of the summer." He climbs out of the car, Blue and I taking our time following him. Cass has already bounded out of the car, eager to escape.

We stroll up the walk, my eyes darting around nervously. My nerves are frayed. Too much time in the Underworld. I expect something bad to happen at any moment.

The boys lead the way, and Cass and I hang back. I wonder if

she's considering running as much as I am. This all seems like too much, too soon. As excited as I am to see Nanda again, I wish it were under better circumstances.

Mostly I wish it didn't involve me fulfilling some impossible prophecy.

I wonder if we wouldn't be better off going into hiding instead of meeting Nanda like this. Prophecy or no, Cass and I are still fugitives. What if the cerberus cross the Rift to find us? The demon dogs could appear at any moment to drag us back to hell. We'd have to fight them in broad daylight in the middle of a pretty nice neighborhood. Not exactly an ideal situation.

We're almost to the door when Cass grabs my arm. "Look at the lawn," she whispers.

I turn around, and my stomach drops to my feet. "Oh, that's definitely bad."

The perfectly green lawn in front of Nanda's house undulates like a flag in the wind. In between the movement, blades of grass grow larger, as though each wave forces them up and out of the soil. Within seconds the blades stretch up into an army of skinny green-clad men with stringy hair and short swords.

"Um, guys," I call over my shoulder. "Is this your aunt's work?" Most vættir have wards, spells of protection, set up to protect their houses. It's just a simple twisting of æther, and even in the Aerie we had wards on things like our weapons cabinets. The last thing you want is someone stealing your favorite sword.

Even though I haven't seen her in a while, I can't imagine Nanda setting up wards that involve her front lawn turning into an army of skinny green men.

Tallon swears and moves next to me. "No. Nanda would never use grass men."

"So, any ideas why the lawn looks like it's about to attack us?"

Blue shakes his head. "No clue."

I sigh. I am so tired of running and fighting. All I want is a shower and food that tastes normal.

But my companions are already jumping into the fray. Cass elbows me. "Stay back. We can't risk you getting hurt." Her hands burst into flames, and she rolls her shoulders like an athlete getting ready to participate in an event. "Grass men. Some things never change."

"Yeah, if you say so," I answer before she runs down the sidewalk and begins throwing flame at the soldiers closest to us.

The front yard turns into a battleground. A giant two-handed sword appears in Blue's hands, its edges coated in bright æther. He winks at me. "Isn't this fun?" He begins slicing through grass men almost as quickly as they appear. Cass is a whirl of flame as she burns the grass men before they even get a chance to rise.

And me? I stand on the sidewalk, frozen with fear.

Tallon stands beside me. His short, curved swords are back. He spins them as he gives me a long look. "No erebos. Stay here and keep out of the way," he says before joining the others. Shame heats my cheeks.

I should help them. I could do something to stop the attack. A simple wave of darkness to rip the grass men apart. But all I can think of is how I lost control back at the pond, how much I liked the idea of hurting the sprite. Tallon is right, even though I hate it. I don't want to use the erebos again. I don't want to feel that destructive.

I don't even want to fight. But I know I can't just stand here and do nothing. And sadly, running is not an option.

The nice thing about grass men is the least little scratch destroys them. Already the sidewalk is littered with charred blades of grass, the remains of the grass men Blue and Cass have cut down. But there are so many of them that a few losses here and there don't really make a difference. Back in the Aerie we had coordinated skirmishes to help us prepare for our Trials. When the wood nymphs brought in their grass men we always lost. It's hard to defeat their sheer numbers.

I take a deep breath and push aside my dread before I pick up a sword dropped by a grass man. I have to do something, and it isn't like I don't have years of training to prepare me for this moment. I swing the short sword wildly at first, awkward as I try to remember the drills from my training in the Aerie. The sword feels light thanks to muscles earned from months of surviving in Tartarus, and the patterns come easily. The spin-slice of Whirlwind. The figure-eight curves of Infinity. The stab and retreat of Strike. When I was in the Aerie, I was never able to see how the sword patterns would be useful in a battle, but now, with the spindly grass men bearing down on me, they are brilliant.

I kill the grass men quickly, using the short sword to cut a path through the horde. The grass men turn toward me. Blue and Cass still burn through them from behind, and Tallon is making a sizable dent in their numbers off to the side, but I am very clearly their target.

Probably because I'm the weakest fighter.

Even with the short sword I'm very quickly overwhelmed. The grass men pile onto me, their swords stabbing and slicing. The basilisk leather blocks most of their attacks, but I'm still taking a beating. I growl, and fight harder. But my reserves are shot from our headlong dash out of hell. After only a few minutes the sword is too heavy. More of the grass men's attacks are getting through, and my arms are covered with dozens of shallow cuts.

My confidence evaporates and fear takes its place. I should've known better than to try to fight. There's no way I could ever hope to measure up to a warrior like Whisper or Cass.

The darkness inside of me answers my hopelessness with a burning. It rises up, offering the power to win, to destroy the grass men. I don't want to answer the siren's call of the darkness. But then I trip and I'm buried by grass men, their swords stabbing and jabbing.

I have no choice.

I release the darkness. It's like opening my hand and setting a butterfly free. At first the shadows seem hesitant, uncertain. They don't know what I want, and I can sense them waiting for my command.

Destroy them. Destroy all of the grass men, I mentally send at them as I try to shove the grass men off me. They don't weigh much, but I'm being buried alive.

There's a far-off rumble of thunder, but I barely notice it in my struggle to escape the attack. Energy crackles across my skin as the darkness responds, and I channel it down my bare arms and outward in a circle. Power sizzles the grass men. They're thrown backward before raining down as charred blades of grass, filling the air with the scent of ozone and burning greenery. The dark lightning radiates outward in an arc of tarnished silver, destroying the grass men and charring the lawn into a smoking black mess.

The grass men fall, and no new ones climb out to take their place.

I give a whoop of victory, standing up and punching the air. Cass and Blue echo my cheer. I did it. We won.

The lawn is destroyed. What was once lush and green is now charcoal. I drop the short sword, and it disappears. The cuts on my arms itch as they knit back together, but overall I'm no worse for wear.

Cass limps up to my side. "That was pretty impressive. Maybe next time you should try that first." She looks like hell. Grass is tangled in her long hair, and several deep cuts show on her bare arms. But like me, she's healing quickly. It's so nice to be back in the Mortal Realm, where vættir healing works.

I grin and bump my shoulder into hers. "Sorry. I'm a Harpy. Magic is sort of a last resort for me."

Tallon grabs my arms and shakes me. His expression is stormy, and my smile fades. "What were you thinking?" he yells.

Everyone stops, and I fight back tears. Low in my belly, the darkness rises up in indignation. "I was trying to not get killed."

"I told you not to use the shadows," he says. His voice is low, but it comes out as a growl.

"She didn't have much choice, Tallon. They were kicking our ass," Blue says, coming to my defense. But his words just make me feel worse. I'm trying very hard not to cry, and I'm not sure why. I can't be this upset just because Tallon is a jerk.

Tallon releases me and sighs, speaking slowly like I'm stupid. "You used dark lightning. Using the erebos brings the Acolytes. Surely you can't be that dense."

"Don't talk to me like I'm a child," I say. I blink my tears away and take a deep breath. I'm more angry now than upset, and the shadows inside of me roil. They want out, to wreak a little more havoc, and I clamp down on the darkness but not on my emotions.

"Well, maybe if you'd stop acting like one and think a little I wouldn't have to. It's been almost ten years and you haven't changed a bit."

My anger leaves no room for any other emotions. "Apologize." My voice is equally low, and Tallon's eyes widen in surprise.

"Apologize for what? Trying to keep us from waking up to a battalion of Acolytes on the doorstep? If anything, you owe everyone an apology for putting them in danger and for being a brat."

Before I even think about it I'm swinging at Tallon. It's a good punch. He isn't expecting it, and my fist connects with his chin. His head snaps back, and before he can recover, I follow it up with a quick punch to his middle.

He stumbles back, gasping for air. I take up a defensive stance, while around us everyone freezes. "Whoa," Cass says.

Tallon straightens, rubbing his jaw. Wisps of darkness rise off my hands, like smoke. He watches me, and his expression changes slightly. Then he does the last thing I'd expect.

He grins at me.

The smile completely transforms his face, like storm clouds parting to reveal a bright blue sky. I'm so surprised by it that my hands clench into fists. "What's so funny?" I snap.

Tallon shakes his head, grinning. "I forgot what a temper you had."

Blue walks in between us, his giant sword resting on his shoulder. The bright fire is gone, but the metal still smokes. He looks around the neighborhood. None of the neighbors have come out to see what caused the smoking ruin of Nanda's front lawn. "If you two are done, we should probably go find Nanda. I'm hungry, and as much as I'd like to watch you kick Tallon's ass, there's probably some sort of family code that says I'm supposed to step in."

"The only family rule we have is to never piss off a Harpy. Looks like your brother was dumb enough to break that one today," says a raspy voice from behind us. We turn. A woman stands on the porch. She has the same dark skin as me, but the locks piled on top of her head are forest green and tangled with bright green beads. Her eyes are golden, and she wears a purple sweat suit and running shoes.

My heart soars when I see the giant emerald wings rising off her back. "Nanda."

The woman grins. "Well, don't just stand there, missy. Come here and give me a hug."

I run up the stairs and launch myself into her arms, emotion crashing through me. I'm happy and sad and scared all at once, and it's only the pressure of Nanda's arms squeezing my middle that keeps me from bursting into tears. "I missed you so much," I mumble into her shoulder. It's strange to be the same height as her, but it doesn't change how good it feels to hug her again.

She smoothes the snarled locks of my hair and kisses my cheek. "I know, sweetling. I was sorry to hear about Whisper. I wish I could have been there for you." There are a dozen unsaid things in her voice, but I file my questions away for later. We have a lot to talk about.

I pull away and take a step back. Blue sends his sword away before climbing the steps and giving Nanda a kiss on the cheek. "Hi, Aunt Nanda. We brought some friends home for dinner."

She grins. "So you did."

I gesture to the lawn. "I'm sorry about your grass."

Nanda waves away my apology. "Don't worry about it. Some nymph will be by before the end of the week offering to grow it back for me. This neighborhood is filthy with vættir. All of Ulysses's Glen is."

I turn around when Tallon clears his throat. My anger has faded, and I watch him quietly as he moves toward me. He stops a few inches away. "I'm sorry. I let my temper get the best of me." I'm so surprised that he actually apologized that I just stand there openmouthed as he walks past me and onto the porch.

Tallon follows Blue's lead and gives Nanda a kiss on the cheek. "Hi, Aunt Nanda. I want you to meet Cassiphone Pellacis."

Nanda's expression turns stormy. "A Pellacis?"

I turn to look at Cass, who hangs back. "What's wrong?"

"Pellacis are dangerous vættir. They're liars and cheats, as dishonest as they are pretty." Nanda's eyes burn into Cass, who says nothing. Probably because Nanda's speaking English, not Æthereal. I don't translate because I want to know why Nanda is so mad first.

Nanda crosses her arms. "Cassiphone Pellacis is the name of the Betrayer. If she is the woman who killed the last Nyx, someone had better tell me what she's doing standing in my front yard."

CHAPTER ELEVEN

AFTER AN ARGUMENT, IN WHICH I ASSURE NANDA THAT CASS IS trustworthy and lay out several prime examples where she saved my life down in the Pits, Nanda relents. She grudgingly shows Cass and me to a spare bedroom, giving Cass a suspicious look as she walks by. I sigh. Nanda may have dropped the matter for the moment, but I know it will come up again.

But before that, I need to find out from Cass what the hells is going on. All this distrust is getting old.

After we're in the spare bedroom, Nanda disappears for a moment before returning with towels and some clothing. "If you put these on, I'll be happy to wash your clothes for you." Her expression doesn't show the least bit of her distaste, and I have to admire her restraint. Even after the dip in the pond, Cass and I still smell faintly like an outhouse.

"Thanks," I say.

Nanda sets the clothes on the bed and pauses a moment. Her eyes are sad, and the scent of roses decaying floods the room. "They took your wings," she says in a low voice.

I swallow past the lump in my throat and nod. "It was the price

I paid for passage to Tartarus." A Harpy's wings are her most prized possession, so losing them was a big deal. It still is. There are days when I wake up from a dream of soaring over treetops only to realize that I will never fly again. It's like losing them all over again.

Nanda nods, and gives Cass a pointed look. I know she's wondering what Cass lost for her passage to the Underworld, but even though she's in a mood, she's still polite enough not to ask. "It's good to see you again, dear," Nanda says before leaving the room.

Once the door has closed, I let out a sigh. "Wow, so that was intense, huh?"

When I turn around, Cass stands in the middle of the room, examining the furniture like it might grow horns and attack her. She looks at me, and her expression is as blank as always. "It was to be expected."

"Ummm, maybe you could tell me why?" I don't want to pry, but I've never seen Nanda act like that. All this talk of Cass being the great "Betrayer" is kind of making me nervous.

Cass sighs, and crosses her arms. "Pellacis isn't just my family name; it's what I am. The Pellacis were once a great line of vættir, known for our beauty and power."

"Gee, that's kind of vain."

Cass gives me a sidelong glance. "We earned that reputation. Some of the greatest heroes were Pellacis. Circe, Heracles, Theseus, Pereseus. Humans and vættir alike revered and feared us."

"So you're from a long line of heroes, then?" It makes sense. As powerful as she is, it only seems right that her family would've done extraordinary things.

"No, I'm from a long line of liars and cheats. It's just a coincidence that the most dishonest vættir tend to make the best heroes."

I laugh, because I don't know what else to do. "Yeah, tell me about it."

Cass watches me. "Do you know why the Pellacis were so good at exploiting others?"

I shake my head. I have a feeling she's going to tell me.

Cass stares at the ground, her shoulders slumped. "Like you, we Pellacis have a secret ability that we don't usually share." She looks up at me and shrugs. "But since you've shared your greatest secrets with me I feel like I should do the same."

I take a deep breath and let it out. "Okay."

Cass walks over to me, so that only a few inches separate us. "We Pellacis have the ability to read the heart's desire. We can see down to the essence of any human or vættir and see what it is that they want more than anything else." Cass pokes me in the chest a few times to emphasize her point. "Our ability to easily trick others has given my kind a bad reputation, one I'm afraid we've earned. It's surprisingly easy to manipulate people when you can see what motivates them."

I want to ask her what she sees in me, but I know what the answer is. I have a desperate need to succeed, to atone for my past failures. It's why I have to find Whisper, and make sure she gets to the afterlife.

So instead of asking Cass what her ability shows her, I incline my head and smile. "Thank you for sharing that with me."

She shrugs. "It's the least I could do." She pauses, as though she's carefully choosing her next words. "Do you mind sharing why you lost your temper with Tallon?"

I study my nails, because I'm not sure how to answer. I finally sigh. "I'm not quite sure what happened." In the Aerie we're taught to suppress our emotions. Harpies are vicious and deadly because we don't get mad, or scared, or really feel anything. We just act.

But I get scared all the time, and the anger I felt when I hit Tallon was so strong that I couldn't even think. When we were kids, Tallon used to make me so mad because he always treated me like I wasn't tough enough to hang out with him and Whisper. They were both older, and they always tried to get me to stay with Alora, Nanda's daughter. She was more likely to play with dolls than go on an adventure. I hated getting stuck with her. Maybe some of that childhood resentment was what was fueling my temper.

Or maybe it was something else. Was my anger a by-product of using the erebos?

Cass glances away, and I wonder if she's thinking the same thing. I decide it's a good time for a change of topic. "You know, you're taking this being in the future thing pretty well."

Cass tilts her head to the side as she examines me. "What do you mean?"

"I mean, I would totally be freaking out right about now. I did freak out when I got to Tartarus, remember? And I'm more than a little freaked out by the idea that I have some big prophecy to fulfill. Yet here you are, thousands of years from when you left the Mortal Realm, and you haven't even batted an eyelash."

Cass sighs and settles down on the floor, cross-legged. "Zeph, I think it's time I told you something."

There's a weightiness to her words that gives me pause. "Oh. Okay." I lean against the doorframe. I stay silent, letting her take her time. Even though I can sense from her tone that she's about to tell me something very important, I don't smell the burning-coffee smell of anxiety. It should bother me, but it doesn't. Mostly because it's Cass. I trust her with my life.

"I have not been completely honest with you since I met you. My personal history was only a little piece of that. But since we are now in the Mortal Realm, I think it's time I shared something that I could not share while we were in the Underworld." She pauses, as though she's carefully choosing her next words. "I've spent all of this time protecting you because the Messenger asked me to keep you alive."

I blink stupidly a few times before her words sink in. "What?"

"Before you arrived, the Messenger asked me to return to the Pits and keep an eye on you. He knew who I was, since he was at my trial so long ago. I was living in the Du'at, searching for a way into the Elysian Fields, when he appeared and offered to take me to Elias if I could keep you alive until it was time. Once I saw you, everything made sense." She looks at me, her metallic-green eyes flat. "I've escaped to the Mortal Realm before now. The last time I was here, I heard the Prophecy of the Promise, which is why I believed you were the Nyx. I suspected you were the one referred to in the texts the first time I met you, but it wasn't until you survived Hades's dark wave that I was certain."

"I . . . oh. So you escaped the Pits before." My brain is trying to make sense of her words, to put what she's telling me into the context of our friendship.

All of a sudden I'm feeling less like Cass's friend and more like a charity case.

"Of course. But the Elysian Fields were where I wanted to be. I thought going there, seeing Elias, that it would fix me. That's why I accepted the Messenger's offer."

Embarrassment heats my face. Of course someone as badass as Cass wouldn't really want to be my friend. "Okay. Well, thanks for keeping me alive," I joke, but my hurt makes my voice crack.

Cass shakes her head. "That wasn't it at all. I had to get into the Elysian Fields, and this was before I met you. I had no idea what kind of vættir you even were." She pauses and sighs. "Remember when I asked you what you smelled from me, and how I wondered why you never told me about your ability to smell emotions?"

The conversation is too fresh for me to do anything but nod.

"Well, everyone pays for their passage to the Underworld. You paid with your wings, and that satyr that came in a little after you paid with his horns, and so on."

I nod, because I remember when the satyr arrived. A couple

of Cyclopes took him out during sleep time. The sounds of his screams still haunt my memories.

I watch Cass, waiting. I always wondered what they took from her, but I never dared to ask. There was something about her that never invited much in the way of conversation, and I was so happy to have a friend, especially one as strong as Cass, that I didn't bother prying.

Now I wish I hadn't trusted her so easily. Because Cass's confession that she kept me alive because of a deal with Hermes makes me feel like I'm an idiot for thinking she could've wanted to be my friend.

It's not a good feeling.

Cass looks down at her hands. She manifests a ball of fire and begins tossing it back and forth. "I thought at first maybe they'd taken my magic, but æther and the mortal elements can't be used in Tartarus, and when I returned to the Mortal Realm, so did my abilities, so I didn't think it was that. It wasn't anything physical that I could tell. I felt perfectly fine. It wasn't until the night a Mer tried to rape me that I understood what I was missing."

I swallow, because I didn't know that Cass had gone through something that bad. Sure, she'd warned me that we needed to sleep in shifts, and the nights we were lucky enough to have some sort of shelter we barricaded the doorway. I never stopped to consider why she was so cautious.

Cass continues. Her words reveal nothing of her feelings. "I managed to fight him off by hitting him with a rock until he didn't move. And then, because his dead body was in the way of my sleeping spot near the dark fire, I dragged him into the tree line. Later that night when the basilisks came to feed, I threw a rock in the direction of his corpse to scare them off. Not out of some respect for the dead, but because they were loud and I was trying to sleep."

Horror makes my chest tight, and I take a deep breath. "Gods, Cass. That's . . . I don't even know what to say. I'm so sorry you had to go through that." Emotion clogs my throat, and if Cass's spine wasn't so rigid I would give her a sympathetic hug. Instead she looks like she's bored.

"That's the problem, Zephyr. You feel bad about what happened, and you weren't even there. I knew it was bad, but I didn't feel anything. I wasn't angry that someone had tried to assault me, I wasn't upset that I'd just killed a man, I wasn't even disgusted that basilisks were feeding on a dead body a few feet away."

Something clicks in the back of my mind, and I finally get what Cass is trying to tell me. At least now I understand why I've never smelled her emotions. She doesn't have any.

Cass watches me expectantly, so I drop the last piece of the puzzle in for her. "They took your ability to feel when they sent you to Tartarus."

"Yes. I have no emotions, Zeph. I know that I like you, my brain can register the fondness that should be there, but the feeling is absent. I can't feel anger, or guilt, or any of the other emotions that make us vættir."

I nod. So much suddenly makes sense. Her matter-of-fact responses to death in the Pits, her lack of frustration or any kind of judgment when I mess up, her flat green eyes. It all ties back to her inability to feel anything.

Now that I know her secret, I feel like an idiot. I've never gotten the slightest whiff of scent from her. I always thought that maybe she was just able to control her emotions, the way good Harpies can. Or maybe she was just barely human, one of those vættir who are closer to the gods than to humans. But she's neither.

Cass stands. "My point isn't to make you feel sorry for me, Zephyr. It's to show you that you're my friend, even though I might not be very good at telling you or showing it. I wanted to go to the Elysian Fields to find Elias, because I loved him. I thought maybe seeing him would fix me." Her flat green gaze meets mine. "Emotions are very important to us as vættir. It's what makes us better than the gods. It's why we're adaptable, and they aren't. Not having emotions . . . I know it's turned me into a terrible person. I did things while we were in the Pits that I never would've done when I could still feel."

I say nothing, and Cass continues.

"My reasons for seeking you out were selfish, but I want you to know that I would never betray you. You're my friend, and the Nyx. Your success is all that matters now, and I will do anything to make sure you fulfill the Prophecy of the Promise. I hope you will think of that before you decide to cast me out."

There's a long moment of silence while I mull over her speech. I shake my head and snort. "Oh, Cass. You're the best friend I have,

and you know the old saying about beggars being choosy, right?"
I force a smile, even though in the back of my mind I know that
things will never be the same again. Still, I have to try to move past
this. Cass is the only friend I have.

I sigh in frustration and push off the doorjamb and head into
the bathroom, gesturing for Cass to follow. "Come on," I say. "I'll
show you the shower."

I give Cass a quick rundown of how everything works in the
bathroom. Her eyes widen and she almost smiles a little when I
show her the commode. "That is amazing," she says, running her
hand across the furry toilet-seat cover. If she could feel emotions,
I'm pretty sure she'd be jumping up and down like the big winner
on a game show.

"They didn't have indoor plumbing the last time you were here?"
She shakes her head. "Time passes strangely in the Underworld."
I think of my lost year and nod. "I know."

I run a shower for Cass and then retreat back to the bedroom
to give her some privacy. I think about lying down on the bed for a
hot minute before I remember the perma-stink that clings to me.
I wonder if I'll ever be able to wash the stink of Tartarus off me.
Ugh, I hope so.

Because my mother taught me that it's rude to stink up someone else's house, I opt for the floor instead of the lovely looking
bed. Neither the hard floor nor my burgeoning doubts about Cass
keep me from falling asleep.

CHAPTER TWELVE

I WAKE TO CASS KICKING MY FOOT AND HER HAIR DRIPPING WATER ON me. "I like showers," she says, and I laugh.

"Yeah, they're okay." I climb to my feet and enter the bathroom, my muscles aching from my few minutes on the floor. By tomorrow I'll feel good as new, but right now I feel every inch of my time sprinting through Tartarus. Weeks? Days? I don't think we were on the run for more than a couple days, but who knows.

I make my way to the mirror over the sink. I avoided it when I was in here showing Cass how to use everything, but now that I'm alone, I let myself study my reflection. I haven't seen a mirror since the day Whisper was killed, and looking at my image feels like I'm breaking some ancient taboo. I'm surprised by what I see in the mirror.

I look exactly the same.

I'm expecting to appear as different as I feel. Time may not truly exist in Tartarus, but every minute I was there felt like a year. After the things I've seen I expect my face to be as lined and wrinkled as one of the seasoned warriors back in the Aerie. Instead it's as smooth and brown as it was before Whisper died. My silver eyes are still wide and surprised looking, the light color startling in my dark face. The only difference is my hair. The blue, ropy locks are slightly longer than before I was sent down to Tartarus, frizzy near my head where the new growth hasn't been properly twisted. Everything else about me looks exactly the same.

Except I have no wings.

I peel off the basilisk-leather shirt and twist around to look at my back. Nanda's soft, pitying words come back to me. *They took your wings.* Dusky lines crisscross my back, scars from my fall into Tartarus when the razor-sharp edges from my feathers cut me as they swirled around, ripped free from my shredding wings. Two large black lines run parallel to my shoulder blades. Once my wings would've been there. Now there are just a few tiny blue pinfeathers, pathetic reminders of what I've lost.

Not that I'm keeping track.

The black scars from where my wings aren't wind over my shoulders and down my arms a little, stopping halfway between my shoulder and my elbow. I do a double take and trace the black, scrolling lines. There's no way it was caused by the loss of my wings; the placement is all wrong. They look like inky vines. What in the realms could cause such a marking?

What if I got some kind of Underworld disease? What if it's from the waters of the Styx? Or maybe it's some side effect from eating that funky fruit. For a single panicked moment I imagine the black markings spreading across my body, eating away my vital organs and turning me into some kind of gelatinous blob.

I poke at the lines, which don't feel any different from the rest of my skin. Overall I feel fine, just a little tired and hungry. I try to push the worry away. I don't know what the black marks are, but maybe Cass will. I make a mental note to ask her about them, shuck off the rest of my Underworld clothes, and jump into the steaming shower.

I crank the hot water as high as it will go, sighing as the heat penetrates the hundred and one achy spots on my body. I would bet money that the Elysian Fields aren't half as good as a hot shower after months of getting beat to the hells and back.

While I'm showering, I can't help but think about Whisper. I'm feeling relaxed from the heat of the spray, and my mind wanders to one of the last moments we spent together. It was a few days before the start of my Trials, and I was so nervous that Whisper finally decided she'd had enough. I was in the middle of running through the One Hundred Ways for the fourth time when Whisper threw down her magazine and stood. "You need a break."

I paused in the middle of pretending to break an unseen adversary's neck and stared at her. "Should I practice my sword work?"

"No. You should get dressed. We're going out."

I stared at her blankly, not understanding what she was saying. "Out to the training area? I think I'm okay on land navigation."

Whisper sighed. "No, out of the Aerie. Come on, we're going to town."

As soon as she said the word "town" I was up the stairs and getting dressed in what I called my norm clothes. A pair of jeans, a

T-shirt cut to fit around my wings, and sneakers that were a little too small. They were relics from the last time we'd snuck out. None of the clothes were new, but they were better than the tight-fitting leathers that were the standard Harpy uniform.

Once I was dressed, we climbed to the roof and flew off. Neither of the sentries challenged us, but that was probably because they recognized Whisper's wings. As an assassin in the Omega Corps she was always coming and going. As soon as we were over the fence and into the countryside, the weight that pressed down on me disappeared, and I felt freer than I had in months.

I followed Whisper as she landed on a loading dock behind an ugly glass-and-steel building. "What is this place?"

She grinned. "The mall. I have some extra cash from my last job. We're going to get you some clothes that don't look like they came from the thrift store."

I flushed, because my jeans *had* come from the thrift store. I never had any money, mostly because I hadn't been assigned to a line yet. But once I passed my Trials and had regular work, I would have a little money to spend.

First we made sure our glamours were in place, mine courtesy of the æther stone in my pocket. Then we walked inside. For the first few seconds I couldn't breathe. The scent of all those emotions made me dizzy. Whisper gently guided me to a bench so that I could sit down.

"You need to learn to breathe past it. After a while, you won't notice the smell so much. At least here the emotions are mostly happy. Try heading into somewhere like one of their prisons. It's terrible."

While I waited for my nose to adjust, I took in the view. It looked just like all the shows on TV. Boys and girls traveled in flocks, their bags swinging happily. Tired-eyed mothers pushed their children along in giant strollers weighed down with purchases, while distracted dads stared at their phones. It was beautifully normal. Average. It was everything I'd ever wanted.

And it was nothing I'd ever get to have.

Whisper and I went from store to store, trying on pants and eyeballing shirts that would have to be altered if we were ever going to wear them. A boy held my gaze for too long in a store plastered with posters of shirtless guys on a beach, but when he headed over to talk to me, Whisper grabbed me by the hand and dragged me off.

"I want you to have some fun, but that is a distraction you don't need. Trust me."

The rest of the day flew by in a blur, so when Whisper recommended getting a pretzel and heading home I'd been crushed.

"I can't believe it's time to go already." My anxiety returned, the fear of my upcoming Trials almost crippling. The scent of my emotions must have been overwhelming, because Whisper wrinkled her nose.

"You'll do fine, Peep. There's no sense in freaking yourself out about it."

"But what if I don't?" I asked Whisper as we adjusted our purchases in preparation for flight. We walked to the edge of the parking lot. Our glamours would hide our take off, but that was the least of my problems. I knew I wasn't going to pass my Trials. My heart wasn't in it. I hated the Aerie, despised the way it controlled our lives and kept us from the real world. The last thing I wanted was to spend the rest of my years rotting away inside of those strictly regimented walls. But I couldn't tell Whisper that.

She loved the routine, the safety. She was just like our mom in that way.

My sister looked down at me, and her expression softened. She laid a protective hand on my shoulder. "Zeph, you'll pass or you won't. And if you don't," she began, halting my interruption, "we'll figure it out. There are lots of things you can do in the Aerie that don't require fighting. We'll find a position for you."

"Maybe I should leave the Aerie."

Whisper laughed. It sounded like my hopes crashing to the ground. "Leave the Aerie? Don't be silly. Life is too dangerous to go it alone. No, if you fail your Trials, we'll just find something else for you to do. But it doesn't matter anyway, because you're going to pass your Trials. Now let's get home while there's still daylight."

We took off then, flying back to the Aerie in silence. And I knew that if I failed my Trials, Whisper would be disappointed. I vowed that I would do everything I could to pass.

But it didn't matter. I still failed. I let down the only person who ever had any sort of faith in me.

I won't do that again. I will find Whisper's shade and send it to the Underworld. Or I'll die trying.

The water turns cool, pulling me from the memory. I hurry to wash up before it goes icy. I don't move fast enough, and I end up washing my ropy snarls of hair under a frigid spray. But I can't complain. It's my first shower in more than a year.

I turn off the water and wrap myself in a towel. When I walk out to the bedroom, Cass is still wrapped in her towel. She holds a pair of the shorts Nanda left for us. Cass's expression is a bit forlorn.

"I don't think I can wear these," she says, holding up the running shorts. "They're . . . indecent."

I look around the room, and the bed gives me an idea. I pull off the bedspread and tug at the sheets, handing the top one to Cass. It has wide green and blue stripes, but it's not running shorts. "Can you make this work?"

She nods before looking down at the shorts again. "Does everyone wear such tiny clothes?"

I shrug. "I don't know. In the Aerie we wore leathers. We switched them out for jeans, which are these canvas kind of pants, when we went to town. But the people on TV wear stuff like this all the time."

Cass stares at the clothes, like she can't believe people would willingly give up wearing togas. "Can you help me cut this down to size?" I nod and extend one of my talons. Nanda's going to be pissed that we're destroying her bedsheets. But I can't let Cass run around in the dirty toga. It's a pungent reminder of hell, and I'd like to forget Tartarus as soon as possible.

I help Cass cut down the sheet, then quickly pull on the clothes Nanda left for me, a shirt advertising a 5K and a similar pair of running shorts to what Cass held. I feel strange walking around someone else's house barefoot, but my boots smell like ass. Hopefully once the leather dries out, the stink of the Styx won't be so noticeable.

There's not much I can do with the snarled locks of my hair, so I bind it in a high ponytail with a leftover length from Nanda's sheet. Once Cass has finished securing her bed sheet toga with a couple of creative knots, we gather up our towels and dirty clothes and follow our noses to the kitchen.

Blue sits at the kitchen table, scraping the remainders of something that smells amazing from his plate into his mouth. Tallon is nowhere to be found. My mouth waters, and I think I recognize the smell, but I'm not sure. The combination of everyone's emotions and the cooking food make for an interesting scent. Birthday cake and bacon. Coffee and too-ripe strawberries. I don't bother trying to parse them out. I just hope at least one of the smells is on the menu.

Nanda stands at the stove, overseeing several skillets at once. She sees Cass and me and gives us a wide, welcoming smile.

"Laundry room's over there, Peep. Just toss those dirty clothes on the floor. I'm making bacon and eggs, so do you want scrambled or fried?"

Nanda speaks English, so I translate for Cass. She's still confused, and I realize that she's probably used to much different food. Has Cass ever had bacon? What the hells did people eat in the olden days? Porridge?

I answer for both of us. "We'll have our eggs scrambled, thanks. Oh, and Nanda, don't forget Cass doesn't speak English. You'll have to speak in Æthereal." I respond to Nanda in Æthereal, so that Cass will know what I'm saying.

Nanda smacks her forehead with her hand. "That's right. Sorry, completely forgot." But her words are flat and insincere. She's obviously not as over Cass's dubious history as she's pretending to be.

I'm also having a little trouble trusting Cass right now.

I force a grin and shrug. "It's okay. Hanging out with Cass has really improved my Æthereal."

Nanda watches Cass with a dark, assessing gaze. "So I guess Blondie doesn't know what bacon is then, huh?"

Cass watches Nanda with her usual blank expression. "No. I've never heard of bacon."

Nanda gives her a feral grin. "Honey, you are in for a treat."

I toss the dirty towels and clothes on the floor of the laundry room, praying that I'm not going to have to referee a cat fight. When I return, Cass has already taken a chair at the kitchen table. A heaping plate of scrambled eggs and bacon sits in front of her, and she's shoveling it in like a champ. I take the other empty chair, Nanda sets a full plate in front of me, and then I get to work as well.

No one says anything for a few long minutes, and when I look up, everyone is watching me. "What?" I say around a mouthful of food.

Blue's lips twitch, and his sapphire eyes sparkle. "Are you hungry?"

I look down at my plate and realize I've eaten everything but a forkful of eggs. I swallow the food in my mouth. "Yes, but I always eat like this. You snooze you lose in the Aerie," I say. Cass frowns in my direction and I shrug. "It sounds much better in English than it does in Æthereal," I tell her.

We finish eating, and when I'm done, my belly is painfully full, stretching out the T-shirt. I feel amazing. I can't keep the blissful smile from my face. "Nanda, you are awesome."

She laughs and picks up my plate. "That's just the bacon talking."

Nanda loads the dishwasher, and Cass watches with her head tilted to the side, like an inquisitive dog. I reach across the table and tap her. "Dishwasher. It washes dishes."

Cass nods, but the perplexed look doesn't really leave her face. Nanda notices and frowns.

"Cass, how are you with wards?" Nanda asks, remembering to speak in Æthereal this time.

"Fairly good. What are you looking for?"

"Well, I had a decent 'don't see me' ward set up to protect me from Hera's Acolytes, but I think one of their seeker spells may have damaged it." Nanda gestures to Blue, and he stands without a word, giving up his chair so that Nanda can collapse into it with an audible sigh. She turns to me and says, "That's how I'm figuring she sent the grass men after me. Hera's been chasing me for nearly twenty years. Her Acolytes send out seeker spells to try to find shadow vættir. It was just my good luck she found me on a day when you kids were strolling up the walk."

"You're a shadow vættir?" I ask.

Nanda nods. "Yep. Not something our kind like to advertise, but there are still a few of us running around." At my shocked look she laughs. "Every vættir race has its dark and its bright members, even Harpies. It's less about who you are and more about where you get your power from."

I bite my lip, because everything I learned in the Aerie tells me the shadow vættir are unnatural, and that their strangeness is what led to them dying out. But that can't be true, because Nanda is a shadow vættir.

And so am I.

Cass climbs to her feet. The lost expression on her face has faded away, which I'm pretty sure was Nanda's goal. "I could definitely strengthen the spell, maybe add a few layers that would trigger a warning. How do you feel about a backlash spell? You know, just in case someone tries to tamper with the ward."

Nanda grins. The twisting of her lips is more devious than friendly. "Blondie, I like the way you think. Blue take her outside and help her fix the ward. Two layers, at least. More if you're feeling ambitious. Tallon's out there already, but you know how bad he is with æther."

Blue nods, and then he and Cass file out the back door.

Now Nanda and I are all alone.

I look at her, and time fades away. It could've been just yesterday that she was arriving at our house in the Aerie like a tropical storm, bearing cookies and promises of fun. Nanda was the only person I knew who could make my mother laugh. Their friendship went back to when they were kids, and I always thought my mother must've been a much different person when Nanda met her. Otherwise I can't imagine the two of them ever becoming friends.

Nanda leans back in her chair. Her posture seems relaxed, but I can see the telltale tension in her shoulders. She's Harpy trained, after all. Even now, so far from the Aerie, it shows. She could kill me before I even have a chance to move. "Why did you stop visiting?" I ask before I can think twice.

Nanda throws her head back and laughs. The birthday-cake scent of her amusement is genuine. "You always did get straight to the heart of the matter. It was one of the things I adored about you."

I smile. "You didn't answer my question."

"No, I didn't, did I?" She sighs. "It was your mother, mostly. She began to take a turn, one that put too much of a strain on our friendship. We grew up together, you know?" I nod, because I remember their stories of "back in the day." They were one of my favorite parts of Nanda's visits, the chance to see my mom as something more than a fierce general.

Nanda shrugs and continues. "She used to see the Aerie as a

necessary evil. As she got older, she lost the sense of adventure she'd had when she was younger, clinging more and more to the traditions inside those walls. When she told me that she didn't think it was a good idea for Alora and Tallon to come the next time I visited, I knew I'd lost her. As brave as Harpies may be in battle, they're terrified of the outside world." Nanda shakes her head sadly.

There's no doubting the truth of her words. I remember how our field trips to town stopped as I got older. I always thought it was because my mom got too busy once she was promoted to general. But now I realize it could've been motivated by fear as well.

"Why don't you like Cass?" I ask, changing the subject.

"The old stories say that she's the reason the last Nyx was killed. She's the great Betrayer, and I don't trust her. It has nothing to do with liking her."

I shake my head. "I don't understand."

"No, I don't suppose you would, growing up in the Aerie and all. It's not like they teach all of the old stories there." Nanda sighs. "Perhaps this story is best if I start at the beginning."

"Okay."

Nanda clears her throat and begins speaking in Æthereal. "In the old days there was chaos. Gods and men mingled freely, and the darkness and light ran rampant. Time was nonexistent. Man and Æthereals both lived many lifetimes. The first among Titans, Cronus, was angered by this. He despised humans and felt they didn't deserve to live as long as the gods. He decided that the worlds needed to be brought to order and he would do this by splitting up the realms. The majority of the bright æther and his favorites would go to the most perfect reality, the Æthereal Realm. Those he disliked or thought inferior, and the erebos that he couldn't control, would go to the lower realm. See, Cronus was only going to create two realms, but then he was betrayed by the drakans."

I prop my elbows on the table, thinking of the one I encountered in the Underworld and its chuffing laughter. I can't see a creature that massive bending to the whim of anyone, even a god.

Nanda continues. "Cronus had a deal with the drakans to create a space of emptiness, a boundary between the realms that we now know as the Rift. The boundary was supposed to keep the bright in the highest realm and the dark in the lowest realm. Cronus planned for mankind to be destroyed utterly, since humans cannot live entirely in either of the realms for too long. Mankind needs balance, and that is not something that the Æthereals are good at providing.

"Cronus, who was indeed an old and crafty god, had overlooked just how many Æthereals loved humans, and vice versa. Even the leader of the drakans had human companions, and it refused to contribute to the annihilation of mortal kind. So the drakans betrayed Cronus and created three realms instead of two, trapping enough of the erebos and æther in the Mortal Realm that mortals would be saved. And then they created portals between the realms that would allow a few chosen ones to travel between the realms."

This part of the story I know. "When the humans heard how Cronus wanted to betray them, they forsook him and took up worship of his children instead."

Nanda smiles and nods. "And in retaliation Cronus cursed the Mortal Realm with time. That's why we age here. And it's why Cass could survive in Tartarus for so long. There's no time in the Underworld or Æthereal realm."

I nod. "Okay, I get that. But how does all that tie in to the Nyx?"

"For a while humans and vættir were united behind Zeus and Hades to fight Cronus and the rest of the Titans. But once they were defeated, humans began to fight the Æthereals. The Exalteds thought of the Mortal Realm as their playground, manipulating some vættir for their own amusement, enslaving others. It didn't take long before that got old."

I nod. Not much has changed since then, from what I can see. Most of the contracts taken on by the Aerie were for one god or another, invisible wars that most mortals never knew about. "So the vættir joined with the humans in fighting the Æthereals."

"Yes. In those days the vættir weren't hidden like they are now. So the vættir and humans began to fight the Æthereals, pushing them out of the Mortal Realm. The average human has no chance against an Æthereal."

Understanding dawns on me. "But an army of vættir could."

Nanda nods. "Zeus and the High Council refused to give in to the demands of the vættir army. But Hades and his dark lords had had enough of war, and they agreed to retreat to the Underworld permanently. It looked like the Æthereal-Vættir War would go on forever, but then Zeus fell in love with one of the vættir generals, Circe. The two of them would meet along the river Styx, where Zeus would proclaim his love to her."

I wrinkle my nose because I've been to the Styx. Not the most romantic place for a hookup.

Nanda is still talking, so I push aside the remembered stink of dead fish and focus on what she's saying. "She made Zeus swear on the Styx that he would help her end this war, and even go so far as to appoint champions that would protect the vættir from the tyranny of the Æthereals. In a moment of weakness he agreed, even though his promise enraged the rest of the High Æthereals. The first champions, Heracles and Tischa, were born a few years later."

I blink. "Wasn't Heracles Zeus's kid?"

Nanda smirks at me. "The Exalteds fall in and out of love very quickly."

I snort. "I bet. Who's Tischa?" I ask, pronouncing it like she does with a *sshh* sound.

"Tischa was the first Nyx, the champion of the shadow vættir. See, the Mortal Realm, unlike the Æthereal Realm and the Underworld, is all about balance. There were two champions: one of the dark and one of the bright. These champions were gods given flesh, just as powerful as the Exalteds but restricted by their lifespans. Every hundred years, there was a new champion chosen by the dark, a complement to the champion chosen by the light. But not all of the shadow champions were strong enough to be called the Nyx, just like not all bright champions are strong enough to be called the Pandarus. The last true Nyx lived over two thousand years ago."

"Until he was murdered by Odysseus Oathbreaker." Nanda and I both look toward the door, where Cass stands. She comes to the table and sits down.

Nanda clears her throat. "I take it the ward is repaired?"

"Yes. It's a good ward." Cass leans back in her chair and plays with the ragged end of her hair. Is she nervous? Can she even get nervous? She clears her throat. "Did you tell her that my father is the Pandarus who set off the Dark Prophecy?"

Nanda shakes her head, and maybe I imagine it, but I'm pretty sure I see the briefest flicker of fear in her expression. The whiff of spoiling grapefruit confirms her panic though. Nanda clears her throat. "I've said nothing. I didn't, um . . . get to that part."

Cass can't smell the fear in Nanda's words, but I can. Is Cass really that scary?

I think of her family line. Circe, who talked a god into ending a war; Perseus, who killed the Medusa; and Heracles, who killed a cerberus with his bare hands. Heroes, all of them. That might be a little intimidating.

"Please let me tell it. After all, I lived it." Cass turns to me, her green eyes wide and guileless. She somehow looks younger right now than ever before, even though she just stood up to Nanda. "My father was appointed the champion of the bright, and for a few years he was happy fighting monsters and keeping the dark ones in line. But then Hera approached him, promising him an Æthereal for a wife if he were to betray the dark champion. My mother had passed on a few years before, and my father thought I needed a mother to ensure a good marriage."

I nod, even though my knowledge of ancient vættir customs is woefully lacking. I'm guessing that arranged marriages were pretty common?

Cass sighs. "What Nanda probably did not tell you is that the dark champion is much stronger than the bright. Always has been. The dark lords were happy to remain in the Underworld, so there were few problems for the champion of the bright to deal with. Just a random monster birthed by the Rift every now and then. But the High Council was still angry at having their war ended early. They were hungry for power after their victory over the Titans, and they were determined to rule the Mortal Realm as well. The only thing stopping them was the vættir."

"So what, your dad went and killed this dark champion guy?"

Cass stills, like a snake about to strike. Her voice is low when she speaks. "Elias was supposed to meet me. We were running away to be married. My father found out and summoned Hera, saying he would accept her deal. By then a few of the Oracles were talking about a Dark Prophecy and a time of fear and pain for the vættir. They saw a Pandarus setting the events in motion, and even though my father knew about the Dark Prophecy, he didn't care. He arrived at the meeting place before I did and killed Elias right in front of me. I killed my father in retaliation, and it was only as he lay there dying that he confessed he'd done it out of some obligation to me."

I want to reach out to Cass and comfort her, but her eyes are dry. From her expression she could be relating a recipe for cookies. I feel a pang of sympathy for her. She lost so much when she lost her emotions, but maybe it's more a gift than a curse. It would be hard to live for thousands of years with the weight of what she went through.

Nanda shifts in her chair and clears her throat again. "With both of the champions dead, things became very bad for the vættir. We tried fighting back against the Exalteds, but by then Hera had begun recruiting vættir and low-level Æthereals to serve her. She called them her Acolytes. After a thousand years or so the Pandarus was reborn and aligned himself with the Acolytes, as did his successors. Most vættir were too afraid to fight the Acolytes, so we all became very scattered. Then, fifteen hundred years after the death of Elias, an Oracle announced that there would be a new dark champion, the Prophecy of the Promise. He said the new Nyx would be a daughter of the dark. She would lead the vættir out of their oppression."

I stand and begin to pace. "That's supposed to be me?"

Nanda sighs loudly. "Yes."

"That doesn't make sense. Why wasn't a Nyx born sooner? I mean, you said that there have been several Pandarus since Cass's father."

Nanda's expression is grim, and her lips tighten for a moment before she speaks. "Since the prophecy, Hera and her Acolytes have been killing anyone they find to have an affinity for the erebos. It could be that a Nyx was born before now, but just never came into their full abilities. Most shadow vættir are in hiding and have been for centuries. They don't speak to other vættir, and they don't use their powers. A few of us have set up a system of safe houses to help those who are outed. I'm a part of that system. In the past few months things have gotten even worse. Where it used to be two or three shadow vættir killed a month, it's now up to ten or twenty. Pretty soon the shadow vættir will be wiped out."

"And then Hera will move on to the bright vættir," Cass says. "She'll enslave them like the old days, and eventually move on to the general human population. The vættir who follow her are fools."

I shrug. "Won't the Pandarus protect the bright vættir? That's his job, right?"

Nanda shakes her head slowly. "Hera killed the last Pandarus about twenty years ago. She then appointed the Ramuns as her generals, which you already know. Right now there's no one to protect the vættir."

The room falls silent as I try to process everything I've learned. Prophecies have never been something I understood. There's a lot of room for error. I mean, I could be the Nyx, but it could all just be a coincidence. The person who actually needs to fulfill the prophecy might be running around in diapers right now, waiting for the stars to align. You never know with these sorts of things.

Anyway, I'm not sure I believe everything that Nanda and Cass just told me. But I'm just too tired to argue about it right now.

I yawn widely. Nanda catches me and grins.

"You know, you girls have been through hell and back, literally. Why don't you go get some rest, and we'll work out what your next steps should be. We have time."

I nod. "That sounds great. Cass?"

She shakes her head. "I would like to spend some time with Nanda, getting caught up on things. I'm very behind, I think."

"Girl, you have no idea." Nanda laughs, but there's a nervousness to it. I make a mental note to try to convince her that Cass is not a threat, despite the niggle of doubt in the back of my mind. Even though Cass kept a few important details from me, I refuse to believe she's dangerous. She's still the girl who has saved my life too many times to count.

I leave the two of them whispering together like old ladies. I head upstairs, my feet feeling incredibly heavy. I've barely sprawled across the bed before my eyes are closing.

My last thought is that everyone is going to be very disappointed when they find out that I'm not really the Nyx.

CHAPTER
THIRTEEN

I WAKE TO SOMEONE SHAKING ME. FOR A LONG, TERRIFYING MOMENT I think I'm still in the Pits. I flail, fighting off my attacker. It's only after I land a punch and the person shaking me lets go with a loud "Ow!" that I remember I'm at Nanda's, safe and sound in the spare bedroom.

I sit up and rub the sleep from my eyes while Tallon holds his face. Darkness presses in from the room's window. The lamp beside the bed casts the only light. I sigh and push my snarls back from my face. "What time is it?"

"A little after midnight," he says. I'm finally waking up, and the first thing I notice is that he isn't wearing a shirt. Dark zigzags radiate out from his shoulder like an angry sun, and I remember admiring them at Lyss's pond. It surprises me a little. I never would've thought Tallon would be a tattoo enthusiast.

I pull my gaze away from his shoulder long enough to notice the way his pajama pants hang low on his hips. I don't think pajama pants have ever looked so amazing. But instead of acknowledging the uncomfortable fluttering sensation in my belly, I point to Tallon's pants and say, "Wow, I never took you for a cat person."

He looks down at the pattern of kittens frolicking and sighs. "They were a gift from Alora." I'm pretty sure that I see a smile play around his lips, and the awkward feeling disappears.

"What's going on?" It doesn't seem like we're under attack or anything, and Tallon must've woken me for some other reason than for me to sit here and admire his muscles.

"You were spilling darkness all over the house. It woke me up and now Cass is sleeping on the couch."

I yawn. "What do you mean 'spilling darkness'?"

He points at me, and sure enough darkness ripples off my arms like smoke. I will it away and the wisps disappear, but not before worry makes my stomach churn.

"How do I keep it from doing that?"

Tallon crosses his arms. "You have two choices. You can force it to submit to your will, or you can make the dark your friend."

"I don't know that I can." How does Tallon know this? Does he use the dark somehow? He can't be a shadow vættir. I've seen him use æther before. Maybe he's just being his usual bossy self.

More important, why is my erebos rising up now?

Tallon sighs and sits at the foot of the bed, his eye surrounded by a fading purple bruise. The spot is healing, but my guilt weighs heavy. "I'm sorry."

He looks at me with a raised eyebrow. "For what?"

"Hitting you. Now and earlier today."

He shrugs, but amusement tugs at his lips again. "It's okay. It was kind of nice. It reminded me of the old you."

I grin at him, the years seeming to fall away for a moment. "Remember that time when me and Whisper dropped the eggs on you and Alora?" I was young enough that I wasn't allowed to fly by myself, so Whisper had convinced me to help her steal a few eggs from Aerie kitchens and drop them on Tallon. I was so excited to have a chance to fly that I agreed.

He nods, his darks eyes sparkling in the low light. "She was so mad. But I got you back with that rotten tomato."

"We didn't think you'd be able to throw that far." I laugh when I remember how Whisper screamed when the tomato hit her in her face. But the memory quickly shifts into pain, and my laughter fades, leaving a raw ache in my middle.

Tallon watches with his too-dark gaze. "I'm sorry she's gone."

"Yeah, me too." I look down at my hands and fight back the tears that threaten to overwhelm me. I haven't even had a chance to mourn her. After her death I went on the run, and then there was my trial, followed by the never-ending fight to stay alive in Tartarus. I feel like I never really got a chance to say good-bye to her.

Tallon pats my hand awkwardly and stands to go. With him gone I'll be left alone in the dark with my memories of Whisper, memories that still bring more pain than joy.

Before I can stop myself, I reach out to Tallon, grabbing his wrist. He stops, dark eyes widening slightly. "Wait. Can you, um . . . can you lie down with me? Just for a little bit until I fall asleep?" When I was younger, I was terrified of the dark.

During his visits all of us kids would sleep out in our yard, holding mini campouts. While Alora and Whisper mocked my fear, Tallon would always scoot his sleeping bag next to mine to help me feel brave. It's that long-ago feeling of security that I'm thinking of when I ask Tallon to stay.

But when he looks at me, I remember we aren't kids anymore. I'm seventeen, eighteen if you count my lost year. And Tallon? Tallon is definitely not a kid anymore. Embarrassment heats my face, and I suddenly feel very silly and oh so exposed.

"Never mind, it was a stupid question." I let go of him, but without a word he climbs into the bed next to me. The mattress is large enough to hold two people. Tallon scoots all the way against the wall, space and a layer of blankets between the two of us. We don't touch, but I am still hyperaware of him.

I turn off the light and lie in the dark, listening to his even breathing. But having him here is almost worse than lying by myself. All I can think about is the way he looks without his shirt, and how he's now a more masculine version of the somber kid he once was. A kid I spent most of my childhood chasing after.

When my mom told me Nanda wouldn't be coming for any more visits, it was Tallon I cried for, not Nanda. Nanda may have been my sunshine, but Tallon was my world.

My restless thoughts make me toss and turn until Tallon finally throws an arm across my middle and pulls me close. "Go to sleep, Peep," he says, an echo of those campouts so long ago.

And at his soft urging I finally do.

CHAPTER FOURTEEN

I WAKE NEXT TO SOMETHING WARM AND SNUGGLY. I'M NOT QUITE READY to get up, so I burrow into the warm spot, hoping to go back to sleep. This is the best sleep I've had in months. I'm not going to give up on it that easily.

I'm happy when the warmth shifts toward me. I'm about to fall back asleep when my warm spot pulls me close. "Go back to sleep, Peep."

I sit straight up in bed, and Tallon cracks open one of his dark eyes to look at me. "What?"

My stomach feels strange, like when I used to turn into a dive too quickly while flying. "Oh, nothing, just you know, ready to get up and attack the day!" The words come out in a rush and my heart pounds. Sunshine streams in through the window, and in the daylight asking Tallon to sleep with me seems like a much bigger deal than it did last night when I was scared of my memories.

Tallon props his head up on his fist. "That's funny. Since when are you a morning person?"

Since now. "Oh, you know, since forever. I mean, I've got a big prophecy to fulfill. I should get on that, don't you think?"

Tallon watches me intently. "The vættir have been waiting for over two thousand years for the Nyx to return. I think they can wait a little while longer."

I shake my head, wrapping my arms around my middle. I'm fully dressed, but having him here with me in my bed makes me feel naked and vulnerable. I decide it's not a feeling I like. I tear my eyes away from his dark gaze.

That's a mistake, because then I remember that he isn't wearing a shirt. I'm in full-fledged panic mode. I can't seem to stop staring at his muscles, which he has more of than any guy should. His skin is golden, not pale like when we were kids. My fingers itch to see if his arms are as firm as they look, and that's when I know I'm in trouble.

Harpies do not have crushes, especially on their childhood best friends.

My wayward thoughts force me out of the bed too fast. The sheets wrap around my legs, and I fall onto the floor. Tallon leans over the edge of the bed, his curtain of dark hair falling across his face.

"Are you okay?" he asks, concern tingeing his voice. "You aren't getting freaked out because we're in bed together, are you?"

I'm so surprised by his response that I can't answer him. Why would he think that? Am I really that obvious? More important, why am I so panicked? Is it because I like him?

Pffft. Of course I like him, that's why I'm about to have a minor freak-out.

Tallon watches me with his dark gaze. "What's going on with you, Peep?"

I want to tell him everything. How I cried for days after my mom told me he wasn't allowed back in the Aerie. How I made myself forget him because my memories hurt too much. Or the way I sometimes imagined him showing up and helping me escape the Aerie when things were at their worst. And more recently, the way my heart jumped into my throat when he saved me from the drakan in the Underworld. I want to tell him all these things, to let him know that the years haven't changed me as much as he thinks.

But I'm not brave. Never have been, never will be. So I mumble some excuse about breakfast and kick away the sheets. I jam my feet into my stinky boots without even looking to see if they're on the right feet, and I run out of the room.

I'm halfway down the stairs before I pause, leaning against the wall and trying to catch my breath. My heart thrums in my ears, and I feel like I was running for my life. I have no idea why I'm so keyed up. It's like I just woke from a bad dream.

That's when I realize that I'm afraid. Not that I'll die, like I usually am, but of Tallon. I'm afraid he'll see how much I like him. Because I like him. A lot. What I'm feeling is strange and unwelcome, an emotion that belongs on a TV screen, not to me.

I feel so fragile right now that Tallon's rejection could break me.

I hide my face in my hands and try not to laugh. I am such a loser. Why do I have to have a crush on a guy who once put jelly and birdseed in my hair? Why can't I like Blue, who's friendly and easygoing? Why does it have to be Tallon, who studies me like I'm about to do something stupid?

Because it wasn't Blue who made me feel safe, who could convince me to go on any of the harebrained adventures Whisper came up with. It was Tallon. He was the one who picked me up when I fell down. It was always Tallon who was there to catch me.

And now? Now I want that, and more.

My middle squirms with nervous anticipation when I imagine kissing him. I push the mental image away in disgust and go downstairs. No wonder I failed my Trials. I'm not even a Harpy. Feeling this turmoil and sick excitement over the mere thought of kissing Tallon proves what a failure I am. Harpies never fall for anyone. They definitely never fall in love.

The thought stops me on the staircase. Love? No, not love. That's much bigger than what I feel for Tallon. It has to be. But I definitely have a bad case of being in like.

I think of Whisper and the one boyfriend I ever saw her with before her doomed relationship with Hermes. Mom was still alive then, mapping out our limited free time with drill after endless battle drill. Whisper hadn't yet taken her Trials, and I was still too young to leave the Aerie by myself. Sneaking out hadn't been easy. But I was determined to know where Whisper went every night after lights-out. So one night after our mom went to bed I opened my window, climbed the oak tree to the roof just like Whisper had, and flew out toward town.

It was easy finding Whisper. The mint-cookie scent of her happiness led me right to her. Learning the scent of emotions isn't easy for most Harpies, and we only learned the most basic in our Aerie-sponsored training: fear, anger, sadness. Those are the most common in a battle, and we were drilled on their different incarnations constantly. But Mom thought it was important to learn more than just the basics, so every night after dinner she and Whisper tested me on some of the lesser-known emotions. I knew the scent of Whisper's happiness because I'd been trained on it. The smell clogged the air like a giant neon arrow, and I found her with a boy next to a fountain in a park.

When I looked down at them, their arms were wrapped around each other as though they were a couple of strangling vines. I was so surprised to see them twined together that I over-corrected for a slight updraft. The mistake cost me my equilibrium, and I crashed into a nearby tree.

I fell through the branches, the noise bringing running feet. The two of them arrived, Whisper's face twisted with anger. I could barely smell the burning-plastic scent of her rage. The boy's orange-Creamsicle surprise nearly canceled out everything.

"Hey, she's got wings," he exclaimed to Whisper, pointing at me. His eyes didn't reflect the light like Whisper's. That's when I realized he was human. "Whisp, tell me you see what I'm seeing."

"Yes, I see it." Her rage melted away, and the rotting-floral scent of her sadness was so strong that I could barely breathe. I stumbled to my feet just as Whisper summoned a bright ball of æther and sent it at the boy. His eyes went flat before he fell into a heap.

"Did you kill him?" I asked, brushing pine needles from my pajamas.

"No, it's a spell of forgetting," she said a split second before she punched me in the stomach. I doubled over in pain, gasping for breath. It was more the surprise of the attack than the pain that stunned me. I was used to my mother hitting me, but not my sister.

But my physical discomfort faded quickly. Thanks to vættir healing, even pain doesn't stick around for very long.

When I stood, she was a few feet down the path. I ran to catch up to her. She was just sitting there, staring at the fountain. A scent I didn't recognize wafted off her before she got ahold of her emotions and clamped it down. It smelled like fruit punch left out in the sun.

"If you were going to set up a secret meeting, you should've picked a better place." Whisper turned to look at me, and I was too stupid to shut up and step back. Instead I just continued. "There were several avenues for attack, and anyone flying overhead would easily see you guys. This place blows as defensive positions go."

I should've seen the second hit coming, but I didn't. I like to think she pulled the punch at the last moment, but even so the left hook caught me on the chin and made me see double the stars overhead. I fell flat on my back. As Whisper stepped over me, I heard her say, "I didn't pick it because of some tactical advantage. I picked this place because it was pretty."

By the time I made it home, the sky was brightening. The Harpy on sentry patrol over the Aerie spotted me and escorted me home to my mom, who was expecting me. She didn't hit me, but I was grounded for a month, which meant no flying except for school drills and no TV at all. It was the worst punishment I'd ever gotten.

I still got off easy. Whisper was grounded until her Trials, three months later. She didn't speak to me for a week. It finally sank in that I'd somehow betrayed her. I tried to make it up to her by stealing a pie from the community kitchens. It was apple, her favorite. I left it on her pillow before I went to bed. She came in, picked it up, and hurled it out our open window.

"You don't get it, Peep," she said, taking off her boots and sitting heavily on her bed.

"Are you mad at me because you loved him and I ruined it?"

"I don't think I loved him. But I liked him. I liked him a lot. And that was enough."

I rolled over and sat up. "But if you didn't love him, why are you still mad at me?"

"Love isn't the only reason to enjoy being with someone. It was enough that I liked the way he made me feel. He made me happy. True love, like in the old stories? That doesn't happen for us. Not like for other vættir."

I rolled over and looked at her. I couldn't tell what she was feeling. Her emotions were on lockdown. "It happened for Mom."

Whisper sighed. "If you think Mom slept with our fathers because she loved them, you have a lot to learn. You need to stop watching so much TV. We don't fall in love, Zephyr. We can't.

Love will get you killed." It was an old saying among the Harpy. It came true for Whisper. The Acolytes killed her because she let herself fall in love with an Exalted. I remind myself of that as I stumble down the stairs and into the living room.

If I'm distracted by Tallon, how can I focus on the other things I need to do? Becoming the Nyx, finding Whisper's shade, fighting a prophesied war, and avoiding death at the hands of Hera and the Æthereal High Council . . . these aren't exactly small tasks. I can't really see myself having a lot of time for dating.

I just don't need the distraction of Tallon. I need to focus on not failing. That's going to be hard enough for me to do without getting all twitterpated about a boy.

And with that thought I push Tallon out of my mind and swear that I won't let myself think about him again. Nothing lies down that path but trouble.

NANDA AND CASS ARE IN THE KITCHEN WHEN I ARRIVE, CHATTING easily. There's something strange about the whole thing, and it takes me a moment before I figure out what it is. Cass's hair is different. It no longer hangs in jagged hanks. Instead it swings around her face in chunky layers that make her look younger and prettier all at the same time.

"What happened to your hair?" I ask, interrupting Nanda's discussion about Gorgons and their nasty tempers.

Cass turns to me with a frown. "What do you mean?"

I make a chopping motion next to my face. "You cut it."

"Yeah, Nanda cut it last night. She's a hairstylist. She thought it would be a good time for a change, and I agreed." Cass shrugs. "I thought you'd like it."

"I do. It looks good." Too good. It's easier to see how pretty Cass is now, and it makes me nervous. Harpies aren't really anyone's idea of beautiful, and standing next to Cass with her shampoo-commercial hair just makes it more apparent.

It also reminds me how outclassed by Cass I am. She's thousands of years old, comes from a long line of heroes, wields magic like an Æthereal, and is beautiful. Next to her I feel pretty insignificant.

Nanda puts a plate of French toast on the kitchen table, and the smell is heavenly. "You girls better hurry up and start eating before Blue and Tallon come down. Those boys are bottomless pits."

My face heats as I think about Tallon. Ugh. I'm supposed to be forgetting he even exists, not swooning at the mere mention of his name.

I collapse in one of the kitchen chairs and put my head on the table, covering it with my arms. I groan. What is wrong with me? I went seventeen years without going crazy over a boy. Why does it have to happen now?

Nanda sets a plate near my head, and I sit up. She watches me with a worried look, but luckily I'm close enough to the French toast that all I can smell is cinnamon. "Is something the matter?" she asks, pulling out a chair and sitting down.

"Ummm," I say, debating how much to tell her. I can't mention that Tallon spent the night in my bed, even if nothing happened. She'll freak. Hells, I'm freaking out.

So instead of telling Nanda the truth, I change the subject. "I'm worried about Whisper." I quickly relate to her my visit with Hades, and the revelation about Whisper not being in the Underworld. There's enough truth in the story that she doesn't notice my lie of omission. Because there *is* something wrong, but a hopeless crush isn't exactly breaking news.

Cass takes the seat on the other side of me and begins loading up both of our plates. "Did you want to try scrying for your sister today? That's usually a good place to start. It would at least give us a basic idea of where your sister ended up."

Nanda sits across from us and frowns. "Maybe you girls should go talk to my neighbor first. Kyra's a Hecate, and they know more about the journey of the dead than any other vættir."

"That's a good idea. I can see if she's noticed a lack of shades on the Paths recently." Cass puts a bite of food in her mouth. She's remarkably dainty, considering she's eating with her fingers.

We eat in silence for a few minutes before Cass suddenly pushes her chair back and stands. "I'm going to talk to Kyra now. You almost finished?" I want to ask Cass why she's in such a hurry, but then I remember Hermes's promise to take her to see her dead boyfriend in the Underworld. Is helping me find Whisper's shade also part of the deal?

Bitterness surges through me, and I'm surprised by the emotion. I push it aside. I shouldn't care what her motivations are as long as she's helping. Besides, maybe she's really just helping me because we're friends.

But I'm not ready to leave yet. My plate is still half-full. I've been daydreaming more than I've been eating. There's just too much going on. It's overwhelming.

I start to stand, but Nanda gestures for me to sit back down. "You finish eating. Cass can go by herself. We need to catch up, anyway." The dismissal in her voice is clear, and Cass nods.

"I'll fill you in when I get back." Nanda gives Cass directions to Kyra's house, and then she's gone.

Cass has only been gone for a few minutes when Nanda sits down at the table. "Tell me how you met the Pellacis." Her tone is harsh, and in that moment she reminds me of my mother.

I shove a forkful of French toast in my mouth to give myself time to answer the question. "Why?"

Nanda shrugs. "Humor me."

I sigh. "I met her when I first landed in Tartarus."

Nanda shakes her head. "No, I want you to tell me everything. It's important."

I nod. And I tell her the entire story.

Once Hermes dragged me to the Æthereal Realm, my life was pretty much over. After I spent a couple of days in a cell, the Æthereal High Council took a remarkably short time to find me guilty. But instead of killing me, a few of the dark lords spoke on my behalf, and I was sentenced to eternity in Tartarus. No sooner had the sentence passed than I was pushed through the portal to Tartarus, my wings shredding as I fell through the abyss. The pain was incredible, fire along my back. But it was nothing compared to my despair. Wings are the pride and joy of a Harpy. To lose them, after I'd already lost so much, was more than I could handle.

I grabbed for the razor-sharp feathers as they swirled around me, cutting my exposed skin. But I couldn't stop the destruction of my wings.

I slammed into the mud of Tartarus broken, bleeding, and utterly hopeless.

My first few moments in Tartarus I didn't do much more than struggle to breathe. The hard landing had knocked the wind out of me, and when I finally managed to gasp, I gagged. The air tasted like iron and sulfur. It was heavy and damp, and the landscape was something out of a nightmare.

The sky had a twilight cast to it, the color somewhere between gray and a bruised purple. The dark shapes of trees pressed in all around me, even though the spot I lay in was clear. I'd landed in a clearing, close to the tree line. I rolled over and stood up.

A few feet away a group of about twenty people watched me, their expressions ranging somewhere between pity and triumph. A mixture of emotions drifted off them, the burned-popcorn scent of excitement, the crap-and-iron smell of bloodlust. I couldn't pick out where each of the scents came from, but it didn't matter. There was a predatory air about them that set my heart pounding.

"Godslayer!" someone screamed. A Cyclops ran forward, his shovel held high over his head. I stared at him openmouthed, and somewhere in the back of my mind a little voice told me that I was about to die. This strange Cyclops was about to bash my head in. No more than a few breaths in Tartarus and I already had my first assassination attempt.

I never even got a chance to react. A blond girl broke free from the crowd and tackled my attacker. She moved faster than anyone I'd ever seen before, a deadly whirlwind of motion. The Cyclops landed face-first in the muck, and the girl jumped to her feet before severing his head from his shoulders with a clean stroke of her shovel. Behind her people murmured and moved back. I swallowed hard, my heart beating out an erratic rhythm against my ribs. There was no way I would stand a chance against this girl.

I took half a step back as she moved toward me. She bent down and grabbed the dead Cyclops's shovel and held it out to me. I took it reluctantly.

"A Harpy? In Tartarus? That's new," she said in heavily accented Harpy. I hadn't heard the language of the Aerie since I'd fled. Not many spoke it, since it's all clicks and whistles, and the sound made me smile.

"Not many speak Harpy," I responded in Æthereal. It was a more common language, and easier to speak.

"I'm not like many people," she said, hand out. "Cassiphone."

"Zephyr. I think you just saved my life." I clasped her arm in the way of warriors meeting each other on a battlefield. Cassiphone's eyes brightened.

She tilted her head as she examined me. "Zephyr Mourning? The Godslayer?"

I nodded, and took back my hand.

"Well, Zephyr Mourning, welcome to Tartarus. Try not to die."

Nanda sits back as I finish the story, her expression a mystery. She's silent for a long moment before she says anything. "How did she know who you were without your wings?"

I shrug. "No idea." The lie sits woodenly in my mouth. But I'm not about to tell Nanda about the deal Cass struck with Hermes. There's no need to add napalm to the fire. Nanda already doesn't trust Cass.

A tiny voice in the back of my head says maybe I shouldn't either.

"She must've noticed your eyes."

I frown. "What's wrong with my eyes?"

"Nothing," Nanda says, shaking her head. "But the eyes always tell."

I don't know what she means by that, so I say nothing and just keep eating.

Nanda sighs. "Let me fix up your hair," she suggests when I push my syrup-covered plate away. I nod, and she disappears to get what she needs.

When she returns, she doesn't say anything. She unwraps my hair and spreads it out across my shoulders, her fingers deftly finding the path of the snarls. Once she's done doing that, she opens a pot of styling cream, dipping her fingers in and using the stuff to twist up the loose curls nearer to my scalp.

"Your locks look a little rough. Who was taking care of your hair before you went to the Underworld?" Her hands move quickly, the rhythm hypnotic.

"Whisper."

She doesn't say anything, then finally there's a long sigh and her hands still. "She's not her, you know."

I turn in my seat to meet Nanda's eyes. "Who's not who?"

Nanda straightens my head and goes back to twisting up my locks. "Cass. She's not Whisper. You don't owe her the same loyalty. She's not family."

"She's my friend," I say as Nanda tugs at my hair.

"You can't trust her, Zephyr. You need to surround yourself with people you can trust right now."

"Cass kept me alive in the Underworld."

"For a reason, Peep. She kept you alive because she knew who you were!"

Nanda's words skim too close to the truth. I don't say anything, but Nanda says enough for both of us as her hands move across my scalp, twisting up my errant curls.

"What's to say she wasn't just using you, huh? Waiting for the chance to either kill you or to con you into helping her. She's a Pellacis, Zephyr! Her people were the worst of vættirkind. They stole the Golden Fleece and put minotaurs in mazes for their own amusement. They hunted their own kind and put them on display to make a statement. There's a reason they call her the Betrayer, Zephyr. She killed Elias, sure enough. Don't let her fool you."

Rage courses through me, swift and strong. I want to slam my fist on the table, to proclaim Cass's innocence. I'll tell Nanda to stop criticizing her, that she's got her all wrong.

But I don't. I tell myself that I keep my mouth shut because I'm a guest in her house and it would be disrespectful to argue with her. But the truth is that I don't say anything because I'm wondering if maybe she's right. What if Cass wants more than just some time in the Elysian Fields? After all, she could've just killed herself when she got back to the Mortal Realm if that was her plan. Death is a one-way ticket to the Elysian Fields usually. Maybe Cass hasn't told me everything.

Maybe she isn't really the friend she pretends to be.

I sit there quietly like the coward I am, doubting the one person who I owe more than anyone else. I hate that I no longer trust Cass, and I hate that Nanda isn't helping the situation.

After a while Nanda sighs and taps me on the shoulder. "All done." I force a small smile.

"Thanks," I say. Then I head into the living room to find a mirror, fleeing Nanda's critical gaze.

Tallon is coming down the stairs as I walk into the living room. A single panicked glance in his direction and I know I'm not ready to face him, or the turmoil in my heart. So I walk past him and toward the door.

"Hey, where are you going?" he calls.

"Out!" I yell before hurrying through the front door. The early morning sun is bright. But I don't bother waiting for my eyes to adjust before I run down the stairs and away from Nanda's house.

CHAPTER SIXTEEN

I HAVE HALF AN IDEA TO GO FIND CASS, TO TELL HER WE NEED TO SPLIT town, strike out on our own. I feel like I could be successful in the world with Cass by my side. We survived Tartarus, didn't we? Maybe when it's just the two of us, my doubts will disappear. I think I could trust her again if I didn't have Nanda telling me otherwise.

But then I remember that Cass didn't even know what a dishwasher was. She won't be any better at surviving the Mortal Realm than I am after a lifetime spent behind the walls of the Aerie. Not only that, but I have no idea where she even is. I wasn't paying attention when Nanda gave her directions to Kyra the Hecate's house.

So instead of finding her and taking off for parts unknown I walk down the street, my boots clomping loudly while I wish I was wearing something more substantial than running shorts and a flimsy T-shirt.

While my feet move, I mentally work through Nanda's latest salvo against Cass. I thought this was settled yesterday when I told her that Cass was my friend and I vouched for her. Nanda and

Cass were sitting at the table chitchatting when I came down, for goddess' sake. How can Nanda say one thing and do something completely different?

I stop, realization sinking in. It isn't Cass who reminds me of Whisper right now. It's Nanda. I've only been here a day, and already her expectations are starting to weigh on me, plans that probably don't include Cass. That's what this is really about.

I start walking again, my mind turning over the conversation with Nanda. Her suspicions niggle at me even as I increase the distance between me and the house. Have I been wrong to trust Cass all this time? I always knew there were things that she hadn't shared. But it wasn't an issue, because I always had my secrets too. But now, after she's confessed all the things she never shared before, I trust her even less. It doesn't make any sense. Where is all this doubt coming from?

Cass is dependable, and she's loyal. Her actions should speak louder than anything else, and even when it has seemed hopeless, she has stayed by my side. She could've left the Pits at any time, promise or no. But she didn't. She stuck it out with me. Cass said I was her friend, and I believe her.

That should be enough to let me move past all this, but I can't. Instead I want to toss aside everything I know about Cass in favor of Nanda's opinion, which is based on rumor and myth.

Why do I let others' opinions steer my life? It's the Aerie all over again.

After my mother died, I no longer wanted to be a Harpy. All

I could think of when I studied for my Trials was the Matriarch. She had come to our door at dawn, as is customary when serving death notices. As soon as I heard the single knock, I knew what it meant. We were taught to celebrate our dead, not mourn them. But when the old Matriarch with her drab green snarls and plain brown wings handed Whisper the wooden box, I wasn't proud. The small box that Whisper held would contain nothing more than a single flight feather from our mother, proof her days of soaring had ended.

My sadness was so strong that it weighed me down, pulling me to my knees. I began to cry, deep sobs that racked my body. Whisper and the Matriarch looked at me in revulsion.

"I thought you'd be stronger," the Matriarch said, her creaky voice heavy with disgust and disappointment. Not a single scent of emotion wafted off her, though. That's how disciplined she was. In that moment I knew I couldn't stay in the Aerie forever. I would never be like them. I couldn't blindly follow custom or turn off my emotions so easily.

And I didn't want to.

Whisper trained me day and night. She made me read texts on battle tactics and drilled me on scenting out emotions. We practiced the One Hundred Ways until I tired of pretending to rip an adversary's heart out with my talons. Whisper did everything she could to show me how to be more Harpy. The afternoon we spent at the mall, one of my favorite memories of my sister, was the exception, not the rule. Most of our time together she was a drill sergeant. I was going to pass my Trials, whether I wanted to or not.

"You won't disgrace our mother's memory with your failure," she said when my initial evals came back low. But we both knew the truth. I was never cut out to be a warrior.

And I'm probably not cut out to be the Nyx.

It's too easy to imagine Nanda looking at me and saying in her twangy drawl, *I thought you'd be stronger.* This thing with Cass is just the beginning of Nanda trying to manage my life, to force me to live according to her expectations. I love Nanda, but I can't go through that again.

Assuming I'm not too afraid to tell her how I really feel.

I kick a rock and swear. The memory lets go of me, and I look around. I lost track of both the time and my direction, and now I have no idea where I am. It looks like it's still part of Nanda's neighborhood, but I am hopelessly lost. I should turn around and go back, but then I'd have to face Nanda and all her expectations. Maybe another lecture about what a terrible person Cass really is.

But it doesn't really matter who Cass is, if she's a villain or a friend. I know how this story will end. I'm going to let Nanda down. The bitter scent of her disappointment will slam into me, burned coffee and rubbing alcohol, just like Whisper's. And then she'll give me that look, the same look that Whisper gave me the day I failed my Trials. An expression of sadness and surprise, like I was a stranger who'd just tried to mug her.

I let people down. It's what I do. Yay me.

A scream shatters my thoughts, followed by a woman sobbing.

It's the kind of sound that sends shivers down my spine and makes my arms break out in goose bumps. Sharp words slice through the quiet morning. I don't understand the language at first, but then I realize it's some bastardized version of Æthereal. Answering shouts echo, followed by a child's scream that rips through my middle. The sound is the by-product of pure terror.

Normally I would head in the opposite direction, looking for help. But I run toward the sounds of scuffle and fighting. My darkness already boils in my middle, anxious for release. It's spoiling for a fight more than I am.

I round the corner, and there, in the middle of a front yard, are a woman and a little girl. The pink-haired little girl hides behind the woman's giant wings, which are midnight shot through with silver. Her locks have been cut off in favor of a short halo of bright red curls. Her skin is pale instead of dark, but there's no mistaking that she's a Harpy. It surprises me, because the only Harpy I've ever known to live outside the Aerie is Nanda.

I guess I'm not the only Harpy to dislike the restrictive customs of the Aerie.

The strange Harpy swings a sword wildly. "Stay back," she yells at the men circling her and the little girl. Up and down the neighborhood people have come out on their porches to watch. From the look of them they're vættir as well. Nanda said there were very few full-blooded humans in the town, and those who do live here are connected to the vættir in some way.

So if they're vættir, why in the hells aren't they helping the woman?

The men wear uniforms. Short black jackets paired with brilliant purple pants and knee-high black boots. On their shoulders is the distinctive peacock feather insignia of Hera's Acolytes.

Back in the Aerie, they would come to recruit once or twice a year. Whisper and I would always make fun of them and their effeminate uniforms, especially their too-tight pants. But there's nothing funny about them now that I know firsthand what they're capable of. I don't know what they're up to, but I know it can't be any good.

One of the men reaches for the little girl, who screams and rakes her talons down the man's arm. He laughs and dances backward. The Harpy swings the sword at him, but she's hopelessly bad with the blade. It's a claymore, one of the largest weapons Harpies use. She's too small to wield the sword properly. She knows it. And so do the Acolytes.

They're just playing with her.

Rage silences the voice that begs me to go find help. My heartbeat pounds in my ears. Everything is so twisted together in my mind. Whisper's death, my past failures, and my burning shame that I couldn't save my sister. Time slows and all the sound bleeds away. There are only the Acolytes and the scared face of the little girl trying to hide behind her mother's wings.

I run forward, catching the nearest Acolyte and jumping on his back. He's so surprised that he goes to his knees. I cup him under the chin and yank his head to the left. Inside, part of me shrieks. I've just killed a man. But the rest of me remembers the move as one of the One Hundred Ways. Number 43: Broken neck.

The darkness is jubilant.

It's an unfamiliar sensation, but also welcome. In the heat of the battle I don't question the feeling; I embrace it.

The other men turn around. There are five of them, not including the one lying on the ground by my feet. Six, the sacred number of Hera.

"You're going to pay for that," the tallest one says, a pale Fae with shining green eyes and copper-color hair.

The darkness rises up, eager to destroy. It makes me brave. It makes me reckless. "Says you."

Distantly I know this isn't me. I am never this calm, especially in the face of danger. But I don't have time to contemplate the change. All five of the Acolytes charge me, coming at me all at once instead of one at a time like in the movies. It doesn't matter. They're already dead. They just don't know it yet.

The first Acolyte reaches me, a guy who smells like the ocean and bloodlust. A Mer. In Hera's Acolytes. What is the world coming to? I see his webbed fingers just as his fist slams into my jaw.

The punch connects, slamming my head back. The pain is so far away that I laugh. I feel so alive. The crippling fear is gone, and there's only the excitement of the fight. I find the shadows in my middle, churning and willing, and ask them if they would like to come out and play.

The Mer before me pauses and takes a step back. I look at the others, who've also frozen, their faces identical masks of shock. They stink of rotten oranges with a hint of ozone. The scent of terror. I turn my head and see a wisp of darkness out of the corner of my eye. One look down at my hands shows them shrouded in darkness as well.

The shadows laugh, and it is the greatest sound I have ever heard.

I grin, and they all backpedal. "Someone owes me an apology," I say. Then I send forth my darkness.

The roiling black cloud surges forward, wrapping around them like ropes made of shadow. It catches all five of them easily, their screams splitting the air. A couple of them beg for mercy, a couple others blubber. Only one stands there silently. The tall Fae who spoke earlier. He says nothing, even though I can smell the burning-rubber scent of his pain.

Deep down inside, I'm thinking I should let them go. I've already taught them a lesson.

But Tallon isn't here to stop me this time, and I'd much rather destroy them.

And so would the dark. Its need is a physical ache, and it purrs and coos like a well-behaved pet. How can I say no to that?

The darkness swarms over the Acolytes, entering their noses and open mouths like some black plague. Winds whip around us, but I barely notice. Instead I am focused on the erebos. I can feel it searching, seeking out what it wants most. The silver shining brightness of their æther. The darkness finds it like a hungry dog digging for a buried bone. There's a second of triumph when the erebos reaches the æther and a moment of hesitation as it waits for permission.

Good doggy, I think. Then I let it off the leash.

Everything stops. The world holds its breath. Darkness boils forth, engulfs me and the Acolytes. I feel their final screams reverberate through my chest, pulsing in time to my heart. I am absolutely invincible.

And then the darkness collapses back in on itself, slamming into my chest. I take a stumbling step back, blinking. When I look around, the Acolytes are gone. The only people left on the street are the Harpy and the little girl clinging to her wings.

And about a hundred eyes watching from the rest of the vættir in the neighborhood.

A woman comes crashing out of a nearby house, her hair a writhing mass of snakes. Her eyes flash, and I look away before she can freeze me. But she isn't trying to attack me.

"Thank you!" she says. She grabs my hands and kisses them, her snakes an agitated mess. I try to take a step backward, but she won't let go of me. She grabs me up in a hug, her snakes actually nuzzling into my hair.

I really don't like snakes.

She releases me suddenly, and the little Harpy girl is there, tugging on my shirt. "Are you the Nyx?" she asks, eyes wide. Her question sends a hush across the gathering crowd, and I shake my head.

"No, no, I'm not—"

My protest is cut off by a Cyclops who breaks from the crowd and grabs my hand, pumping it up and down. "You're real. I knew you were real. My grandmother used to tell me about you. I knew you'd come for us. I knew it!"

"No, I'm sorry, but I'm not the Nyx."

I don't have a chance to argue before I'm spun around to face the Harpy. She grins at me, her happiness a bright chocolate-chip-cookie scent. She presses a flight feather into my hand, the sharp edge cutting my palm a little.

"I am in your debt, Nyx. Me and my daughter." I look down at the flight feather, and a lump forms in my throat. A flight feather is a huge sign of gratitude. And here I destroyed the Acolytes just as much because the darkness wanted to as for anything else.

I nod and try to give her back the flight feather. "It's not a big deal." She won't accept the feather, just pushes it so it cuts a little deeper into my palm.

"You have to take it. Please. You saved Freesia's life. You know that's a debt that must be repaid."

I nod, because she's right. Harpies are very strange about repaying debts to the people who help them. I can't help but think of

Cass. She's saved my life on more than one occasion. If I had flight feathers to give her, she'd have at least a dozen.

I frown. "Wait, what do you mean I saved your daughter's life? What did the Acolytes want with her?"

"The Acolytes kill any vættir who can wield erebos," the Cyclops answers. He points to a large, rust-colored spot on the sidewalk a little ways down. "Too bad you weren't here last week. They've been busy lately."

"Wait, what?" Sudden nausea makes me unsteady, and the more I look at the brown spot on the sidewalk the worse I feel. That could've been the little Harpy girl. My brain helpfully supplies an image of the last time I saw Whisper to put in her place. So much killing. Why can't I escape it?

I look around at all the smiling, happy, hopeful faces. It's almost a tangible thing, their expectations. It steals my oxygen and makes it hard to breathe. Not even the frowns of the few skeptics in the crowd can remove the hope of all those people looking at me, wanting me to be the answer to all their problems.

I can't save them. I can't even save myself.

I don't want to be the Nyx. I just want to find out what happened to my sister's shade.

An arm slips around my waist, steadying me. I look up in surprise at Blue, who gives me a quick nod before saying, "Maybe Nanda didn't tell you, but the Acolytes kill anyone they suspect of being able to use erebos."

"But . . . children?" I glance over at the brownish spot again before my eyes slide away. "And in the middle of the street?"

"They killed my brother Owen a few months ago," he says, leading me through the gathered crowd with a tight smile. Despite the forced friendliness I can smell his sorrow, rain on hot asphalt. "We were coming back from a movie, and we weren't careful. He started showing off with his magic for one of his friends. The Acolytes found him and slit his throat in the middle of the street. He was ten."

"I didn't know you had a younger brother." The words are barely a whisper. What I really mean is that I didn't know Tallon had another brother. This is the second time I've been surprised by a revelation about Tallon's family ties. What other secrets is he keeping?

Tallon's angry words come back to me. *Using any kind of erebos brings the Acolytes.* Now I feel even worse for blowing up at him.

"I'm sorry," I say, stopping. Blue stops too. His eyes are sad, but he forces a smile.

"Now you know why we want you to be the Nyx so badly. We need you." Blue's usual teasing tone is gone, his words serious. Vættir crowd around us, some of them reaching out to touch me reverently, others murmuring in disbelief.

I shake my head. "I don't know that I am the Nyx," I confess.

Blue grins. "That's okay. We do."

He gently nudges me so I'll start walking again. My legs feel like overcooked spaghetti. I wish Blue would carry me, but instead he just navigates us through the crowd. I can barely stand, so I lean heavily on him. He keeps his voice low as we walk. "That's why we came to Tartarus, you know. After the news spread about Ramun Mar, people began to talk about you being the Nyx. No one else thought it was anything but a coincidence, but Nanda was convinced. When Alora had her vision, Nanda said it was time to find you."

Nanda sent them to find me, but only once she thought I was the Nyx. Not because of my mom or because she's my nest mother, but because I might turn out to be important. I knew that already, but now that I take the time to consider it, the reality of her motives kind of bothers me. Who is Nanda to preach about trust and the hidden intentions of others?

"Nice of her to wait so long," I mutter to myself, but Blue hears me.

"Nanda was going to try and cross over herself, but Tallon refused to take her."

"Why?"

Blue grins at me. "Because she complains too much. More than you, in fact."

"Ha." We've made it past the crowd, who thankfully decided not to follow us. I'm not sure how far it is to Nanda's house, but I can't wait to get there. All I want to do is spend the rest of my years in hiding. To keep my mind off everyone staring at me I say, "So, you guys decided to take a trip down to hell because your aunt asked you nicely?"

Blue gives me a look. "Nanda's meaner than she looks. Tallon eventually just told her we'd go so she'd quit harassing us. I went along because even though Tallon's the dude with the ability to trip the Rift, I'm a dragon." Blue grins and flexes the arm that isn't wrapped around my waist. "Never go down to hell without a little firepower."

"And yet, you ran from the drakan just like everyone else."

He grins sheepishly. "I agreed to go before I realized that there's no æther down there. Tallon might be of the dark, but I'm of the bright. No æther, no badassery."

I nod, but I'm completely unable to speak. Instead I'm thinking of all the things I've learned about the people I thought I knew. Tallon had not one, but two brothers. Nanda only cared about rescuing me after she thought I was going to fulfill the Prophecy of the Promise. And Cass only kept me safe in Tartarus because she wanted to see her boyfriend. My stomach does that weird lurching thing again, and I fight back tears.

I stop walking, and Blue stops as well, looking down at me. "Are you okay?" he asks.

I shake my head, because I'm not okay. I'm off-balance and out of control, afraid of all the things I still don't know and feeling more alone than ever. It isn't fair.

Blue must sense my sadness, because without a word his arms wrap around me, enveloping me in a guy-scented hug. "It's not that bad, you know. You have me and Tallon. We'll help you. You don't have to do this alone."

I sniff, because it's exactly what I was just thinking. I tighten my arms around him and sigh. "Thank you."

"If the two of you are finished, we should get back to the house."

Blue and I break apart, and Tallon's stormy expression causes my face to heat. Blue laughs. "We were on our way back." Blue looks at me with a sly grin. "Someone was saving the day."

Tallon rolls his eyes and points to a small red Honda. He seems mad, but it doesn't make any sense. Blue was just giving me a hug, not making out with me. What's his problem?

"Let's go," Tallon says, still not looking at me. "Nanda wants to move forward, and she wants to talk to you about it first."

Blue helps me walk toward the car, even though I'm feeling better. I frown. "Move forward?"

Tallon shrugs. "It seems like we aren't the only ones who thought you were the Nyx; we just got to you first. Now that the other vættir in town know you're here, they want to talk about the future, and how to fight the Acolytes."

Blue gives me an apologetic smile. "News travels fast in Ulysses's Glen."

It looks like I'm about to get a lot more popular.

CHAPTER
SEVENTEEN

AFTER TALLON'S REVELATION THE CONVERSATION DIES. I'M STILL NOT convinced that I'm the Nyx, but the more people believe I am the more it seems to be the truth. It's hard to think so many people could be wrong.

The turmoil I feel makes my stomach hurt and my head pound. I just want to lie down, close my eyes, and pretend the world doesn't exist.

We get in the car and head back to Nanda's house. We're farther away than I thought we would be, which means I was walking longer than I thought. It's late enough that Nanda is putting lunch on the table when we walk in: fried chicken with greens and mashed potatoes.

She gives me a grin as I enter the kitchen. Her eyes shine with pride, but it doesn't make me happy. It just makes me feel anxious. "I heard what you did. The whole neighborhood's talking about it. I figured you'd be hungry."

I nod, sitting down and digging in. I'm hungrier than I've been in a long time. I'm halfway through my first plate of food before I realize that Cass isn't at the table. "Hey, where's Cass?"

"She already ate. She said she had something to look into and said she'd talk to you when she gets back." Nanda gives me a meaningful look, like this is why I shouldn't trust her. But I don't know that she's doing anything wrong. What if she's just trying to track down what happened to Whisper?

But what if she isn't? a little voice says. A little niggle of doubt begins to creep in. Everyone around me has secrets, and I'm not sure I know all of Cass's.

Guilt clenches my middle. No. I won't fall into Nanda's trap. Cass is my friend. She's out there trying to find out what happened to Whisper. That's where I should be. Helping Cass, not stuffing my face.

But I don't get up, because Nanda's refilling my plate. So I feed my guilt along with the gnawing, hollow ache in my middle. I've eaten two more pieces of chicken and another helping of both greens and mashed potatoes before I finally feel full.

I sit back and sigh. Tallon looks at my empty plate, chicken bones piled high. "The erebos takes a lot out of you. You're going to have to eat like that every time you use it."

The knowing tone in his voice irritates me. "What are you, the food police?"

Hurt flashes across his expression, and I immediately regret my sharp words. But before I can say anything, he pushes back from the table and leaves.

Nanda begins cleaning up the kitchen, and I jump to my feet to help her. Blue finishes his food and gives Nanda a peck on the cheek. "I'll help Zephyr clean up here. You go sit down. You deserve a break."

Nanda beams at Blue, and her fondness fills the kitchen with the scent of bubble gum. She nods at me. "We'll talk later," she says ominously before walking out.

Blue loads the dishwasher while I rinse off the dishes. He seems nervous, and I can smell the burned-popcorn stink of his anxiety. We work in silence until the dishwasher is loaded. Once it's full, Blue clears his throat and leans back against the dishwasher.

"Can we talk?" he asks, and I nod.

"Sure. What's up?" I turn off the water and dry my hands on a nearby towel. It's amazing how nice it is to have something normal to do. I never thought I'd actually enjoy cleaning. It's funny what a few months in Tartarus can do for your appreciation of mundane things.

Blue runs his hand through his hair and sighs. "What's going on with you and Tallon?"

"Oh." I force a laugh, convinced my feelings are all over my face. "Nothing, just old friends. Why?"

"If you're just friends, why did he sleep in your room last night?"

My face is on fire, and every possible lie dies in my throat. "Uh . . . um . . . how did you know?" I croak.

Blue grins. "Well, I happened to catch someone sneaking out of your room this morning."

"Nothing happened," I say. Too quickly perhaps. Blue gives me a slow smile.

"Was that your choice or Tallon's?"

I sigh and put my hands to my burning cheeks. "What's this about?"

"Nothing, just brotherly interest."

"Well, there's nothing going on, okay?"

Blue's head tilts as he studies me. "Oh, I'll be the judge of that. How does Tallon make you feel?"

I start to lie, but something about Blue makes me feel like I can confide in him. "I don't know. Aggravated, confused, followed by this melty feeling, and then I wonder what it would be like to kiss him."

Blue smirks. "You do like him."

I bury my face in my hands. "Promise me you won't tell him."

"Nope."

I drop my hands. "You're joking."

Blue puts his hand over his heart. "Of course I am. Watching the two of you dance around each other is going to be too much fun."

I cross my arms. "Really?"

"Yes."

I watch his face, sniffing for the lie. He's telling the truth. "You are evil."

He laughs. "Yeah, maybe a little." His expression turns serious. "Just make sure you don't break his heart. Tallon's had enough pain in his life. He deserves to be happy for a change."

I want to ask him what he means, but Tallon walks in and the conversation halts.

Blue tries to look nonchalant. "Hey, Tallon."

Tallon doesn't even acknowledge Blue. "If you're finished, Cass is back. She's been looking for you."

"Okay. Thanks." I can't even look at Tallon. I wonder how much of our conversation he heard. He seems put out about something. He wouldn't be all pissy if he knew I liked him, would he?

I think of the boy he used to be. He did once put gum in my hair. So anything is possible.

I walk out into the living room, where Cass is making notes on a piece of paper. She looks up when she sees me. "Wait until you hear what I've learned."

I plop down next to her on the couch, trying to forget the drama I just left behind in the kitchen. Why did Tallon look so mad?

Cass shows me the piece of paper she was scribbling on and begins going on about crossings and Rift cycles and a hundred other things that mean absolutely nothing to me. I'm not really listening to her. Instead I'm trying to imagine what it would be like to kiss Tallon. Would he wrap his arms around my waist, or would he cradle my face in his hands like they do on TV? I wonder if his lips are as soft as they look.

Cass stops and glares at me. "Are you listening?"

I startle. "What? Yes, what's going on?"

"I just told you. Jeanine told me that the crossings have gotten fewer and farther in between. She thinks someone's taking shades. So maybe the something that happened to your sister's shade is happening to everyone's. Not just hers."

"I thought the Hecate you were supposed to see was named Kyra." I hate the suspicion that creeps into my voice. Somehow I need to find a way to get over my doubts before she notices. It's stupid and not fair to her, and even though Cass can't really feel anything, I still don't want her to know that I'm having trouble trusting her.

Cass turns her flat green gaze on me. "She wasn't there. Jeanine told me she fled, along with a bunch of other vættir. Things are happening, Zephyr. Big things."

That gets my attention. "Okay, so what's happening? And what does this have to do with Whisper?"

"Her shade isn't the only one that's disappeared, and traffic on the Paths to the Underworld has been drifting off. Plus, a bunch of vættir have fled Ulysses's Glen. There's definitely something going on that we're not seeing."

I nod, my brain trying to internalize everything. "I knew about the vættir fleeing. They're running from the Acolytes. So, the shades of vættir are also disappearing on a large scale. What does Jeanine think is happening to them? Does she have any ideas?"

Cass shakes her head. "No. But she agreed it would be a good idea to attempt a scrying as soon as possible. I talked to Jeanine about it, and she showed me her calendar. The full moon is ten days from now, and I think that would be the day to try it. The erebos will be weaker than usual, and we won't have to worry about it blocking our ability to speak with the dead."

I shake my head. "What are you talking about? I thought erebos was tied to death."

"It is, but it's also what keeps the dead from communicating with the living until they cross over. The living belong to the bright, the dead to the dark." Cass gives me a look that makes blood rush to my face. "What are they teaching the vættir in the schools these days?"

She sounds so much like Whisper that my heart aches for a moment. I shrug, and Nanda walks into the living room just in time to hear the end of our conversation. "Zephyr, didn't you go to an Aerie school?" I nod, and Nanda turns to Cass. "Don't blame the poor girl. The Aerie schools only teach the basics. They spend more time focused on killing and battle tactics than on the finer differences between æther and erebos." It's clear that Nanda's defense of me is tied more to her dislike of Cass than anything else, but I still don't say anything. I should let go of my doubts about Cass and stand up to Nanda. I should be a better friend. I should be braver. But I'm not.

Even though I really want to be.

Either Cass doesn't pick up on Nanda's tone or she just ignores it. Instead she nods and gives me a look. "Well then, maybe it's time you learn more than the basics."

Nanda turns to me. "We still need to talk. I've been getting nonstop calls from the leaders within the vættir community. The Aeries' Council of Matriarchs, the Fae's Queen's Council, even the King of the Cyclopes had his assistant call me. They all want to meet you and to find a way to move forward against the Acolytes. Especially after this morning."

"Wow, word really does travel fast." I fight back a sigh. I should've known there would be some sort of fallout from my little hero stunt earlier today. But I can't see a way around this. "So, road trip?"

Nanda shakes her head. "I don't think meeting with everyone is really such a great idea right now. We're going to have to figure out what to do with you. Otherwise I'm going to have every Acolyte on the East Coast pounding on my door. I'm going to call Alora. This is her vision I've been chasing. It's about time she provided some input into how we handle things. For now, get comfortable."

Tallon walks into the living room, and I give him a sidelong glance before I collapse back onto the couch. At least now I know why he's in such a snit. It looks like he was right after all. Saving the little girl and her mother, and using erebos, is going to bring the Acolytes to Nanda's front porch.

I don't know what I hate more, the fact that he was right or that I'd do just about anything to chase away his frown.

I am so messed up.

CHAPTER EIGHTEEN

CASS MAKES GOOD ON HER PROMISE TO TEACH ME ABOUT ALL THINGS magic. For the next three days she spends every waking hour teaching me the difference between erebos and æther. "Small magics should be easy to control," she says. Cass is right. Small amounts of magic should be easy to control.

But I can't summon the erebos because it would call the Acolytes.

And I couldn't summon æther if my life depended on it.

The only time we don't spend drilling in magic and æther theory are the couple of hours a day that Cass lets me watch my soap operas with Blue. Whisper and I had a TV in our house in the Aerie. It wasn't anything special, but I loved it because it was a window to the outside world, a world that I'm still not allowed to be a part of. Soap operas were my favorite, probably because they reminded me of the old stories, where heroes fell in love and villains were punished. It's surprising that after a year I'm still pretty caught up on the storyline. I went to the Underworld and came back, and nothing in the soap opera world has changed.

To be honest, nothing in my life has changed. I'm still training for a role I'm not sure I want.

We've been at Nanda's house for a week when Cass disappears for a whole day. I have no idea where she went, and Nanda wastes no time drilling me on her whereabouts. "Where's the Pellacis? Shouldn't she be teaching you magical theory?"

I shrug. "She said I could take today off to rest. Don't worry, she'll be back." I'm only half paying attention to her. I'm mostly watching the couple on-screen argue.

"They're totally going to end up doing it," Blue says next to me, shaking his head. "This has been going on ever since she came out of her coma."

I blink, confused. "But what about Caitlin? I thought Allie was staying away from Grayson because it would dishonor her memory."

"Caitlin's not dead anymore. They found out she's being held in a secret government facility. So all bets are off."

Nanda sighs. "You need to keep an eye on her, Zephyr. It's just a matter of time before she betrays you."

I nod as Nanda stalks off, but the truth is I'm listening more than I want to. Even though Cass has spent the past few days helping me understand my powers, there's still a tiny tendril of distrust in the back of my mind. It's like a splinter under my skin. Every time I think I've forgotten about it, something nudges against it and I remember all over again.

I like to think that if Cass were hiding anything, I would've known about it by now. Besides, why would she work so hard to get me to control my abilities if she was a traitor? It just doesn't make sense.

The next day Cass is back to hounding me about learning every small detail about my powers. We sit at the kitchen table where she quizzes me on the things that we've learned over the past few days. "What are the principles of erebos?"

"Darkness, rage, and . . . um . . . death." She gives me a look and I shrug. "Dying?"

"Destruction. Death is destruction of the form. Erebos thrives on destroying. Remember that."

"Why? Why do I need to know any of this, Cass?"

She stares at me until I squirm. Cass is really good at this teacher thing. "You know all of the weird norm trivia, but you don't know the basic tenets of magic." I'd tried teaching Cass about all the different shows on TV. That was a disaster. She couldn't tell the difference between eighties sitcoms and reality TV.

"TV and movies are fun, Cass. This is boring."

"Maybe. But knowledge is power, Zeph. Remember that."

I do feel smarter about magic after working with Cass. I still can't summon the æther at all, and that seems to worry her as much as anything does. Every single time I call the power it's like trying to hold on to a fish with my bare hands. And that's when it comes at all. Most of the time it's nonexistent.

As much as I see Cass and Nanda and Blue, I rarely see Tallon. He makes a brief appearance at mealtimes, but that's it. He arrives after we've all sat down and then eats his food leaning against the counter, quietly and quickly. He doesn't even look at the rest of us. And before anyone can even ask him what he's been up to, he's gone. I don't think he even tastes the delicious meals that Nanda makes for us.

And I feel like his behavior is all my fault.

I hate to admit it, but his constant absence just makes me think about him even more. I replay the moment when I woke to find him in my bed, only in my daydreams I kiss him instead of freaking out. My overactive imagination creates battle plans, until I know that if I get the chance to kiss him again, I won't waste it.

After a week and a half of safety and security in Nanda's kitchen I almost forget what it's like to be afraid. It's amazing how quickly I've forgotten the fear and uncertainty of Tartarus.

The day of the full moon arrives almost without notice. Cass and I sit at the kitchen table. She's trying to show me how to summon the mortal elements of fire, air, water, and wind. As usual, I suck.

Cass watches me try to call fire for a moment before she shakes her head. "Summoning is easy. You need to use æther to call the element into being, and then use it to fuel the element. For example, fire." Flames appear on Cass's hands. "If you look closely you can see the æther under the flames. That's what's fueling the fire. Æther isn't just a magical element. It can also work as a power source. The same is true for the erebos."

I try to summon æther and flames. If Cass's hands look like

torches, mine look like a match. I can only summon enough energy to make a single flame dance on my fingertip. And that feels like trying to push a car by myself.

Cass releases her magic. "Maybe you should try it with the erebos."

"I can't, remember? Acolytes."

Cass's golden brows knit together. "Okay. Maybe you could try it with the æther one more time."

"It's going to have to wait," Nanda says, walking into the kitchen with a girl who looks like she just stepped off the cover of a magazine. Her long dark hair hangs down her back in carefully crafted waves, and her violet eyes don't have the shine of Æthereal blood, but they're strange nonetheless. She wears a dress that hugs her curves and makes me feel incredibly dumpy in the hand-me-down jeans and T-shirt I wear. I'm lucky that Nanda keeps a stash of clothing on hand for the refugees that she takes in, but I still feel like a charity case next to Miss September. She's polished and sophisticated in a high-priced-hooker kind of way.

Gods, I hate her just as much now as I did when we were younger.

I have a memory, a crystal clear shining moment that became the defining point for my and Alora's relationship. We were outside, Whisper off studying for some test or another, so that it was just me, Alora, and Tallon. We were playing some pretend game where Tallon was an evil wizard and she and I were princesses. Only once Tallon was out of earshot, she turned to me and said,

"You can't be a princess; you're going to have to be a servant. Princesses can't have Harpy hair. They have to have pretty hair." I'd wanted to hit her, but like always I just nodded and went along with what I was told.

"Zephyr, you remember Alora, right?" Nanda's face shines with her love for Alora. Tallon and Blue may be Nanda's nephews, but Alora is her one and only child. Jealousy curls through my middle. I wish my mother had looked at me the way Nanda gazes at Alora.

Cass and I stand as Nanda continues talking. "Alora was sent down by the Oracle to meet with you." Nanda's excitement floods the kitchen with scents of waffles and maple syrup. I sniff again. No, not excitement. Anticipation. Nanda expects something good to come out of this meeting.

Maybe she's forgotten the time Alora took a pair of scissors and tried to clip my wings because she needed feathers for a picture she was making. Because I haven't.

Alora smiles at me, and for a moment I think maybe she's changed. It has been a while since I saw her. She has to be nineteen now, just a year or so younger than Tallon. I smell nothing from her, which I take to mean she's trained herself to lock down her emotions. "Zephyr! It's been too long," she says. She holds her arms open for a hug, and without thinking I do the same.

But as soon as she touches me, I can tell that something's wrong. I hiss and shove her away. A bit of darkness wisps off my fingers and snaps at her as I step back, the way a mother would slap a child's hand to keep her away from a hot stove. Alora hugs her hand to her chest with wide eyes, and I smell the citrusy tang of her fear.

"Don't ever do that again," I say. I don't even know what it is she did. I just know I didn't like it.

"I'm sorry. It's just habit. . . ." She trails off and stares at Cass for a long moment before she clears her throat and smoothes her hands down her sides. "I apologize. I shouldn't have snooped." She inclines her head in a sign of respect, and Cass comes from around the table to stand by my side. Alora is very careful not to look at Cass. I wonder why she's suddenly acting so cagey. Did Nanda already give her the rundown?

"What was that?" I can't forget the sensation, like someone sifting through my most intimate thoughts and fears with grimy hands. I feel dirty. I already didn't like Alora. This isn't helping.

Alora doesn't answer, and she looks uncomfortable for the first time that I can remember. Even as a kid she was confident and self-assured. Now she looks like she wants to ask for a do-over.

Next to her, Nanda's smile is starting to look brittle. Did she forget how Alora and I didn't get along? Did she think that would change just because a few years have gone by? Knowing Nanda, she's wondering what food she can make to save the situation. I bet she's rearranging the lunch menu as we speak.

Alora looks at me, still ignoring Cass. There's a flash of irritation in her eyes before she regains control of her emotions. "I'm a Fate. We work with the Oracles to help navigate the Paths and guide events. It's only natural that we would examine the Strands of Time and how they relate to the people around us." And there it is, the same haughty tone I remember from so long ago.

"You tried to see my future?" I say, a little in disbelief. Part of me wants to hit her for prying, but the other part of me wants to know what she saw.

Behind me, Cass snorts. "They're busybodies," she mutters. "They try to piece together the information they steal from people to form predictions."

"We do not make predictions; we see the possibilities. There's a difference," Alora snaps, still not making eye contact with Cass. It's almost distracting how carefully she's avoiding her gaze. Is she afraid of Cass? I kind of like the idea that someone can intimidate Alora.

"I know what they do," I murmur back to Cass, crossing my arms. Like many vættir, I don't really like seers. I like to think that maybe some things aren't destined. My mother hated them. Although she was never rude to Alora, she always looked at her the way someone would a strange dog, like she was just waiting for her to crap on the rug.

It always seemed odd to me that Alora wasn't a Harpy, since usually the line breeds true. But the one time I asked about it, Mom had shaken her head. "Some lines are stronger than ours. It's a disgrace, really, that Nanda would've bred with someone who couldn't give her a strong daughter. But that's where love will get you." She'd seemed more sad than angry when she told me that, and it was such an odd response that I dropped the matter entirely.

We had a few Fates and our own Oracle back at the Aerie. Most of the larger Aeries did. The Fates would predict which jobs would end up most profitable and help the Matriarch negotiate terms. Since Harpies are basically hired killers, they like to know where the chips will fall before they sign on to a cause. There's no harm in fighting for a lost cause, just as long as you get out before too many of your people get killed.

I take a deep breath and try to put on my best manners. "Look, what do you want? In case you haven't noticed, I'm trying to figure out how to fulfill some Promise here."

Alora sighs. "That's why I'm here, Peep. I'm going to guide you to the Oracle. She'll help you understand what your next steps should be."

I blink. "Oh? And what if I decide I don't want to go see this Oracle?"

Tallon walks into the kitchen, halting a few feet inside the door. My eyes flicker over to him, and Alora turns around to see who I'm looking at. I give Cass a sideways glance. If Alora was so able to predict the future, shouldn't she have known it was Tallon without looking?

Before I can make a snarky comment about her lack of future-seeing skills, Alora lets out an earsplitting scream and launches herself into Tallon's arms. He catches her with a grin, and my talons actually slide out of their nail beds. I want to claw Alora's eyes out.

It's just like old times. The biggest obstacle between me and

Tallon when we were kids was Alora. While playing pretend, she always had to make Tallon her pet dragon, or her prince, or something that would pit him against me. From the way he glares at me over her shoulder, some things never change.

I shake my head and take a deep breath. My talons slide back under my fingernails. I'm being silly. Alora isn't out to get me. I may not like her, but her Oracle is going to be my best bet for figuring out how to get this prophecy thing over with and getting on with my life. Because that's what I need to do, just save the world and get on with my life.

The thought of me saving anything is so funny that I laugh at myself.

Cass lays a hand on my arm and gives me a questioning look. "Are you okay?" she asks, and I nod. I don't bother looking at her. Instead I'm watching Alora and Tallon talk like old friends. He's even smiling. Why can't I make him smile?

Ugh. Why do I care?

I feel reckless and out of control and maybe more than a little crazy. I'm half-tempted to insert myself between the two of them, although it would probably just earn me a glare from Tallon. We haven't spoken in more than a week. I want to know what I did to piss him off. It had to be something.

Why won't he just talk to me?

And why is he smiling so much at Alora? She doesn't deserve his smiles.

Nanda moves over to talk to Alora and Tallon. While they're

occupied, Cass pulls me toward the back door. Once we're outside, she sighs. "Emotions are a difficult thing. Especially where love is involved."

I blink. "What? What are you talking about? I don't love Tallon. I barely know him."

"Uh-huh. I may no longer have my own feelings, but I know a smitten Harpy when I see one." Cass puts her hand on my shoulder. "Sometimes the suddenness of our feelings can make them seem even more wrong."

"It doesn't matter, Cass. I'm wasting my time mooning over him. Did you see him? He was actually laughing and joking with her. All he does when he sees me is scowl like he's afraid I'm going to steal the good silver." I cross my arms, because it pisses me off. Why can't he be like that with me? Why does he always have to be all frowny faced? I know Alora's his cousin, but it doesn't make it any less annoying.

"Well, you did punch him in the face. I don't think that is an endearing trait." Leave it to Cass to break it down like that.

I sigh and collapse on a decorative bench. Nanda has one of the nicest backyards I've ever seen. It looks like a park, and I realize I should spend more time out here enjoying it. I pick a daisy and tuck it behind my ear. "Do you think he's still mad about that?"

Cass shrugs. "Probably not. But you don't have time for romance anyway. We need to talk about tonight," Cass says. I straighten, because in my irritation over Alora I'd completely forgotten that tonight was the big night.

Tonight I would find out what happened to Whisper's shade.

I lean back and take a deep, steadying breath. I can't believe I let myself get distracted from finding Whisper. What kind of sister am I? "Okay. What do we need to do?"

Cass quickly outlines the plan, which involves a lock of my hair, some of my blood, and fire. Easy enough. Most summoning spells involve something personal. Since it's my sister, I should contribute the necessary ingredients.

But something about her expression makes me think she's holding something back, and I'm pretty sure it's not just my paranoia this time. "Okay, so what's the big deal?"

Cass sits next to me on the bench. Instead of answering right away, she fiddles with the knots at her shoulders. Even after more than a week in the Mortal Realm she still wears a bedsheet toga. She can't get over the idea of pants. I think they kind of gross her out.

Personally, I'm glad to have jeans, even if they're too-big hand-me-downs Nanda got at the local thrift store.

"Cass," I say, drawing the word out.

"There's something you need to know about the spell."

"Is it going to kill me?"

"Not directly, no."

I sigh. "Please, no guessing games. I'm getting a little fed up with piecing out information."

Cass nods and clears her throat. "There's a chance that the spell could pull in anyone looking for you."

That doesn't sound good. "Explain."

"When you do a summoning spell, it's kind of like sending out a message of where you are, like that thing Nanda showed me on the glowing box."

I frown until I put her words together. "You mean the map? On the computer?" Nanda had been trying to explain to Cass exactly where Virginia and Ulysses's Glen were in relation to the tiny Greek island where Cass had lived. The entire exercise was a failure as a whole, since Cass couldn't comprehend a whole other country, much less continent. Cass had been pleased to know that Greece was still a country, though she was dismayed when Nanda had gleefully shown her the ruins of the temples.

After that Cass quit asking about the outside world, and we quit telling her. She didn't need any additional complications. There was plenty of time for her to get used to the new world.

Cass's expression twists in confusion again, and she nods. "Yes. Like how the little flag told Nanda where we were? You're going to be the flag for anyone looking for you."

I take a deep breath. "So anyone looking for me will be able to find me." I take a quick inventory of the people looking for me. The cerberus. Maybe Hermes and the Æthereal High Council. Probably Ramun Sol. After all I'm sure he's heard by now that I've escaped from Tartarus. Also, there's the small problem of the Acolytes I killed a few days ago. My stomach clenches with guilt when I remember how easy it was to break the one Acolyte's neck.

Number forty-three, I think. It's easier than thinking of it as murder. Just an act attached to a number. It's a nice way to distance myself from the way his vertebrae grind together. Because if I think about the killings too hard, I start to wonder what kind of people they were. What made them join the Acolytes? Maybe that guy had a wife and kids. What about the other five? What happened to them? There wasn't even dust left behind after the darkness was finished with them.

I take a deep breath and think about the little girl clinging to her mother's wings. The Acolytes made their choice. Who knows how many children they murdered, innocents like Blue and Tallon's little brother? I did the world a favor getting rid of them.

I have to believe that, otherwise the guilt could rise up and bury me.

"Zeph!"

I shake my head and give Cass a wan smile. "Yeah, I get it. So how long will I be waving the 'Here I am!' flag after we do the summoning?"

Cass shrugs. "Don't know. Because of your strange abilities the spell could be stronger." Cass glances back toward the house. "We may want to try to leave the house to do the spell. You know, go somewhere where we don't have to worry about others getting hurt."

I nod. Cass is right. If the cerberus turn up, it wouldn't be a big deal. But Ramun Sol or Hermes? I imagine Nanda lying on her patio, the way Whisper was when I found her. I shiver, despite the warmth of the day. I can't put her in danger. She's all the family I have left.

"All right, do you have any ideas?"

Cass nods. "Yes. When I was talking to the Hecate, she told me about all of the empty houses in the neighborhood. One belonged to a Fae family that fled after an Acolyte raid a few months ago. There's already a few strong wards around the building that I can fix to suit our needs. We can cast the summoning spell inside. That way if anyone besides Whisper's shade answers the call, we can trigger the wards and buy ourselves some time."

It sounds like Cass has been thinking about this. "Great. But what's the plan after that?"

She levels a look at me. "We run, Zeph. Just like before. Only this time, we do it alone."

Her words sink in, and a surge of panic rips through me. "You mean, just leave everyone behind?"

"Yes. They've helped us enough. If you do this and then return here, you'll put them all at risk. I'm willing to put my life on the line to help you find out what happened to your family. Do you want to put them in danger as well?"

I open my mouth to object, then shut it. Cass is right. I can't ask that of Nanda. She's already done enough to help me. They helped me escape the Underworld, after all. That's more than enough. I won't put them in any more danger.

Because it's really just a matter of time before one of the people who want me dead shows up. And I'll do anything I can to make sure I don't see anyone else I care about get hurt.

"So then, I guess that means we're leaving tonight, huh?"

Cass nods slowly, her green eyes deep pools of calm. I envy her. Inside I'm in turmoil. Leaving feels like I'm abandoning the Promise and the whole messy prophecy. It's almost like I'm giving up on the vættir. Because it's not just the shadow vættir who are in trouble. Eventually all of the shadow vættir will be gone, and then the Acolytes will come for the bright, too.

But I push aside all my doubts and force a smile. "So what's the plan?"

Cass starts talking, and I let my mind wander. I try not to let my doubts about leaving show as Cass relates her plan. Even though I know it's the best thing I could do for Nanda and everyone else, I don't want to go.

For the first time, running away feels like failure.

CHAPTER NINETEEN

AFTER DINNER CASS AND I KILL TIME WATCHING A REALITY TV SHOW. IN the kitchen Nanda, Blue, Tallon, and Alora relive some funny story about the last time she was in town. Alora goes to some college for Fates, where they study the Strands of Time and buy dresses that barely cover their boobs. Not that I'm jealous of all the attention everyone is paying to Alora. Because I'm not.

All right. Maybe a little

I punch the couch pillow in my lap and watch the flickering screen. I'm not quite sure what's going on, I just know that it has something to do with people living in a house and basically being completely awful to each other in between bouts of drinking. Cass can't understand what they're saying; her grasp of English extends to "yes," "no," and a few choice swears that Blue taught her. Still her face scrunches up as she watches the show with me. Some things you don't need to understand the language to figure out. It's not a program I'd normally be interested in, but I need something to distract me from tonight's planned activities.

Have I mentioned how much I dislike magic rituals? They're just as likely to go horribly wrong as they are to work.

Besides the summoning, I also have our escape to worry about. Right now the plan is to wait until everyone goes to sleep and then sneak out without disturbing the wards too much. Cass wanted to put the house under a sleeping spell, but I worried that if something happened, they wouldn't have a chance to defend themselves. After all it was only about two weeks ago that we arrived to Nanda's house under attack. Who knows what will appear when we trigger the summoning spell?

The show goes to commercial, and there's a knock at the front door. Cass and I look at each other, debating whether or not to answer it, when it comes again.

"What happened to your wards?" I ask her.

She shrugs. "They weren't triggered. Must be a friend."

The knock comes again, a little more frantic this time. I get up, and as I pull open the door, my mouth drops open in shock. There have to be about fifty people in the front yard, all vættir. I recognize the Harpy with the little girl and a few others in the crowd from the day I killed the Acolytes. The Gorgon at the door isn't familiar though.

"Are you the Nyx?" she says, not even bothering to introduce herself. The blue snakes of her hair hiss in agitation, and I lean back.

"I don't know."

My answer sets off the crowd behind the Gorgon. People begin murmuring, while others shout quotes of some sort. I hear "She will come to you in a haze of uncertainty!" and someone else shouts, "If she's the Nyx, why did the Acolytes just attack my cousin in Canada?" I take a nervous step backward, and Nanda is there, pushing me behind her.

"Marnie, what a surprise," she says, her voice not at all friendly. "I thought we agreed to wait on this." Nanda closes the door behind her as she and the woman on the porch begin to argue. I turn around, and Alora and Tallon are there, Blue and Cass hovering in the doorway to the kitchen.

"What's going on?" Tallon asks, the first words he's spoken to me in what feels like forever. I shrug.

"I don't know, angry mob coming to kill the Nyx?" I'm only half joking. There weren't any torches or pitchforks, but I'm pretty sure I've seen this before. And it never ends well.

"If they meant you any harm the wards would've been triggered," Blue says. Cass watches us, her calm expression making me wary. But then I realize she doesn't know what's going on because we're speaking English. I slip back into Æthereal.

"The wards seem to be holding, for now," I say. "Who knows what will happen if the riffraff decide they're no longer just here to ask a few pointed questions?"

From out on the porch there's a crashing noise and some yelling. Tallon opens the door and rushes out, Blue on his heels. Alora pushes past me to watch the scene on the porch through the living room window. A hand pulls me backward, and I look over at Cass.

"Perhaps this would be a good time to go," she murmurs, and I nod. Everyone is distracted by the commotion out front. We can use the opportunity to slip out, instead of waiting for everyone to go to bed.

I run upstairs to grab my pack, which is shoved under my bed. I debate leaving a note, but there isn't time. Besides, what would I say? That I'm afraid to be the Nyx? Thanks for letting me crash here, but I'm bailing?

I come downstairs to find Alora and Cass talking. Alora's hands gesture wildly, while Cass listens with her arms crossed. They see me and freeze. Alora's expression turns guilty before she slinks off toward the living room window. Cass comes over to me.

"Are you ready?" Cass asks.

"Yeah. What was that about?"

Cass shakes her head. "Nothing important. Let's go."

I glance over at Alora, who stares out the window with an intensity that seems false. "Don't you think she'll say something?"

Cass adjusts her pack. "No, she'll keep her mouth shut." There's an edge to Cass's voice that scares me enough that I clamp my lips closed.

We quietly exit through the kitchen, slipping out the back door without incident.

And then we're off.

The layout of the house two down from Nanda's turns out to be nearly the same, thank the gods. We enter through the kitchen, which has been ransacked. Cupboards hang open; dishes and utensils are strewn about the floor. I quietly snag an overturned bowl before we make our way into the living room. This room looks a little better, but the tang of the family's fear scents the room. They must've been very scared for their emotions to still cling to the walls.

"Do you know how long ago this family left?" I ask Cass as we head upstairs.

She shakes her head. "Before Tallon and Blue came to the Underworld to find you. Alora said that things had been getting worse."

I frown. "Alora?" How many times did she and Cass powwow?

"Yes. We spoke at length today while you were watching your soap operas with Blue."

My face flushes because I hadn't even noticed the two of them talking. "What else did she say?"

"Nothing of import," Cass says, the edge back in her voice. I take that as a cue that it's none of my business and drop it.

We climb the stairs slowly. There are two bedrooms upstairs instead of the three that were in Nanda's. "I think we should do the summoning spell on the roof," Cass says.

I stare at her. "Seriously? The roof?"

Cass nods. "You aren't afraid of heights, are you?"

"No, but . . . never mind. We can do the spell on the roof. We should be able to climb onto it from one of the bedroom windows." It'll be uncomfortable to sit on the sloping roof for very long, but if Cass wants to cast the spell up there, then that's what we'll do.

The first bedroom we check has a window-unit air conditioner blocking the only window. The second has two unblocked windows, and I'm hoping one of them will lead to the roof.

We slink through the room in the near dark. The streetlight outside provides some light, but not much. Like the rest of the house, the place is trashed. Dolls lie on the floor, a few trampled underfoot. A tiny stuffed dragon lies facedown in the middle of the chaos. For some reason seeing the thing makes me sad. This was probably a little girl's room. The shelves hold a collection of dolls with ceramic faces and eyes that are a bit too lifelike. It's creepy, especially since the rest of the room has been destroyed.

I open the window and lean out. The opening is close enough to the sloping angle of the roof that I can grab the edge and pull myself up. I bite down on the edge of the bowl so that I have two free hands, and then I'm out and up.

Once I'm on the roof, I lean over the edge to help Cass up. She weighs next to nothing, but the angle is awkward, and I have to strain to help her climb up. By the time she's next to me, we're panting from the effort.

Getting onto roofs was much easier when I had wings.

From here we have an almost clear view of Nanda's house. The crowd is beginning to break up, although there are still knots of people here and there. I wonder what they're all talking about.

And I wonder how long it'll take Tallon to notice that I'm gone.

Ugh, why do I even care?

I settle onto the roof, the bowl next to me. It's tricky because the roof slopes, so I have to draw up my knees and plant my feet on the shingles to keep from falling off. Cass sits beside me, her leather sandals loud as they scrape across the rough surface of the shingles.

"Do you know what that is?" Cass asks. She stares at my arms. The dark swirls are just now beginning to peek out of the bottom of my short-sleeved shirt. I pull the sleeves down, trying to cover the markings. The material just bounces back up, the curving edges once again visible.

I shake my head. "It just started after we got here. I forgot to ask you about it." And my doubts about Cass made me hesitant to bring it up. But she doesn't need to know that.

Cass traces one with her finger, and I jump at the sudden contact. She pulls back her hand. "Elias had the same marks. It's from the erebos."

I look at the marks. "What does it mean?"

Cass shakes her head. "He never told me." There's sorrow in her words, and I study her. Her mouth has the slightest downturn, and I actually get a whiff of her sadness. It smells of lavender and powder with a tinge of rain.

I wonder if Cass is starting to get some of her emotions back. If she is, then maybe my wings could grow back. I want to ask her, but now is probably not the time. I swallow the words I want to say. "So, how do we do this, again?"

Cass walks me through the steps. I haven't done a summoning in a very long time. And like most magic, I'm not very good at it.

The night I killed Ramun Mar, it took me three attempts to get ahold of Hermes. By the time he showed up, I was light-headed and blubbering from the blood loss.

I hope this works the first time.

I extend a talon and slice open my hand before I think too much about it. Blood wells up, dark and shining in the moonlight. I hold my hand over the bowl, making a fist to squeeze as much out as I can before it seals over. The cut was deep, and about half an inch of blood fills the bowl before it heals. I pray it's enough to get Whisper's attention.

My middle twists and tangles with anticipation. I've waited so long for this moment. Now I just hope I can get the answers I'm looking for.

I balance the bowl carefully on my knees, while Cass saws off the bottom few inches of one of my ropy locks with a steak knife. The snarled hair falls into the bowl. She tucks the knife away into the folds of her bedsheet toga and then looks at me.

"Are you ready for this?" she asks.

"Yes. No. Maybe." I sigh. "Let's get this over with before I throw up." The nervousness churns my stomach now. I really wish I hadn't had a third pork chop at dinner.

Cass nods. "Say the words of binding."

I lean over the bowl and repeat the words that Cass taught me, high Æthereal that basically says that I freely give up this little bit of me. The words tangle on my tongue, but I can sense the power in them. This spell is much more complicated than the silly little summoning spell Hermes taught me to call him. This feels powerful.

The bowl begins to feel heavy, like it holds more than some blood and hair. I turn to Cass. "Can I get a little flame, please?" I could try to do it, but I don't feel the need to embarrass myself when I know she can conjure flame without much thought.

With a nod Cass produces a handful of fire and drops it into the bowl. It flares up when it hits my hair, and the blood sizzles up into a thick dark smoke. I blow the smoke away and hold my breath before I say, "Whisper Mourning, you are summoned!"

The smoke billows around us, and for a moment I worry that someone might see it and call the fire department. But then it swirls and coalesces into a female figure with giant wings, her short, ropy locks pulled into pigtails. My heart leaps.

"Whisper," I say, and the smoke figure turns to me. Her expression is sad and angry at the same time.

"Peep, what have you done?"

Screaming echoes down the street toward us, and Cass scoots to the edge of the roof. She turns back to me. "Acolytes. In the street. They're running this way."

I turn back to Whisper, and she shakes her head sadly. "He was just waiting for you to do this, Peep. Now you've led him right to you."

I grip the bowl tightly. If I drop it, Whisper will leave. "Wait, who? Why aren't you in the Elysian Fields?"

Whisper's smoke form wavers, like a TV screen on the fritz. "Because he has us. So many of us. All to stop you."

I don't know what she's talking about, but the sounds of fighting filter down the street toward me. I should go help them, but I need to know what Whisper is talking about. "Who, Whisper? Who has you?"

"I do."

I drop the bowl and scrabble around on hands and knees in the direction of the voice. Behind me, with a knife to Cass's throat, is a man with pale skin and a long, drooping mustache. His hair is completely white. He wears the purple uniform of the Acolytes, a radiant sun emblazoned on his chest. His brother's uniform bore the wavy lines of the sea. Nearby, a golden monkey-type creature hisses at me. A kobalos.

"Ramun Sol." I've never met the Æthereal, but he looks exactly like his brother, Ramun Mar. The first person I ever killed.

But not the last.

Rage surges through me, hot and sharp. The darkness rises up, fast and hard, ready to destroy. I gasp at how easily the power comes. Wisps of darkness curl around my hands and up my arms. There's comfort in its strength.

Ramun Sol laughs. "Ah, now it all makes sense. You were here all along. The Æthereal High Council has been wringing its hands and asking Hades to turn you over, like a bunch of simpering old women. Meanwhile you've been running around the Mortal Realm like some mythical hero. Do you actually believe you're the Nyx?"

"Let her go," I say. His words sting. They're exactly the same doubts that I've had all this time. The darkness surrounding me hesitates at my uncertainty.

I won't let him be right. He can't be right. I have to be the Nyx. I have to be able to kill him.

The people screaming in fear on the street below are counting on me.

Ramun Sol opens his mouth to say something, but before the words leave his mouth, Cass pulls out the knife tucked into her robes. She jams it into his thigh, twisting the blade viciously. Ramun Sol screams as Cass summons her fire, feeding it down the knife blade and into the wound. He releases his hold on her, and Cass is tilting her way across the roof toward me.

"Hurry," I say, holding my hand out to help her over the apex of the roof. She gives me a smile, and for a single moment her face is more than just pretty. She's radiant.

"I believe in you, Zephyr. I always have." Something furry jumps at my face, screaming. I swat at it, and it isn't until I bat the creature away that I realize it was the kobalos. Damned demons.

I drop my hands in time to see the kobalos jump on Cass's chest, propelling her backward into Ramun Sol's arms. He laughs and grins at me as he holds a knife to Cass's throat.

"No. Please," I say, panic slamming my heart against my ribs.

"Her shade shall help to burn away the shadow vættir, once and for all."

Without another word, he parts her throat with the knife.

Time slides to a stop as Cass's toga turns scarlet. My heart beats once, and again. The bright smile at Cass's throat is garish and outlandish. My brain refuses to see it, refuses to acknowledge what it means.

No. Oh gods, no.

Cass isn't just Cass anymore. In my mind she's Whisper, lying on the patio, sightless eyes staring up at the night sky.

I've failed her. I failed both of them.

The kobalos jumps on Cass as Ramun Sol releases her. It parts her chest easily, pulling out her heart and devouring it. The golden creature turns and screams at me, its muzzle covered with blood, then it runs off across the roof, disappearing in a bright, camera-like flash.

Cass's body slides off the roof, landing below us with the sound of crashing branches. All this has taken maybe seconds, and I haven't moved. I can't breathe, and the old panic surges back. He killed Cass. Cass is dead.

Cass, who saved my life. Cassiphone Pellacis, who helped me escape hell, who believed I was the Nyx. Cass, who never even knew that I was having doubts about her loyalty. My best friend is dead.

It's more than I can handle.

Ramun Sol is still perched on the roof. He smiles at me again, his golden eyes seeming to glow. "Now we settle our grudge."

"No, asshole. Now you die." My voice is far away. I can't feel anything. My entire body's gone numb, and everything feels like it's happening to someone else. Without even realizing it I'm up and running across the roof, the darkness rising around me. I catch a glimpse of fear in Ramun Sol's eyes before I tackle him around the middle. We fall backward over the edge of the roof, and Ramun Sol drives the knife he killed Cass with into my back. I ignore it.

The darkness is too hungry to even acknowledge the pain.

We fall off the roof, crashing into the yard below. Ramun Sol tries to scramble away, but I'm on top of him. I'm not going to let him go anywhere. The darkness tears at his exposed skin, and he screams like a wounded animal. He summons his power, æther as bright as the sun, and just as hot. It explodes around us, lighting up the night.

The solar flare throws me backward off him. The darkness retreats into me to avoid the bright. My clothes burn away, leaving behind blistered skin and agony. My eyes can't see anything, the light damaging the retinas. I hear the crackle of fire as the nearby trees and house go up in flames. But the darkness protects me. It wants to devour the brightness, and I laugh.

I've never been so excited by the idea of destroying something. I unleash the darkness.

I blink as my eyes repair themselves, and the pain disappears from my skin. I've just healed faster than ever before.

I climb out of a bunch of scorched bushes near the house. The darkness swirls around me, eager to fight. But Ramun Sol is gone, and rage sweeps through me. I scream out my frustration.

Around me the houses are burning, several destroyed by Ramun Sol's solar flare. But my anger has left me spoiling for a fight. The sounds of battle filter to me from the street out front.

If I can't kill Ramun Sol, I'll tear apart his Acolytes.

The darkness swirls around me, hiding my nakedness as I calmly walk around the side yard and into the middle of the street. The Acolytes are fighting the people gathered in front of Nanda's house. The vættir are sadly outnumbered, but it looks like they're trying to defend themselves against the swords and clubs of the Acolytes. Bodies litter the street, most of them vættir from the neighborhood.

Blue swings his giant sword at a knot of Acolytes chasing a woman. Tallon has his own battle going on, his smaller blades whirling in a deadly circle. Even Alora fights, tiny throwing knives that reappear in the bandolier she throws them from. Infinity knives. That used to be my weapon of choice back in the Aerie.

The darkness snaps around me, anxious for release. It wants to hurt, to kill. My pain is its pain as well, and it aches for my loss. The shadow's bloodlust should scare me, but it doesn't. Because I want the same thing it wants.

I want to destroy everything.

I send the darkness out, tendrils of it spiraling through the street. I can sense the Acolytes acutely, their corrupted brightness like rot on a piece of fruit. The first couple of Acolytes go down easily. The darkness understands the need for stealth and speed. It kills the Acolytes quickly, consuming their brightness without touching their physical forms. After the first dozen or so I realize that the darkness is saving its appetite. After all, you don't want to stuff yourself on the first course of the meal.

I walk toward the battle, sending the darkness out farther and farther. First down past the end of the street, then over to the next street, where the Acolytes stalk a sleeping family. Farther and farther I send out the darkness. To the next street, and the next. The shadows spread out from me like a dark plague, killing those Acolytes it finds. A barrack of sleeping Acolytes in New York. A party of Acolytes at some college nestled among giant pines. Farther and farther the darkness goes, seeking out Acolytes, stretching impossibly far.

They killed my sister and they killed my Cass. All my fear has disappeared in my burning need for revenge.

I fall to my knees. I'm exhausted. I can feel my heart slowing. But I still pour everything I have into sending the darkness out to find the Acolytes and stop their hearts.

Because Cass is gone and my heart is broken.

Someone shakes me, and I turn my head slowly. Tallon kneels next to me. His dark eyes are filled with worry. He isn't wearing a shirt, and I dimly realize it's because I'm wearing it. I look down, but my eyes don't want to focus.

"That's enough, Zeph. You have to call it back."

"Call back what?" My brain doesn't want to work. I'm so sleepy. Why won't Tallon just let me sleep?

"The darkness. Please. Everyone else has fled. You have to call it back."

At first I don't know what he's talking about, but then I feel it, tiny tendrils of death snaking out across hills and valleys, searching for more Acolytes. So many gone. And it's still hungry.

I close my eyes and urge it to come back. At first it doesn't want to listen, like an errant puppy sniffing out a rabbit trail. But then I tell it how much I miss it, and how much I need it, and it comes rushing back.

All of the darkness comes rushing back.

I gasp as the power slams into me. The shadows are glutted and huge, fat from the deaths of so many. It's too much. Too much destruction, too much darkness. I did this. I gasp as the swell buries me under a wave of erebos. I'm drowning under the weight of my own power.

Then Tallon is there, siphoning it off and using it. His hair whips around his head as he pulls in the darkness, and I turn my head to watch him. Smoky tendrils wisp around his eyes, and he grits his teeth as he pulls in the power so that it won't kill me. I didn't even know he could use the erebos. Suddenly the design on his shoulder makes sense. Not a tattoo, but shadows etched into his skin. A halo of darkness surrounds him. He is absolutely gorgeous.

I smile at him, and it's enough to get his attention. He looks down at me. "Too much, Peep."

"No. It will never be enough," I say. And then I surrender to the shadows.

CHAPTER TWENTY

I WAKE WITH A START, JOLTED BY A DREAM OF CASS. IN IT SHE SMILES at me with garish red lips. She keeps mumbling and talks out of a mouth in her throat. Only every time she tries to speak, blood sputters forth, and I can't understand what she's trying to tell me.

Finally she shrugs sadly and falls backward into darkness. I scream and reach for her, but she's falling and I can't get to her.

I startle awake when I realize it isn't a dream.

Cass is dead, I think.

I open my eyes and sit up. I'm on the couch in the living room, and gray daylight streams through the window. A tattered quilt covers me, and the stink of worry permeates everything. It smells like a musty closet mixed with lemon cleaner and sweaty gym socks. The scent is so cloyingly strong that I turn in the direction of the doorway to the kitchen. Nanda stands there. Her eyes are red rimmed.

"How long was I out?" I ask.

Her lips purse. "Two days. The boys have been strengthening the wards daily. You pissed the Acolytes off but good."

I vaguely remember the fighting in the street. "How many of your neighbors were hurt?"

"Not many. We lost Marjorie, an old Fae woman, and a couple of others. But it's nothing compared to the blow you dealt the Acolytes. Alora said from what she can read in the Strands of Time, you killed at least a thousand of them up and down the Eastern Seaboard before Tallon got through to you. Maybe more. The Strands are snarled right now."

I want to puke. A thousand Acolytes gone because I let my darkness loose. I can't even imagine that many vættir. The Aerie only had about a hundred of us at our fullest capacity. There were fifteen of us in my year group. A thousand . . . it's so many.

I'd kill three times that to bring Cass back.

"Cass is dead," I say.

"I know. Blue found what was left of her."

My head snaps up. "What was left?"

"Ramun Sol completely incinerated the house and the surrounding area. It took six hours to put out all of the fires." Something in my expression must show my emotions, either that or she can smell the horror I feel.

"I'm sorry, Zephyr." There's so much pity in her voice that it undoes what little control I have. A sob hitches in my chest, and I cover my mouth. *A Harpy doesn't cry,* I remind myself. But I'm not a Harpy.

I'm the Nyx.

Nanda walks over and sits next to me on the couch. "I was wrong about her. She was loyal. I wish I could've seen that before it was too late. But I'm glad you did," she rasps. I can't answer. Words won't force themselves past the lump of guilt in my throat, and if I open my mouth, I'm pretty sure that the only thing that will come out is a scream.

I wrap my arms around my middle and try not to cry, but it's hard. Tears slip down my cheeks unchecked, and Nanda lays an arm across my shoulders.

I should've done more. I should have done *something*.

I saw what Ramun Mar did to my sister. I shouldn't have hesitated.

My stomach lurches and my heart seizes with pain.

It's my fault Cass is dead.

Nanda sighs. "Your hair is gone as well. It was badly burned from the flare Ramun Sol attacked you with. I had to cut off most of your locks. I saved as much as I could."

I shrug. "No big deal. I'm not a Harpy anyway." I look in her eyes and confess. "I failed my Trials right before I was sent to Tartarus."

Nanda laughs, the sound sharp and short. "You think those antiquated tests are what make a Harpy? Please, child. You've fought more battles than most of the Matriarchs. You're more than a Harpy. You're the Nyx."

Her words should make me feel better, but they don't. All I can think is that I should've been able to save Cass. She was my friend, and I doubted her. I let her get killed.

My thoughts must show, because Nanda puts her hands on her hips and sighs. "It's not your fault she's gone, Peep. But I'm smart enough to know that's something you've got to come to terms with on your own. I'm going to go make you something to eat. Things tend to look better with a full belly."

I nod, and she moves off into the kitchen. I'm not sure there's enough food in the world to close the hole in my chest.

Why did Cass have to die?

I wipe away my tears, but fresh ones take their place. At the doorway Nanda stops and turns around. "I know it probably doesn't seem like it, but you did everything you could. You saved a lot of people, Zephyr. I was wrong about Cass, but she wasn't wrong about you. Cass always believed in you. I do too."

She disappears into the kitchen, and I pick at lint balls on the quilt. I sniff and force myself to stop crying. Would Nanda still believe in me if she knew that my selfishness is what brought the Acolytes to Ulysses's Glen? What would she say if she knew that I was the one who got her neighbors killed?

Ramun Sol never would've found me if I hadn't done the summoning spell. No matter how I look at it, Cass's death is my fault.

And so are the deaths of all the other vættir.

The front door opens, and Blue walks in, his arms full of bags. Behind him is Alora. The two of them chatter happily, and I recognize a few of the names on the bags. They're all from mall stores. An ugly feeling rises up in my chest.

Cass is dead, I'm unconscious, and they decide to go *shopping*?

Blue stops short, stumbling forward a little when Alora runs into him from behind. He gives me a wan smile. "You're awake."

"Yeah. Surprise, surprise. Did you find any good deals?" Sarcasm drips off every word, and Blue winces.

Alora steps around Blue and gives me a wide grin. I've never wanted to hit someone so much. "We actually went shopping for you. You know, since your clothes burned up while you were fighting Ramun Sol." Her matter-of-fact statement just makes me angrier.

"Wow, thanks for your concern. But I'm sure I could've borrowed something from your mom."

Alora plops down on the couch, completely oblivious to the death glare I give her. "I know you could, but the Nyx cannot meet the Oracle wearing running shorts and an old T-shirt. Look," she says. She reaches into the bag and pulls out a slinky summer dress in a bright blue shade. "What do you think?"

"I think you are out of your mind. There is no way in the seven hells I'm wearing that."

Blue snatches the dress out of Alora's hands and puts it back in the bag before pulling her up off the couch and taking her place. It's such a smooth move that she doesn't even have a chance to look put out.

"I'll put these in your room, Nyx," she says, picking up the bags and climbing the stairs.

I turn to Blue. "Anyone else calls me 'Nyx' and I'm going to gut them."

Blue laughs and leans back against the couch. "Gods, what a

week." He turns to me, the lavender-vanilla scent of his concern rolling over me. "How are you doing?"

"Gee, my best friend is dead, I just killed about a thousand people, half the neighborhood saw me butt-ass naked, and the Acolytes are trapping the shades of the people they kill. How do you think I feel?"

"Well, no one saw you naked except for Tallon." Blue waggles his eyebrows, and my face heats. He laughs. "Relax. He was the only one strong enough to get through the erebos without getting swept up into it. I doubt he was really checking out your goodies at the time. The rest of us just saw you looking like some badass avenging goddess cloaked in darkness."

"Well, that's a relief," I say, completely insincere. My fingers tingle, and my stomach is unsteady at the memory of Tallon next to me, talking me through pulling the darkness back. It would be a memory I'd cherish if it wasn't tied so closely to Cass's death.

Blue continues. "As for the Acolytes, well, they're not worth worrying about. Half of them are murderers, and the other half are deviants that get off on bullying others. They're barely human."

"Blue, all vættir are barely human."

He gives me a look, and the forest-fire scent of his anger surprises me. "No, we are human. That's why the Æthereals fear us. Because we're human, and our emotions make us dangerous."

I open my mouth to argue, but then reconsider. "Okay. So no one saw me naked, and the Acolytes deserved to die because they were all murderers."

"And deviants."

I wave my hand. "Whatever. But that doesn't make me feel better about the trapped shades or Cass."

"What do you mean, the trapped shades?"

I quickly fill him in on Whisper's missing shade, the summoning, and what Whisper told me on the roof about her and so many others being held captive. Blue frowns. "That doesn't sound good."

"No. And now they have Cass as well."

Blue leans forward, a small frown pulling together his pale brows. "Do you know what they're stockpiling the shades for?"

"No."

"It sounds like the old magics." The front door slams, and Tallon walks into the room. "There are some spells that use shades as a power source. It's nasty stuff, the kind of magic the Hecates used to do in the old days."

My heart does a swan dive as Tallon comes to stand next to the couch. He's gorgeous, his long dark hair pulled back in a braid. Even with dark circles shadowing his eyes, he looks amazing.

Blue scrubs his hand over his face. "We should find Kyra and ask her what she knows about this."

I shake my head. "Cass said Kyra had fled. She spoke with a Hecate named Jeanine. But I don't know how she found her." Tears threaten to well up, because it seems so hopeless. "Gods, what do we do now?" I can barely breathe, and I want nothing more than to just hide until this is all over.

Tallon levels a gaze at me, a muscle twitching in his jaw. "First of all, you stop panicking. You're the Nyx. So act like it."

His tone snaps me out of my self-pity, anger rising up sharp and hard. "I just killed a bunch of Acolytes, and my best friend is dead. The last thing I need right now is your attitude."

Something flashes across his face. Satisfaction? "You're right. I'm sorry." His tone is contrite, and I don't know what to say. Next to me, Blue makes a choked sound. Tallon sighs. "I'm worried and I took it out on you. How are you feeling?"

"How do you think?" I'm not ready to call a truce so quickly. He can't snap at me and be a jerk and expect me to fall all over myself when he apologizes.

He nods, and his expression softens. "Take a shower. Get dressed. Eat something. I know Jeanine. I'll go down and talk to her, see if she knows of any spells that would require such a large number of shades to be invoked, okay?"

A spark of memory flares. "And kobaloi. Ramun Sol had a kobalos with him. So did Ramun Mar, the night he killed Whisper."

Blue frowns. "A kobalos?"

"Minor demon used by some of the Exalteds for errands in the Æthereal Realm. But they don't usually cross into the Mortal Realm," Tallon adds.

I'm surprised he knows what they are. I only know because Harpies are required to have a working knowledge of the entire Æthereal bestiary. The more you know about creatures the easier it is to kill them.

But how does Tallon know that bit about them being used as

servants in the Æthereal Realm? Has he spent some time there?

I stretch, and my stomach growls. "So I go get pretty, you talk to the Hecate, and then what?"

"And then we go and see this Oracle of Alora's," Blue says with a shrug. "If she doesn't know what's going on, no one will."

Tallon heads toward the front door. "Don't dawdle. We need to get moving as quickly as possible."

He says it like I'm still that little kid chasing after him, begging him for a piggyback ride. "What's your deal, Tallon? Huh? Maybe you should back it down a notch."

He gives me a sympathetic look. "I know you're upset, Zeph, but you need to think beyond your own hurt right now. You know your sister's shade isn't the only one the Acolytes have. They've killed a lot of vættir over the past few years. Who knows what will happen to their shades once they do this spell? You can let your sister be devoured by the Rift, but I'm not letting that happen to my brother."

Too late I remember Blue talking about their youngest brother, and how the Acolytes murdered him in the middle of the street. Shame heats my cheeks. And here I didn't think it was possible to feel any worse. "Gods, I'm sorry. I didn't think."

"No, that's the problem, isn't it? You never think. All you do is react." Tallon takes a deep breath. "Look, I'm sorry I spend so much time yelling at you, but we have a lot to do. Alora said we have to go all the way to Pennsylvania to find this Oracle. That's like an eight-hour drive from here. Get cleaned up, and I'll talk to the Hecate." Tallon leaves without another word, the door slamming behind him. My shoulders slump.

Why do I always ruin everything?

Blue stands and wraps me in a hug. "Don't worry about him. He's just on edge because he was worried about you. He didn't think you were going to make it. There was so much darkness. . . ." Blue trails off, and I hug him back.

"I'm going to go take a shower," I say. I pull myself free and climb the stairs to the extra bedroom, where Alora is laying out the clothes they bought for me on the bed. She turns with a grin when I enter.

"I got you several different bras, since I wasn't really sure what size you were. There are also three different kinds of underwear. You struck me as more of a boy-short kind of girl, but you never really know these days—"

"Out," I say, pointing at the door. She opens her mouth to argue, and I shake my head. "I am not discussing underwear with you. Please get out."

She clamps her mouth shut and scurries out. Just before she closes the door, I call her name. "Alora."

She ducks her head back into the room.

"Thank you."

She grins. "Anytime. It's an honor to help you fulfill the Promise." She closes the door behind her, and I groan.

I have the awful feeling that living up to other people's expectations is going to get me killed.

I strip off the running shorts and T-shirt and walk into the bathroom to start the shower. I'm shocked by the glimpse of my reflection that I get. My entire body is covered in the twining black vines now. They curve up my neck, stopping just short of my face. I look down at my arms and legs, which are also covered with the dark lines. I look over my shoulder at my back reflected in the mirror. The swirls seem to be concentrated the most where my wings used to be, covering the scars in between my shoulder blades. It's beautiful and terrifying, a physical manifestation of how much I'm changing.

I should ask Tallon about the marks. His angry zigzags must be tied to the erebos. Since he knows everything, he probably knows what the markings mean. Cass said Elias had the marks as well, but the memory of our last conversation makes me well up. It takes a few moments of deep breathing to fight back the tears.

I swallow down my loss and continue to study my reflection. My hair is also different, but I was expecting that. The long ropy snarls are gone. In their place is a halo of blue curls that stick out in all directions. After the solar flare that Ramun Sol generated I'm lucky I even have hair. The tiny curls are a nice change, and the lack of hair makes my silver eyes look huge.

I feel different, and now I look different. It seems to be a fitting change.

I shower quickly and search through the clothes that Alora and Blue picked out for me. There's a lot that I will never wear. The underwear and bras I need, but there's no way I'm wearing any of the dresses. There are several pairs of jeans, and after pulling on underwear, I settle on a nice pair of jeans in a dark wash that fit like they were made for me.

The bras are a disaster. Most of them are lacy push-ups in bright colors that make me want to swear vengeance on their makers. I finally find something cute and cotton that doesn't seem like it could double as some sort of torture device. My choice of top is easy: a blue short-sleeved shirt with four-inch-high letters that spell out OVER IT. I'd bet money that Blue picked it out.

I pull on socks and gray, soft leather boots, and I'm ready to go.

Alora is going to have a fit. The thought actually makes me smile.

There's not much to do with my hair, so I do nothing. The smell of something delicious fills the room, and I head downstairs to eat. There's a massive hollowness in my middle. I seriously need food.

I hope Nanda is ready for me.

Tallon shows up just as I'm finishing enough sausage and pancakes to feed a small army. He enters through the back door, and a tall, willowy girl in a sundress follows him. Her golden eyes widen as she sees me. I slowly put my fork down as a tendril of jealousy unfurls in my middle.

"Hey," I say. My words are directed at Tallon, but my eyes are on the tall girl. Her straight brown hair hangs down to the middle of her back, and her skin is pale. She's pretty in a bland sort of way.

"Hey," Tallon says, sitting at the table. He looks at my plate. "There any left?"

"In the oven. Nanda actually went to the store to get more food. I think she's worried that I might start eating her plants."

He nods, and the willowy girl hovers behind him, her eyes on me. Tallon pulls out a chair and gestures for her to sit down. "Zephyr, this is North, Jeanine's daughter. She's a Hecate."

I give the girl the stink eye and a slight nod. "Hey."

"Hi." Her voice is tiny, like a little kid's. She looks around the kitchen nervously, and I sigh.

"Do you want something to eat?"

She shakes her head and continues to stare at me like I might grow another head.

"What?"

"Are you really the Nyx?"

Ugh. Well at least that explains her skittishness. I shrug. "That's what they tell me." I turn to Tallon. "Did you find out about the deal with the shades?"

"That's why North is here. I just wanted to tell everyone at once, and she can explain it better than me."

I roll my eyes but don't say anything else. I could seriously do without all the buildup for once.

Tallon gets up to find out where everyone is, and I sit with North in the kitchen. We don't say anything for a few long moments. She clears her throat. "Are you from around here?"

I shake my head. "No. I grew up in an Aerie out west in California."

She leans forward, and a spark of interest lights her eyes. "Really? What was it like?"

"I don't know. It seemed normal. I went to school, I learned how to kill people, and I watched TV. Every once in a while my sister and I would go to town and eat ice cream or something. The townies all thought we were just part of some weird religious cult."

North shifts in her chair. "That must be different. Not going to regular school, I mean. Of course, even here the public school's not exactly normal. I mean, it's all vættir. The whole town is populated by vættir. People don't even bother to wear glamours most of the time."

"Yeah, I noticed that. It must be pretty cool."

North shrugs. "Maybe. The only time we get to pretend to be normal is when we go to the city. I almost wish we spent more time being just regular people, you know?"

I nod, understanding what she means. In the real world you can just be how you are. But in the vættir world you are what your lineage says you are. Gorgon? Well, then you have snakes for hair and a quick temper. Harpy? You must love killing and hate men. There really isn't a whole lot of room for the truth, just stereotypes.

It's exhausting, always caring about that kind of thing.

Tallon returns with Alora and Blue in tow. Blue and Alora sit at the table while Tallon stands. He gestures to North. "You may as well get started. My aunt won't be back for a few hours. Grocery shopping is serious business."

She clears her throat. "Okay. Well, my mom wanted me to come and explain things because I've spent more time working with the pathways than she has. Mom is kind of a psychopomp, just ferrying the dead to the Underworld. I actually traverse the Paths and patrol them to make sure they stay in good repair."

Everyone else is nodding, but I have no idea what she's talking about. I raise my hand. "Yeah, uh, what are the Paths? I've never heard of them."

"They're sometimes called ley lines. They're underground currents of energy that flow through the worlds. In the Underworld they're all erebos, in the Æthereal Realm, æther. Here there are dark Paths and bright Paths. We use them to get somewhere really fast."

"How fast?" And why haven't I ever heard of these Paths before?

North shrugs. "I don't know, maybe half the time as a plane trip? Hecate usually stick to the dark Paths, but there aren't many of us left who can actually use the dark Paths anymore. The Acolytes"—her voice drops, as though saying their name can make them appear—"well, they've been killing a lot of our kind. We can usually use the ley lines to escape, but they've recruited a few of our kind to watch the Paths, so that's been out of the question."

I nod. "Okay, got it. Ley lines, awesome way to travel. But what does that have to do with the missing shades?"

North shifts in her seat and clears her throat. She tucks a strand of hair behind her ear. "There was a theory that came out around the same time as the Promise. It said that the vættir fed their abilities by being near the Paths. It's why Ulysses's Glen was founded on a Node, which is kind of like a junction of the Paths. We're attracted to the power of the Nodes. Glory Kirkcutt, the woman who came up with the theory, thought that if you flooded the Nodes with power, it would actually have a transportal effect on vættir."

I blink. "What? What does that even mean?" My voice comes out sharper than I intended. I'm almost sure that she's just making words up.

I hate being confused.

Blue interrupts to explain. "What she's saying is that if you put enough erebos or æther into a Node you could use it to draw in all the nearby vættir. Kind of like turning it into a vacuum cleaner." Blue mimics a sucking sound, and North nods so hard I'm afraid she'll pull something in her neck.

"Yes, exactly. Shades are essentially the erebos that remains after a person dies. I believe that the Acolytes are going to use the shades to turn a Node into a magnet for vættir. Since like attracts like, they're going to use the shades to pull shadow vættir down the Paths to wherever they are."

I shake my head. "And then what? Kill them? Why?"

There's a long moment of silence, as though talking about such a terrible thing will make it real. It's Tallon who finally speaks. "Many reasons. There are folks who believe the shadow vættir are evil. That's the reason a lot of vættir join the Acolytes. But Hera wants the shadow vættir dead, because once they're gone there will be no one to oppose her and the rest of the bright Exalteds."

Tallon's lips thin into a narrow line as he thinks. "The bright vættir aren't a threat. The bright Æthereals can easily overpower any vættir that uses æther. But the erebos is deadly to the bright Æthereals. Even a small amount could kill them."

I shake my head. "But there aren't that many shadow vættir left, right? Why would she even bother?"

Tallon's dark eyes seem to bore into me. "It only takes one person to change the world."

Alora nods slowly, her lavender eyes far away. "Tallon's right. The Strands seem to indicate the possibility of a great catastrophe. I see a knot, and the potential for many Strands to be cut. Human and vættir."

I turn to Alora. "Human?"

Tallon laughs, the sound humorless. "Of course. Why else would you need to get rid of anyone who can stop you? She pretty much already rules the vættir. But the shadows are the only thing stopping her from ruling the world."

Alora nods, her eyes still looking at something within the Strands of Time. "It would be just like the old days. The dark days, when humans worshipped the Exalteds and the vættir were the Æthereals' slaves."

North slouches in her seat, looking miserable. "There are old stories of those days, when the Hecate worked to ferry the lower Æthereals all over the world. It was a bad time." She shakes her head and wraps her slender arms around her middle. "Definitely not something we want to repeat."

I think about Cass, her toga soaked with blood. She lived long after the dark days, and yet she still ended up suffering at the hands of the Æthereals. I can't let this continue to happen.

"Fine," I say. "How do we stop this?"

Tallon looks at me, a smile playing around the edges of his lips. "You're the Nyx, Zephyr Godslayer. You tell us."

"Me?" Everyone is looking at me now and doing this slow nod. The last piece of the puzzle clicks, and I stand so abruptly that my chair falls over. "You want me to kill Hera."

Blue shrugs. "How else are we going to stop the bitch-goddess? She's been hatching scheme after scheme for thousands of years. The only way we can be sure that it's all ended is to kill her."

Tallon walks over, the sunlight from the kitchen window playing across his face. I'm surprised to realize that all this time I've been wrong about his eyes. They aren't black like I thought, but a purple so deep that it appears black. There's a metallic sheen to them that's never been apparent until now, and being so close to him makes my mouth go dry. I expect his usual mocking glint, but there's only sincerity there. "You're the only one of us with half a chance, Zephyr." He takes my hand and traces the dark vines twining around the inside of my wrist. "You're more powerful than anyone I've ever met, and you wield erebos like an Æthereal. If you can't kill Hera, no one can."

I don't know what to say. Everyone is suddenly looking at me, and my palms go from nice and dry to embarrassingly damp. Their expectations weigh me down like a ball and chain.

I know what they want from me. They all want me to be the

hero. But that's not me. I'm the coward. The girl who runs first and worries about the consequences later.

I could walk away. I could just leave, the world be damned. But that would mean turning my back on Whisper and Cass. They both believed in me. And it feels like it's time to stop letting them down.

Not only that, but Tallon is watching me. He isn't glaring at me like I'm about to screw up something important. He's looking right at me like he finally thinks that I can do this.

Strangely enough, I really don't want to let him down.

I snort and shrug off his backhanded praise. "You don't really believe that. But I'm not about to sit back and let Hera use my sister and my best friend in some twisted science experiment." I take a deep breath, because I know I'm about to make a promise I'm going to regret. "I'll do it. Just tell me when and where."

Everyone nods. It's not the kind of announcement that deserves a cheer. Maybe because they're all thinking the same thing I am.

Me against an Exalted? Yeah.

I am so dead.

CHAPTER TWENTY-ONE

AFTER MY BRAVE, AND COMPLETELY INSINCERE, ANNOUNCEMENT, everyone disperses. Tallon takes North back home, and Alora goes off to try to contact the Oracle, whatever that entails.

Blue and I sit in the living room, watching TV. Well, mostly watching TV. I'm trying not to think about Cass and Whisper. Are they suffering? Do shades feel pain or discomfort? My worry sours my stomach, and I idly dig my talons into Nanda's couch cushions until Blue stops me.

"Hey, Nanda's going to freak if you keep doing that," he says, pointing to the tears in the fabric.

"Oh, dammit." I fold my hands in my lap so I don't unconsciously destroy anything else.

Blue turns the TV off with a sigh and turns to me. "Do you want to talk about it?"

I shake my head. He studies me for a moment. "Is it about Tallon?"

I blink. "What? What about him?"

"I know you like him. I thought maybe you were planning on making a move or something."

I shake my head. "Blue, I have so many other things to worry about right now that Tallon is the least of my concerns." I don't add that I'm starting to wonder if the Tallon I knew as a kid even exists anymore. Maybe all of these feelings are tied up in the memory of him, and not the reality. Because from what I can see, the Tallon I knew grew up to be kind of a jerk. A hot jerk, but a jerk nonetheless.

"Look, I know my brother can be a little intense. But you don't know him like I do. He deserves to be happy, and it's hard for him to let go and do that."

"What's that got to do with me?"

Blue grins at me. "You made him smile, Zeph. That has to count for something."

I shake my head. "He doesn't need me, Blue. He needs to have the stick removed from his ass."

Blue laughs. "Maybe. Or maybe what he needs is someone he doesn't have to worry about losing. Since our brother was killed, Tallon has kept himself cut off. He's scared to let anyone in. Maybe you're just what he needs to show him that it's okay to care about people again."

"Me? Why me?"

Blue ruffles my curls. "Zeph, if anyone can take care of herself, it's you. You're more powerful than just about anyone I've ever met. Plus, you and Tallon have more in common than you think. I'm not saying the two of you have to run off and get married, but you should try talking to him. You know, like regular people do when they like each other."

I don't get a chance to answer Blue because Alora comes through the front door, slamming it behind her. Worry creases her face, and she's gnawed the lipstick off her bottom lip. It's the first time I've ever seen her look less than perfect. I sit up and stare at her, a tiny, ugly part of me glad that she looks like hell. "What's going on?"

"We have to leave tonight," she says, collapsing into the nearby recliner. "It took me forever to find out how to get in touch with the Oracle, and then when I finally did, she told me I needed to leave tonight." Alora kicks off her heels with a sigh. "There's something going on with the Strands. The pattern's changing, but I'm not good enough to read why."

I smirk. "I thought you were some sort of psychic."

"I'm not a psychic; I'm a Fate. I can read the Strands of Time, but I'm only an apprentice. Some things are easy, like deaths and births. And sometimes things hit you over the head out of nowhere, like your Prophecy. But the Strands are all snarled right now. I can't even figure out if skinny jeans are in or not. It's hopeless." She groans. "This is why we need to go and see the Oracle. She'll be much better at reading those sorts of things. And she can tell us how to stop whatever it is that the Acolytes are doing with the shades."

Blue stands and stretches. "I guess we'd better pack then. We can leave first thing in the morning."

Alora shakes her head. "No. We have to leave tonight. I was given the name of a hotel that we're supposed to stay at."

He raises a single eyebrow. "We? Who all's going?"

Alora uncrumples a piece of paper in her hand and reads from it. "You, me, Zephyr, and Tallon. Mom's supposed to go visit 'the relative who rarely speaks,' if that makes any sense. I have no idea who that is."

"I do. It's Saundra. She's a siren, so she tends to keep quiet," Tallon says, entering the living room from the kitchen. "Where is Nanda, by the way?"

"Gone." Alora yawns and continues. "I called her as soon as I knew what the plan was. She's already on her way over there, with a car full of groceries."

Tallon nods, like it's normal for people to just up and go unexpectedly. I look at each of them, but no one really seems troubled or even all that excited.

"So this is really happening, huh?" I say.

Tallon frowns at me. "What do you mean?"

"We're really going to leave just because of Alora's half-baked prediction?"

Alora straightens, and the skunk scent of her irritation filters toward me. "My predictions aren't half-baked."

"If you say so. Look, why don't we just spend the night here and drive up to see the Oracle tomorrow. You said it's like an eight-hour drive? We can do that in a day." I'm not ready to charge into the next chapter of my life. Part of it's fear that the next chapter will be the final chapter. But mostly I'm just irritated that we're all going to follow Alora like she's anything more than some shallow, self-centered fashionista. It's childish, but I can't let go of my childhood dislike of her. Nanda warned me against trusting Cass, but it's Alora who I don't trust.

As much as I can't let go of the past, Alora seems to be oblivious to it. She waves the little piece of paper at me. "Zephyr, I got my directions from the Oracle. We're supposed to spend the night at this hotel. If we don't leave soon, we won't make it."

Anger surges through me. I lean forward and snatch the paper out of her hand. Then I tear it into little pieces that drift down onto the floor. "And now I just changed the future. We are now free to sleep wherever we want. And I pick here."

Alora scrambles to pick up the pieces of paper. I stand, ignoring the looks Tallon and Blue give me. I know I'm acting like a brat, but I can't help it. I hate how she's so certain about what the future will hold, when I don't even know what's going to happen in the next five minutes.

I hate that she's here and Cass isn't. It's not fair. Why does everyone I care about leave?

I get a whiff of some emotion off her. Lavender with a tint of rot. I don't know what the scent is, but Alora's on the verge of tears. "My predictions are right. No matter what you believe, they always come true. I worked really hard to get that information."

I shrug. I'm feeling mean, and the guilt and pain over Cass's death still weigh on me. "Yeah, well, now we can make our own predictions. I predict that I will go upstairs and take a nap." I turn and head upstairs, ignoring the rank odor of Blue's disgust. My conscience tells me I should apologize, that I need to give her the benefit of the doubt.

But I don't. I just keep walking away.

"Cass thought my predictions were right," Alora calls. I'm half-way up the stairs, but I stop and turn around.

"What did you say?"

Alora's on her feet now, her hands clenched into fists. The rotting-lavender smell still wafts off her, but now there's a deeper scent of iron and hot garbage. I'm not sure what the lavender scent is, but I know the scent of someone spoiling for a fight. If Alora wants a brawl, I'm more than happy to give it to her.

Blue tries to maneuver in between the two of us. "Look, maybe we should all just calm down. We can take some time to pack, Zeph can get in a nap, and we can leave later this evening."

Alora shakes her head. "No, we need to leave now."

I cross my arms. "I'm not going anywhere until you explain why you think Cass believed your predictions."

Tallon shakes his head, moving next to Blue. "Now's not the time Zephyr. You're angry, and you're starting to leak." I frown, unsure what he's talking about. But then I see my hands. The swirl-ing dark lines are actually emitting darkness, the tendrils wafting up like I'm on fire. Huh. So that's what the swirls do.

Alora puts her hands on her hips. "I think now's the time. I've done nothing but try to help her, and all she does is treat me like crap. After all these years she's still a spoiled little bitch."

"I'm a spoiled little bitch—" I start, but I don't get to finish because Alora keeps talking.

"I know my predictions are good because I'm the one who warned Cass to stay off the roof that night." She's flushed, and when she drops her hands by her sides they ball into fists.

I laugh, the sound dark and dangerous. I can feel the erebos urging me on. I'm not the only one spoiling for a fight. The darkness wants loose, and I want to give it what it needs. "What are you talking about? We went up on the roof to find out what happened to my sister's shade."

Alora shakes her head. "Do you really think that's why Cass wanted to go onto the roof? To do a summoning? You could've done that anywhere. I told her what would happen if she went on the roof, and she believed me."

The darkness around me stills. I'm confused. "Why would she do that?"

Alora smirks. "Because she knew that for you to be the Nyx you needed a reason to fight Hera. Ramun Sol killing her was the Strand most likely to lead to your success."

Her words sink in, and my rage snaps back, fresh and hot. The darkness rises up around me, the tendrils forming a cloud. I take a step down the stairs. I want to kill her.

Tallon curses. "Dammit, Alora, why couldn't you just keep your mouth shut?"

Alora takes a step back, her eyes wide. I growl low in my throat.

"You knew that there was a chance Cass would die, and you didn't tell me?"

"Cass was going to die, Zephyr. Every single one of the options led to her death that night. Her doing the summoning on the roof and being killed by Ramun Sol was the only one that led to you coming into your full power. You're the Nyx! The vættir need you." Alora is babbling, but I barely hear her. All I can think is that there might have been a way for me to save Cass that night, and I never even got a chance.

"You should've told me. I would've been able to keep Cass alive."

Alora stops, and her eyes flash violet. "No, you wouldn't have."

Her words undo me. I launch myself off the second-to-last step, using the growing cloud of darkness to propel me over Tallon and Blue. I land in front of Alora and smile. Her fear hits me in a blast of spoiled lemons.

It feels too good to hit her.

My fist connects with her jaw, and Alora goes down. She curls up in a defensive position. Blue grabs for me, but the darkness keeps him away, picking him up and throwing him through the living room's plate-glass window. Tallon tries to fight through the darkness, but my shadows are much stronger than him. That makes me happy. Because now I know I can kill Alora without any interference.

I pick her up by the throat, and she sobs. "You should've told me," I say. My anger is so great that I feel calm, like I'm standing in the center of a hurricane.

"I'm sorry," she says. Her mascara runs down her face, leaving black trails of tears.

"Tell it to Cass," I say.

Tallon's arm snakes around my throat, and I drop Alora. She scrambles away as I struggle against Tallon. "Calm down," he says, his voice next to my ear.

"Don't tell me what to do," I snarl, bringing my elbow back and driving it into his stomach. His grip relaxes enough that I can maneuver free. He surprises me by wrapping his arms around my middle and holding me close.

We stand in the middle of a cloud of darkness. My erebos lashes out at him, whipping at him with thin tendrils. The shadows open up cuts on his arms, cuts that don't heal. He doesn't let me go, just grunts in pain. If I really wanted to, I could wield the darkness like a knife and open up his throat. But I don't want to. I want him to let me go.

He's not the one I want to kill.

I fight to get loose of him, but he's physically stronger than I am. "Let me go," I grit out.

"Not until you calm down. You can't kill everyone who pisses you off."

"She killed Cass, Tallon."

"No, she didn't. Alora wasn't the only one who knew about the danger to Cass that night. We all did."

His words leave me chilled, and the world seems to hold its breath. "What?"

"We didn't say anything because Cass asked us not to. She knew you'd never do something that could lead to her death. She believed in you enough to sacrifice herself, Zeph. Cass chose your future over her own life."

His words undo my anger, and I go limp in the circle of his arms. I manage to turn around until I'm looking at him. His expression is calm, even though I just tried to kill his cousin. That bugs me, but my sorrow is too vast to acknowledge anything but the weight of my loss. "I'm all alone again," I say, my throat clogging with tears.

Tallon shakes his head. "Aw, Peep, how could you think that? I'm here," he says. Then he kisses me.

The darkness stills when his lips touch mine, and my eyes drift closed. His lips are soft and warm against mine, and my arms go around his neck automatically. I sigh, because he makes me feel like I'm flying. Only kissing him is better than soaring above the treetops. It's better than anything I've ever experienced. I've never felt so alive.

The darkness wraps around Tallon as well, healing him and pulling him close. His lips open slightly in surprise, and I take the opportunity to nibble on his full lower lip. He groans and hugs me tighter before ending the kiss.

"You are a pain," he mutters, before giving me a peck on the forehead. I blink and take a step back. The darkness retreats, purring like a cat as it settles in my middle. I hug myself. It's a little lonely standing outside the circle of Tallon's arms.

"Yeah, well . . ." I trail off, unsure what to say. I turn around, where Blue and Alora watch us from the corner of the living room. Nanda's house is a disaster area, and shame heats my face. I'm going to owe her a new living room. Blue's arm lies protectively across Alora's shoulders, and guilt burns through me. He glares at me.

"Are you finished?" Blue snaps. I nod. I still don't like Alora, and I'm glad I hit her. But I definitely don't want to kill her.

"I'm not sorry I hit you," I say, and Alora starts to sob all over again. "But I'm sorry I tried to kill you," I hastily add. I feel bad about making her cry. "You should've told me. About Cass."

She nods. "I know. Can we go now?"

I sigh and nod. I can't exactly say no after trying to kill her, can I?

Tallon sighs and runs his hand through his hair. During the storm of erebos his braid came undone, and now his hair hangs loose. "Well, on that note, let's get the hells out of here before anything else goes wrong."

We all hurriedly grab a couple of changes of clothes before we pile into Blue's SUV and hit the road. Alora keeps looking over her shoulder as we head out, like she's afraid that something is going to attack at any minute. She doesn't bother sharing what she's afraid of with the rest of us, and no one bothers to ask. I think we're all a bit on edge after I lost control. Even I'm a little afraid of myself.

Tallon sits in the backseat with me. He's the only one even remotely strong enough to handle me if the darkness rises. We each sit stiffly, not touching. The tension of unsaid things is a physical presence between us. We don't mention the kiss in the living room, just stare out of our windows like the scrub grass next to the highway is the most interesting thing we've ever seen.

I rest my head against the window and think about Cass. She had enough faith in me to give up her life.

How do I repay that kind of a debt?

CHAPTER TWENTY-TWO

I WAKE SLOWLY AND SIT UP WITH A GROAN. MY HEAD POUNDS. I DON'T know where I am, but I feel like crap. The bed is hard, and the worst artwork I've ever seen decorates the walls. It smells like stale cigarettes. Tallon sits at the foot of the bed, watching TV. He turns around.

"Hey, you're finally awake."

I nod, but moving my head in any way hurts. I groan. "What happened?"

"You fell asleep in the car. I think you're still recovering from using the erebos the night Cass died. We tried to wake you up when we stopped, but you wouldn't budge. You missed dinner."

I sigh. "Of course I did."

He gives me a sympathetic smile and hands me a bottle of orange juice. "Here. I also grabbed you a sandwich, if you want it. Is ham still your favorite?"

"Yup. But just the orange juice is good for now." I open the juice and drink it in a few gulps. I twist the cap back on, and Tallon takes the empty bottle, going to a grocery-store bag next to the TV and taking out another one. He flings it at me, and I catch it one-handed. I drink half of it before putting the cool bottle to my aching head.

"I feel like hell," I mutter.

Tallon smirks. "You should, the amount of erebos you've used over the past couple of days. Even Æthereals can't use magic without paying a price." It's a curious thing for him to know, just like the line about the kobaloi. I want to ask him what else he knows about Æthereals, and about using the erebos. But I don't, because I'm not thinking about magic, I'm thinking about being in a hotel room with Tallon. Just the two of us.

I look around the room and finish the rest of the orange juice. "Where are we?"

"A crappy hotel about an hour or so away from where the Oracle wants us to meet her." He gives me a pointed look. "You know, the magical hotel on Alora's scrap of paper?"

"Oh."

"Yeah."

"Is she still mad?"

Tallon laughs and comes to sit next to me on the bed. "Well, knowing Alora she's only going to stay mad at you until she remembers how popular she's going to be once she can tell everyone that she knows the Nyx. But she refused to share a hotel room with you, and there were only two rooms left. So you're stuck with me."

I raise my head, slowly, and study him. "Why do you say it like that?"

"Because I know you're mad at me for not telling you what Alora saw about Cass."

I sigh. "I don't hate you. I wish you would've told me. But I don't hate you. I could never hate you, Tally." The nickname slips out, and my face flushes. I sound like a little kid.

He watches me, his dark gaze intent. "You're so different from what I remember. And yet, you're exactly the same. It's weird."

I nod, because I know what he means. But then Blue's advice comes back to me. Maybe he's right. Ever since I got back I haven't really talked to Tallon. When we were kids, we talked all the time. Not about anything important, just about stupid things.

"Do you still like black licorice?" I ask suddenly.

He smiles. "Of course. It is the superior licorice."

"Ugh. And I bet you still think yellow cake is better than chocolate."

"Yeah, because it is."

"Oh, come on," I say. "Yellow cake? It's the lamest of all cake. It's like the cake that wasn't cool enough to be banana. It's just yellow. That isn't a flavor—it's a color."

He snorts. "Look who's talking. Do you still scrape the frosting off your cake before you eat it?"

"Yes, because the frosting is a distraction. I like to taste my cake, thank you very much."

He shakes his head. "You are the only person in the universe who thinks that."

We sit there, grinning at each other like idiots for a few long seconds. I bite my lip as I consider my next words. Even though I know I should keep them to myself, I can't help but tell him.

"I thought I would die when you stopped visiting the Aerie."

A shadow settles over his expression, and for a moment I regret bringing it up. But his next words change that. "I know. I know how you felt."

"Why? Why did you guys stop coming to visit us?"

Tallon tugs on one of my curls, pulling it straight before letting it go with a sigh. "Your mom found out what I was, and she didn't want me around you anymore."

"What do you mean? That doesn't make any sense."

His dark gaze finds mine. "I'm a monster, Zephyr. Your mother never knew that, not until that day when you and Whisper dropped the eggs on me and Alora."

I think back to that day, the last time Nanda came to visit with Tallon and Alora in tow. After that she came by herself a couple of times before she stopped visiting altogether. "I don't remember anything."

He smiles sadly and traces the dark lines on my arms. A chill runs across my skin. "I started to leak, like you sometimes do. I was so mad at Whisper, because I knew she put you up to it."

"Please. I wanted to drop the eggs on Alora. You were just collateral damage," I say, grinning and trying to lighten a conversation that's gotten way too serious.

But Tallon shakes his head. "It didn't matter. When I got mad, I lost control of the darkness in me. Your mom saw, and she went ballistic. She called me an aberration and told me I needed to get out before she put me out of my misery."

I think of how Whisper freaked when she found out about my ability to use erebos. Now it makes sense. She wasn't afraid of the Matriarch or any of the other leaders in the Aerie finding out what I could do. She was afraid of what my mother would do.

My heart aches for Tallon, for what he must've gone through when my mother yelled at him. I know how her insults made me feel, and I could convince myself that she was just saying those things because she wanted me to be a great Harpy. Tallon didn't have that excuse. "I'm sorry. But you know you aren't really a monster, right? Because if you are, what does that make me? And I'm too cute to be a monster," I joke. I want to wrap my arms around Tallon and hold him. But I'm afraid. What if he pulls away?

Tallon shakes his head, as though he doesn't believe we're having this conversation. "You're right—forget about it." He raises his hand, his thumb tracing my lower lip. I freeze, afraid he'll stop if I so much as breathe. "I wish you smiled more. I wish I could make you laugh like I used to."

My heart shudders to a stop. When it starts up again, too fast and too hard, I feel different. Tallon's confession makes me brave. I lean toward him. He meets me halfway, his lips touching mine hesitantly at first. The taste of him, orange and mint, unleashes a wildness in me. I grab his shirt and pull him with me as I fall back across the bed.

As he kisses me, as I kiss him, I think back to the night I found Whisper with her boy from town. No wonder she was so mad. I can't imagine what I would do if someone came between me and Tallon. This thing between us, this hunger, it makes me feel murderous. I want him to be mine.

His hair tickles my cheeks, and I push it back as I open my mouth. I want to taste him, to feel him. My hands fumble for his shirt buttons even as his hand is snaking up under my shirt. When his fingertips brush across my stomach, I growl and wrap my leg around his waist. I break the kiss and nibble at his ear before kissing the hollow of his throat. His hands are splayed across my rib cage, warm and possessive. He suddenly pulls back, breathless.

"No, stop. We have to stop."

The darkness rises all around us, and it doesn't want to stop. I know what it wants, and I want the same thing. I want to understand the mystery of it all. I want the answer to why my sister would give herself to an Æthereal when she knew it would never amount to anything except her death. I want to understand what kind of emotion is strong enough to make Cass kill her father and wage a battle against an Exalted, a battle she knew she would never win. I need to know what it's like to love, to feel something that strongly.

I want to know it all. And I want Tallon to show me.

The darkness wraps around him, rising off my arms. My hands reach for Tallon's waistband, and he suddenly lurches back and away from me. I sit up. My lips tingle, and I feel cotton headed and confused. "Tallon?"

"I'm sorry, Zeph. We can't. It's just . . . no. I'm sorry. I won't ruin you." Before I can say anything else, he flees the hotel room, the door slamming behind him. I stare at it a long time before I realize that he isn't coming back.

I hug my knees to my chest, the ache of want still thrumming through me. The darkness tries to comfort me, but it can't. Because everything I want right now has just fled.

I consider going to him, asking him what I did wrong. What did he mean "ruin" me? What, like I'm some maiden to be delivered to an altar as a sacrifice? The whole idea is silly, even among the vættir. We stopped sacrificing virgins at least a thousand years ago. He had to have meant something else.

Maybe I just scared him. I know it's too soon, that the feelings between us are too new. Maybe he still sees me as that little girl, tagging along behind him, begging to be carried when my legs got tired. Maybe I need to give him more time to really see me, for him to know me as more than just his childhood friend.

But I don't want to wait. I'm not sure how much time I have left, after all. Tomorrow I go to see the Oracle.

And after that? Well, I'll most likely die heroically in a climactic battle. Isn't that how it always goes?

I stay up for a little while, waiting for Tallon to come back. But he doesn't. Whatever I did wrong is enough to make him spend the rest of the night somewhere else. I eventually take a hint. I turn off the TV, turn out the lights, and lie on the bed until I finally cry myself to sleep.

CHAPTER TWENTY-THREE

THE ORACLE LIVES IN A TRAILER PARK AND NOT A NICE ONE. BLUE navigates the car down a narrow gravel road while Alora directs him past the run-down mobile homes. Tallon and I sit in the backseat, ignoring each other. I think we've pretty much agreed to pretend the incident in the hotel room didn't happen.

That's unfortunate because it's all I can think about.

When I woke up this morning, Blue was banging on the door, yelling at me to hurry up so we could get back on the road. My magic hangover was gone, but my eyes were all puffy and my nose clogged from crying myself to sleep. I didn't even bother taking a shower, just grabbed my backpack from where it sat on the floor and walked outside. Blue paused mid-knock, his eyes wide. I didn't even have to sniff the air to sense his curiosity.

"What happened to you?"

"Magic hangover," I muttered. What I should've said was, *I've never had a boyfriend and Tallon's a tease and now I'm all confused so I slept like crap.* But I didn't. It's old news. Plus, it isn't Blue's fault his brother runs hot one moment, cold the next.

Blue watched me and shook his head. "Something's going

on with you, Zeph. You seem to be really on edge. Just watch it, okay? I mean, yesterday with Alora was kind of . . . alarming." His expression turned pensive, and I knew he was remembering the incident at the pond.

I didn't say anything after that, just followed him to the car where everyone waited. Tallon was stuck in the backseat with me again. He didn't even look at me as I got in, just kept staring out the window like the hotel parking lot was the most amazing thing he'd ever seen. The cold shoulder shouldn't have hurt, but it did.

I force Tallon from my mind and look out the window as we roll slowly through the trailer court. It's better than sneaking glances at him out of the corner of my eye like I have for the past hour. The houses are only ten or twelve feet apart from each other, sardine cans that are sardine close. The sad patches of land that separate the mobile homes range from bare dirt to overgrown weeds. Grimy little kids play in between the houses, some game that involves running and screaming at high decibels. A woman sits on the steps of one of the houses, smoking a cigarette as she bounces a baby and talks on the phone. I'm disgusted even as I'm impressed by her multitasking.

"This is it right here," Alora says, pointing to a dilapidated green-and-white trailer. Blue parks the car and we get out.

"Is this a vættir neighborhood?" I ask. The feeling here is very different from the Aerie, where everything was orderly and regimented. It's even different from Nanda's neighborhood, which had a feeling of community, with an undercurrent of fear. Here there's a sense of desperation, and as we walk up the sidewalk, the neighbors watch us with suspicion in their eyes. I'm starting to realize how good I had it, growing up in the Aerie.

Alora shakes her head. I don't know if she senses that something happened between me and Tallon or she saw it in her Strands. Either way she's been super polite to me today. I've been trying really hard to be equally civil. "No, just a regular place. Oracles can't live around vættir. Our æther tends to cloud the View," Alora says, refusing to meet my gaze. Even though we're playing at being nice, she hasn't looked me in the eye since I hit her. The bruise on her jaw has faded since yesterday, but my anger at her for not revealing what she knew hasn't. Now I really don't trust her.

Blue raps on the trailer's screen door. From inside come the sounds of the TV, and there's a creaking as someone gets up to answer the knock. A huge woman appears behind the screen. She's wider than the doorway, her flowered purple dress blocking out any view of the house.

"Yeah?" she says.

Alora clears her throat. "Parnassus," she says, which I'm guessing is some sort of password.

"What?" the lady barks out.

Alora shifts from high heel to high heel. "Um, Parnassus. I was told to come to this address and say the word 'Parnassus.'"

The large woman stares at us a moment longer before turning her head and yelling, "Jimmy! There's a bunch of kids here to see you." She waddles away, and a hyper skinny guy takes her place. A dark scruffy beard covers his cheeks. He wears a white T-shirt and chinos that hang low on his hips. With the bright red bandanna wrapped around his head he looks like a cheap Hollywood version of a drug dealer.

The only giveaway that he's more than he seems are his deep violet eyes. They're the color of grapes with a lavender sheen. I smell nothing from him, probably because of the high concentration of Æthereal blood.

Even though we're supposed to be here to see a woman, I'm willing to bet my new boots that this guy is the Oracle.

"Yeah?" he says, slouching and giving us a look like we're all wasting his time.

I sigh, because I'm tired of this game. I push Alora, who looks confused, to the side and stand in front of the door. "Look, we're here to see the Oracle. And since that's you, I'm guessing you knew we were on our way before we left an hour ago. So are you going to talk to us or not?"

The guy glares for a moment longer before his face splits into a wide grin. "Yeah, come on in. I should've known I couldn't fool a Harpy." He pushes open the screen door, and I walk into the house, Blue and Alora following closely behind. Tallon stays outside.

"I'll keep an eye out for trouble," he says. Blue shrugs and lets the screen door slam shut behind him.

A skinny black girl sits on the couch, her hair a riot of blue curls. Just like mine. It takes me a moment before I realize that she is me. My copy winks. "Sorry. I couldn't help myself. Wanted to take you for a test drive."

I'm not offended. It's actually kind of cool being able to see what I look like from this angle. The black swirls on my arms are kind of badass. "Shape-shifter?"

She shakes her head. "Nonesuch."

"What's the difference?"

She stands, and it's a little surreal to see a mirror image of myself holding out a hand to shake. The only difference between the two of us are the eyes. The Nonesuch's are a pale green, only the faintest hint of a metallic sheen. "Shape-shifters can turn into anything they want. I'm pretty much stuck with humans. Females, to be specific." She winks and holds out her hand. "I'm Ricki."

"Zephyr," I say. It's strange, because I thought I'd learned everything I needed to know in the Aerie. But I'm realizing that I know less than I thought the more time I spend in the real world.

We follow the Oracle, Jimmy, to the bedroom in the back. Heavy-metal posters decorate the wall, and the room has a smell to it that I can only describe as burning foliage. He gestures for us to take a seat on the unmade twin bed, and we sit down. Alora grimaces at the dirty sheets and smoothes her skirt before perching daintily on the edge. I actually feel kind of sorry for her. I'm sure she didn't think her precious Oracle was a stoner in a trailer.

Jimmy sits on a beanbag chair across from the bed and lights a cigarette. Blue grimaces. Jimmy blows the smoke right at him. Blue says nothing, just waves it away. I have to admire his restraint.

There's something about the Oracle that makes me want to slap him silly.

Alora coughs a little. "Oracle, we're here because we believe Zephyr is the Nyx. We know that Hera's going to use the shades of vættir that she's been gathering to draw the remaining shadow vættir to the Paths and into a trap."

Jimmy leans back with a grin. "Wow, really? That's pretty messed up. Like genocide, you know?"

I glance over at Blue, and from his expression I know that he's thinking the same thing I am: *This guy's supposed to help us?*

Alora clears her throat and nods. "Yes, um . . . that's why we're here. We need to know where and when she'll strike."

"Oh, the when is easy." His eyes glaze over and then snap back into focus. "Looks like it's going to be during the new moon."

Blue nods. "Makes sense. That's when the erebos is the highest. You do a spell that big when the æther is down." I'm impressed by Blue's knowledge of magic theory, but thinking about magic reminds me of Cass. The hollow feeling in my middle reopens, gaping wide with loss. I stare down at my hands in my lap and vow not to let her death be in vain.

The Oracle clears his throat. "As for where . . ." He drops his cigarette in a soda can and cracks his knuckles. "Let's see if we can find out."

Energy crackles through the room, and the Oracle gets a far-off look. His eyes glow a royal purple, and I realize how much stronger he is than Alora. Lavender smoke leaks from his eyes and wreathes his head, and when he speaks, his voice is much lower.

"The end of the vættir, bright and shadow, will come at the strongest Node. The crossroads of the realms."

I lean over to Alora, who watches the Oracle while gnawing on her bottom lip. "Do you know where that is?"

She shakes her head. Jimmy continues.

"There's more there. I see Exalteds, all of the bright, and a great approaching army. Clad in the plumage of a peacock."

"The Acolytes," I mutter.

Alora leans forward. "What are we supposed to do?"

The Oracle looks at her, his head turning oddly. "Do?" His voice has changed. It sounds feminine, and the purple drains away from his eyes. Suddenly they're a reddish brown, the same rust color as the blood on Cass's toga so long ago. The voice clicks into place, and I jump to my feet.

"Hera," I growl.

The Oracle turns to me, his expression smug. "There is nothing you can do, Godslayer. You think you can defeat me and my army of Acolytes? I've been planning for this day for centuries, and you are not going to stop me. You will be dead by nightfall."

Just as quickly as it appeared the rust color bleeds away. Jimmy blinks at me, his deep purple eyes back to normal. "Um,

I think you should run," he says, color draining from his face.

"What? Why?"

He doesn't answer me. Instead the trailer shakes, and there's the screech of metal giving way as something tears through the side. From where I stand in the bedroom I can see all the way to the living room, so I'm the first to see the cerberus push through the newly widened front door.

"Gah!" I slam the bedroom door closed and look around the room for a weapon.

Blue is already on his feet. "Is that what I think it is?"

"Yeah. Hera knows where we are, and now so does the High Council. I'm still supposed to be a prisoner. They must've sent it after me."

"So she gets you out of the way without lifting a finger or endangering any more of her Acolytes."

I nod. From the other side of the door comes screaming, and too late I remember Ricki in the living room. "Dammit, we have to help her."

Blue manifests his giant sword with a grin. "Leave this to me." I open the door, and he dashes down the narrow hallway to the living room. I close the door behind him. Jimmy and Alora both gape at me.

"We need to get out of here."

Alora stands and tears off the miniblinds on the room's lone window. She struggles to open it before she swears and kicks it out. It gives way with a crack. I can't help but grin at her. "I'm impressed."

"Yeah, well, you aren't the only badass here. Help me with this. We have to protect the Oracle."

We break away the remaining shards and push out the screen. I stick my head outside. Blue's sword moves in a silver arc as he fights the cerberus in the middle of the street. I wonder if anyone's keeping the norms from seeing this.

I can already see the headlines in the tabloids.

I duck back in the room. "Blue's distracting it. Let's go."

Jimmy stands and shakes his head. "You two go. I've got to go check on Ricki." Alora starts to argue, and he raises his hand for silence. "There's no need to worry. We'll be fine." He says it with a confidence that makes me think he might've just taken a peek at the future to make sure.

I nod. "Good luck," I say. He doesn't have to tell me twice.

I launch myself through the window. I hit the ground on the other side and roll, rocks digging into my bare arms. I slowly climb to my feet with a groan, and someone steadies me. It's Tallon.

"You need to get out of here."

"Me?" I say as Alora comes flying out the window. She's much more graceful than me, even in a dress and heels. No wonder I'm jealous.

"Yes, you. The cerberus is after you, not us. If you guys can get to the car, you can maybe lose it."

"Too late," Alora says, pointing down to the edge of the yard. The cerberus has turned. Blue continues to attack the thing, which is already bloodied from earlier sword strikes. It ignores him and stalks toward us, healing as it goes.

"Oh, I think I should maybe listen to the Oracle and take off."

"Good idea," Alora says, slipping out of her heels. "I'll try to distract it."

I take a single step backward. Alora starts waving her arms around and yelling at the demon dog. "Hey. Hey! Yeah, you. Here, puppy, puppy, puppy."

I take another step back, and then another. I've just made it to the back of the trailer when the cerberus sprints toward me, barking.

I turn tail and run.

I weave between the trailers while the cerberus breathes heavily behind me, snuffling as it keeps track of my scent. I cut around a trailer and through a weed-choked yard, the heads of the demon dog barking excitedly as the beast runs me down. Skidding around another corner gives me a few feet of breathing room. The cerberus doesn't corner so well. It slams into trailers and shaves off corners in a screech of metal. The beast's clumsiness is the only reason it hasn't caught me yet. That, and it's about as smart as the average mutt.

I gasp for breath as I round another corner. I need a plan. I can't just keep running through the trailer park willy-nilly. I won't be able to keep this up forever.

I slide around another corner and come face-to-face with a chain-link fence. I take a step backward before turning to run back the way I came. The demon dog is there, the tongues of all three heads lolling out in doggy grins as it stalks forward. Panic flares in my chest, and the darkness begins to rise off my arms like angry black snakes. I wonder if erebos will work against Hades's pet.

There's a flash of white light behind me. I look over my shoulder, and I'm surprised to see Hermes leaning against the chain-link fence. He wears designer jeans and a fashionably distressed T-shirt. The sight of him causes an ache to rise in my chest. He looks exactly the same as he did when he came to visit Whisper. I'm surprised to realize that I miss him. I lost him the same time I lost my sister. There's been too much loss in my life.

He grins at me. "Hey, Peep."

I turn and look back at the cerberus. The giant dog sits down, letting out a trio of puppy whines. What in the hells is going on?

"You have a choice, Peep," Hermes calls. "Up or down."

I don't answer, and for a long moment the only sound is that of my labored breathing. I look at Hermes, and then back to the cerberus. Of course. Why didn't I see it? The High Council wouldn't send a cerberus after me. Hades would. The High Council would send Hermes, just like they did the night Whisper died. The night I killed Ramun Mar.

I can't help but look down at the erebos still rising off my arms. No way I'll get a fair trial this time.

I take a step toward the cerberus. Hades's words come back to me. *I would not let any harm come to you in my realms.* If I go with it, Tallon and everyone else in the trailer park will be safe, and maybe I will be too. My stomach clenches as I debate my options. Hermes was right. I know now that he kept his promise, and I think Hades will too. Nothing bad happened to me while I was in the Underworld. I'm not sure how much of that is because of Cass, but I like my chances there. What are the chances I'll get a fair shake in the Æthereal Realm? Not good, with Hera leading the charge against me.

Hermes gives me a slight nod, as though he knows what I'm thinking. "I won't be able to come after you in the Underworld this time, Peep. There's a war brewing, and Hades has locked down travel between the realms. If you go with the cerberus, there's no way the High Council will be able to come after you."

I want to ask Hermes what war he's talking about. Hera's pending attack against the vættir? Or something worse?

What could be worse than an attempt to annihilate the shadow vættir?

I don't ask him any questions, though. I don't even apologize for thinking he abandoned me. Now I know he was looking out for me all along, but there isn't time for a heartfelt reunion. Maybe later, gods willing.

I run toward the cerberus. The beast stands and licks me affectionately. I lean backward to try to avoid the slobbery tongues, but it gets me anyway. I turn around and look back at Hermes, who is smiling sadly at me.

"Thank you," I say, my voice choked with unsaid things.

"Take care, Nyx," he says before flashing out of sight. I stare at the spot where he stood for a long while, then I climb onto the cerberus.

"Let's go," I say. And then we are gone.

CHAPTER
TWENTY-FOUR

ONE MOMENT I'M IN THE TRAILER PARK, THE NEXT I'M IN ONE OF THE halls of Hades's palace. The cerberus lies down on the black marble, and I slide off. My boots echo eerily as I walk toward a doorway bleeding light. It's so much like my last trip here that I have a moment of déjà vu.

Dark fire burns in fire bowls in between the giant columns of æther. The columns seem to retreat as I walk down the hallway, and the darkness inside of me likes that. It feels more awake now, churning through my belly like a bad case of indigestion. I ask it to settle down, and I get a sense of amusement from it. But then it does as I ask, and the sick feeling fades a little.

I wonder if Tallon's erebos feels like a creature inside of him. I'll have to ask.

If I ever see him again.

The doorway is closer than it appears. When I walk through it, I enter a room unlike anything I've ever seen in the Underworld. The marble floor is covered with thick rugs, and the furniture around the room has a modern look. The columns of æther are more numerous here, casting the room in a sunshinelike brightness.

Plants, real Mortal Realm trees and flowers, grow in riotous abundance. Nanda would love this room.

Sitting in the center of it all is Persephone.

She smiles and stands when she sees me. "Oh, good. I was afraid that Hermes would get to you before the cerberus."

"No. I mean, the cerberus got to me first, but Hermes let me go. He gave me a choice. . . ." I trail off, because I'm suddenly not sure what I'm doing here. I was expecting Hades. Not Persephone. "Did you send for me?"

She grins, and for a second she looks like a little girl about to steal the last cookie. But there's a glint in her eyes that I don't like. I'm kind of wishing I would've gone with Hermes instead. Or kept running.

"Oh, I sent for you, Zephyr Mourning. I have watched you for your entire life, waiting for this moment."

I take a step backward, away from Persephone. "What moment?"

"The moment you meet your father."

My brain short-circuits, and I stand there dumbfounded. While I'm frozen in shock, Persephone moves, quicker than anyone I've ever seen. Before I even process her words, she's up from the cushions and behind me. I don't even realize she has a knife in her hand until the tip of it digs into my throat. I swallow convulsively, afraid to move.

Her voice is loud in my ear. "Do you know how long I believed the lie? Do you? He told me nothing ever happened, but he is a liar just like the rest of them. They promised me so much, and all I was given was hell." She sounds on the verge of tears, and the knife at my throat wavers. There's a sharp pain, then the sensation of blood. It's all the darkness needs to rise up.

The erebos is stronger here. It swarms quickly, a living creature beyond my control. It engulfs me and Persephone. The pain at my throat disappears as the darkness heals it, and Persephone screams as the shadows pick her up and throw her to the side. I grapple with the shadows, trying to reel them in. If they kill Persephone, I will definitely be next. Hades will kick my ass, promise or not.

Persephone stands. She's shaken, her hair tousled and her expression confused. The black leaves woven through her hair wriggle in agitation. She takes a step toward me, and the darkness whips out, snapping at her like a whip. She freezes.

"Stop," I say. "Let's talk about this." Gods, I sound like a therapist on a talk show.

"There is nothing to talk about. I know who you are, what you are. As long as you live, the rest of us will suffer." Her words don't make any sense, and I'm starting to wonder if maybe Persephone is just as insane as the rest of the Exalteds.

"What are you talking about? Why did you bring me here?" I demand. Her lips press together, and she takes another step forward. I relax my hold on the darkness enough to let a tendril whip across her face. She stills as a cut opens up and doesn't heal. I clamp down on the shadows before they can do any more damage. She's of the bright. Her kind can't heal themselves down here in the Underworld.

"That is enough." Hades walks into the room with purposeful

strides. The darkness surrounding me leans toward him affectionately before retreating.

"Traitor," I mutter as the shadows curl around me. They snuggle close, but they don't disappear.

Hades gives me a bemused look. "You have learned much since you left the Underworld."

I look down at my arms, which are wreathed in darkness. "I didn't really have a choice."

Hades turns to Persephone, who has slumped to the floor. She cries loudly, the sobs racking her body. I'm half convinced that she's faking it. "I think you should return to the bright for a while, my wife."

She shakes her head. "I want to stay with you."

Hades gives her a pitying look. "You made a promise. A promise you broke."

She cries harder, and around us the plants begin to shrivel and die. I wrap my arms around myself and step away from a pot of geraniums as they suddenly wither. Okay, so maybe she really is upset.

"I am sorry," Persephone sobs. "I should not have touched her. It will not happen again."

Hades sighs. "No. It will not. I think you should stay with your mother for a spell." A cerberus comes padding into the room. It walks over to Persephone and nudges her. She puts her arm around it, still crying. A circle of darkness opens up around them, and they are gone.

I blink and look around the room. It's dismal without her, a dank room full of dead plants. I want to ask Hades why he sent her away, where she went, and why she tried to kill me. It must've been personal for her to send the cerberus after me like that. Otherwise she could've just let the Council deal with me.

Hades looks at me. "You have questions."

"Yeah, a few."

He catches the edge of my sarcasm and smiles. It's a terrifying expression. "Come with me."

Darkness opens up and we step through it. Just like that we're in a new room, one similar to the round chamber where I first met the King of the Dead. This one is also round, but the windows are real windows. We're high on the side of a mountain, looking down on a dark forest. In the distance is the confluence of the Acheron and the Styx, and it's strange to think that less than two weeks ago I was there, running with Cass to the Mortal Realm. Grief clogs my throat, and I have to swallow hard to force it down. So much has happened in such a short time.

Hades gestures for me to sit on one of the easy chairs, and I do. It's strange to see such modern furnishings in the underworld. I guess even Hades likes to be comfortable.

He sinks into the chair opposite me. The darkness writhes around him. My own darkness is held tight to me, and as I watch, part of Hades's darkness detaches itself and floats over to me. He watches it with a bemused expression. "So, is that how it is going to be?"

The dark cloud hovers before me, and I get the sensation that it's studying me. I open my arms a little in a welcoming gesture. The cloud zips down my arms, joining with the rest. The thin tendrils of darkness on my arms are now a little fuller, the tattoos more prominent. I blink. "What just happened?"

Hades waves his hand. "It is the nature of darkness to be fickle. That bit of erebos knows that it will be well cared for with you."

I look down at my arms, at the writhing black markings, and the cloud of darkness they emit. "Can you please tell me what is going on?" There's an edge of hysteria in my voice, and I choke down my panic.

Hades sighs and leans forward. "Yes. But perhaps you should start with what you already know."

"Okay, yeah. I know that there was some sort of promise made a long time ago, and there were two champions. One got killed by the other, and that little snippet of Cass's history that you showed me was her going all rage on Hera because she organized the whole thing. Once the dark champion was gone, the bright Exalteds started screwing over the vættir, so most of them went into hiding of some sort. Then there was some sort of vision, this messy Prophecy about the Nyx that no one is really all that sure about."

Hades nods, not stopping me. I take a deep breath and continue. "And now everyone thinks I'm the Nyx, and they want me to go and kill Hera because she's getting ready to use shades she's been amassing for a while to kill all of the shadow vættir so that no one stands between her and complete enslavement of the Mortal Realm."

Hades props his cheek on his hand and nods. "That is very nearly everything."

"Oh? What did I miss?"

Hades stands and begins to pace, his cloak of darkness swirling around him. "First, you *are* the Nyx. You are the new dark champion, and you will be responsible for righting the balance."

"Brilliant," I mutter. A crushing disappointment hits me. I'm flattened. All this time I was kind of hoping that everyone was wrong and I was just a really strong shadow vættir. I could deal with that. But I'm not. I'm the Nyx. Being the Nyx has all kinds of expectations attached to it. It's not something I want.

But it doesn't look like I have a choice.

"Are you sure?" I ask. It's the last-ditch effort of a drowning girl. Hades just gives me a side-eyed look, and I realize if anyone would know, he would. He's practically made of shadows.

"What else?" Fine, I'm the Nyx. That sucks, but I'll get over it. Too many people are counting on me to spend my time boohooing about it.

Hades stops pacing and looks at me. "Persephone wanted to kill you because she knows what you are. But that also means she knows the truth about you."

Something in his expression makes my stomach drop out. "What truth?" I whisper. But I already know what he's going to say.

"Zephyr Mourning, I am your father."

I can't breathe. There's no air and I can't breathe. So I just sit in the chair, my mouth opening and closing like a fish on the riverbank.

Hades is speaking, and I should be listening, but all I can think of is my mother's scolding words: *You're the daughter of an Æthereal, Zephyr. Act like it.*

I shake my head, refusing to believe it. "No, it doesn't make sense."

Hades studies me, his expression impassive. "How is there confusion? You are my child, of that I am quite certain."

I glance down at the darkness rising off my arms. His point is clear, but my brain refuses to believe what I'm hearing. I take a deep breath and let it out. "But I don't understand why. I mean, did you love each other?"

Hades frowns at me. "Love? No. Æthereals do not love, at least not in the way that humans do. We have our dalliances, but for the most part we do things for a reason, not because of an emotion. The prophecy was clear that the Nyx would be the child of the Dark Lord and a warrior. When your mother sought me out, I knew that she was the one to help me fulfill the promise. It made sense to conceive a child with her."

His words make me feel cheap. Most Harpies are born from business arrangements. Whisper's conception was a contracted affair. After all, that's how Harpies procreate. They find an interested party and pay them. If the child is male, it's sent off to live

with the father. Females grow up in the Aerie with their mothers. But me, I'd always hoped I was different, mostly because I
never fit in with the rest of the Harpies in the Aerie. I wanted to
think maybe I'd been born out of something other than business.
I wanted to be different.

Turns out I'm not.

Once again Whisper's words come back to haunt me. *Love
really isn't for our kind.*

But then I think about Hermes asking Cass to protect me so
that he could keep a promise he made to Whisper. Surely he didn't
go to all that effort for a "dalliance"?

I decide that maybe Hades isn't being completely honest with
himself. Otherwise why would Persephone have been so upset?

I turn to Hades. "What about Persephone? What was all of
that about?"

His expression shutters. "That is not something you need to
concern yourself with."

I laugh, the sound bitter. "She brought me here and then tried
to kill me. I think maybe I should be concerning myself with that."

His lips quirk. "You do make an excellent point. Let us just say
that the vættir are not the only ones with prophecies. We shall
leave it at that."

I'm not really happy with his answer, but the last time we got
into an argument, it didn't turn out so hot for me. So I clear my
throat and change the subject.

"What would've happened if I'd been a boy?"

Hades pauses, considering. "We never spoke of it. Your mother was certain she would conceive a girl child."

I shake my head, trying to maintain a shred of control. He says it in such a matter-of-fact way, but I feel like everything I've ever known has been a lie. My entire world has been unraveling ever so slowly since I was sent to the Underworld. And now I feel like I'm coming undone.

Hades watches me. I wonder if the concern on his face is real. "Perhaps you should speak with your mother."

I laugh. "Why? Like talking to her has ever solved anything before?"

Hades gives me what I figure is his best disapproving-father look. It's pretty good. "Yeah. Okay. Fine, I'll talk to her."

A darkness-filled doorway appears, and I stand. Hades gestures for me to walk through first, so I do. There's a moment of icy darkness, and then there's . . . singing?

It takes a few long moments for my eyes to adjust to the brightness of the Elysian Fields. Everything seems lit from within. The trees and grass and even the damn butterflies sparkle. When I was younger, my mom once bought me a box of glitter crayons. The pictures I drew back then would've fit right in here.

"Wow. It's very . . . bright." The sky is too blue, and the rainbow up above is pretty unbelievable. It's a kid's cartoon come to life. The darkness in me shrinks away from the unnatural beauty of the place.

Behind me, Hades sighs. "It is pure æther right here, a pocket that never made it across the Rift. The rest of the fields are not quite this bright. Follow me."

We walk along a pathway through a meadow. All around us are quaint houses, cottages that would make Snow White and her dwarves proud. Everything is a little too colorful and a little too happy. A woman sings as she sweeps her front walk, and children chase one another in the street, skipping and calling out in chirpy voices. This is what it would be like to live in an amusement park.

As we move along the pathway, I notice that Hades's own shadows have retreated as well. Today he wears modern clothing, jeans and a polo shirt that look out of place on him. His arms are bare. Like mine, they are marked with black tattoos. But his designs are much thicker, almost covering the skin. He notices me looking and holds his arm out toward me. "Your markings will grow as you get stronger."

"What are they?"

"It's how the darkness anchors itself to you. Erebos is not like the æther. It is sentient. It will become your friend, but it can be willful. It takes discipline to be able to control such a weapon. Væance may be born to their aspect, but we Æthereals are given the choice. Bright, dark, or a weak ability with both. Few choose the erebos, even though it can be more powerful than æther." He drops his arm and looks away. "It is so much easier to choose the light." Sadness laces his voice. It sounds like he's speaking from experience.

I think of the jagged lines on Tallon's shoulders. They're not tattoos. They're the telltale markings of erebos use. But that just creates another mystery. Nanda had Tallon fixing the wards with Cass our first day back. Most wards require æther, not erebos. So what kind of vættir is Tallon that he can not only trip the Rift, but also use erebos and æther?

And does Nanda have similar erebos markings hidden somewhere under her clothing? How many other vættir are marked like me?

There is too much that I still don't know. But they're questions for another, less hectic time, and I file them away for later.

We continue along the path a while longer. The brightness fades, and the landscape becomes less cartoonish and more familiar. A little too perfect to be the Mortal Realm though. The darkness inside of me doesn't feel so skittish anymore, and I'm kind of beginning to enjoy my stroll through paradise.

Hades stops before the door of a house painted in shades of cream and lavender. He turns to me. "The woman you knew as your mother is gone, but her shade resides here. She is the same person, but different. An echo of who she was in life. Do you understand?"

I consider his words and then nod. I don't really know what he means by that, but I guess I'll figure it out.

Hades knocks, and a woman with giant wings, dark skin, and candy-apple red hair answers the door. "Yes?"

"Mourning Dove. I have brought our daughter. She wishes to speak with you regarding her conception."

My face burns at the way he puts it, and the woman at the door smiles wide when she sees me. "Darling, how are you? Oh, you have grown since I saw you last." The woman gathers me up in a cinnamon-sugar-scented embrace, and I awkwardly hug her back. I can't ever remember hugging my mom, and she never called me darling. But this strange woman looks just like my mother.

She stands back and smiles at me. I take a step back, unsure how to react. "Come in, won't you? I was just making a pie." She steps back and I start to follow her in. Hades doesn't move.

"I will fetch you when you are done," he says, before disappearing in a swirl of shadows.

My mother closes the door behind me. She gestures at the kitchen table. "Please, have a seat."

I take the only chair, and as soon as I sit, another one appears across the table. It startles me, and she laughs. "That's the Fields for you. Always providing what you need."

She sits across from me, all smiles. It's seriously creeping me out. I can't remember my mother wearing any expression except for a scowl. "Are you all right?"

"Me? Of course! Why do you ask?"

"You, um . . . you're smiling a lot. I don't remember you smiling this much when you were alive."

"Oh well, that's because living is pain. But this is death. And death? Well, it's painless." She sighs, but it's the kind of breathless sigh people give when they're happy. "Some days I miss living, but then I remember what a struggle it was. Always worrying and fighting. Here we only fight because it's something to do."

I nod like I know, but I don't. Now I know what Hades meant

when he warned me about this woman being an echo of my mother. My mom would've kicked this smiling woman's ass.

I clear my throat. "So, I just found out that Hades is my father. I guess I just wanted to know why."

Mom purses her lips. "Well, let me think. That was a very dark time in my life, so I don't necessarily remember it as well as some of the other times. I came down to Tartarus to save the sister of a friend. A minor goddess who'd fallen for one of the dark lords, a fringe god named Typhaon."

I nod. That sounds like something my mom would do. She was fiercely loyal to her friends. "Okay."

"Well, long story short, the rescue didn't quite go as we planned. I was gravely injured and pretty close to death. As you may know, dying in Tartarus can leave your shade in limbo. So I prayed to Hades for help." Her eyes are far away as she smiles. "It was the only time I prayed to a god other than Athena."

"And Hades answered."

She blinks, and the dreamy look fades from her eyes. "Yes. He was so handsome, all swirling shadows and brooding godliness. Anyway, with his help I made it back to the Mortal Realm with my friend. Three years later, you came along."

I blink. "You were pregnant with me for three years?"

Mom laughs, the sound tinkling and completely foreign. "Oh no, dear. Hades came to visit me in the Mortal Realm. Your sister adored him. He used to create animals out of the shadows for her, and she would chase them around the house."

Another shard of betrayal lodges in my heart. "Whisper knew who my father was?"

"Of course! As did the Matriarch. Hades was in the Aerie more than any other male. The Matriarch almost changed the Aerie's patron deity to the King of the Dead, but she knew it would piss Athena off something fierce. The old bird was a big believer in the Nyx prophecy."

It all makes sense. The Matriarch's disappointment, her pointed statements. I'd always thought I was falling short as a Harpy, but it turns out I was just not the hero the woman wanted me to be.

An entire childhood of misery because of a prophecy I never knew about.

"Why didn't anyone ever tell me?" I hate how whiny it sounds.

"Zephyr, your ignorance bought your safety. The Aerie had some power, but it was nothing compared to the Acolytes. If they ever suspected who you were, you would've been dead. The fewer people that knew the better."

Something occurs to me. "What about Nanda? Did she know?"

Mom purses her lips as she thinks. "Well, I suppose she must've. I think she suspected when you were younger, but things didn't really come to a head until later . . . ah, yes, now I remember. It was that child you were so fond of. That's what caused me to tell her."

"What child? You mean Tallon?"

"Yes! I saw him using erebos during one of their visits and told Nanda never to bring him back again. If you had come into contact with the shadows, it would've ruined everything, and you weren't ready to be revealed yet. You just weren't strong enough."

I frown as I try to make sense of her words. "The erebos? What would've happened if I'd come into contact with his shadows?"

My mom stares at me, her eyes bright with unshed tears. "Why, the seal your father put on your powers when you were born would've been destroyed. There would've been no way to hide you from the Acolytes, and you would've been dead within a few months. They would've killed you."

"But I used the erebos once, when I was younger. For a magic test."

She purses her lips as she thinks. "Perhaps the binding was flawed. Although I do remember that danger was supposed to let you utilize the erebos. So maybe you were scared enough to pull power through the seal."

I consider her words. It makes sense. I was terrified of my mother, so failing magic class would've been scary enough to allow me to access the power. Killing Ramun Mar the night he murdered Whisper had been a mistake, and my desperation must've somehow managed to break through the binding placed on my dark powers. The day I first met Hades, he must've removed the remainder of the seal. That's why I felt so out of control when I returned to the Mortal Realm.

But that doesn't help me make sense of everything else. My mom slept with the King of the Dead to help fulfill a prophecy. She never really wanted me, she just wanted to save the day.

I was her ultimate weapon, a sword to be forged and honed

and eventually wielded in battle. Meeting with this bright, smiling woman who is the echo of my mother has only managed to make me feel even more alone.

I stand too quickly, and the chair falls over before disappearing. A flicker of worry crosses my mother's face. Her wings droop a little. "What's wrong?"

I shake my head and force a smile. "Nothing. I just need to get back. Hera's Acolytes are stirring up trouble, and I need to take care of it."

And just like that her worry is gone. She grins at me. "Of course. Tell your sister I said hello."

It hurts to smile, but I do it anyway. "I will," I say. The lie scrapes along the hollow in my chest. Whisper should be here with her. It's a reminder that I still have so much left to do.

I smile and give the stranger who is my mother one last wave. Then I escape out the front door.

Once I'm back outside, I call for Hades, hysteria in my voice. I need to get back to the Mortal Realm. I need some space to think, to work through the things I've learned.

Everyone has lied to me. It's enough to make me want to scream.

Hades appears. "Ready?"

It's a loaded question. I sigh and bury my face in my hands. "So, what's next? I go and fight Hera?"

"Yes. She and Ramun Sol have my shades. I want them back."

I look at Hades. He sounds like a bad breakup song. Nice that he made this about him and not the annihilation of the shadow vættir. "What about after?"

He frowns. "After what?"

"After I destroy Hera, after I keep her from doing this spell or whatever. What comes after?"

Hades levels a gaze at me. "I do not believe there will be an after."

Oh, this just keeps getting better. "You think I'll die?"

"Yes. But you should not worry. Death is not so bad. Look how happy your mother is." I give him a look of disbelief. My mother is not happy; she's a completely different person. "All things die," he says. He doesn't even sound like he believes the halfhearted pep talk.

I want to scream. Not even the bright shiny version of my conception that my mom just gave me makes up for the knowledge that I was born to fulfill some stupid prophecy. I want to rail at the gods, to smite them and manipulate their futures for my own amusement. I hate them. I hate their childish games and the way they suck unwitting mortals into their games of power. If I could, I would make them know how it feels.

But I don't have that kind of power. As angry as I am, I know I can only play the hand that I was dealt. They have a saying in the Underworld: *Life's a bitch.* But I kind of think dying, even hero-ically, might be worse.

I stretch. "Fine. So I go back, try to stop Hera, maybe die. Any ideas of where she might strike?"

Hades's mantle of darkness flares around him. Another bit of darkness detaches itself and writhes over to me. I accept it without a word. Nice to know someone has some faith in me.

"She will need a powerful Node to conduct the spell she is attempting. I would look at the confluences of great rivers. They are very powerful places."

"Great. Thanks." That only leaves the entire world. How many confluences are there in the world? Five? Fifty? I wish I was better at geography. Who would even know the answer to that? I'm pretty sure that the Oracle is not going to be happy to see me again, considering what the cerberus did to his trailer. North or one of her Hecate friends might have a better idea. Maybe someone can give them a call. At this point I'm running out of options. Not that I had many to begin with.

I glance around, looking for a door or something. There's nothing but cottages and butterflies. What is up with all of the butterflies? I swat at one in annoyance.

I clear my throat. "How am I supposed to get back to the Mortal Realm?"

Hades closes the distance between us. He rests his hands on my shoulders, and the movement is both reassuring and disconcerting. It's strange to think of this man and his constantly shifting darkness as my father, but at the same time it makes me hopeful. Hades is the most fearsome of all the Exalteds. Maybe I actually have a chance at success.

Hades pulls me close for a quick hug. His darkness swirls around me affectionately for a moment. My own rises up in response, not as strong, but just as fierce. "You have far exceeded my expectations, Zephyr Mourning, Godslayer and Lady of Darkness. Best luck in fulfilling your Promise," he says. His words fill me with confidence.

Before I can thank him, he picks me up and throws me. I fly through the air, through a cold darkness that I figure is the Rift, and land hard on a road. I roll around in agony until the pain fades, gravel crunching beneath my body.

I much prefer Tallon's way of traveling the realms.

I open my eyes, and my heart leaps. The Oracle, Ricki, Blue, and Alora all look down at me, their eyes wide with shock. I force a grin.

"Hey, guys. What did I miss?"

CHAPTER TWENTY-FIVE

AFTER MY TRIUMPHANT RETURN BLUE RUNS OFF TO FIND TALLON, WHO has apparently made it his mission to figure out where I went. I've been gone for almost two weeks. What seemed like an afternoon for me was ten days of searching and scrying for Alora, Jimmy the Oracle, and Blue.

I'm not sure what Tallon's been up to. Everyone kind of just looks away when I mention him.

"We didn't know what happened to you. We thought the worst," Alora says. We sit amid the chaos of Jimmy and Ricki's ruined trailer, drinking warm beers out of an ice chest. Jimmy hangs around outside waiting for Blue's return, and Ricki picks things out of the wreckage and stuffs them into a backpack. Today she looks like a female version of Jimmy: lank brown hair, pale skin, and skinny to the point of looking sick. I get the feeling that's her true appearance. Alora told me Ricki and Jimmy are siblings, so it makes sense they'd look alike.

The ruined trailer became the base of operations while everyone tried to figure out what happened to me. Most of the trailer park was abandoned after the cerberus attack. The cover story is that a tornado damaged most of the trailers. The residents are all currently living in a nearby hotel or staying with relatives since the trailer park was evacuated and most of the homes condemned.

"Do you guys have somewhere to go?" I ask Ricki. I hate that they're homeless because of me. It's not like I have somewhere to live either, but I feel like the least I can do is ask.

Ricki nods and grins. "Oh, yeah. Jimmy's the Oracle, so he can call in a bunch of favors. We're thinking of heading south. He's been talking to Blue about Ulysses's Glen. It sounds like a nice place, you know?" Ricki touches her hair gently. "It might be nice to be around our own kind for a while." She hefts the backpack and gives me a weak wave. "See you around."

I nod and take a deep drink of my beer. I've never had one before, but seeing as I'm supposed to die pretty soon, it seems like a good time to try it out. The beer is bubbly and it makes me burp, but that's about all I can say for it.

Blue and Tallon walk up the ruined stairs as Ricki slides past them out the gaping doorway. Tallon looks tired. Dark circles surround his eyes, and his steps seem to drag. He brightens a little as he sees me, and a rush of excitement trills through me. "You're back." There's a tinge of something in his voice. Relief? Was he actually worried about me?

I take another drink of my beer to hide the emotions that well up inside. Hope and embarrassment tangle around whatever I feel for Tallon. "Yeah, I'm back. Woo-hoo." My voice is flat, and I focus on thinking about how much it hurt when he vaulted off the bed and ran out the door. I will not feel anything for him but apathy.

Tallon gives me a long look and reaches into the ice chest for his own beer. He's all scratched to hell, and I pat the couch cushion next to me. I am the coolest cucumber ever. He gives me a hesitant look before plopping down on it. And no, my heart doesn't race the tiniest bit at having him near me.

He pops open the beer and takes a drink. "So, what's new?"

After everyone got over their initial shock, I'd filled them in on what happened, leaving out the part about Hermes. He kept his promise, but now I have more questions. Did he know that Hades is my father? Did he love Whisper? And did she really die because of her relationship with him? Or was it because of me? Was Whisper killed because the Acolytes suspected I was the Nyx?

I'm not sure I want to know the answer to that.

Everyone was surprised when I told them Hades was my father, except for the Oracle. Jimmy just grinned at me. "Oh, there are all kinds of secrets swirling around you. I can't wait to find out what they are. You're going to have an interesting life."

That gave me some hope that maybe I'd survive my confrontation with Hera.

Until I remembered that Jimmy hadn't been able to figure out where she was going to attack, or anything else even remotely useful.

I tilt my head and grin at Tallon. "Hmm, what's new? Let's see . . . I rode a cerberus to hell, found out Hades was my dad, talked to my dead mother who is now a bowl full of sunshine, and lost ten days. Good times."

Tallon slurps at his beer. "Rode a cerberus, huh?"

I shrug, like finding out the King of the Dead is my dad doesn't make me question everything I know about myself. What other lies was I told? I push my questions aside and give Tallon what I hope is a carefree smile. "Yeah, no big deal. You can do that sort of thing when you're the Nyx."

Tallon drains the entire beer and then tosses the can to the side. It bounces off the broken TV before landing next to the rest of the debris. "Wow."

"Yup." I take a gulp of my beer and grimace. I'd really prefer a soda instead. It would taste better.

Alora props her chin on her fist and watches us from her perch on a nearby footstool. "I don't suppose the Dark Lord was able to tell you where Hera and Ramun Sol will strike?"

"Actually, he did. He said it would have to be a powerful Node. I guess the most powerful ones are near the confluences of two or more rivers."

Alora groans. "How many of those are there in the world?"

I shrug. "Maybe North would know? With a name like that it seems like she might be good at geography."

Tallon gives me a look. "Tell me you aren't making fun of other people's names, *Zephyr*," he says. Not in a snotty way, but teasing like he used to back in the day.

"Whatever, *Tallon*, just see if she has any ideas."

He pulls a cell phone out of his pocket with a grin. "I'll call North. She and the other Hecate might have noticed some activity at one of the bigger Nodes. There's only a day until the new moon. It seems like the Acolytes should be making preparations right about now."

Tallon stands up and moves away as he dials North's number. He has it memorized? A stab of jealousy zings through me. I want to know why he has her number memorized. Did he date her at some point? Is she just more his type? Is that why he bolted back in the hotel room? Was it because he couldn't imagine himself with me?

I swallow a groan. I need to just stop. I shouldn't even be thinking about Tallon; I should be focused on Hera and Ramun Sol. That's more than enough to worry about.

Blue watches us with his arms crossed. "We should probably get going. We need to get back to Ulysses's Glen before Nanda gets worried about us."

Alora stands and stretches. "Yeah, I need to get back to the university. They're going to want to know how the meeting went." She groans and hides her face. "How am I supposed to tell them that the Oracle is trailer trash?"

Blue gives her a dirty look. "Hey, everyone comes from somewhere. Besides, he really helped us out the past few days."

I drop the half-full beer on the ground next to me. I've had enough. "Oh?" I'm intrigued by Blue's response. He never gets short with Alora, and the trailer's exploded with the bleach-and-pine scent of his indignation.

Tallon tucks his phone into his pocket and laughs. "Ignore Blue. He's just smitten. Jimmy just gave him his number before he and Ricki left. Even a little kiss good-bye." Tallon grabs another beer, pops it open, and drains it. It's hard not to watch him. His movements are so fluid and hypnotizing. Tallon catches me, and I look away, my face hot. Sadly, I can relate to what Blue's feeling. Against my better judgment, I'm also feeling pretty smitten.

Alora snort laughs as she stands. "Aw, Blue, it's okay. The Oracle was kind of dirty hot."

Blue's expression is calm, but the burning-flowers stink of his hurt feelings is overwhelming. I sigh. "Shut up, Alora. Stop being such a snob."

She clamps her mouth closed and gives me a worried look. The darkness has risen up at my irritation, and thin tendrils of black smoke rise up from my arms. "I'll be in the car," she says, pushing past Blue and out the door. The rancid-orange stink of her fear lingers even after she's gone.

"Thanks." Blue gives me a worried look. "Should you be leaking like that?"

I glance down at my arms and shrug. "Who knows? This is nothing compared to Hades's mantle of shadows. It's probably normal."

"Tallon doesn't emit like that."

Tallon gives Blue a pointed look. "Zephyr is much more pow-erful than I am."

Blue nods, but the moldy-bread smell of his worry just gets

stronger. "Okay. Well, it's good to have you back, Zeph." He gives Tallon a pointed look. "You guys hurry up so we can get going." Then he follows Alora to the car.

"What was that all about?" I ask, standing and stretching.

Tallon shrugs. "I don't know." He leans against the broken refrigerator. He looks like a magazine ad for expensive cologne, a hot guy standing in the middle of wreckage. He catches me staring at him again, and I clear my throat at the unspoken question in his raised eyebrow.

"What did North have to say?"

Tallon's brows knit together. "Who? Oh, North. She's going to check on it. She said they've noted some activity on the Paths, mostly just the Acolytes. No different than usual, though."

I move toward the door, and Tallon maneuvers in front of me, blocking my path. I cross my arms and sigh. "What?"

Tallon shifts from foot to foot. It's the first time I've ever seen him uncomfortable. "I have something I need to say." I can see the guilt forming in his eyes, and I suddenly feel sick. If he apologizes for kissing me, I will kill him.

The darkness surges around me, and I fight to calm it. "Save it, Tallon. There's nothing I need to hear from you."

"No, you do. I owe you an apology."

I shake my head so hard that I make myself dizzy. I can't do this. Fear and hurt collide in my middle, and I'm angry and sick. I don't want to hear whatever it is he has to say. "No, don't do this. There's nothing you need to apologize for. We're just friends. I get that. Let's just get this whole thing over with so we can go back to our lives." I don't give him a chance to respond. I push past him and stumble out of the trailer. Tears well in my eyes, because I can fill in the rest of what Tallon was going to say.

Rejection doesn't hurt any less when it comes in the honey-coated words of your childhood best friend.

I blink my tears away and climb into the back of the car, slamming the door so hard that Blue turns around to look at me.

"What's going on?"

I force a smile. "Nothing. Why?"

Blue frowns at me but doesn't say anything, just turns back around. I study my cuticles so that I won't have to make eye contact with anyone. The darkness settles, fading away so that the only sign of it are the swirling designs on my arms. Tallon opens the door and climbs inside the car, but I don't look at him. I can't. If I did, I might cry.

"So, what's next? Lunch?" I say. I'm trying very hard to act lighthearted. Inside, I'm dying a little. All I can think of are Whisper's words to me so long ago.

It looks like she was right after all. Romance isn't for vættir like us.

WE STOP AT A ROADSIDE DINER FOR LUNCH. IT'S THE KIND OF PLACE where you can pretty much figure on getting a good dose of food poisoning. The outside looks like a cross between a bomb shelter and a trailer. Inside the floors are sticky, and our sodas are flat, but it's far enough off the beaten path that we probably don't have to worry about any witnesses if we have to fight off an Acolyte attack.

I order pancakes, figuring there's no way anyone can mess those up. After living with Nanda, I'm spoiled. My mouth waters as I remember her cooking. Even though I'm a little miffed she didn't tell me what she knew about my birth, I still miss her. I hope she's doing okay.

Alora gets a salad, while Blue and Tallon each order cheeseburgers. We're the only ones in the restaurant, so our food arrives quickly. Alora's salad is a plate of brown iceberg lettuce with a few shards of carrot and a couple of tomato slices that have seen better days. It looks so sad that I push my plate of pancakes into the middle of the table between us. "Here," I say, cutting the stack in half. She gives me a look of surprise, and I sigh. "Don't say I never did anything nice for you."

She considers it for a moment before picking up the syrup and covering her half of the pancakes. "Thanks," she says.

While we're eating, Tallon's phone rings. He answers it before going outside to take the call. Hearing his voice next to me is like nails on a chalkboard. Being in the same car, and now the same restaurant with him, is slow torture. Like having bamboo shoved under your fingernails, or being forced to listen to elevator music. All I want is for him to grab me and kiss me until I'm breathless. I want it so badly that my middle aches with the need to feel him against me again.

But that's never going to happen. And that just makes it all the more painful to sit next to him. With sadness I realize that we'll never be just friends again. It hurts too much to be around someone I can't have.

Tallon returns and slides into the booth with a sigh. I swear he sits closer to me than before, and I inch closer to the wall. "That was North. She says that a couple of Hecate covens are reporting increased activity at a Node in Pittsburgh. She thinks that might be our best bet."

Blue nods. "Three Rivers. There used to be a stadium in Pittsburgh called that. It was named for the Allegheny and Monongahela rivers, which come together to form the Ohio River there."

Alora bumps her shoulder into Blue's. "Look at you, with your geography knowledge."

"Actually, it's sports knowledge. The Steelers used to play at Three Rivers Stadium before moving to Heinz Field."

I barely register their banter, instead I'm thinking about the shades and Hera's spell. Fear leaves me cold, and goose bumps form along my arms. "So that's where Hera is going to strike."

"Do we even know if she's the one actually conducting the spell?" Alora asks. She runs her fork across our empty plate, then licks the syrup off the tines. The short-order cook watches her in open-mouthed fascination until he catches me giving him a dirty look.

I shrug. "Hades was pretty clear that she was the one who had the shades. He said that I had to kill her to set them free. But I guess Ramun Sol could be doing the actual spell." I try not to think about Hades's certainty that I'll die.

Tallon shifts on the seat next to me, and every nerve ending goes on alert. I should've sat next to Blue. I would've, but he plopped into the booth next to Alora when we sat down, leaving Tallon with the option of sitting next to me or leaving. I didn't want to make a big stink about it when he sat down next to me. I can tell he still has something he wants to tell me, but I don't want to hear it. I'm pretty sure my fragile emotional state couldn't handle an apology from him. Kissing him is one of the best memories I have. At least right up until he ran out of the room. I'm not going to let him ruin what I have left.

I'm so busy remembering how it felt to kiss him that I almost miss his next words. "North thinks she might know where Ramun Sol is."

My heart pounds in my ears. The darkness swirls as I imagine ripping out the Æthereal's heart. "Where?"

Blue glances at the kitchen staff and clears his throat. "Maybe we should continue this discussion where we don't have an audience."

The waitress storms over and glares at us. "There's no smoking in here," she says, before looking at us in confusion. The darkness has snapped back into place, and we all smile at her like we're just a bunch of innocent kids enjoying lunch.

"Can we get our check?" Alora says, her voice all honey.

The waitress nods and digs it out of her apron before looking at us again. "I'm sorry, I thought I saw smoke."

Blue digs a few bills out of his wallet and throws them on the table. "No big deal. Keep the change," he says. Then we escape outside.

Tallon takes a deep breath. "North says that one of the Hecates she spoke with remarked upon seeing a bright streak on the Paths near Pittsburgh. That could be Ramun Sol. If we can get him to come to us, that might give us the edge."

I snort. "And how are we supposed to do that? He took off running the night he killed Cass. He knows I'm stronger than he is."

"Maybe. But I'm willing to bet that he wants revenge more than anything. If he thinks he has an advantage over you, he might be convinced to attack." Tallon scowls, his lips pursed. I want to kiss him. Blue grins.

"Oh, I know that look. You have a plan."

Tallon nods. "I do. And if it works, we'll be able to stop Hera and kill Ramun Sol."

CHAPTER TWENTY-SEVEN

TALLON DECIDES THAT HE NEEDS TO MAKE A FEW CALLS BEFORE HE finalizes his plan, so we find a place to stay for the night. I'm not tired, but Blue, Alora, and Tallon don't look like they've gotten much sleep since I left for the Underworld. When Blue declares that he wants to spend the night somewhere, no one argues.

Especially when he pulls into the parking lot of a really nice hotel.

"We're staying here?" I ask, looking at the fancy fountain in front of the hotel and the impressive entryway.

"Yes. I am sleeping in a big, comfortable bed," Blue says, putting the car in park. "If we're about to ride off to some 'epic battle'"—he draws air quotes with his fingers—"I want to make sure I'm well rested. That's not going to happen on a bed that feels like it was a brick in a past life."

Alora looks at the hotel and sighs. "I'm with Blue. After two weeks of trailer hopping I'm ready for a hot shower and a deep conditioner. Oh, and cable. I need to catch up on my Hollywood gossip."

Tallon says nothing, and I just shrug. "Okay." I don't have any money, so I figure they must have a way to pay for everything.

Blue and Alora turn to look at Tallon, who sighs. "You know we don't have that kind of money."

Blue grins. "Well, I guess you'll just have to work your magic."

We get out and head inside to the lobby. Tallon stands back and waits until everyone else has been helped before he approaches the clerk. When I raise a questioning eyebrow in Blue's direction, he leans in close. "Tallon's the only one who can get a room without anyone making a fuss. He can charm anyone."

"What do you mean?"

Blue jerks his chin to where Tallon speaks in low tones with the clerk. "Watch."

The clerk is shaking her head no, and for a split second I'm certain she isn't going to let us have a room. But then she stills as Tallon keeps talking to her. The tension drains out of her; a small smile ghosts around her lips. After a few taps on the computer in front of her, she slides four key cards across the counter to Tallon.

He walks over and hands them to us with a murmured, "It's over two hundred dollars a night. We need to be out of here tomorrow before they realize the Kensington family doesn't exist."

I look past Tallon at the clerk. She looks happy, if a little out of it. "What, did you just hypnotize her or something?"

Tallon directs a dark look at me. "Yes."

Alora and Blue lead the way toward the bank of elevators, chatting excitedly about what they're going to do first. I frown at Tallon. "How long have you been able to do that?" Tallon didn't have the ability when we were younger. Or if he did, he never shared the secret with me.

He shrugs. "It came along a few years ago. It's something my father was able to do."

I cross my arms. "You didn't ever hypnotize me, did you?"

"I tried," he says, jogging to grab the elevator doors before they close. I do the same, and as I slink past him, a smile plays around his lips. His dark gaze meets mine and he leans in close. "It didn't work."

I open my mouth to ask him what he means by that, but the fact that he's flirting with me short-circuits my brain. While we ride the elevator up, I examine him out of the corner of my eye. He wears his hair braided today, and even all twisted up it reaches his shoulders. My fingers itch to reach out and touch it. I bet it's as silky as it looks.

The elevator dings, jerking me out of my daydream of stroking his hair. I clear my throat and look behind me, where Blue and Alora watch me with identical smirks. Oh gods, am I that obvious?

When the elevator opens, we split up. Our rooms are all right in the same hall, so it's not like we have to worry about trying to find one another later. Tallon ducks into his room without a word, leaving the rest of us standing in the hallway in shocked silence.

Alora sighs. "I hate when he gets like this. Focused Tallon is an annoying Tallon."

Blue shrugs. "You know how he is. When he's scheming, everything else takes a backseat. Honestly, we're lucky he got us rooms first."

I glance at the closed door and try not to feel disappointed. I sigh. "So, what now? We hang out and wait for the brilliant Tallon to reveal his awesome and awe-inspiring plan?"

Blue shrugs. "Pretty much. Hey, at least we have cable again." He takes off into his room, and Alora grins at me.

"I looked at the Strands while we were in the car. Blue's going to sneak out and meet Jimmy. He and Ricki are staying in the hotel as well."

I frown. "How does someone who lives in a trailer park afford a hotel like this?" If it hadn't been for Tallon's hypnotizing skills, we wouldn't be staying here either.

Alora shrugs. "I don't know. Good question, though." She disappears into her room, and I enter mine, wondering if maybe Alora isn't so hot at reading the Strands of Time after all.

I waste no time jumping in the shower, turning the hot water as high as I can stand it. It's a mistake. There's nothing to do but think as the water pours down on me. And I have entirely too much to think about.

Hades is my father. All this time I thought I was the product of some romantic affair, my father a random Æthereal. But instead I'm the offspring of an Exalted. And not just any Exalted, but the villain, the væittir equivalent of the boogeyman. The old stories aren't kind to Hades. Where the other Exalteds, like Zeus and Apollo, are bright and dashing, Hades is dark and terrifying. Knowing he's my father is more than a letdown. It's a little scary. He's the King of the Dead. When he shows up, people die. And now I get that honor.

I'm not really thrilled with that revelation.

Killing Ramun Mar was an accident. But the Acolytes? Their deaths clutch at me, eating away at my conscience in the quiet moments. But not as much as I feel like they should. Almost a thousand people died the night Ramun Sol killed Cass. Shouldn't I feel a little guiltier about their deaths?

I haven't had a lot of time to think about it, but now that I know who my father really is, I wonder if my lack of remorse is because of him. Am I programmed to just not give a damn about the people I kill? Is it part of wielding the darkness, or just a family trait? Harpies kill without remorse, but mostly because they see it as a badge of honor, the number of kills. I'm not proud of the deaths. I just don't really care, like the kind of remorse little kids have about stepping on ants. It happened, and I know I should feel bad about it, but I don't.

Thinking about my lack of regret is actually more depressing than the deaths of the Acolytes.

My brain is too full of questions that I have no answers for, so I turn off the water and get out.

I've just managed to get dressed in fresh jeans and a T-shirt when there's a knock on my door. I drop the towel on the floor and pad to the door barefoot. A quick glance through the peephole reveals a nervous-looking Tallon. My stomach does a swan dive, and my heart beats triple time.

I can't yank open the door quickly enough.

"Hey," I say, trying to look like I'm not about to hyperventilate. "Are we meeting now?"

He shakes his head quickly. "Not yet. Can I come in?"

I want to say no. I could laugh, like I'm too cool for his games, before slamming the door in his face. But I don't do any of that, because the truth is that I'm just glad he's here.

I step back and he walks past me into the room. I close the door behind him and take a deep breath. The last time we were in a room by ourselves I threw myself at him. That's not going to happen this time.

Maybe.

When I turn around, Tallon wears a sad smile, and I tilt my head to the side. "What?" I ask.

He shrugs. "Come here." His voice is slightly above a whisper, and huskier than normal. It turns my legs to mush, but I still manage to stumble over to him.

He cups my cheek with a sigh. My breath flutters in my chest, and I have the wild irrational thought that maybe I'm dreaming. There's no way this beautiful boy could be in my hotel room, looking down at me with eyes of the darkest violet. I have to be asleep.

But then Tallon leans forward, his lips brushing mine. Such a simple act. Lips touching. But the result is pure magic.

Electricity.

The contact sets off a flurry of tingles low in my belly, and I tip-toe to deepen the kiss. Tallon pulls back, and his expression is like a bucket of cold water to the face. The corners of his lips tug down, twisting his normally guarded expression into one of sadness.

"Tallon?" I move to step back, but he grabs my arm, squeezing too tightly.

"I'm sorry," he says, voice low. At first I think he's talking about the kiss, and a wave of hot rage crashes through me. But then I feel the cold bite of metal as the cuff locks around my arm. I look down in openmouthed shock. Tallon just banded me with a damper.

"No," I whisper, pulling for the darkness. It's far away, useless. The damper is a mute button on my abilities. Tallon has just crippled me.

What kind of a game is he playing?

I can't reach the magic, but I don't need it. I extend my talons and swipe at him, catching his cheek and parting the skin.

Tallon's head jerks, and he looks over my shoulder at someone behind me. "Trust me," he murmurs. I'm so angry that he's just thrown a damper on me that I don't even acknowledge his words. I scream and reach for him, but someone grabs my arm from behind.

"Temper, temper, little bird." I throw my head back, catching the person behind me with the back of my skull. Hopefully I just broke someone's nose. They dance away, and I spin around, my rage drowning out my normal fear. I blink, because I can't believe what I'm seeing.

Ramun Sol stands in the middle of my hotel room wearing jeans and a T-shirt. He looks completely normal without his Acolyte getup on. Cass's murderer is here, and I'm completely powerless.

The rage evaporates, an icy cloud of fear taking its place. I try to pull the damper off, clawing at my skin. I dimly register the pain, blood welling up and around the dark metal. Ramun Sol laughs at my panic, the sound high and mocking.

"Uh-oh, it looks like our little friend isn't so brave without her shadows."

He's right. I'm terrified. The spirals of darkness on my arms have retreated into thin gray lines. I can't even sense the darkness, much less call it.

I collapse on the floor, utterly hopeless. Tallon. He's betrayed me. "Why?" I whisper.

Tallon doesn't answer me. It's Ramun Sol who dances close, his face inches from mine.

"Why? Because he knows that the bright will win. We're the good guys. Don't you get it? The world needs the light. The darkness is an aberration." Ramun Sol shoots Tallon a knowing grin. "It also doesn't hurt that our friend over there wants to get on grandma's good side."

I look at Tallon and then back at Ramun Sol. "I don't understand."

Tallon's eyes lock on mine. "Hera is my grandmother. Typhaon is my father."

There's not enough oxygen in the room, and I struggle for breath. In the old stories Typhaon was a monster birthed by Hera in a fit of rage over one of Zeus's affairs. Hades took pity on the creature and let it live in the Underworld, where it was responsible for keeping the drakans contained. But so many of the old stories are wrong. This one can't be true, can it?

But it can. I remember my mother was just talking about a mission to the Underworld to save a friend from Typhaon. And Nanda and Mom were friends from way back. Did Nanda and Mom go down to the Underworld to save Tallon's mom? Is that why Mom was so angry when he started to manifest darkness? Because she knew he was the child of a monster? It can't all just be a coincidence, can it?

"No," I say, shaking my head. Tallon's father might be a dark lord, but I can't imagine Tallon has sold me out to Ramun Sol.

Tallon shrugs, as though betrayal is a common part of his life. "I told you I was a monster."

He did. It's something he's said to me more than once. I thought he was being dramatic. I should have known better. Tallon isn't one for melodrama.

But looking up at Ramun Sol, I'm starting to think maybe Tallon is one for a little treachery.

Ramun Sol sighs. "Are you finished? Because I'd like to kill her now, if you don't mind." Ramun Sol strides forward and lifts me up by my hair. I clutch at his hand, trying to get him to let go. I hate the whimpers of pain that manage to escape.

Tallon doesn't even look at me. "Yeah, whatever. Where's my grandmother?"

Ramun Sol laughs. "You really think I'd tell you?"

"I gave you what you wanted. Are you going back on your word?"

The Æthereal shrugs. "So? What are you going to do—tell your granny? Do it, and then we'll see what the old woman thinks." For some reason that cracks him up, and he begins to laugh. It's the same sound as when he slit Cass's throat, and something gives way inside of me. I don't know whether it's Tallon's betrayal, all the lies I've been told, or the ache of being held up by my hair, but I snap. After all, I might not have my darkness, but I still have years of Harpy training.

One of the old sayings comes back to me: *A Harpy goes where Æthereals fear to tread, so a Harpy shall fear no Æthereal.*

I'm already dead. Might as well take a little bit of Ramun Sol with me.

I let go of Ramun Sol's hand and use my talons to swipe at his eyes. He drops me, and as I fall, I kick out at his midsection. He doubles over in pain, and from my spot on the ground I kick up, catching him in the face.

I have never had this much fun kicking someone.

I quickly climb to my feet just as he recovers. He reaches for his solar flare, and I instinctively run toward him. There's a saying in the Aerie: *Do the last thing your opponent expects.* It's good advice, and I manage to catch Sol in a flying tackle. The attack is enough to send him sprawling, and I kneel on his chest as I use my talons to rend his face.

Ramun Sol screams. The slices from my talons heal slowly, and he shudders as though each touch burns. At first I think his reaction is because of the pain, but then I realize he's laughing. His eyes open, brightness like the sun leaking from them. "By the Rift, you Harpies are stupid." I have a moment of shock before a flare of light sends me reeling backward.

I moan, each nerve ending on fire. Sol stalks slowly toward me, but I'm helpless to do anything but writhe around in pain. Without a word he picks me up and hurls me across the room.

I smash into a barrier, and then I'm lying on the balcony. Glass rains down on me. As I struggle to my feet, I dimly realize that he just threw me through the sliding glass door. Pain blossoms bright and hard, and takes too long to fade. I roll around in agony. Ramun Sol crunches over broken glass, his steps slow and deliberate as he approaches. I try to get up, to run away. But everything is slow to respond, and before I can climb to my feet, Ramun Sol is next to me. His boot presses into the small of my back, crushing my spine and forcing the air from my lungs.

"Oh, I am so going to enjoy breaking you down piece by itty-bitty piece. You're going to pay for what you did to my brother, vættir bitch."

"Not now, Ramun Sol." A woman's voice carries out to us from inside the hotel room. "Honestly, one would think that you were vættir, the way you continue to pander to this notion of revenge." The pressure on my back disappears, and I roll over in relief. But the sensation is short-lived. My vision fills with a woman's smiling face looking down at me. There's no mistaking who she is. Hera, Queen of the Æthereals.

Despair washes over me. Things just went from bad to impossible.

"Exalted, I didn't realize that you were going to be in the area." Ramun Sol's voice quavers.

"Am I to now coordinate my movements with you, Ramun Sol? Are you my event planner?" Hera's face disappears. She steps over me like I'm a discarded gum wrapper and approaches Sol. I manage to roll over enough to watch her approach the minor Æthereal. Hera wears tight white pants, white knee-high boots, and an equally white blouse. Her dark hair is pulled up in a high ponytail and hangs down to the middle of her back. She looks like something out of a comic book.

So that's what a goddess wears to a genocide.

Hera stops a few feet away from Ramun Sol and studies him. "I await your response, Ramun Sol."

He falls to his knees, his eyes downcast. "No, Exalted. Your movements are none of my concern."

Hera looks over her shoulder at me. Her too-red lipstick reminds me of blood. "Gather the Nyx and the monster, summon my Acolytes, and meet me at the Point. With her darkness to power the spell, we no longer need to wait. Tonight the vættir will be abolished."

Hera disappears in a flash of light, and I groan as I try to sit up. Tallon is there, trying to help me to my feet, but I shake him off.

He gives me a look before reluctantly letting me go. Yeah, like I want the boy who betrayed me to help me kill myself.

Because I heard what the bitch-goddess said, and there's no way I'm letting Hera use me to power her spell.

Sol forgets about me long enough to turn to Tallon. "You brought her here."

Tallon shrugs, his lips twisted up in a smirk. "Yeah, maybe. I did ask you nicely to call her. You should learn about keeping promises. There might be a way around a lot of things, but there's no way around a promise."

"A promise kept," I mutter. I glance up at Tallon. Without looking at me, he taps a couple of times on my damper. My brain is slow, but I'm pretty sure it's some sort of sign. Especially since he just gave Sol a lecture about promises. Did Tallon plan this whole thing?

I glance down at the damper encircling my arm, and it hits me. The dampers were created by the Æthereals to control vættir. But I'm not just any vættir.

I'm the Nyx. I am a dark goddess made flesh.

And it's time I started acting like it.

I climb unsteadily to my feet. Ramun Sol looks at me and laughs.

"You really don't know when to quit, do you?" he sneers. He begins to glow, summoning his solar flare again. I run forward and tackle him around the middle, eyes squeezed shut against the glare of him. We slam into the balcony railing. He groans, and I take the opportunity to shove my hand up under the T-shirt he wears. I call for the darkness, and I'm surprised and relieved when a thin tendril of it comes rushing back. I send it racing along Ramun Sol's bare skin, and he screams.

"Get her off of me!"

"Tell me what Hera was talking about when she said to take us to the Point," Tallon says. He sounds bored.

"It's a park with a fountain. It sits right on the Node where the three rivers come together in Pittsburgh." Ramun Sol screams again, and I laugh. The wisps of darkness rising off my bare arms are getting thicker. Stronger. And so is the tendril tearing at the Æthereal's skin.

Elation washes over me. My shadows are back.

Ramun Sol sees them the same time I do. "No. No, it can't be. The damper—"

"Those dampers were designed for the average vættir, offspring of minor Æthereals like you. Do you really think something like that would work on Hades's daughter?"

Ramun Sol looks at me and shakes his head. "No. No, it can't be. You'll destroy us all."

I can't help it. I smile. "No, just you." I lean close so that only he can hear my next words. "I hope this hurts. A lot."

I clamp my hands around his throat, and I think about Cass, the way she looked as he took her life. The darkness swells forth, shadows gobbling up the light and leaving us in deepest night. Around us the lights explode, swaddling the hotel in complete darkness. It's only when shadows remain that the dark actually attacks Ramun Sol.

His screams are loud enough to shatter the windows.

The darkness clutches at the brightness of him, devouring it and growing stronger. I can sense that it wants more; it wants freedom to hunt like it did before. Part of me wants to give it that freedom, send it out into the world to hunt the Acolytes. But that won't help me stop Hera, and it won't free Whisper and Cass's shades.

"Not yet," I whisper to the erebos, soothing it like a pet. The darkness seems to like that. It curls around me, healing the last of my injuries before settling back into the markings on my skin. "Soon."

I blink, and the world slowly comes back into focus. Tallon is hauling me up from where I've slumped onto the balcony. "Come on, we need to get going. Hera is expecting us."

"How'd you know the damper wouldn't work?" I ask.

"Someone tried to damper me, once. It didn't go so well."

I open my mouth to ask him more, but he cuts me off. "We have to find Alora and Blue and get out of here."

I let Tallon pull me from the balcony and into the room. His grip is firm on my upper arm, his fingers warm. A chill sweeps over me as he reaches down and snags my backpack, slinging it over his shoulder. But then his touch is back, and we're out of the dark room and into the hallway, which is dimly lit by the emergency lamps on the wall. Blue and Alora stand near the stairway, their faces worried.

"What's going on?" Blue asks.

Tallon shrugs. "Just tying up some loose ends. I'll fill you guys in on the way."

"Way where?" Alora asks, looking mussed and a little put out.

"We found out where Hera's taking the shades. We have to get going, though. We don't have much time." He steers me toward the stairs, and I push him away.

"I can walk," I say. I'm unsteady, but I'm still the first one to the stairs. I pause and turn around, looking over my shoulder at everyone. "What?"

"Where are we going?" Alora asks, tugging at her hair.

I lean against the doorframe. My head is dizzy, like I just got off a carnival ride. I take the ruined damper off my arm and drop it on the floor. "We're going to stop Hera," I answer, even though that isn't what Alora meant. I take a deep breath, and to myself I say, "I've got a promise to keep."

CHAPTER TWENTY-EIGHT

WITH A LITTLE HELP FROM THE INTERNET ON TALLON'S PHONE WE discover that the Point is actually the name of the park. Point State Park in Pittsburgh.

"It looks like we're about an hour away," Tallon says. He sits in the front seat next to Blue, playing navigator for a change. From Alora's posture she isn't happy to be stuck in the backseat with me, and I share the feeling. I have some things I want to say to Tallon, but unless I want to share them with the entire car, they're going to have to wait.

So as we drive, I stare out the window and fume.

Why didn't Tallon tell me that his plan was to pretend to give me up to Ramun Sol? If I was a little more prepared, maybe I wouldn't have freaked out so much.

But more important is the fact that Hera is Tallon's grandmother. How does that work? Especially since he's working just as hard as the rest of us to see her fail.

We stop for gas and all pile out to go to the bathroom. We don't know what waits for us in Pittsburgh, but if I'm going to die I want to make sure I don't end up wetting my pants in the process.

In the ladies' room I corner Alora, who looks at me with startled violet eyes. "Don't hurt me," she says. The lime scent of her fear is no competition for the funk of the bathroom.

"Pffft, I'm not going to hit you," I say.

"Yeah, but that's the same look you had on your face last time. Sorry if I'm a little unconvinced."

I get a glimpse of myself in the mirror and sigh. My hair sticks out in all directions like a crazy woman's, the blue curls looking unkempt. My silver eyes are too wide, and darkness leaks from the corners of them. I close my eyes and reopen them, and the darkness disappears. I force what I hope is a reassuring grin.

"Sorry, just a little on edge. Look, I wanted to ask you what you know about Tallon's father."

Alora looks away. "We don't talk about that."

I cross my arms. "Well, we're talking about that. I want to know how his mom ended up getting pregnant by T—" Alora clamps her hand across my mouth and looks around.

"Don't say his name. I'm serious. If you do, he'll be able to find Tallon." I nod, but Alora doesn't remove her hand. "Promise you won't say his name."

"Mmmpphhhff," I say.

Alora removes her hand and sighs. She begins talking, her words coming fast and hard. "Tallon's father is one of the lowest of the dark lords, the monster-that-will-come-when-called. Janda, Tallon's mom, was carried off by him in the middle of a mission. She used to work with our moms a lot on missions. Like Tallon, she could trip the Rift."

I frown. "Tallon's mom was a Harpy?"

Alora shakes her head. "No. She was a minor Æthereal. Not strong enough to be Exalted, and too weak to survive in the Æthereal Realm. She's my mom's half sister, and she's the one who convinced Mom to move to Ulysses's Glen when the Aerie threw her out." The Aerie threw out Nanda? I suspect there's a story there, but it'll have to wait for another time. I don't want to interrupt Alora.

Her eyes get a faraway look. "By the time our moms found Janda she was pregnant and convinced she was in love with the creature. No one really knows how Tallon was conceived; it should've been impossible."

She swallows hard and continues. "Most of the healers thought that he would die in the womb. His mother was pregnant with him for over a year. One of my cousins says that when he was born, his eyes were all black, no white at all, and his teeth were pointed." Sadness crosses Alora's face and she shrugs. "A lot of the family still won't talk to him. They just refer to him as 'that dark one.' Janda sent him to live in the Æthereal Realm with one of her sisters when he was little. She wasn't very strong, and she was scared of him."

I shake my head. How did I not know any of this? "But what about when you guys came to visit? I can't remember a time when Tallon wasn't there."

Alora shrugs. "He would run away a lot as a kid. Every time, he would show up at our house and stay with us until someone came for him. I don't think my mom ever told yours who Tallon was, and when she finally did, they stopped talking."

I nod. That would've been the day my mom saw Tallon use the erebos. My mother wasn't a kind woman, but she was shrewd. It wouldn't have been hard for her to figure out that Tallon wasn't the poor orphan vættir she thought he was.

Alora adjusts her hair in the mirror and continues. "When Janda died, Blue and Owen moved in with us, and Tallon did too. No one came to take him back to the Æthereal Realm. I think they knew that he didn't belong there. I mean, Tallon is strange. Not only can he use the Paths like a Hecate, but he can cross the Rift. And he wields erebos like one of the lords of the Underworld. Who knows what else he can do? It's not many Æthereals that have that much power without being an Exalted."

Alora's words freeze my brain. Tallon is an Æthereal. Not a vættir. It's difficult to breathe, and not just because of the funky bathroom air. Why didn't I put that together before now? Did I just not want to see the truth? Tallon's ability to trip the Rift, to use both the æther and the erebos. Tallon is an Æthereal. Anything I feel for him is "forbidden," just like Whisper and Hermes.

And I don't care.

My shock must show on my face, because Alora's gaze meets mine. The sadness is gone, and all that remains is a fierceness. "I've seen the way you look at him. I was always jealous of how close the two of you were when we were little, but now I think you could be really good for him. Tallon needs someone who won't fear his darkness."

"Oh," I say. That's not something I ever expected to hear from Alora. Maybe I've misjudged her.

Alora sighs and pats my arm. The darkness there rises up to stroke her, and she yanks her hand back with a nervous laugh. "Power like Tallon's makes others jealous, and mean. I know you think Tallon's cold and distant, but he has good reason. Life really hasn't given him a lot to smile about. Hopefully you can change that."

I stare at Alora as she walks out of the rest room. Is that why Tallon freaked out on me in the hotel room? Did he think that he was somehow going to ruin me because he's really a god? If so, then he's an idiot. I'm not going to let some archaic law stop me from being happy.

I hope I have a chance to set Tallon straight.

I leave the bathroom, confused and on edge. Back at the car, everyone is waiting for me, and I get in without a word. As we drive the last few miles to where Hera and her Acolytes wait for us, I'm not thinking of my impending doom or the army waiting to kill us.

I'm thinking of the boy in the front seat, and wondering if I make him feel as conflicted as he makes me.

WE PULL INTO THE PARKING LOT OF THE DESERTED POINT STATE PARK.
Signs warned us that the park closed at dusk and that violators
would be prosecuted, but we continued on. I think we all figure
that preventing genocide justifies a little trespassing.

We get out of the car and sort of look around. It's warm out, even
with the breeze coming in off the water. Trees edge along either side
of the park, which is in the shape of a giant triangle. At the tip a
fountain shoots water up into the air. We all look to Tallon for direction, since he has the phone with the Internet connection.

"It looks like this is definitely the place. This website says
French settlers built a fort here back in the day. Fort Duquesne.
The foundation is the only thing left."

Alora's gaze gets distant and she nods. "Oh yeah, the Strands are
really tangled around this place. Lots of lives passed through here."

I want to point out that we're smack-dab in the middle of
a major city, and that maybe the Node has nothing to do with
the Strands. But Alora was nice enough when I asked her about
Tallon. So I keep my mouth shut.

I look out across the grass, but there's no sign of anything except maybe some rocks far off. "You think they knew it was a Node?"

Blue shrugs. "A lot of the first settlers were vættir trying to escape persecution in Europe. It makes sense that they would've chosen a Node along one of the Paths. That way they could return home if they needed to."

I nod and swallow a sigh. Nerves make my hands shake, and my stomach is sick. I want to be anywhere but here, but I need to see this through. I have to set Cass and Whisper free, if nothing else.

Tallon looks back at the rest of us. "You guys stay hidden while I check it out. Hera's expecting me, but if she sees the rest of you, she'll know something is up."

"She's Æthereal, Tallon. Won't she know something is up anyway?" Tallon gives me a look that screams, *Shut up*. I throw my hands up in the air. "Fine. Never mind."

"Wait," Alora says, putting her hand on Tallon's arm. "Let me check the Strands first." Alora's gaze focuses on something far away. I shift from foot to foot, anxious for something. Maybe she'll tell us we were wrong. Maybe this has all been a huge misunderstanding. I cross my fingers and hope that I won't have to die.

But I'm not that lucky. After a long moment Alora finally sighs and shrugs. "I can't see anything. The Strands are too jumbled."

I swallow hard, my fear souring my stomach. I'm trying very hard not to be sick. "Is that a good thing?"

She purses her lips. "It isn't a bad thing. For now we should probably just go along with Tallon's plan."

We duck into the trees while Tallon walks toward the fountain and the remains of the fort. As he walks across the open area, the tiny hairs on my arms stand up straight. He's so exposed. If Hera were to attack right now, there wouldn't be anything to protect him. The erebos crawls under my skin, trying to reassure me. I rub my arms, but the sensation doesn't go away. Blue bumps his shoulder into mine.

"What's wrong?" he whispers.

"What do you mean?"

"You're jumpy as hell. More than usual, in fact. You're making me nervous."

"Sorry. I just feel . . ." I grab Blue's arm as something runs toward Tallon. "Do you see that?"

Blue squints toward the field, shaking his head. "See what?"

"There! The kobalos running toward Tallon."

He looks at me like I'm crazy. "That's a kobalos? Are you sure? It looks like a monkey."

"Blue, why would a monkey be running around a park in Pittsburgh?"

His lips tighten. "We have to warn him."

The longer I watch the kobalos run across the grass the more I see Cass's last few moments. The memory is too much, and the erebos urges me to action. I break cover and sprint toward the kobalos loping toward Tallon.

I run full out, my arms swinging and a stitch forming in my

side. It's not a large distance, but the kobalos is much closer to Tallon than it is to me. If I don't hurry, it will attack him from behind.

"Tallon, watch out!" I scream. I will the darkness to attack the demon spirit, and it happily obliges. Strands of darkness shoot from my hands, wrapping around the kobalos and snuffing out the æther of its life force. The thing disappears before my eyes, and as I draw even with Tallon, he turns to glare at me.

"What the hell is wrong with you?"

"The kobalos, didn't you see it?" I gasp, my hands braced on my knees as I fight to catch my breath.

Tallon sighs. "I didn't see anything." He looks around, his hands on his hips. "It doesn't matter. There's nothing here. Hera tricked us."

"Oh, I did, but not in the manner you think." Hera stands behind me in the middle of the ruins of Fort Duquesne. Her white outfit glows in the low light, and the darkness inside of me jumps in anticipation.

The dark is much more anxious to get at her than I am.

Tallon shoves me behind him, and his twin swords flash into existence in his hands. "Where are the shades?"

Hera's lips twist into a slow smile. "And why would I tell you that?"

Tallon grins, the expression cold. "Good. So you do have them. I wasn't sure about that."

Hera's smug expression twists into one of rage. "I should have killed you while you were still in your mother's womb," she says. She points a single finger in my direction. "But I will settle for destroying your girlfriend."

Hera moves, faster than either of us could have ever imagined. She's a blur of white as she knocks Tallon to the side and grabs me by the throat. My feet dangle in the air. Tallon jumps to his feet, but some kind of invisible barrier keeps him from me and Hera. Far off, Alora and Blue come running out of the woods, a golden wave of kobaloi bearing down on them. I want to warn Tallon, to make him turn to help them. But I have my own problems.

I gasp and struggle, and the bitch smiles at me, like I just told a joke. "Where is it?" she asks, her voice a singsong. "Show me your darkness, little Nyx." As though she called for it, the darkness leaps off my arms, swirling around us.

I pry at Hera's cold fingers as my shadows rise up, trying to attack her. Æther leaks from her eyes, shining and bright, and she laughs. The darkness seeks out a weakness in her defenses, more and more of the erebos swelling forth in response to her æther. The erebos should be devouring the æther, but the more dark I summon the more the bright blinds me.

Hera is too strong. Spots begin to appear in front of my eyes. My blood pounds in my ears as the dark rises up, undisciplined and unruly. I think about Cass and Whisper. I've failed them.

Beyond Hera the kobaloi climb all over Blue and Alora,

burying them in an angry golden sea. Too late Tallon sees the danger and runs to help. My friends are outnumbered a hundred to one. They're no match for the angry spirits. And I'm in this cloud of æther, slowly dying, the darkness swirling around me without purpose.

I've failed everyone.

I'm not the Nyx.

My eyes meet Hera's, and she grins at me. It's a smile of triumph. "I thought you would be stronger."

Her words cut through me, unleashing something red and hot and angry. Her ridicule mingles with so many others', and the bitterness from a lifetime of failing to live up to expectations rises within me.

I will show them all.

I failed their Trials, but it means nothing. Because no matter what they say, I know who I am.

I am the Nyx. But first and foremost, I am a Harpy.

I extend my talons and dig them into Hera's wrist. Then, before she has a chance to react, I move my hands quickly outward. She screams as I sever the tendons in her wrist, dropping me and taking a few steps back. I gasp for air and drag myself to my feet, calling the darkness back to me. I don't know what Hera's up to, but she wants the darkness. My darkness.

She's not getting it.

The darkness comes quickly, swirling around me anxiously

before settling around my head and shoulders like a hooded cloak. Hera's hand repairs itself, and she laughs.

"So, the little bird's beak is sharper than it looks. Excellent. I worried your death would be boring." She holds out her hand and the æther swirling around us coalesces into a giant sword. I swallow hard.

"Oh, it's that kind of party." I jump backward as she swings the thing at me.

"It is, indeed, that type of party." She twirls the sword faster and faster, chasing me around the inside of the barrier. If I don't do anything, I'm going to be very dead, very quickly. I move out of the way a split second too late, and she opens a line on my chest. The æther burns, and it's all I can do not to scream in agony as I dance backward.

Hera pauses to laugh at me. "See? Even heroes bleed."

I'm going to be a dead hero in about two seconds. *I need some sort of weapon*, I think. The darkness answers, and I jerk as a couple of throwing axes appear in my hands. Throwing axes? I would've preferred infinity knives, but now is not the time to be picky.

I duck out of the way of Hera's next swing and respond by throwing one of the axes at her. Her body shimmers for a second, and the ax flies right through her. She then resolves back into a solid form. "Throwing axes. How quaint."

I don't say anything, because I can see what she can't. The first throwing ax has lodged into the barrier separating me from my friends. Dark energy crackles along the invisible wall. I throw the second ax just as Hera parries with her silver sword. The ax lands next to its twin, the dark energy radiating across the bright nothing until the barrier shatters with a scream.

"No!" Hera screams. The dark's response is immediate. It shoots out from me, seeking out the kobaloi and devouring their brightness. A few of the creatures try to run, but the darkness is fast and hungry.

I run away from Hera and into the crowd of kobaloi, wading through the quickly disappearing creatures and trying to find my friends. I know they're somewhere beneath the golden, writhing bodies. I've just gotten a glimpse of Tallon when Hera grabs me by the back of my neck.

"I am tired of this game, little bird. Now it ends." A sharp coldness rips through my middle, and I look down. The pain is too much for me to do anything but gasp. The silver sword glimmers at me, my blood streaking it gaily. I wrap my hands around the blade jutting out from my stomach. I'm not quite sure it's really there.

"No!" The shout draws my attention toward the field of retreating kobaloi. Alora lies on the ground, dead or unconscious. Blue has gone dragon, his giant jaws snapping up what few fleeing kobaloi he can grab. Tallon sprints toward me and Hera, his dark hair streaking out like a comet's tail. Behind me, Hera laughs.

"You are too late. Her blood shall unlock the Paths. She will do what I have been working toward for centuries." She pulls the sword out, and the pain is excruciating. I scream and clutch at the blade. A few weak shadows lash out, but I'm no match for Hera now. The darkness tries to repair the damage to my middle, but there are some things that even væettir healing cannot fix.

This might be one of them.

Hera releases me and I fall to the ground. She takes her bloody sword to the center of the fort's remains. I roll over to watch her. I clutch my stomach, as though I can stop my life from draining out between my fingers. She shoves the sword into the center of the Node, burying the thing up to the hilt. I have the urge to laugh. With that kind of strength there was no way I ever had a chance of defeating her.

Tallon skids to a stop beside me just as Hera begins to recite something in a language I don't understand. His hands find my middle, pushing down over mine. "It's okay, it's okay. We'll fix it. The dark will fix you."

I shake my head, tears leaking from the corners of my eyes. I can't bear to tell him that there's something wrong with me. The sword was made of æther, and that element has never been my friend. I can feel it killing me from the inside out. I don't have much time left.

"What's she saying?" I ask. Tallon turns to Hera and then turns back to me.

"It's High Æthereal. She's asking the spirits to open the gate, to bring the blood of her blood to her. But we don't have time for her. We need to get you somewhere safe."

I shake my head. "No, she's doing it. She's going to kill the shadow vættir. We have to stop her."

Tallon shakes his head. "You need a healer."

"No, I need to see what she's doing. Help me sit up." I have a feeling. It's just a hunch, but something that Hades told me about the shades niggles at the back of my brain.

Tallon scowls at me before lifting me into a sitting position. I swallow a moan and watch Hera, and it all suddenly clicks. She needed the shades to power the spell, but she needed my blood to summon them through the Paths.

"Those are my shades," I murmur, remembering my father's words. It all makes sense. Hera may have trapped the shades and kept them from traveling to the afterlife, but she couldn't command them to do what she needed them to do. That would take a dark lord's power.

Or the blood of the daughter of a dark lord.

Everything slips into place. Hera must have suspected that either Whisper or I were Hades's daughter, since Persephone knew about his fling with my mother. When Whisper didn't go along with Ramun Mar's questioning, he killed her. Not because she was sleeping with Hermes, but because Hera wanted the blood of Hades's daughter for her spell. But Ramun Mar made a mistake, and I walked in on the aftermath.

Hermes must have known the truth about my parentage, which

is why he told me Whisper was killed because of their relation-ship. Like my mother, he was counting on my ignorance keeping me safe until I was strong enough to fulfill the Prophecy of the Promise. Well, that and Cass's protection.

Hera would've known that I was Hades's daughter after I killed her Acolyte with the dark lightning. Plus she had Whisper's shade all this time. She would've been able to question her, and she would've known that I used dark lightning to kill Ramun Mar. Since I was in the custody of the High Æthereal Council, Hera just had to wait for them to hand down a death sentence. It must have pissed Hera off when the High Council gave me a sentence in Tartarus instead of death. I wonder how much Hermes and Hades had to do with that bit of good luck.

I hope my good fortune can hold for a little longer.

"Help me up," I say, trying to struggle to my feet. I'm bleeding all over the place, and even though the darkness is trying to heal me, I can sense its frustration. The æther in my belly burns like acid. I imagine it eating away vital organs, and force the thought away. I have one last thing to do. To fulfill a promise.

This all started with Hera. If I beat her, I can end it once and for all.

I push Tallon away, and stumble toward Hera. He grabs me by the arm and hauls me back. "Don't," he says, voice rough. "If you try to stop her now, you're dead."

"Tallon, I'm already dead." Pain shoots through my middle again, but I'm careful not to let any of my distress show. There's too much of the dark in me now, and Hera's bright sword has done more damage than it should've. But I don't tell Tallon any of this.

I gently remove his fingers from my arm. Behind him, the darkness is beginning to whip around Hera. I can sense the shades approaching down the Paths, pulled from wherever Hera's kept them hidden. I have to get to her before they do.

I shuffle toward Hera. I've only gone a couple of steps before I start to go down. I brace for impact, but Tallon is there. He scowls at me. "You need help."

"I can't ask you to do that. She's your grandmother."

"She's an insane goddess bent on once again ruling the Mortal Realm, Zeph. Besides, she's never even sent me a birthday card." His grin is slow and wicked, and sadness floods me.

I'm going to miss him most of all.

I clear the lump from my throat. "I need you to throw me into the air. If I can get high enough, I think I can dive at her. Can you do that?"

He nods and moves behind me, his hands on my waist. I draw as much of my darkness to me as I can. His breath is warm on my ear. "I'm going to lift you onto my shoulders, and then launch you from there. Just like the old days. Okay?" I nod. We used to do something similar back in the Aerie when I was small, before I could take off on my own. It was one of my favorite games.

I brace myself, but I'm still not ready for the pain that knifes through me when he lifts me up. Still, my feet manage to find his shoulders without kicking him in the face.

"On the count of three," he yells. His hands are under my feet, ready to throw me. Hera is only a few feet away from us, completely absorbed in whatever she's doing. I can do this. I can stop her.

"One, two, THREE!"

I crouch and jump at the same time that Tallon pushes up on the bottom of my feet. The result is that I'm airborne, but falling too quickly to reach Hera.

Wings. I need wings, I think. And like before, the darkness obliges.

There's a tingling along my spine, and then upward movement. A coordinated flapping of wings behind me, and I'm soaring. It feels like coming home, gliding through the sky again. But I don't have time to savor the feeling. I have a prophecy to fulfill.

The pain in my middle fades a little as I focus on Hera. I climb a little higher. Up high, the ruins of the old fort are clear, as is the darkness pulsing along the lines of the old walls. It radiates off into the night. From here it's easy to see how this place could be more than what it seems. Each of the corners of the fort terminates in a diamond shape instead of a normal corner. It's unusual and beautiful.

I take a deep breath. I don't have time to admire ancient architecture. Holding my hand out, I ask the darkness for a short sword, the kind we train with in the Aerie. It's slow to respond, and instead a long, slender knife made of midnight appears in my hand. The darkness is fading, pulled down to whatever Hera is doing below.

That's my cue.

The wings ride the currents as I seek the best place to strike. The magic is stirring up the winds now, and Hera stands in the calm center of a storm of erebos. A thin layer of bright æther protects her from the dark magic, which is probably why I wasn't able to hurt her before.

But my talons were able to strike her just fine.

I loosen my grip on the long knife and angle my shadow wings into a dive. Hera doesn't move, but her magic senses the impending attack. The bright reaches out for me, but a bit of the dark magic swirling around Hera detaches itself and intercepts the bright. I swerve to avoid the next missile, and then I'm beside Hera.

Æther leaks from the Exalted's eyes, the only sign of the amount of energy she's expending. "They are coming. And they will bring every last dark creature with them."

"Let them come," I grit out. Hera still grips the sword she buried in the ground. It must be her link to the spell she's casting. I slice at her arm with my talons. The æther pulls back, revealing the pale skin of her arm and a thin bloody cut. Before the æther can recover I plunge the dark knife into the gash.

Hera's scream of pain rips through me like a sonic boom. My shadow wings disintegrate at the same moment that she lets go of the sword. She clutches at the knife in her arm, but already the darkness is devouring her from the inside out. Dark lines run up her white arms and the column of her throat. She turns wide eyes on me.

"No. It cannot be. You . . ." She never finishes, stumbling back-ward into a bright column of æther and disappearing.

That's when all the hells break loose.

The rushing sound of a freight train approaching echoes around me. The erebos has been let loose, the magic wild without Hera to control it. The ground vibrates. Tallon runs up next to me, his eyes wide. "You have to take control," he says, yelling to be heard over the noise.

I groan. I just want to lie on the ground and die in peace. "What?"

"Look!" He points behind me, and I slowly turn. A dark cloud spirals into the sky like a tornado. Only the cloud has faces. The thing shifts, and I get a glimpse of Cass before she's sucked back into the maelstrom.

A funnel cloud of the dead is about to destroy Pittsburgh.

"I got it," I say. Pain radiates through my middle again, and I moan. Tallon starts to move toward me, and I shake my head. "I have to do this myself." He nods and takes a step back. I close the distance to the sword without a backward glance.

The swirling mass of shades is anchored to the sword, courtesy of my blood and Hera's spell. The sword is no longer bright, but blackest night. It oozes erebos, and the thing calls to me like a piece of unattended chocolate cake. I limp toward it. But it takes me years to reach it. The bright æther in my middle is spreading throughout my body. My leg has gone numb, and the side of my face tingles. I'm going to die from this.

I hope Hera is going through the same hell.

I tentatively touch the sword, and the darkness leaps for me. My arms are bare, silver lines arching across them from the poisonous æther. The erebos doesn't seem to mind, and dark lines form right next to the bright. I take a deep breath and put my other hand on the sword. I gasp as the dark rushes toward me, fast and hard.

I am drowning in a sea of shadows.

It's just like when Hades sent his dark after me, but worse. There's no violence this time, no intent to punish. There is only the dark's willingness to serve. It wants what I want. It wants me to be happy.

Right now it thinks that means pulling every shadow vættir in the world down the Paths and straight into the Node.

I try to tell the darkness to stop. But it's too loud. It's like shouting at a crowd of screaming fans. Telling the darkness not to pull in the shadow vættir isn't going to work.

I have a moment of despair before I take a deep breath, and I close my eyes. I think about Whisper and Cass and all of the other shades swirling overhead. I think about Alora lying facedown in the grass and Blue gorging his dragon form on kobaloi. I even think of Tallon, waiting to catch me like he always did when I was little.

He won't get the chance. This time I'm going to save everybody else.

The darkness is so close, and I reach for it. It comes like an eager puppy. It wants to heal me, but the bright is too far entrenched. I know there's no use in worrying about that, so I try to clear my mind of all my doubts, all my worries. I send the darkness one final, crystal clear thought.

Home, please. Send everyone home.

The shadows hesitate for a second, trying to interpret what I mean. Then the dark storm of shades slowly stops swirling. The column of them stretches and narrows, before shattering into a flurry of dark butterflies. They flutter and flit for a second before winking out one by one.

One of the shades brushes against my cheek before it goes. I want to think it was Whisper, but I know it's more likely it was Cass. She always believed in me.

The shades fade away, and so does the darkness. My legs go numb, and as I collapse, Tallon is there to catch me.

Just as I knew he would.

"Peep, what did you do?"

I can't breathe, the æther moving through me faster and faster. I try to force a smile, but instead a sob tears through me. It hurts so bad. Now that I know I've stopped Hera, it's hard to focus on anything else. "I told the darkness to send everyone home. I'm sorry." I say it because I don't know what else to say. Tears leak out of the corners of my eyes.

"Not yet, Zeph. Not yet," Tallon says, but I can't answer him. I look up, surprised to see the darkness hovering above us. Tallon's right. I can't die yet. That much darkness let loose in the Mortal Realm will upset the balance. There's too much. If I try to take it all, it will kill me.

But I'm already dead. The bright will see to that. I can't just leave the shadows here for Tallon and everyone else to deal with.

"Go. I have to take the darkness from the Paths," I tell Tallon. This close he'll be hurt if something goes wrong. But he doesn't listen.

"I'm not leaving you. We need to get you to a healer," he says, his jaw set. I reach behind him for the sword, connecting with the darkness that way. Then I use the dark power to shove him away and copy Hera's barrier move from earlier. It's easier than I thought it would be. He yells at me, but I'm not listening. I'm focused on the darkness still pulsing down the Paths.

"Come here," I say, calling to it. I use the sword to haul myself to my knees. It's the best I can do. The darkness moves along it and into me, healing me and battling the æther in my veins. But there's too much bright.

More. I need more.

I'm not trying to heal myself. I'm just trying to soak up as much of the erebos as I can before the bright wins out. Hopefully when I die, the erebos will be carried to the Underworld with me. The darkness floods through me, and the black lines on my arms grow thicker, the shadows deeper. I take in more. I'm bloated with the energy. My heart thrums, loud in my ears, and the pain of the æther is sharper, closer.

I close my eyes, pull in more erebos. More and more. For a single brilliant moment the pain fades away, and I open my eyes.

On the other side of the barrier Tallon, Blue, and Alora watch me, their mouths hanging open. I smile, feeling truly wonderful for the first time in a very long while.

This is what it's like to win.

It's the last thought I have before the darkness overwhelms me.

I break into a million pieces.

CHAPTER THIRTY

THE AFTERLIFE BLOWS.

I sit on a grassy mound above a gently sloping field. It's skirmish time, and far below, my mother and Whisper lead a contingent of shadow vættir against a horde of Hera's Acolytes. It's all in good fun, since there are no grudges in the Elysian Fields. Memory is a tricky thing when you're dead. No one remembers the petty arguments that were so important in the Mortal Realm.

That's a good thing, since a lot of the Acolytes down below were sent here by me.

Someone blows a horn, and the two sides run screaming toward each other. I catch a glimpse of Cass and Elias throwing spears alongside a score of Amazons, their aim deadly true.

The two of them cheer as their spears bury themselves in a couple of satyrs. Elias, the dark champion, looks nothing like I thought he would. His hair is the orangey red of the setting sun, and his skin is covered with freckles. But Cass is crazy about him, and even death hasn't erased their love for each other.

On the other side of the field the goat men go down, writhing around in their death throes. Then after a few minutes they jump up, pull out the spears, and chase after a couple of nearby nymphs. I can hear their laughs all the way up on my hill.

Skirmishes in the afterlife are just to pass the time. What's the point? Everyone's already dead.

I look away from the battle, which will go on until it's time to eat again. It's hard not to appreciate the view. Every day is perfect, the sky a shade of blue that makes my chest ache. Time actually seems to exist here, although it's a lie. But there's a day and a night. We sleep under the stars when the sky darkens or in one of the cottages that spring up at a thought. In the morning we're greeted by a perfect sunrise. Everyone's dead down here, so I'm not plagued with the stink of emotions. Although I suspect that if I was, it would be the smell of never-ending birthday-cake happiness.

I don't know if I could handle all that joy when I'm as angry as a hornet's nest.

I watch as Cass picks up a set of bolas and swings them above her head before releasing them. They tangle around the legs of the satyr chasing a nymph, and he goes down. Elias high-fives Cass, a move she taught him. I sigh.

"What, don't they let you play?"

The voice strikes a chord deep in my belly, and I hate the way my breath catches. This is the third time he's found me, but not the third time he's come looking. He's been down in the Elysian Fields so much that the dead have given him a nickname. The Dark One. It's fitting.

Every time I see him, it's the same nervous flutter of hope and excitement. I swallow the ache that blooms in my chest. I will not do this to myself.

"No. I'm not allowed to participate in the battles. The last time I fought alongside them, I changed the entire landscape. Hades said that until I learn to control my powers, I'm not allowed to use them anywhere but Tartarus. He doesn't like cleaning up my messes."

Tallon collapses on the ground next to me with a sigh. It's an exhalation of pain, and I can't help myself. I look at him.

"Oh my gods, what happened to you?" He looks like he was beaten with a sock full of quarters. His face is scraped up, and his lower lip is swollen. He moves like he's in agony, slow and stiff. He isn't healing, which is unusual.

"I had to cross the river Styx to get here this time. And, you know, a few other choice places. You ever fight a hydra? Yeah. Me neither. I got my ass kicked."

He looks so sad that before I can help myself, I reach out and touch his lip, using my darkness to lower the swelling and ease his pain. He could've healed it himself, but instead he made me do it.

"Why aren't you healing?"

He grins. "I was hoping maybe it would make you feel sorry for me." I pull my hand back, but he catches it and places it against his cheek, his eyes closing. I let myself enjoy the contact for a second before pulling my hand back.

"Why are you here, Tallon?"

He grins. Just the tiniest bit of power, and already his face is knitting back together. In a few seconds he'll be flawless once again. Either way, he still looks wonderful to me. "I'm here to take you home, Peep."

I shake my head and put a few inches between us. "I am home."

He snorts. "You aren't dead. You don't belong in the Underworld. You belong with me. In the Mortal Realm."

I look away from him toward the battle going on in the field below. I don't want his words to make me feel as happy as they do. I want to be numb inside. I want to feel like I deserve to be exiled to this place of endless boredom.

I should be dead, even though I'm not. The erebos saved me. And like everyone else, it sent me home. To the Underworld.

Whisper's team has started to mop up the remainder of Hera's forces, who are now running back to their base with whoops and laughter. I smile as Mom raises her sword in the air and screams out her victory, the sound echoing like that of a falcon. Whisper is right next to her, and they put their arms around each other and laugh. It's been a good series for them. Their team is three for four.

Not too far away, Hermes waits for my sister. He sees me looking at him and waves. I do the same. Whisper sees him and runs over, a wide grin on her face. I'm starting to think he really did care for her. Especially since Hermes travels down here to see her all the time.

I think I've been wrong about Æthereals. I think they can feel. It's just easier for them to deny their emotions than to live with the messy consequences of feelings.

Maybe one day I'll ask Hades about him and my mom again. I wonder if he'll tell me the truth this time.

"Zephyr."

I turn to Tallon, to the raw emotion in his voice. "What?"

"Please say you'll come back with me. You've had enough time to recover. Blue misses you, Nanda keeps making food that no one eats, and the entire neighborhood is looking for you. We need you. All of Ulysses's Glen needs you." There's an edge of desperation in his voice.

"Tallon, I can't go back; you know that." The darkness is a part of me, but there's more of it now. After that last battle with Hera I took in so much power that I can no longer keep it contained. It flares around my head like a dark aura. Even Hades doesn't know what will happen if I go back to the Mortal Realm. It could be dangerous.

Tallon shakes his head and grabs for my hand. Our fingers tangle together, but I don't pull away this time. He takes a deep breath. "Say you'll at least think about coming back."

I am thinking about it, damn him. And now that I am, I desperately want to see my friends again. Maybe even give school and all that a chance. I don't know that a normal life will ever be mine, but I'd like to at least try.

I glance down at my arms, and the darkness holding the bright æther at bay. The deadly power still moves through my body, the shadows holding it in check. Here in the Underworld the effects are barely noticeable. But what happens if I go back? "I don't even know if I can go to the Mortal Realm, Tallon."

Something in my voice must give him hope. "We can try. Besides, it's not just me that needs you. Hera's gone, but her Acolytes are beginning to gather again. It's just a matter of time before they try something new. And there are other problems. The entire vættir community is in chaos. You're the Nyx. The vættir will need you to lead them, and you need to be ready." He kisses my knuckles, and I can't help but remember those lips in the hollow of my neck. The memory makes me feel flushed. Tallon raises his head and smiles at me. Such a simple thing, that smile. And yet it undoes all of my resolve. "Come back with me. The world's better with you."

I think of the possibilities, of all the things that wait for me if I go back. Danger, definitely. But also friends. And maybe . . .

Maybe love?

I take a deep breath and let it out. "What did you mean, back in the hotel room? When you said you didn't want to ruin me?"

Tallon swallows and sighs. "I'm a monster, Zephyr. My father is a monster and one of the dark lords. One day I'll be a dark lord as well. I'm of the dark, and I didn't want to hurt you by pulling you into my world." He looks away, his gaze far-off. "I may live in Ulysses's Glen, but it's not the vættir that I belong to. I'm an Æthereal, and one day I'll have to answer that call. I know what happens to those who make the mistake of falling for one of my kind."

I shake my head and look out at the few vættir left on the battlefield, some of them chatting, others wrestling or joking around. "What does that have to do with anything, Tallon?"

"I remember what you were like as a kid, Peep. I didn't know if you were strong enough to handle the complications of being with me. I didn't want to put you through that if I could help it, even if it killed me to push you away."

I turn to study him, my heart in my throat. "And now?"

He laughs. "If anyone is strong enough to stand with me, it's you. You stopped Hera and saved the shadow vættir. You can handle my darkness."

I don't tell him that's because I am the dark. The shadows course through my veins, whispering to me as they move through my body. The dark is a living thing within me, and I think I like it. It's something I'm still getting used to.

Besides, a girl has to have some secrets.

I grin at him. "Maybe I've changed my mind. Maybe I don't like you anymore."

He pushes me so I fall over, just like he used to when we were kids. "Well, maybe I don't like you, either. Do you think Whisper would make out with me if I asked her?"

I sit up with a snort. "I think you'd have to fight Hermes first."

"I could take him."

I shove him. "Jerk." Before I know it we're wrestling, and then he's tickling me, and I'm laughing so hard that my middle hurts.

"Stop, stop!"

"Admit you still like me," Tallon says, finding the ticklish spot in my side.

"Okay, I admit it. I still like you." He stops tickling me, but his hand is still splayed across my middle.

He grins down at me. He knows the battle's almost won. "So, are you going to come back to Ulysses's Glen with me?"

I push him over so we're lying side by side in the tall grass, the too-blue sky above us. I rest my head against his shoulder, and his arms wrap around me. Right now I refuse to think about anything but how good it feels to be in the circle of his arms. I won't think about the future, or about all the things people will want from me if I go back to the Mortal Realm. I refuse to think of anything but the boy who crossed the Rift to save me, the boy who was there for me when I was small. The one I hope will be there for me in the future.

So I don't answer Tallon's question. Instead I just enjoy the moment.

And for now, it's enough.

ACKNOWLEDGMENTS

So, I'm not very good at thanking people. Mostly because it always comes out sounding a little insincere. But there are tons of awesome people who made this book (and *Vengeance Bound*) possible, and it would be terrible of me not to say thank you.

First, thanks to my editor, Navah Wolfe, and everyone at S&S BFYR, who made sure that my books were the best they could be. You all rock, and I totally appreciate your help. Especially the copyeditors, the unsung heroes of publishing. THANK YOU!

Thank you to my amazing agent, Elana Roth, who always answered my rambling, semi-incoherent e-mails with tact and aplomb, and never told me once to put on my big-girl panties and get over it. Thank you. Your steadfastness makes me feel less crazy, and that is saying something.

Thank you to anyone who has ever read my book, thought about reading one of my books, or just likes books in general. I think you're swell.

A big squishy non-hug for The Lucky 13s and all of the amazing authors I've met. You make me feel less alone. And that's nice. But I still don't want to hug you.

Thanks to my family and friends, who bought copies even though they had no idea what a YA was. Thanks to my weekly writing partner Jon Weidler, who never (okay, maybe once in a while) pointed out we did more talking about movies than writing.

Mostly, thanks to my husband, Eric, who endured my many moods and was always there to pretend to care about the latest publishing kerfuffle and listen to me talk out plot problems to myself. You're a jerk, but you're also my happily ever after. I love you.

ACKNOWLEDGMENTS